THE DEPARTMENT OF DEAD ENDS

14 Detective Stories by
Roy Vickers

Selected and Introduced by
E. F. Bleiler

D1610350

DOVER PUBLICATIONS, INC.
NEW YORK

Published in Canada by General Publishing Company, Ltd., 30 Lesmill
Road, Don Mills, Toronto, Ontario.
Published in the United Kingdom by Constable and Company, Ltd., 10
Orange Street, London WC2H 7EG.

This Dover edition, first published in 1978, is an unabridged republication
of the following stories by Roy Vickers, first published as individual stories
under his copyright in the publications listed below:

"The Rubber Trumpet," (*The American Mercury*, 1935)
"The Man Who Murdered in Public," (*Ellery Queen's Mystery Magazine*,
    July, 1944)
"The Parrot's Beak," (*EQMM*, January, 1946)
"The Yellow Jumper," (*EQMM*, June, 1946)
"The Henpecked Murderer," (*EQMM*, January, 1947)
"The House-in-Your-Hand," (*EQMM*, May, 1947)
"The Case of the Social Climber," (*EQMM*, June, 1947)
"The Nine-Pound Murder," (*EQMM*, November, 1947)
"Kill Me, Kill My Dog," (*EQMM*, November, 1949)
"A Man and His Mother-in-Law," (*EQMM*, February, 1953)
"Little Things Like That," (*EQMM*, September, 1953)
"A Fool and Her Money," (*Six Murders in the Suburbs*, published for The
    Detective Book Club, by Walter J. Black, New York, in 1955)
"A Toy for Jiffy," (*EQMM*, August, 1956)
"Marion, Come Back," (*EQMM*, March, 1958)

A new introduction has been written especially for this Dover edition by
E. F. Bleiler.

International Standard Book Number: 0-486-23669-2
Library of Congress Catalog Card Number: 78-52587

Manufactured in the United States of America
Dover Publications, Inc.
180 Varick Street
New York, N.Y. 10014

INTRODUCTION

There have been many Scotland Yards in English literature. There is the Scotland Yard of Inspector Lestrade, somewhat vague and occasionally romantic, and there is its opposite, the realistic Scotland Yard of Inspector Richardson (by Sir Basil Thomson), where the budget has the final say. There are Scotland Yards inhabited by mid-19th-century thugs and bullies, Scotland Yards that vie with Dr. Thorndyke, cooperate with Hercule Poirot and toadie to Lord Peter Wimsey. In fact there are so many different versions of what goes on at New Scotland Yard that to describe them would be to survey most British detective fiction.

Among these Scotland Yards of probability and improbability one that stands out in the mind of aficionados, second only to the one tormented by Sherlock Holmes, is the creation of Roy Vickers in the Department of Dead Ends.

The Department of Dead Ends at Scotland Yard is in a way a philosophic concept as well as a physical place. It is a special department of the Yard where the detritus of unsolved crimes is stored until some larger time when it may be utilized or discarded. It is not a museum, not an artifact file, not a laboratory; it is simply a bureaucratic rubbish pile. Here rests the old suitcase that the murderer used, gold-plated fittings and scratches and all; there the broken toy found near the corpse; on that shelf the toilet articles from the hotel room; against the tier of shelves the framed print abandoned carelessly by the murderer. Through chance, or some weird periodicity factor, or even through a mistaken conclusion by an investigator, this material sorts itself out and is itself the ultimate solution.

By thus elevating the benevolence of chance to a separate depart-

ment of Scotland Yard Roy Vickers wrote a series of short stories
that almost all critics have rated as the best inverted detective stories since the work of R. Austin Freeman, and that many have considered the best British detective short stories of the 1940's and
1950's.

II

Altogether Roy Vickers wrote at least 38 stories that are precisely
concerned with the Department of Dead Ends and a few more that
are peripherally associated with a Scotland Yard abutting on it. I
say "at least" since Vickers was a man of large output in varied
places, and it is always possible that a few stories are still to be
located.

The first Department of Dead Ends story was "The Rubber Trumpet," which appeared unheralded in *Fiction Parade* in 1935. It was
followed by several other stories in the same magazine. These stories
attracted little attention, however, and it was not until several years
later, when they were reprinted in *Ellery Queen's Mystery Magazine* that readers and critics suddenly discovered that one of the
finest contemporary short story writers had been working quietly
among them, without fanfare of trumpets, rubber or otherwise.

The question arose, "Who is Roy Vickers?" and today, about
thirty years later, the question is still mostly unanswered, except in
barest biographical information. Vickers, an Englishman, was born
in 1889 and died in 1965. He attended Charterhouse, a well-known
public school, and studied at Brasenose, Oxford, but dropped out
without a degree. He then enrolled at the Middle Temple in the
Law Courts, in London, although it is not clear whether he
planned a legal career or was simply trying to save money while
learning the writing craft. As he told Ellery Queen, for 2/6 a day he
could eat well at the Temple. During these early years, which must
have been in the second decade of this century, Vickers served var-
iously as an insurance salesman, a real-estate salesman, a stationery
salesman, a ghost writer for would-be authors and politicians, a
crime reporter for a newspaper, and a contest editor for a weekly, at
which last job he was highly unsuccessful: almost everyone who
entered his contests won. Eventually, however, he became a com-
mercially successful freelance writer. His first book, *Lord Roberts,
The Story of His Life* appeared in 1914.

Vickers's second book and first novel to be published in book form was *The Mystery of the Scented Death* (1922), a shocker in the manner of Sax Rohmer's Fu Manchu stories. It was fairly popular and went through several printings in Great Britain.

Over the next forty years or so Vickers wrote at least 72 more books, as well as much material for the periodical press. It is not possible to be precise about his output, for apart from the difficulty of tracing ephemeral publications, he wrote under several pseudonyms. It is known that Sefton Kyle, David Durham and John Spencer were Roy Vickers, but it is also possible that Vickers wrote under still other names. In many instances Vickers's stories first appeared under a pseudonym, then were reissued under a different name, so that the same book is to be found under two different authors. Such was the case with the famous *Exploits of Fidelity Dove*, which was first printed in 1924 under the name David Durham, then reprinted in 1935 as by Roy Vickers.

Since Vickers is known in America almost solely for his later work, like the Department of Dead Ends stories, it would be well to say something about his earlier work, which by and large was not published in America. His earlier books are extremely rare, having been pulped for the most part during World War II. To anticipate, they do not have the quality of his later work, but they do offer points of interest.

All in all Vickers wrote 74 books that I have been able to trace. Most of them are mysteries of one sort or another, but there is a fair assortment of shopgirl romances and general fiction based on topical situations.

The long list of Vickers's novels reveals several points that make one wish that more were known about Vickers as a personality. On the technical side, it is immediately obvious that he was much more skilled at writing short stories than novels. On the personal side, it is equally obvious that Vickers matured very late as a writer (not until the 1940's) and that his earlier work can often be discounted as journalism aimed at the thriller market to which his chief publisher, Herbert Jenkins, Ltd., catered.

Much of Vickers's earlier fiction plays with ideas that were potent in the sensational fiction of the twenties and thirties: social ostracism because of criminal parents, the horrors of unwitting bigamy, the superior wisdom of the young, and the mad race of the Depres-

sion. Other novels, however, are adventure mysteries in the manner
of Edgar Wallace or E. Phillips Oppenheim, with masterminds and
gangs, gun battles, raids, impostors, clean-cut young secret investi-
gators, hidden wealth, and femmes fatales, often on the fairy-tale
level. These mysteries vary considerably, from flimsy thrillers which
Vickers must have written tongue-in-cheek and finished off in
extraordinary ways, to elaborate mystifications with very complex
plotting and attempts at sophisticated characterizations.

None of these earlier novels is completely satisfying, yet even in
Vickers's less substantial work there is often something rewarding,
something emergent that shows that Vickers could have done much
better things, as he was later to do.

Sometimes this is a characterization; amid the simple dash-and-
dare types a well-rounded character will appear. Such is the color-
less maid Slene, who stands behind the criminal activities in *Against
the Law* (1939) or the remarkable Ant of *The Radingham Mystery*
(1928). The Ant is a lady criminal who has received her nickname
for her patience in working out large schemes. She is a ruthless
killer, yet still a pleasant, refined, intelligent member of the British
upper middle class. In *The Gold Game* (1930), which is otherwise
somewhat foolish, there are two fascinating characters, the mealy-
mouthed schemer Malmesbury, and the ancient criminal master-
mind Jabez Winterbourne, who is worthy to stand beside Professor
Moriarty and Counts Fosco and Jalacki as one of the most interesting criminals in the literature. Vickers must have recognized Winterbourne's qualities, in retrospect, for he reused him, with some small
variations, in *Hide Those Diamonds* (1935), despite the fact that
Winterbourne had been found out in the earlier novel and had committed suicide.

Vickers's ability to create a complex plot also deserves some comment. He employed a very unusual technique to carry the reader
along: for each development he soon provided a counterdevel-
opment. The result can be a plot of great intricacy, as what begins
as a simple story divides and bifurcates endlessly, so that the reader
is perpetually tossed back and forth and shunted from one solution
to another. When Vickers works on a sophisticated level and is at
his best in such manipulations, as in *Murdering Mr. Velfrage* (1950,
American title *Maid to Murder*), few authors have been his match
at concealing what every mystery writer wants to conceal.

Some credit should also be given to the earlier Vickers for imaginative criminality. The activities of Fidelity Dove, in *The Exploits of Fidelity Dove* come to mind here. Seldom have more ingenious crimes been perpetrated, what with art swindles, chemical novelties, and that great tour de force, the light bulb that has been hollowed out to conceal gems.

Yet most of these themes, techniques and approaches that I have mentioned for the novels—writing down to semiliterate markets, imitating popular authors, interweaving complex subplots, inventing dazzling tricks—are not to be found in the Department of Dead Ends stories. Indeed, it is sometimes difficult to believe that the same man could have written, say, *Terror of Tongues!* (1937) and *The Bloomsbury Treasure* (1933) and the later work.

The Department of Dead Ends stories are formally very unusual, removed from the conventions of mystery or detective fiction. Displaying many of the characteristics of the factual crime article, they tend to avoid the scene structure of most fiction and move along in a sparse, direct narrative style reminiscent of Hammett's in its complete avoidance of involvement. Each story is a personality study and a life history, in which crime and its roots are symbiotically interwoven and interblooded. Ranging widely over British society they present the matter of dozens of novels in compressed, capsulated form.

It has sometimes been said that Vickers's stories are based on R. Austin Freeman's inverted detective stories, but I think that the resemblances can be overstated. Dr. Freeman told certain of his stories in two parts: first, the criminal accomplishes his crime, leaving in full view of the reader certain minimal traces; then a skilled scientific detective, Dr. Thorndyke, uses the methods of the laboratory to reconstruct the crime from these minimal clues. For Roy Vickers, who does not seem to have been a humanistic optimist, however, there is no faith in scientific method, and no clues, as such, to be examined by a scientist. The reader is usually not aware of what will be significant. There is simply a world of chance, a fatal cloud chamber, in which particles cycling around aimlessly sometimes collide. Occasionally their collisions are observed and interpreted. There is no mystery involved, except the greatest mystery of all, the trend of a human life.

III

On the trivial side, however, there is a mystery associated with the Department of Dead Ends and its personnel—particularly Detective-Inspector Rason, which name I would imagine is not pronounced "raisin" but "Rawson."

The name Rason keeps bobbing up in Vickers's work (along with other names that he seemed to like—Bissett, Aspland, Stranack, Marples, Kyle), and there are at least three detectives Rason in his fiction.

There is the Detective-Inspector Rason of the Department of Dead Ends. He has no first name, and he is something of an oaf with an occasional touch of shrewdness. On his head Fate is pleased to drop titbits now and then. He is the Rason of this book.

There is also another Detective-Inspector Rason of Scotland Yard, who is described in *Hounded Down* (1923). J. Rason: "A little above medium height . . . a powerful physique was the only thing which might conceivably suggest the police force. Of good family and liberal education, he had during the war held the rank of colonel in the Intelligence Department, and at the Yard he was regarded as a future Chief Commissioner." This Rason, who also appears in *Bardelow's Heir* (1933) and elsewhere, is a clever, resourceful, superior detective. Is he also the same Rason of whom Fidelity Dove made such a fool?

The third Rason is a poor, shabby Rason, who is a private detective for the Mansfield Agency in *The Woman Accused* (1923) and *His Other Wife* (1926).

I leave to others the disentangling of the various Rasons and the anagrammed Inspector Sorran of *The Radingham Mystery*.

                                                    E. F. Bleiler

CONTENTS

A TOY FOR JIFFY

In most civilized countries the procedure in the criminal courts permits every circumstance in the prisoner's favor to be brought out and properly considered. In England—though it is painful to admit it—this does not apply to trial for murder. British law acknowledges two points of favor only—reasonable doubt whether the accused did in fact commit the murder, and, alternatively, proof that he was so mentally deranged at the time that "he did not know that what he was doing was wrong."

Of course, Douglas Baines knew that it was wrong to seize a girl by the throat and try to shake the truth out of her. He did not deny that he had taken twenty pounds from her purse. So the judge colored his address to the jury with a great deal of moral indignation.

But that was because the judge did not know how and why Baines had been caught—five years after the crime had been committed.

Baines was the son of a prosperous architect, practising in York. His mother had run away—eloped—when he was two. But his father had filled the double role so successfully that the boy had been barely conscious of his loss. In 1944, he was eighteen and was therefore swept into the army while on his way to a university to seek a degree in engineering. He had no aptitude for soldiering; but in France he did well enough to be given a Field promotion from the ranks. He was pleased because his father was so pleased.

After the fighting was over, he was sent to London on escort duty, without leave. His job done, he wrongfully took the next train to York—he had not seen his father for more than a year.

After the first glad minutes of reunion, he frankly explained that he was awarding himself a few days' leave. His father's geniality vanished and with it the affection of nineteen years. He ordered the boy to return to his unit at once—or he would himself report to the authorities. The shock was profound. Hating the world and himself, Douglas Baines collected his civilian clothing, emptied his bank account of some fifty pounds, deserted the army and his home at the same time, and came to London.

A deserter—without the identity card and the ration book which were then in force—was in much the same position as an escaped convict, except that there was no publicity and he was not actively hunted. Meals could be bought in restaurants. But it was impossible to obtain lawful employment.

When he was halfway through the fifty pounds, he met Daisy Harker, a waitress in a cheap "caff." She guessed what he was doing. She stimulated his waning courage, gave him practical advice on how to scratch a living, and fell in love with him—as much as Daisy Harker could fall in love with any man. Daisy was spirited, more than a little motherly, and passably good-looking.

He joined forces with her, adopting her surname, and drifted into the life of a "spiv." He was not exactly a crook, though few of his activities would bear the full light of day. It was a life of street-corner deals, of shady little commissions, of sudden repairs to a car, with no questions asked. He endured it contentedly enough until Daisy bore him a son. Thereafter, his single purpose was to wriggle himself into a legitimate business.

It so happens that the whole of his life for the next four years is compressed and, as it were, photographed in the last half hour of Daisy's life.

It was early evening of a foggy day in November. He clattered down the stairs to the basement flat, in a slum area near Euston Station. The clattering alone was significant, for the years of spiv-ing had given him a catlike walk. He was carrying a neatly wrapped parcel bearing the imprint of a toy shop. He had the air of a man who has won a sweepstake and is warning himself to keep his head.

The house—a tumbledown Victorian survival—was let by the floor. It was damp and drafty, but at least it provided space. The kitchen-living room was like two rooms in one. In the kitchen half was the stove, overhung with a wash line on which underclothes were drying, and an oilcloth-covered table at which were three chairs, the third being a young child's high-chair. The sitting room part contained two aged armchairs and a settee in faded plush.

He called to Daisy, received no answer, and promptly forgot her. He sat at the table and with slow enjoyment unwrapped the parcel. From the carton he took a tumbler doll, a garish clown made of tin: it was so weighted that when it was pushed over from any angle, it would noisily wobble back to a standing position. Baines pushed it and giggled happily as it wobbled back.

Daisy came in from the bedroom. She had reached home only a few minutes before himself. She was still wearing a neat outdoor skirt and her best blouse, and carried her purse bag in the crook of her arm. She looked from the toy to the paper in which it had been wrapped.

"Did you *buy* that thing?"

"Paid cash over the counter—and liked it! Bert paid up this morning and a good time will be had by all." He glanced over his shoulder, to make sure the bedroom door was shut—in case the boy should be awake. "Jiffy didn't know it was his birthday last Thursday, unless you told him, so his birthday is tomorrow, see? Take a look at this, will you!" He poked the toy. "You can't help laughing!"

"Kids don't play with toys like that."

"Jiffy will!" He pushed the toy out of reach. "Listen, Daise, I've got a bit of good news."

"You always have got a bit of good news."

"Hark at her!" A laugh rippled up from deep down. "This is different, Daisy. This is a real opening at last!"

"I'm sure it is." She was bitter. "You met a man in a pub who has a gem of an idea and enough dough to get it started. And it's legitimate business—or next door to. And in a month you'll have an office of your own and we'll get a decent place to live in. You'll go on having that bit o' good news all your life."

"Say it all!" His eyes were smiling. "Only this time, duckie, you'll be wrong. This man is in a good way of business."

"Did he happen to ask what you've been doing these last few years? . . . Whatcher tell him?"

"I told him I deserted from the army and I'm still on the run." He saw that he had shaken her, and pressed on, "Do you know what he said Daise? He said, 'I got browned off on my last leave, too. But I was luckier than you,' he says. 'My missis—she was the girl friend then—she nagged me into going back to duty. And now I've got a repair garage and I'm getting another and I need a manager.' Meaning *me!*"

Daisy was silenced but not convinced. His tales were never downright lies, though nothing ever came of them.

"Think of it, Daisy! It means an end of all this. It means I'll be able to look Jiffy in the face when he's old enough to ask questions." She remained unimpressed. "We're going to celebrate. There's a half bottle of mother's ruin in my coat. And put some grub up, I'm starving."

He got up, moved towards the bedroom door.

"What're you going in there for?" she asked.

"It's all right—I won't wake him."

"Jiffy isn't in his cot," she said sullenly.

"Cor! You oughtn't to've left him at Ma Dawson's as late as this." A second later his good temper returned. "I'll go and fetch him while you get the grub."

"Stay where you are, Douglas!" The tone of her voice stopped him short. "Jiffy's gone. I've fixed it for him to be adopted. I took him along to his new mum and dad this afternoon."

"Say that again!" He was trying to force time backwards to the moment before she had said it.

"I made up my mind months ago. A gentleman friend who's a lawyer told me I have a perfect right and you can't do anything. And he's seen to the law part of it for me. Better get used to it, Doug. You'll never see that kid again."

He was standing where he had stopped on his way to fetch Jiffy. He was not even looking at her.

"They're decent people, if you want to know—real gentry, with money of their own. They'll give him a proper chance. . . . First and last he's my child, don't forget it. . . . I'll own up you'd have done your best for him, but your best wouldn't have been any good. Done him harm, more like . . . If I've never been a good mother to him before, I've been one today."

Slowly the essential question framed itself.

"How much did they give you?"

"Twenty quid, though I don't see what that's got to do with it, I

suppose you want your cut. You do need a couple o' new shirts."
"We're going to pay it back. Tonight. Before they have time to
get fond of Jiffy."

She stormed at him, arguing that the adopting parents would
send for the police if he made a scene and the police would ask
unanswerable questions. Baines was thinking of something else.

"Jiffy will be frightened in a strange place. Betcher he's howling
for me this very minute. I'm going to get him."

That loosed in her the frustration of years and the submerged
hatred.

"You, slopping over that kid!" she shrilled. "Look him in the face
when he's old enough and—kiss-me-foot! Will you tell him you let
his mother keep you when you daren't go to the hospital because of
being a deserter? And you pretending to believe I got all that cash-
on-the-nail as a waitress in a caff! You'd got eyes, same as other
men. You could see where that money came from."

"It doesn't matter what I've been. Everything's different now."
His own words came as a revelation to him. Life was beckoning to
him and Jiffy. "Put your hat and coat on and take me along to those
people—and I'll marry you as soon as you like. It'd be safe now."

"*You'll marry me!* Thank you kindly, Mister Whatever-your-
name-is—I don't know because you've never told me. And you can
drink that half bottle o' gin by yourself because I'm walking out on
you tonight!"

"Okay! I'll settle about Jiffy myself. You're out of it and no one
will blame you. Give me the address and mind it's the right one."

"So's you can make a nasty smell round his new life before it's
even begun! Not me!"

As she passed his chair he caught her wrist and bent it.

"What's the address?"

When she refused, he gripped her round the neck and slowly
applied pressure.

"You'll break my neck, you fool!"

She was not frightened enough—not yet. But as the pressure in-
creased, she screamed. The scream was cut off and he felt a click
that might have come from her bones. Her weight sagged onto his
hands, and he lowered her gently to the floor.

"Daisy . . . Daisy, snap out of it. . . . I'll get you a drink." He
knew it would be absurd to get her a drink. But, again, he had to

reach back—to the moment before he had killed her. He even took the bottle from his raincoat, but was jerked back to reality by the sound of footsteps—shuffling footsteps which he recognized—coming down to the basement.

The new life had not yet begun—the technique of the old still had its uses. He flung his raincoat over the child's high-chair and moved the chair so that a man standing in the doorway would have no line of vision to the corpse. Then he shouted as if he were still brawling with a living woman.

"You got what was coming to you! And now go and wash your face." Then he opened the door to the elderly tenant of the floor above.

"Why, it's you, Mr. Hendricks! Fact is, I lost my temper and dotted her one. She's washing herself up. P'raps you'd like to see her, so's you can tell Mrs. Hendricks it's all right? . . . Hi, Dais-*eel* Here's Mr. Hendricks wants to know what it's all about. Come in, Mr. Hendricks, she won't be a minute."

But Mr. Hendricks, as could be anticipated, declined the invitation and shuffled back up the stairs.

Baines was now fully alert. He found the same shabby old suitcase with which he had left his father's house, and began to pack. As he was about to leave he caught sight of Daisy's purse on the floor. He picked it up, sat at the table, and opened it. From the litter inside he drew a wad of currency notes.

Twenty pounds.

He was stuffing the notes in his pocket when his elbow knocked against the tumbler doll and set it wobbling. It clattered on the table and inside his head. His sense of time slipped—it was as if the clatter would never stop. He tried to put out his hand to stop it.

The fantasy passed. That twenty pounds had been the price paid for Jiffy. He sprang up and went to the stove. In the act of thrusting the notes inside, he pulled up.

"I must show *some* sense. All right! I'll show some sense." The notes went into his pocket.

Turning round, he faced the tumbler doll. He decided to destroy it—and an instant later was horrified at his own decision. He put it back in its carton, then made room for it in the suitcase by throwing out a pair of gum boots.

2

On the following day the total silence in the basement alarmed
Mrs. Hendricks, who told the rent collector, who in turn informed
the police. They traced the recent movements of "Douglas Harker,"
including the purchase of the gin—which he had left behind—and
the tumbler doll, traced through the wrapping paper. The time of
the purchase suggested that he did not know his child had
already gone to the foster parents—which might have been the
cause of the quarrel. The absence of the toy from the basement suggested that a murderer on the run had encumbered himself with a
bulky, mass-produced toy, worth only a few shillings and difficult to
resell. Possible but unlikely—and certainly not helpful!

The dragnet went out for Douglas Harker, with police description, and yielded nothing—because Harker, the streetcorner commission agent, had, in effect, ceased to exist.

The history of Douglas Baines for the next five years is a commonplace one of steady if unspectacular success. The war restrictions
were now gone and a man could move as freely and anonymously
as he liked. His own name, being a fairly common one, no longer
held danger.

True, the first three months at the garage had taxed his abilities.
Encouraged by the faith of his employer, however, he survived and
soon took the initiative. The repair service grew and added a sales
agency, the trade boom acting as Baines's fairy godmother. He was
able to rent a serviced flat in a respectable district.

In appearance he was a tall, well groomed businessman, looking
a little older than his thirty years. His personality reverted to type.
His outlook, his tastes, and his habits became those which one
would have expected from his early upbringing. The years of spiv-
ing seemed to have left no traces—with one exception.

We again receive a telling picture of Baines by watching his
behavior with a woman—in this case, Joan Mencefield. She was
a first-grade secretary who lived in a flat of her own in Chelsea. The
attraction had been mutual—perhaps strengthened by the girl's
perception that there was a shadow in the man's background.

They were having tea in his flat when he asked her to marry him.

"Yes, of course I will!" He had been rather solemn and hesitant
about it. "In June, if you like," she said. "It will have to be a quiet

one—Mother is hard up. You bring two friends and I'll bring two—
that sort of wedding. You don't mind, do you? Why, you're not
listening!"

"I've been trying to ask you for months. But I felt I had to tell
you something about myself, first. I kept putting it off."

"Then don't tell me—I'll tell you instead." She invited his kiss. "My
dear, dear man! Your secret writes itself all over your face every
time your car is stopped at a crossing by—young school children.
Little boys, about seven to nine years old."

"I'd no idea I was giving myself away like that!" He was pleased,
because now they could share his secret. "I'm not always thinking
about him, only sometimes!"

"I suppose his mother is part of the problem?" she asked.

"Oh, no!" It was as if she had asked a pointless question. "She's
dead and out of it."

He had not forgotten that he had killed her. He blamed himself
—much as a car driver who had killed another in a road smash
might acknowledge to himself a measure of blame. The sense of
personal peril had long vanished.

"I want to be told only one thing, Douglas—is the boy alive?"

That shattered his contentment.

"I don't know!" It sounded worse when he said it aloud. "Why
shouldn't he be alive and happy? With people who are always kind
to him? It's just as likely to be that way as—the other."

He suspected that he was telling her about it in the wrong way.
He warned himself to speak calmly and clearly.

"He was adopted. His mother fixed it behind my back. When I
came home one evening he was gone. Gone for good! I never saw
him again. But that's all over—it doesn't affect me now."

"Only sometimes?"

Her sympathy was weakening his grip on himself.

"Five years ago, it was. He was just three. I'd bought him a toy.
And when I got home, he wasn't there. I couldn't give him his birthday present. See what I mean? I never saw him play with it."

She could not fail to notice the change in him and censured herself for stirring memories that still disturbed him. Before she could
turn the conversation, he added:

"Matter of fact, I have the toy still. Like to see it, Joan?"

"Only if you're quite sure you want to show it to me."

Before she had answered he was unlocking a drawer in the writing table. The carton was crinkled now, but the colors of the clown were as garish as ever. He drew a chair for himself, sat at the table, and gazed at the doll.

Joan watched him with deep concern. She guessed that he had slipped into a world of his own. He was smiling now, but not at her. When he broke into speech she observed the change in his voice.

"Take a look at this, will you! You can't help laughing." He thrust with a finger at the clown. "O-ver he goes! . . . Up again and roundabout. Now it's your turn, Jiffy. Knock him over, boy! That's the way."

He was laughing in counterpoint with the clatter of the toy—the timed, mechanical laughter of a self-induced trance in which he was playing with his child.

Without warning he looked up at her.

"That's torn it!" he said quietly. "I didn't know I was as far gone as that, or I would not have asked you to marry me. We'll call it off, Joan."

"You thought I wanted you to say that—but I don't!" She thrust her arm through his and held him close to her. There was a long silence.

"Do you often play with it?"

"No. I can't remember," he faltered. She waited and he added: "Yes. Quite often."

"Let me keep it for you." She sensed his opposition and hurried on. "You know it's bad for you. If you will trust me with it, I'll lock it away. And I promise I'll give it back at once, whenever you ask, day or night."

"Day or night," he echoed. "How could you keep such a promise? You might not be at home. You're going to your mother's next weekend, and you'll not be back until Monday morning."

That told her that it must be now or never.

"Here is the key to my flat—and here's the key of the left-hand drawer of my dressing table. You can keep them—I have duplicates." Before he could speak, she added: "I think it's our only chance, Douglas—if we are ever to have a child of our own."

Her meaning was sufficiently clear. He wanted her very much and would not risk losing her for the sake of a melancholic dream. He put the toy in its carton and handed it to her.

The next time he saw her—which was also the last time—was on the following Monday morning.

3

He was finishing breakfast when he heard her knock. He got up slowly, puzzled, and opened the door.

She stepped quickly over the threshold, took the latch from his hand, and shut the outer door.

"Douglas! I've let you down, though it wasn't my fault. The toy!"

She had feared some kind of breakdown but he gave no sign of distress.

"I was having breakfast," he said. "There's some tea left. Come along."

She assumed he had not understood. She signed to him not to pour out tea and made a new beginning.

"Bad news! While I was away, sneak-thief burglars got into the flat. They took my nice rug, most of my clothes, all my sheets and blankets, emptied all the drawers on the floor, and left all the windows open so that the rain—"

"That's tough luck!" he broke in. "But you are insured, and there need be no loss in the end. I've lots of blankets and that sort of thing which I can lend you."

"Stop, please! I am trying to break it gently. The toy you entrusted to me for safe-keeping is gone."

"No, it isn't." He was standing by the window, looking out. "I have it."

"Do you mean you took it from the flat before the burglary?"

"Yes. There was no sign of a burglary then."

"Oh, Douglas! I don't know whether to be glad or sorry. Less than a week! I did think you meant to make a real effort."

"I did and I do. I feel very bad about this, Joan. I think it was your going away that did it. The feeling didn't start until Saturday morning, when I thought of you getting on the early train. Then it —well, it sort of grew. It was pretty strong on Saturday evening, but I stuck it out. I fought it on Sunday, but after I'd gone to bed I couldn't hold out any longer. So I dressed and drove over to Chelsea."

She was struck with a sudden happy suspicion.

"I can only half believe you. Are you making it all up to save my feelings? Let me see the toy—please, Douglas." When he unlocked the drawer, showed her the doll, and replaced it, she gave up hope of him.

"You despise me, don't you?" he asked.

"Hardly that." His contrition played on her pity. "It's easy for me to feel superior about it, because I've never had the kind of shock you had. Let's talk about it some other time."

She was about to go when there came a knock on the outer door, and she waited for him to answer it. A moment later she recognized the voice of Detective-Sergeant Jarman, who was investigating the burglary.

"Do you want me, Sergeant?" she asked.

"No, Miss. I didn't know you were here."

"Miss Mencefield and I are engaged to be married," said Baines.

"That should tidy it up," grinned Jarman. "It's about your car, Mr. Baines." He quoted the number. "I have a note that it was parked in Graun Street—that's the side street on the east of the flats—at midnight."

"Correct. But it was there for only a few minutes and I think I can clear myself of the burglary. As you know, Miss Mencefield was away—"

"That's all right, Mr. Baines, now that we know the car was not borrowed for the raid. This gang always uses a private car, which they pick up. They always go for a hundred pounds' worth of domestic stuff, and they do two raids a week—small profits and quick returns, you might say. Sorry to have troubled you, sir."

Thus the district police had an amiable exchange with the murderer of Daisy Harker, without causing him a tremor. It would have been fantastic to assume that he had been concerned in the burglary. No brilliance of detection could have linked the position of that car, at that time, with the murder—but it was for this sort of thing that the Department of Dead Ends existed.

4

Scotland Yard was not called in. It was a small case, with no outstanding feature. But the fact that the windows had been left open rated five lines in an evening paper. The paragraph was read by Detective-Inspector Rason.

"Builder Smith!" exclaimed Rason, and promptly set out for the local police station. Some two years previously, in a similar burglary in Plymouth, the porter of the flats had been maimed for life, and his assailant was believed to be an ex-builder who had never been caught. Builder Smith was known to be in the habit of opening all the windows while working, though he generally shut them when he had finished.

The local station gave him all its information, which helped him little but kept up his spirits. The constable who had observed the number of Baines's car had observed nothing else, as he had been "proceeding" along the side street. Rason thought the owner of the car might be more helpful.

Rason had the integrity, but few of the other qualities, of a good detective. But the Department of Dead Ends was greater than its servants and required of them not brilliance but enthusiasm—and a long memory. Rason would lurch along a trail of hopes and guesses, and the success—in this case and in others—was due to the logic inherent in the Department itself.

After surveying the site of the flats, with special reference to the side street, he called on Douglas Baines.

Baines, who had half expected the police would turn up again with supplementary questions, was very genial about it.

"I warn you I've already told all I know," he said as he invited Rason into the sitting-room.

"That's all right, Mr. Baines. I'm working on another angle." Rason liked the look of the flat—nothing showy or antique—good modern stuff—the sort of flat he would have himself if he could afford it. He gave a racy sketch of the life and works of Builder Smith.

"Well, I'd like to help you, Mr. Rason, but I don't see how I can, so let's have a little whiskey."

Rason accepted. He gave instances of the activities of Builder Smith which an intelligent man like Mr. Baines might have observed.

"But the burglars turned up after I'd gone—I was back here a little after twelve thirty."

Rason blinked.

"The local police don't know what time it was done."

"Nor do I," said Baines. "But I can tell you quite positively that the flat had not been burgled when I entered it at about five past twelve."

"You were *in* that flat!" Rason hesitated. "I know you won't mind my asking this sort of question, Mr. Baines, but how did you get in? I understand Miss Mencefield was away for the weekend."

"I know. I got in with a latchkey."

Rason was not suspicious of anything—he was merely bewildered.

"If you knew the lady wasn't there—I mean, what was the point of going to the flat at that time of night?"

"It isn't *that* kind of latchkey!" Baines spoke severely. "We're engaged and expect to be married very shortly. We run in and out of each other's flats, to fetch this or leave that. It's fairly common, nowadays."

Rason tried to work it out. Fetch this or leave that. At midnight. When the other person wasn't there. Fairly common?

"It sounds all right, in a way." He drained his glass. "Were you fetching something or leaving something that particular time?"

Baines allowed himself to show irritation.

"Don't think me starchy, old man, but has that anything to do with your—Builder Smith?"

"You'd be surprised, but it has! I'll give you the lowdown." Rason enjoyed expounding police doctrine—which he himself so rarely followed. "We go out on all sorts of cases and ask all sorts of questions of innocent persons. One of the first things that's rubbed into us as recruits is never to pass an answer which we don't understand —no matter what it's about and no matter what kind of person we're talking to."

"I didn't mean to make a mystery of it," said Baines apologetically. "I was going to fetch something. Something very personal, and I hope you won't ask me for details."

"And something mighty urgent that couldn't wait until the lady came home, so you had to go and fetch it at midnight? Something you had to get hold of there and then?"

"True, in a sense. But it's nothing illegal nor indecent—nor even particularly private. It's just something—well, damned ridiculous."

"So when my chief asks me why you went to that flat at midnight I tell him it was for something damned ridiculous?"

Baines's reluctance had nothing to do with the fact that the other man was a detective. The murder of Daisy was not in his present consciousness. Even if it had been, his attitude to the detective would probably have remained the same. It would have been beyond his conception that the tumbler doll could be a clue to the old murder. It had not been left on the scene of the crime. Nor could he guess that the police had ever known he had ever possessed such a thing.

"Fair enough!" Baines felt as if he were about to strip before a hostile crowd. "It's a toy—a child's toy."

Rason did not laugh. He was surprised only that the other had made all that fuss about a toy—if it really was about a toy.

"Now you've cleared that up, have another drink?" invited Baines, pouring it as he spoke.

"Here's luck, Mr. Baines!" Rason set down the glass and added, "Better let me see the toy and then I can cross it off."

Rason meant no more than he said. Nothing could be further from his mind than to connect this respectable man, in his comfortable flat, with the crime committed by a street-corner spiv five years ago. Nor could the toy itself provide a link. It had not been featured in the report. The only mention of it occurred at the end of the inventory, and it had but a couple of lines: *Objects unaccounted for: Tumbler doll bought by Harker circa 5.45; not received by foster parents*—followed by the latter's name and address.

Baines was unlocking the drawer in his writing table. He took out the carton, removed the toy, and placed it on the table.

"There you are. That's the whole mystery."

The appearance of the doll moved Rason to reminiscence only.

"I know those things—my niece had one when she was a nipper." He poked the doll. "Hm! Amusing! Only you'd get tired of it, wouldn't you! What do they call 'em? 'Acrobatic doll'—no, 'Tin Tumbler'?"

"I don't know what they call it." Baines was gazing at the doll. "It's a clever bit of nonsense. A small child would sort of think it's alive and make a pal of it." He began to put it back.

"It's your property and you lent it to Miss Mencefield. So that she could play with it by herself?"

"It isn't quite like that. Anyhow, she will confirm that she was keeping it for me."

Rason had only one more question.

"I take it, then, that you got a strong feeling in the middle of the night that you must have that—that acrobatic doll—to play with?"

"If you like to put it like that," admitted Baines. "I suppose it's a sort of tic in the brain. You'll understand now why I wasn't keen to talk about it."

Baines replaced the toy in the drawer. As the lock clicked Rason exclaimed, " 'Tumbler Doll'! That's what they call 'em . . . Tumbler Doll," he repeated. "Reminds me of something . . . a case in our files. About five years ago, it must've been. Let's see, now—how did the tumbler doll come into it?"

That gave Baines his first suspicion of danger. But suspicion was not enough.

"I've got it! A murder job, it was. Name of Harker. A small-time crook."

It had come too quickly for him—Baines knew he had flinched. But Rason did not observe this, because he had not yet connected Baines with the old case.

"Harker had a young child—and he seems to have been fond of it. Chaps like that often do turn out to be good fathers, though you'd hardly believe it. Harker must've thought a lot of his because he bought the tot one of those tumbler dolls. When he got home he found his missis had had the kid adopted without telling him. So he broke her neck and hopped it."

Baines relaxed. There was no danger, after all—no more than there had been for every hour of every day for the past five years. His confidence had been strengthened—the police could chat to him about his own crime without the flicker of a suspicion.

Rason was rattling on.

"Funny thing! That tumbler doll wasn't found in the basement, where they lived. Our men never did find it. Vanished. Almost makes one superstitious when you come to think of it."

"I can guess that one," said Baines. "The spiv posted it to the foster parents?"

"No," said Rason. "We checked."

"What sort of people would adopt the child of a spiv?" asked Baines.

"I don't know what they were like—never saw them. We only kept the name and address in case Harker should try to see his child.

Which he never has." Rason got up from the armchair which he so
deeply approved. "Well, I've taken up a lot of your time, Mr.
Baines, and I'll be off."

Rason glanced guiltily at the clock. He had spent half an hour
finding out nothing about Builder Smith.

"Have one for the road," suggested Baines.

"No, really, thanks! I'd like to sit here yarning with you, but I've
got to make a move."

"Just one more!" Baines poured the whiskey. "You won't do any
more detecting tonight, and this is a quick one."

"That's very nice of you. A quick one it is, and I won't sit down
again . . . Cheers!"

"That yarn of yours about the spiv's child who was adopted. Five
years ago, you said. I think I can put a cap on it. Five years ago a
married cousin of mine adopted a boy—took him from surroundings
very close to your description. My cousin's name is Gramshaw and
he lives at Brighton. I bet that's the name in your files."

Rason gaped at his own face in the wall mirror. What was there in
that face which encouraged amateurs to believe they could pull a
fast one on him?

He was silent so long that Baines asked, "Well? Am I right?"

"Yes," said Rason.

This time he was watching Baines, and saw the other's jaw drop
in sheer astonishment. Rason laughed.

"One of the *other* first things they rub into us as recruits is how
to use a trick question and join it up with another." The trick question had given him a new perspective of the man who had to play
with a tumbler doll at midnight. "You're better at it than me. 'What
sort of people would adopt the child of a spiv?' I fall for it—like the
sucker I am—and let you know I know the name and address. But
you overdid it with an imaginary 'cousin Gramshaw.' I did *not* answer with another name and address. When I said 'yes,' you nearly
had a fit. You *had* to have that address same as you have to have
that doll to play with—and for exactly the same reason."

Baines took the second shock steadily.

"And are you going to tell that fantastic story to your chief?"

"Catch me!" smiled Rason. "He'd say it was all guesswork—without a jot of evidence. Won't breathe a word to anybody until we've

checked on your fingerprints and shown you to old Hendricks and all the others who lived above your basement . . . Cor, you must be fond of that child! Why the hell did you have to insist on that last whiskey when all I wanted was to go home?"

THE HENPECKED MURDERER

THE case of Crippen has been retold so often and in so many languages that the facts are known even to those students of criminal psychology who were not born in 1910, when it all happened. That he was the first murderer to be caught by wireless telegraphy, as it was then called, is to-day of less interest than the fact that police, counsel, and finally warders of the condemned cell all agreed that he was a 'decent little man,' a 'gentleman,' in the moral rather than the social sense of the word. Yet he buried portions of his wife under the floor-boards of the kitchen.

Alfred Cummarten had much of the mentality of Crippen. The Cummarten murder, in 1934, was a sort of tangent to the Crippen murder. As he had not read the case, Cummarten made most of Crippen's minor mistakes, avoiding the major mistake of flight. He was not as anxious as the decent little Crippen that no one else should suffer for his sins—a moral defect which brought its own penalty.

There was even a physical resemblance to the original, for Cummarten was a shortish man, with brown, protuberant eyes, a moustache and a waxen complexion.

Moreover, there was, to start with, exactly the same set-up. Gertrude Cummarten, like Cora Crippen, was regarded by her husband with esteem and affection, although she was shrewish, greedy, and wholly selfish. She drilled and bullied him—for Gertrude, too, was physically larger than her husband, and would sometimes strike him in anger. That her attractions were fading at thirty-seven had, really, nothing to do with the case, because the girl, Isabel Redding, appealed primarily to Cummarten's thwarted paternal instinct.

Isabel, as is now known, was of unidentifiable origin. Someone contrived her admission to a convent school, where she acquired a certain ladylike address, if nothing else. She was twenty-two when she applied to Cummarten for employment as a stenographer. Cummarten was a shipping agent with a small but steady clientele. Isabel was decorative, docile, but remarkably inefficient. Cummarten saw in her an innocent child-woman who could be moulded into the kind of woman he would like his daughter to be—if he had a daughter. So he engaged another girl to be his secretary, and kept Isabel on to run the errands and stamp the envelopes.

Being a silly little man (though Scotland Yard would not agree) he asked her for the week-end to The Laurels, his modest house on the outskirts of Thadham, an old market town some twenty miles from London. He was guileless enough to suggest that his wife should elect herself an honorary aunt.

Gertrude's marked coldness did not deter Isabel from spending three more week-ends at The Laurels during 1933, the last occasion being in July, when Cummarten took her to a flower-show and introduced her to most of his acquaintances.

He was deeply shocked when Gertrude said she did not believe a word of his angel-child nonsense, and that, if he could afford a mistress, which surprised her, he might have the decency not to humiliate his wife by flaunting the girl before the neighbours. The truth was that he himself did believe the angel-child nonsense.

Gertrude's allegation that he was spending money on the girl was true. There was her salary, the bulk of which was a dead weight on the business. There were other expenses—not indeed for dress nor for any kind of entertainment, but for a special diet, to build up her nervous system; for massage to cure her insomnia, and even for books to nourish her mind.

Gertrude's accusation lost its horror through repetition. By the autumn of 1933, it no longer seemed outrageous to notice the physical charms of the young woman he had hitherto thought of as his spiritual daughter. In short, under some high-falutin phrase, she became his mistress in fact. In this period she betrayed a certain sophistication which compelled him to revise the angel-child theory, and to wonder what she had been doing between leaving the convent school and applying to him for employment.

By the turn of the year, his expenditure began to alarm him. This, he believed, was largely his own fault. He would discover little needs of Isabel's, and urge her to do the buying. It was he who suggested that she needed a new bag, not expecting that she would order one in crocodile, costing nine pounds. It was he who said she must have new hairbushes. She ordered a dressing table set in tortoiseshell. He had admired it before she revealed that it would cost one hundred guineas.

"You've been swindled, darling!" he gasped. "I've noticed things exactly like this at Harridges—the whole layout for about a couple of pounds."

"But this is real tortoiseshell, darling!" she explained. "It comes from Perriere's, and they said they would always lend us sixty pounds on it if we should ever need the money. But, of course, I'll take it back if you think I've been extravagant."

By ill luck he had knocked one of the scent bottles to the floor, slightly chipping the glass and slightly denting the tortoiseshell. She had been so nice about it—so anxious to cover up the damage so that the set could be returned—that he eventually sent the cheque to Perriere's, feeling that he had robbed Gertrude.

He was now leading a double life, which he hated. To rob it of some of its duplicity, the silly little man confided in his wife. She treated him with scorn and intensified bullying—which made him feel better, because he despised himself and felt that he ought to be punished.

In July, 1934, Isabel gave him the usual reason, true or false, for hurrying a divorce, to be followed by immediate marriage. He said he would put it to Gertrude, but did not, because he was afraid. For an utterly miserable fortnight he stalled Isabel with palpable lies.

On Monday, August 7th, a Bank Holiday, Isabel took the matter out of his hands by turning up uninvited at the The Laurels—at half-past two in the afternoon—for a showdown with Gertrude.

2

Gertrude had been visiting a cousin at Brighton and did not return until about nine o'clock. A light rain was falling and it was getting dark—but not too dark for the neighbors to observe her return from behind their curtains. They had been, in a sense, waiting for her. They had seen Isabel arrive: they had discussed the details of her dress: in particular, a magenta scarf which was unfashionable and strident but, in her case, effective: a crocodile bag, which they opined must have cost Mr. Cummarten a matter of pounds. They knew

Gertrude had been to Brighton for the day. Whatever happened now, there was certain to be a scandal or at least a rumpus.

'As soon as I heard her footsteps I went into the hall and turned on the light,' wrote Cummarten. *"I meant to tell her about Isabel at once, but, of course, I had to lead up to it a bit. So in the hall I just said something ordinary, like I hoped she had enjoyed her day."*

"Well, I did think you'd have the light on in the hall to welcome me home, even if it'd be a false welcome," said Gertrude. "But I expect we have to be careful with the housekeeping bills, now that you're spending so much money on that girl. And since you ask, I didn't go to Brighton for pleasure. I went to Mabel for advice and I'm going to take her advice. Come in here and sit down, Alfred."

She took him into the little room which they called the morning-room because they had breakfast there. He obediently sat down at the table, knowing that he could not secure her attention until she had talked herself to a standstill.

"Mabel says I'm a soft-hearted fool to put up with it and she's right. And it's got to be one of two things, Alfred. Either you sack that girl from the office and break off with her altogether or I'm going to divorce you."

"I was so surprised when she said this after all I'd been through that I said nothing but stared at her like a ninny."

"You needn't pretend it would break your heart, Alfred. I've no doubt that you'd be glad enough to have done with our marriage altogether, after the mockery you've made of it. But Mabel says the judge would make an order for you to pay me at least a third of your income, and perhaps a half, and so you may want to think twice. *Alfred*, whose bag is that over there by the coal scuttle?"

"As soon as she saw the bag I knew she would tell herself everything and I needn't try to break it gently but just answer her questions."

"It's Isabel's bag," said Cummarten.

"So she has been here! I suspected it from your sly behaviour. What time did she go?"

"She didn't go. She's in the drawing-room."

"Then she's going now. I'm going to turn her out."

"You aren't," said Cummarten. "You can't get into the drawing-room. I've locked the door and I've got the key."

The pitch of his voice made her spine tingle. She reached across the breakfast table, upsetting a vase of flowers, and grabbed him by the lapel of his coat.

"What're you trying to tell me, Alfred? Go on! Say it!"

"She's dead," answered Cummarten. "I killed her."

"Oh-h!" It was a long-drawn, whispered moan. "To think that this should happen to *me!* Oh, dear God, what have I done to deserve this!"

Characteristically, she was concerned solely with the impact of the murder on her own circumstances. She sprawled forward on the table, her face on her forearm, and burst into tears. So violent was her emotion that the silly little man went round to her side of the table to comfort her.

"There, there, my dear!" He patted her shoulder. "Don't take on so, Gert! It won't bring the poor girl back to life. Something goes wrong sometimes, and this sort of thing happens. Stop, Gert—you'll make yourself ill!"

Presently she was able to speak, in a voice shaken with convulsive sobs.

"I was twenty-four when you married me and I'm thirty-seven now. You've had the best years of my life. I could put up with your wanting a younger woman, though it hurt my feelings more than you know. But I did believe you'd always look after me in my old age."

"Thirty-seven isn't old age, dear. Now, do calm yourself, because we've got to settle practical matters before I'm arrested."

That caught her attention.

"You haven't got any money outside the business, have you?"

"No. And I'm afraid you won't get much for that. It's largely a personal connection."

"I can't even go back to nursing. No one would employ me after this!" Her imagination still struggled against accepting the fact of disaster to herself. "Are you sure you've killed her, Alfred? Are you sure she isn't fooling you? How did you kill her? I don't believe you could kill anybody without a revolver, which you haven't got."

"I killed her, all right! She made out we had to have a divorce and me marry her. Even if she was telling the truth about that, I've good reason to believe she could have picked on others besides me. There's one she called Len—I've seen him hanging about—big Spanish-looking feller. Never mind!"

"But you didn't have to kill her for that, Alfred!"

"Let me finish! She came down here on her own for a show-down with you. When she offered to say nothing to you and cut out all the divorce stuff if I'd hand over a thousand pounds, I got pretty angry. After a while, she tried to coax me into a good temper by love-making. Real love-making! I suppose I softened up a bit, and then I felt what a worm I was for letting a woman like that wheedle me. I'd got my arm round her neck in some way—can't remember quite how—and she was pretending to struggle. And I thought if I pushed her chin back it'd break her neck—sort of leverage. And I suddenly wanted to do that more than I'd ever wanted to do anything. And I did it. That's all!"

"I don't believe you killed her!" Gertrude was lashing herself into wishful disbelief. "Give me that key!"

She went alone to the drawing-room. Her past training as a hos-pital nurse saved her from the normal revulsion. When she returned she was carrying the magenta scarf.

"You were right," she said. "I didn't think you could've done it, but you have." She went on: "I've brought this scarf, because it's the sort of thing you would leave lying about, same as you left that bag. You'd better put them both together. The neighbours will have no-ticed both. And we'll have a look round to see if there's anything else, before I go."

"What's the use, Gert! As soon as you've gone, I'm going to ring the police."

"I *thought* that was in your mind!" Her self-pity was lost in fury. "Going to give up without lifting a finger to save yourself? And you call yourself a man!"

"I can take what's coming to me without squealing, anyhow!"

"You mean you can take what's coming to *me!*" she shrilled. "You're ready to kick me into the gutter where I shall be branded for life as the wife of a murderer, and all you think about is how brave you are!"

"But what can I do? It's no good running away!"

"You can get rid of her if you keep your head. You can use a spade, can't you! And who's to know she didn't leave the house and run off with a man who's got more money than you—not that any-one will bother their heads about what happens to that sort!"

Cummarten had planned to give himself up, because he had not been able to imagine doing anything else. But already Gertrude had planted in his brain the idea of escape. For thirteen years he had lived under her domination. Always, after his domestic blunders, she had first bullied him and then cleared up the mess. The same process was now at work on a larger scale.

"Suppose something goes wrong?" he objected, in order to receive her reassurance, which promptly came.

"Nothing will go wrong if you do as you're told. I shall have to leave everything in your hands, because I know you wouldn't wish me to take any risk of being dragged into it. I shan't worry about myself. No one need know I've helped you. I wasn't seen coming home to-night. It so happened that I took the bus from the junction instead of waiting for the local train, and no one else got out at the corner and there was no one about, because it was raining. I'll get along to Ealing and spend the night with mother. You can say I went straight there from Mabel's. You can give out that mother is ill and I'm looking after her. As soon as it's all clear, I'll come back."

"You mean we can take up our life again as if nothing had happened!" There was awe in his voice as the idea took shape.

"I'm quite ready to try all over again to make you happy, Alfred, now that you've learnt your lesson."

But she must, of course, take care not to burn her fingers. In a few minutes she had evolved a plan by which all risk was concentrated upon Cummarten. She made him repeat his orders and then:

"I'll slip out to the garage now and get into the car. The neighbours will hear the engine. And if anyone asks you afterwards, which they won't, remember to say that you were driving the girl back to her flat in London. If anyone wants to speak to me they can ring me up at mother's."

3

With a course of action laid down for him, Cummarten's nerve steadied. He made good time to London. In Holborn he dropped Gertrude at the tube station, where she was to take a train to Ealing. He himself drove on to the flatlet, which was in one of the dingier blocks in Bloomsbury. The block had no resident porter—a fact which most of the residents regarded as an advantage. He chose his moment for leaving the car, his sole concern being that no one should observe that he was alone.

The flatlet consisted of a fair-sized room with two curtained recesses. It was clean but untidy. Three large fans nailed on the walls gave it a would-be artistic atmosphere, helped by an expensively elaborate cover on the ottoman bed. For the rest, there was the usual bed-sitting-room furniture.

Acting on Gertrude's instructions with all possible speed, Cummarten found Isabel's suitcase. Into it he crammed her nightdress and other small oddments. Next, "any small articles you've given her that are expensive." The tortoiseshell dressing-table set was certainly expensive though it was not small, as it consisted of eight pieces including the scent bottles. It occupied two-thirds of the suitcase and left no room for any additions.

The magenta scarf he placed 'carelessly' on the folding-table. The crocodile bag, emptied at The Laurels, he put on the floor near the stove, as if the girl had flung it down after emptying its contents into another bag.

By midnight, he was back at The Laurels.

He had brought his tools from the garage and a spade and pick from the adjoining tool shed. He moved the table and chairs from the morning-room into the hall. Then he untacked the carpet in the morning-room and removed some of the floor boards.

This gave him no serious difficulty—he had finished before one. Below the beams holding the floor-boards he had expected to find soft earth. Instead, he found rubble, evenly spread to a depth of some eighteen inches. Clearing this was extremely laborious: he had to work very slowly because the rubble made a dangerous amount of noise. His courage fluctuated: while he was wielding the spade he was steady: but when he rested, which was often, he would fancy he heard footsteps on the garden path and would climb up and listen, to reassure himself.

It was half-past three before he had cleared a sufficient area. Temporarily exhausted, he went into the kitchen and revived his strength with tea. When he re-started work, with the pick, he realised that his own stamina would be a major factor. Though the house had been built before cement was commonly used for the purpose, the foundations had been well laid and the earth was dry and very hard.

In an hour his strokes with the pick became feeble. By six o'clock his physical condition resembled that of a boxer who has just managed to keep on his feet for a twenty-round contest. His wrists were numb and his knees were undependable. It was all he could do to hoist himself back onto the floor of the morning-room. As he lay panting he knew that, in his present condition, he could not possibly carry the body and complete his task before eight o'clock, when Bessie, the daily help, would arrive. If he were to make the attempt and fail he would be worse off than if he were to leave it in the drawing-room.

He was moving so slowly that when he had replaced everything in the morning-room and re-tacked the carpet with his hammer-head muffled, half-past seven was striking.

Having washed, he went upstairs, got into bed for a minute in order to tumble the bedclothes, then did his best to shave as usual. When he heard Bessie arrive he came down in his dressing-gown.

The drawing-room door was locked: the blinds were down, as he had left them the previous evening: the french windows giving on to the garden were bolted on the inside. He had only to keep his head and, as Gertrude had promised, everything would be all right.

"Mrs. Cummarten," he told Bessie, "has had to go to her mother who has been taken ill. If you'll get me some breakfast, that'll be all. You can have another day off."

"All right, sir!" Bessie was not overjoyed. After Sunday and the holiday on Monday there would be arrears of cleaning which would have to be made up later. "But I'd better do the drawing-room before I go."

"You can't," said Cummarten. "It is locked and Mrs. Cummarten has evidently taken the key with her."

"That doesn't matter," returned Bessie. "The key of the morning-room fits."

To keep his head was the first essential. But what was the use if you couldn't think of things quickly, not being that sort of man.

"I'd rather you didn't, Bessie." With sudden misinspiration, he added: "Before Mrs. Cummarten left yesterday morning she started to clean the china. She had to break off to catch her train—and she left the pieces all over the floor. She asked me to keep the room locked."

Bessie stumped off to the kitchen. She heard him remove the keys from the morning-room and the dining-room. Knowing that something was being kept from her, she went into the garden and tried to look through the edges of the blind, but without seeing anything except part of a cushion from the settee lying on the floor.

Instead of leaving for the office at nine-fifteen, Cummarten stayed on in the morning-room, so that she could not clean it. Bessie left at ten. But before going home, she stepped across the road to The Cedars to tell her friend, who was help to Mrs. Evershed, all about the locked drawing-room and the nonsense about the china being on the floor.

Cummarten was dozing in his chair at eleven when Mrs. Evershed knocked at the front door.

"I didn't mean to disturb you, Mr. Cummarten—I thought you'd be at the office. Can I have a word with Gertrude if she isn't busy?"

"Sorry, but she's in Ealing looking after her mother. I don't suppose it's anything much, but the doctor says the old lady had better stay in bed for a bit. Don't know when Gertrude will be back."

Mrs. Evershed delivered the usual polite platitudes, and then:

"Did she leave a message for me about Thursday? She said she'd know for certain by Monday night."

"I haven't seen her since yesterday morning," said Cummarten.

"Oh!" said Mrs. Evershed, who was amongst those who had seen Gertrude return, "I thought she was coming home last night."

"She was, but she didn't. On her way back from Brighton she stopped off at Ealing, then 'phoned me that she would stay there."

Bessie's friend had already repeated to Mrs. Evershed the tale of the locked drawing-room. Mrs. Evershed carried the tale to others. Before noon, there were two more callers for Gertrude, who received from Cummarten the same explanation.

During the afternoon he was left in peace and slept in his chair until nine. By midnight he was at work again on the grave. He was more careful of his strength this time and completed his task by four. The remains of Isabel and the contents of her crocodile bag and of the suitcase he had brought from the flatlet were buried four feet in the earth, with another eighteen inches of rubble on top. The floor boards and the furniture were replaced.

In the drawing-room, the dozen odd pieces of china had been moved from the cabinet and placed on the floor, to give substance to the tale told to Bessie. Cummarten bathed, went to bed and slept until Bessie called him.

At breakfast he was surprised at his own freshness. "I must be as strong as a horse, when I'm put to it," he reflected with pride. That he had killed Isabel Redding ranked in his mind as a tragic misfortune, over which he must not allow himself to brood. He had a moral duty to Gertrude and, so far, had made a pretty good job of it, as Gertrude herself would have to admit.

When he arrived at the office he decided to ring Gertrude and let her know that the coast was clear—was about to do so when his secretary came in.

"Good morning, Miss Kyle; has Miss Reading been in to collect her belongings?"

"I have not seen Miss Redding since Friday last," replied Miss Kyle with some hauteur, "and her belongings are still here."

"She came to my house on Monday and made it clear she would not be working for us any more. I fear," he added, "that Miss Redding has not been a success in this office."

Miss Kyle, who was well aware of their intimacy, said nothing.

Having dealt with his mail, he rang his mother-in-law's flat in Ealing, but could get no answer. He tried again before going out to lunch and again when he returned. Then he rang the porter of the flats—to learn that Mrs. Massell, his mother-in-law, had gone away for the week-end, had not yet come back and that the flat was therefore empty.

"Has Mrs. Cummarten—my wife—been to you to make enquiries?"

"No, sir, there've been no enquiries for Mrs. Massell since she went away last Friday."

Cummarten replaced the receiver and found himself badly at a loss.

"Then where on earth is Gertrude?"

4

Others were already asking that question—including Mrs. Massell herself. On her way back from a long week-end at Salisbury she had stopped off at Thadham to have a chat with her daughter. Arriving after Bessie had left, she was unable to obtain admission to the house. Mrs. Evershed popped out of The Cedars. Explanations were being exchanged in the front garden of The Laurels when Cummarten himself appeared . . .

"That's what Gertrude told me on the telephone," said Cummarten doggedly.

"But she knew I had gone to Salisbury!"

"I'm not saying what she knew. I'm saying what she told me." His mother-in-law walked him, by the sidepath, to the garden at the back of the house.

"You said all that because that Evershed woman was listening. Where is Gertrude?"

"I don't know! That's the maddening part of it!" cried Cummarten in genuine exasperation.

"When did you last see her?"

"Monday morning when she was going off to Mabel's." He added a flourish: "At least, that's where she said she was going."

Mrs. Massell gave him a hostile stare.

"Look here, Alfred, it's no use your trying to hint that she has run off with a lover. She's not that kind and wouldn't need to run when she could easily divorce you, as I happen to know, though you may have thought I didn't. If she has disappeared, something has happened. She may have lost her memory, like those people you hear about on the radio every night. Or she may have met with an accident—she might even have been murdered, for all you know or seem to care."

A long, bitter laugh broke from him, which angered her further.

"You may not care much about her, but I warn you that you will find yourself in a very awkward position if anything has happened to her and you doing nothing about it."

"But what *can* I do?"

"Come straight to the police with me and start inquiries."

"That's no good!" he said sulkily. "The police will take no notice."

"Then I am going myself," said Mrs. Massell and promptly went.

5

In the Crippen case, the very similar lies were exposed within a few days of the murder. Nevertheless, six months passed before the police were able to take even the preliminary steps. But Crippen had no mother-in-law, nor did he employ domestic help.

Mrs. Evershed's maid, in whom Bessie had confided, was being courted by a young constable, to whom she passed Bessie's tale and

Mrs. Evershed's comments. This she did to entertain the young man, not with any idea of informing the police as such—for even at this stage there was no suspicion that a crime had been committed, in spite of the locked drawing-room.

But everyone's sense of proportion was shattered by the arrival of Mrs. Massell. When she was seen to enter the local police headquarters there was hardly anyone in the neighbourhood who was not ready to believe that Cummarten had murdered his wife. In drawing-rooms, in gardens, at the local tennis club, the case of Crippen was recalled, the younger generation tactfully pretending they had not heard it all before.

If the police did not jump to that conclusion, they would seem to have toyed with it. By half-past nine, when he went to The Laurels, Superintendent Hoylock had tapped all sources and primed himself with every available fact, even to the details of Isabel Redding's magenta scarf and crocodile bag. He wanted, he told Cummarten, confirmation of Mrs. Massell's statement, before he could ask the B.B.C. to broadcast an inquiry.

Cummarten took him into the dining-room, which was rarely used. He heard his mother-in-law's statement read and nodded confirmation of each item, inwardly fearing that Gertrude would be very angry at having her name called on the radio.

"When did you last see Mrs. Cummarten?"

"About the middle of Monday morning—before she went to Brighton."

Superintendent Hoylock folded the statement and returned it to his pocket.

"Mr. Cummarten, your wife was seen to enter this house within a few minutes of nine o'clock on Monday night."

It had not yet dawned on Cummarten that he was in immediate danger of anything but Gertrude's wrath. He looked positively angry.

"It's all Gertrude's fault for not telling me where she's gone!" he blurted out spontaneously. In spite of what Gertrude had said, he would now have to admit that she had returned on the Monday night. His anger stimulated him to a certain ingenuity in adapting the story which Gertrude had concocted.

"I'd better begin at the beginning, Superintendent. A young lady I employ at my office—a Miss Isabel Redding—came to see us in the afternoon. She has been here often—spent several week-ends. She looked on us almost as relations. Lately, my wife became jealous, and everything was—well, not so pleasant as it used to be. Isabel came down to talk it all over. She waited until my wife came home. Words passed, and you may say there was a bit of a row. Soon we all calmed down and I drove the girl back to her flatlet. When I got back here—must have been about midnight—my wife had gone. Next morning the neighbours asked where she was. I wasn't going to tell 'em what I've been telling you, so I told 'em the first thing that came into my head. My wife may have walked out on me for all I know."

The story held up under Hoylock's questions, because it covered all the facts known to him—with one exception.

"With one thing and another, Mr. Cummarten, you've set people talking their heads off. There's a tale about something funny in your drawing-room——"

"That must be Bessie, our maid," said Cummarten. "You see, after breakfast on Monday, before my wife left for Brighton, she thought she'd clean the china——"

"So I heard," interrupted Hoylock. "It wouldn't do any harm to let me see that room."

Cummarten produced a number of keys from his pocket, unlocked the drawing-room door. The Superintendent saw drawn blinds, and a litter of china on the floor—also on the floor, near the window, a cushion.

"Shows what people will say!" remarked the Superintendent. "Now I'll tell you what we'll do. If nothing develops by tomorrow morning, we'll put it up to the B.B.C. People really do get lapses of memory sometimes when they're upset. Good night, Mr. Cummarten. Don't you worry! We'll stop people talking!"

Talking! What were they saying?

Why, of course! Why hadn't he seen it before! They were saying that he had murdered *Gertrude!*

And what did they think he had done with her body?

Buried it under the floor boards?

6

On Thursday, as Cummarten was about to leave the office for lunch, Superintendent Hoylock turned up, in plain clothes.

"Miss Redding might be able to help us find your wife," he said. "Can I have a word with her?"

Cummarten explained. He was pleased when Hoylock asked for her address, because he wanted the police to 'discover' the magenta scarf and the crocodile bag.

"It's a bit difficult to find. It'll save your time if I take you there."

Outside the flatlet, Hoylock pointed to three milk bottles with the seals unbroken.

"Tuesday, Wednesday and this morning!" he remarked and rapped on the door. "Looks as if we shan't get an answer."

Cummarten indicated that he was not surprised, and added: "I have a key—she used to like me to have one."

Inside the flatlet, the Superintendent behaved, as Cummarten hoped he would, by immediately noticing the magenta scarf on the folding table.

"Is that the one she was wearing on Monday afternoon?"

"Let's have a look! Yes, that's the one all right."

Hoylock's eye travelled to the crocodile bag lying on the floor near the stove.

"Wonder why she hasn't taken her bag with her!"

"She had more than one." Cummarten picked up the bag and displayed the empty interior. "She evidently shifted her money and whatnots to another bag."

"So *she's* disappeared too!" exclaimed Hoylock. "That's what I call a most peculiar coincidence!"

"Not much coincidence in it, really!" said Cummarten quickly. "When I was up here with her on Monday night she said she was going straight off to a feller."

"There and then? Without telling the man she was coming?"

"I didn't believe it any more than you," said Cummarten. "She started packing things before I left, but I thought she was putting on an act."

"What's the man's name?"

"Don't know. She used to refer to him as 'Len'. I saw him hanging about outside once. Tall, dark chap, thick eyebrows and sidewhiskers. Like a Spaniard. Sort o' chap who appeals to women. Probably a dancing partner by profession."

Hoylock made a note of the description. Next, he opened the wardrobe, then the drawers of the dressing-table. Cummarten wished he would ask if there were anything missing from the dressing-table.

But Hoylock said the wrong thing.

"She didn't take much with her, did she!"

"There was very little room in her one suitcase," said Cummarten, "because she had to take her dressing-table set—brushes, combs, scent bottles—eight pieces in all. I saw her packing them."

"What! All that junk when she'd only got one suitcase! You'd think she'd leave that sort of thing till she came back for her clothes and furniture."

"It was a very valuable set," explained Cummarten. "A present from myself—with my wife's approval, of course! It was real tortoiseshell. I paid Perriere's a hundred guineas for it."

"A hundred guineas!" Hoylock was impressed and elaborated his notes.

Everything, thought Cummarten, was going just right, though he wondered why Hoylock was showing such detailed interest in Isabel's movements.

"Miss Redding," he said, "is certain to turn up in a few days to collect her things. Is it your idea, Superintendent, that she and my wife have gone off together?"

"I don't say they have. But I do say that if Mrs. Cummarten doesn't turn up after the radio appeal we shall have to find this girl."

Superintendent Hoylock returned to Thadham to file a detailed report—Cummarten to his office to spend the afternoon wondering what had happened to Gertrude.

After the nine o'clock news that night, Gertrude's name was called amongst those missing from their home and believed to be suffering from a loss of memory.

Cummarten sat up until after midnight in the hope that she might turn up. It didn't occur to him that her absence might have a wholly selfish explanation. For his peace of mind he forced himself to accept the loss of memory theory. Someone had told him that the broadcasts always found such persons, if they were alive. He saw clearly what his fate would be if the broadcast failed to produce results in a very few days.

7

When Cummarten entered his office the next morning he found a young man chatting to Miss Kyle.

"Mr. Cummarten," said Miss Kyle, "this gentleman is from Scotland Yard."

Cummarten managed to say 'good morning'. But it was a minute or more before he could understand what the young man was saying. "In a boarding house in West Kensington, Mr. Cummarten. We can get there in twenty minutes in a taxi. If the lady is Mrs. Cummarten I can then notify the B.B.C."

The lady was indeed Mrs. Cummarten. She was being virtually held prisoner by the proprietress of the boarding-house, who had been suspicious from the first of this visitor who had paid a deposit in lieu of luggage.

Gertrude had the presence of mind to tell the plain-clothes youngster that her memory was a blank from the moment she left Brighton on the previous Monday. While the report for the B.B.C. was being filled in, Cummarten telephoned a telegram to Superintendent Hoylock.

In the taxi that was taking them to the station, their first moment alone, Gertrude asked:

"Is everything all right, Alfred?"

"Absolutely! Only it would have been everything all wrong if you hadn't been found. I say—did you really have a lapse of memory?"

"Of course not! In the train I suddenly remembered mother was at Salisbury. I daren't ring you up—in case. It wouldn't have been safe to do anything but just keep out of the way. I was getting short of money. I tried yesterday to catch you on the Tube without anybody seeing me."

He failed to perceive her callous indifference to his own fate, contented himself with a modest grumble.

"This time yesterday everybody thought I'd murdered you. In another day or two——"

"Well, then, that's the best thing that could have happened, when you come to think of it!"

In the train, in an unoccupied compartment, he gave her his account. To his surprise, she was extremely annoyed when he told her about the locked drawing-room door and the china ornaments.

"As if anybody would believe I'd be so silly! What would be the sense of putting the china on the floor?"

"I couldn't think of anything else to say on the spur of the moment."

"The less you think about the whole thing now, the better. I shall

pretend I've forgotten everything, and they can't get over that."
The neighbours did not even try to get over it. The prestige of
the B.B.C. had the illogical effect of making everyone believe that
the lapse of memory must have been genuine. Police interest vanished
with the return of Mrs. Cummarten. In a week or so, the neighbourhood, in effect, forgot its disappointment that a major scandal
had failed to materialise.

A month later, Isabel Redding's landlord distrained on the flatlet
for non-payment of rent. A dressmaker complained that Isabel had
obtained a credit of forty pounds by false pretences. The Bloomsbury police, after a perfunctory attempt to find her, reported her as
missing. As missing she appeared in the official police publication.
Superintendent Hoylock, remembering the name, sent a copy of his
report to Scotland Yard.

"Same old story!" grunted the inspector in charge. "You can
never trace these girls. You may pick 'em up by chance some day.
Or you may not!"

With which remark he dropped the report into the basket which
would eventually be emptied in the Department of Dead Ends.

The Cummartens resumed the even tenor of their life together.
Though neither was strong in logic nor in law, they knew, in general terms, that before the police can start digging up a man's garden
or lifting his floor boards, they must establish before a magistrate a
prima facie case that somewhere therein he has feloniously concealed
a corpse.

They knew also that it was now impossible to establish such a case.

8

In May, 1935, the Cummartens went to Brighton to stay for a fortnight with Gertrude's cousin Mabel. While they were away, one
Leonard Haenlin, a tall, dark, handsome scoundrel, remarkable for
his sidewhiskers, was charged by a wealthy spinster with stealing her
automobile and defrauding her in other ways.

The defence was that the car and the other articles and sums of
money were gifts, and it looked as if the defence would succeed.
The police had recognised that this man was a professional despoiler
of women and were working up the case. His rooms were equipped
with a number of expensive articles—including a handsome and obviously expensive dressing-table set of eight pieces, in real tortoiseshell.

When asked to account for the latter, he grinned in the face of Detective Inspector Karslake.

"You think they are not mine. For once, you happen to be right. They belong to a girl friend, who lent them to me. Her name is Isabel Redding." He added the address of the flatlet.

One of Karslake's men went to the flatlet to check up—to be humiliated by the information that Scotland Yard had posted the girl as missing the previous September.

A chit was duly sent to Detective Inspector Rason asking for any available light on the ownership of the tortoiseshell set. Having found the reference in Superintendent Hoylock's report, Rason called on Haenlin, who was on bail, to see the set for himself.

"When did you borrow it, Len?"

"She lent it to me to pawn on July 20th, last year. If you look it up, you'll find that on that day I was fined forty quid for a little misunderstanding in Piccadilly. Perriere's, where it came from, said they'd always lend her sixty quid on it. But one of the bottles had a dent and a chip—the mutt who gave it her knocked it off her table —look for yourself—and they would only spring forty-five."

"A good tale, old man—but you're switching this set with another," chirped Rason. "D'you know where Isabel got her set?"

"Yes. From a funny little bloke with a pasty face called Cummarten. You been a detective inspector long, Mr. Rason?"

"July 20th, you said," returned Rason. "Stand by for a shock! On the night of Monday, August 7th, Mr. Cummarten saw Isabel packing her tortoiseshell set into her suitcase."

"He didn't—he only thought he did," grinned Haenlin. "Listen! I knew I couldn't redeem the stuff for a bit, and Pasty Face might miss it from Isabel's table. So we went to Harridges and paid thirty-seven-and-six for an imitation set, like enough to that one for old Pasty Face not to know the difference. I redeemed the other set last month; you can check up if you want to."

"That's big of you, Len. Where shall I find her to check up?"

"Wish I knew! She's a good kid, that!"

"Very good not to bother you about her tortoiseshell."

"Can't make out why she hasn't been round!" Haenlin scowled. "I'm not sure she isn't holding out on me. She went down to make a row between Pasty Face and his wife, saying she must have a divorce. It's not a sound line as a rule, but sometimes it works. She

reckoned to touch for a thousand. Maybe she got it and is spending
the dough on her own. Can't think of any other reason why she has
kept out of my way."

At Perriere's, Rason learnt that Haenlin's tale of the purchase
and the subsequent pawning was true. Therefore the tale about the
imitation set, which had successfully deceived Cummarten, must also
be true. But it didn't make sense.

"If the girl was off in a hurry with one suitcase, she wouldn't
stuff it with the whole eight pieces of doodah which she knew to be
practically valueless. Even if she had pretended to Cummarten that
she was taking them, she'd have unpacked 'em as soon as he left the
flatlet. Hm! Probably Hoylock has muddled his facts."

At Thadham, it soon became clear to Rason that Superintendent
Hoylock had not muddled his facts. He heard Hoylock's full story,
which included the story of the locked drawing-room and the china.

"So all Tuesday that door was locked—and most of Wednesday?
And the blinds were down?"

When Hoylock assented, Rason asked for Bessie's address. By indirect means he contrived that the girl should show him the china,
of which he noted that there were only a dozen small pieces.

On the way back he surveyed progress, if any.

"The next check-up is whether it's true the girl was blackmailing
Cummarten for a thousand. Hm! Simplest way to do that would be
to ask Cummarten."

9

Two days later, when the Cummartens stepped out of the Brighton
train at Victoria Station they were surprised to find that Bessie had
come to meet them. And Bessie was not alone.

Rason stepped forward and announced himself, positively grovel-
ling with apology.

"I'm very sorry indeed to pounce on you like this, Mr. Cummarten, and I hope Mrs. Cummarten will forgive me. It's about the
Haenlin case—I daresay you read about it in the papers."

Cummarten felt the pain in his breathing apparatus vanish.

"We have a strong suspicion that Haenlin is the man you told Superintendent Hoylock last year that you had seen outside the flatlet
of Miss Redding. By the way, we haven't traced that girl yet."

Cummarten, with something approaching graciousness, agreed to accompany Rason to the Yard to identify Haenlin. Now that the whole thing had blown over, he wished he had never mentioned 'Len' to the superintendent. Still, it had been a wise precaution at the time. He told Gertrude that he would come on by the one-fifteen to Thadham and his lunch could be kept hot.

"Haenlin," said Rason in the taxi, "is charged with swindling women. But we strongly suspect that he knows something about the disappearance of Miss Redding."

"He struck me as a pretty rough type," put in Cummarten, "though I suppose one shouldn't judge on appearance."

"You don't have to," said Rason. "He was working with that girl to trim you, Mr. Cummarten. He knew all about her coming down to try and sting you for a thousand quid—he admitted it when we started work on him. But he wouldn't say whether you had paid her the thousand. Would you have any objection to telling us?"

"I have no objection to telling you," said Cummarten gaining time to reflect that such a payment could be traced, "that I did not. I couldn't afford such a sum."

So it was true that the girl had tried. That altered the perspective of all Cummarten's statements and all his actions. But perspective isn't evidence. There was still a long way to go.

"To show you how he knew all about your affairs," continued Rason, "he even mentioned that you'd given her that tortoiseshell dressing-table set and that you yourself had chipped and dented a scent bottle, thereby reducing its value."

Cummarten was shocked at this revelation of Isabel's treachery.

"I'm not the first man to make that sort of fool of himself," he muttered. "But I didn't know she was playing as low down as that."

Rason's room, normally a disgrace to the orderliness of Scotland Yard, to-day looked more like a store room than an office. His desk had been pushed out of place to make room for a trestle table, the contents of which were covered with a white sheet which might almost have been a shroud.

"We shall have to keep you waiting a few minutes for the identification, Mr. Cummarten," apologised Rason. "Take a seat."

Cummarten sat down, uncomfortably close to the trestle table.

"In the train coming up from Thadham, your maid Bessie made me laugh," chattered Rason. "Told me how she thought once you had murdered Mrs. Cummarten, because the drawing-room door was kept locked. And it all turned out to be something to do with the china being on the floor."

Cummarten, being a silly little man, took the words at their face value.

"Yes. My wife was cleaning it when she had to run for her train, and——"

"Why did Mrs. Cummarten clean the china in the dark?"

Cummarten blinked as if he had not heard aright. Rason added: "Bessie says the blinds were down."

Cummarten opened his mouth and shut it. Rason stood up, towering over him.

"D'you know, Mr. Cummarten, if a girl tried to sting me for a thousand pounds I wouldn't see her home." He drew at his cigarette. "I'd be more likely to murder her.

"And if I had murdered her I might sneak into her flat and plant her scarf and her bag—then carry off her expensive toilet set, to suggest that she had bolted."

Again Cummarten had felt that pain in his breathing apparatus. It passed, as cold fear forced him to self-control.

"I don't begin to understand you, Mr. Rason. You asked me here to identify that man——"

"Still trying to plant the murder on him, Cummarten? You packed that tortoiseshell stuff in the suitcase yourself and took it back to your house. And you know where you put it."

"I deny it!" The words came in a whispered shout.

"You're wasting your breath, Cummarten. Look at that white sheet in front of you, Cummarten. Any idea what's underneath it, Cummarten? Well, lift up the sheet and see. Go on, man! It isn't Isabel—we couldn't bring her along."

Cummarten sat as if paralysed. Rason tweaked the sheet, slowly raising one corner. Cummarten stared, uncertain whether he were experiencing hallucination. For he saw on the trestle table a scent bottle, with a chip in the glass and a dent in the tortoiseshell cap.

He sprang up, tore the sheet from Rason's hand and flung it back. Spread out on the table was a complete tortoiseshell set of eight pieces.

"You know where you put it!" repeated Rason.

With a cough-like sound in his throat, Cummarten collapsed into his chair, covering his eyes with his hands. When he removed his hands he looked like an old man, but he was wholly calm.

"I suppose it had to come some time," he said. "In a way, it's a relief to get it over. I can see now what a fool I've been from the first. That tortoiseshell brings it all back." He smiled wanly. "Paid a hundred guineas for that set!"

It was indeed the set for which Cummarten had paid a hundred guineas—the set which Len Haenlin had pawned and redeemed. Rason had borrowed it when he had become morally certain that Cummarten had buried Isabel—and the imitation set.

But he still had no proof—still did not know precisely where Isabel was buried—could doubtfully have obtained an order to dig at random.

"You made a good fight of it!" remarked Rason. "Weakest spot was that yarn about cleaning the china——"

"First thing that came into my head when Bessie wanted to do the drawing-room on the Tuesday morning! You see, I couldn't finish the job in the morning-room on the Monday night—all that rubble!"

Rason dug under the morning-room. With the remains of Isabel Redding, there was found an imitation tortoiseshell toilet set costing thirty-seven and sixpence.

THE YELLOW JUMPER

THE execution of Ruth Watlington sent a shudder through respectable, middle-class Britain. If she had in some way repudiated her upbringing, by becoming a crook or a drug-addict, or a 'bad woman,' it would have been more comfortable all round. As it was, her exposure created the suspicion that the impulse to murder is likely to seize almost anybody who has enough animal courage to see it through. It was not even a *crime passionel,* although scented hair, moonlight playing on running water, and a wedding became subsidiary factors—particularly the moonlight on the running water.

This is in no sense a love chronicle; but we must for a moment concern ourselves with the romantic vapourings of poor Herbert Cudden, the mathematical master at Hemel Abbey, a girls' boarding-school in Devonshire.

At eight-thirty on May 2nd, 1934, a week before the summer term opened, he was alone in the empty schoolhouse putting the finishing touches to his syllabus. His thoughts kept sliding to a young, modern languages mistress, Rita Steevens, who had come, fresh from the University, a couple of terms ago.

An under-vitalised man, he had been astonished at his own boldness in proposing marriage to her, still more astonished when she accepted. Incidentally, he had been very grateful to his friend and colleague, Ruth Watlington, for inviting Rita to share her cottage.

Daydreaming of this young woman, he visualised her in the dress in which he had last seen her. Now, if he had simply remembered that she had looked delightful in whatever she was wearing, it would have been better for his own peace of mind in later years. He was not the kind of man who understands women's dress.

Nevertheless, he happened to visualise Rita in what women call a pinafore dress, though he did not know the term. He visualised a pale green, sleeveless dress with a short-sleeved underbodice of yellow—the dress that was eventually produced at the trial after the police had, as it were, walked clean over it without seeing anything in it but the bloodstains.

So much for the dress. As for the moonlight—the full moon, which on that day rose at six thirty-seven in the afternoon, was already tingeing the dusk when Cudden crossed the campus and dropped the syllabus in the letter box of the headmistress's house.

Skirting a playing-field, he crossed a spuriously antique bridge over the Brynn, a sizeable trout stream of an average depth of a dozen inches, with many a deep pool which made it dangerous to children, though the swift current would generally carry them to safety. Feeling his thirty-six years as nothing, he very nearly vaulted the stile giving on to the wood—part of the school estate—that ran down the side of the hill to the village of Hemel, where most of the teaching staff were accommodated.

He was wearing a mackintosh. A man of many small anxieties, he nearly always carried a mackintosh. Presently he turned off the track, to Drunkard's Leap—a pool in the Brynn some ten feet in breadth and some forty feet deep. When Rita was half an hour overdue he lit a cigarette. When the cigarette was finished he was not impatient. He sat down on an old bench like a park seat. As he did so, the centre plank fell out.

"Funny! The screws must have rotted out of the bracket." He ran his hand along the bench, noticed, without interest, that the bracket itself was no longer in position. Rita was later than usual.

The stream, tumbling over rocks into the pool, threw up a spray, and for the first time he saw a rainbow of moonlight. He must remember to point it out to Rita. Below the rainbow, the moon shimmered on the turbulent surface of the pool, so that the pool itself seemed to be made of liquid moonlight.

So he described it to the Coroner—liquid moonlight. Then, he said, a light cloud crossed the moon so that the rainbow and the shimmer faded out. Instead, a diffused glow enabled him to see beneath the surface of the pool. And a few feet beneath the surface of the pool, below the current, he saw Rita Steevens.

For some seconds, he supposed, he gazed at the staring eyes, at the hair lightly swaying, as if stirred by a sluggish breeze. Then the cloud passed, and he could again see nothing but the shimmering surface of the pool.

He shaded his eyes, lurched to and fro, trying to escape from the angle of light. He grabbed the loose beam of the bench, intending to bridge the rocks of the waterfall to get a new angle; but he stumbled, cutting his hand on a splinter of the beam, which splashed into the pool and was carried away.

He related that he shouted at himself as if he were someone else. "Pull yourself together, man! You were dazzled by the moonlight, and you've had an hallucination. You were thinking of Rita, and beginning to fear she had met with an accident, and you visualised your fear. How could she be sort of standing up under the water like that?"

He half believed it. The other half sent him scurrying from the pool down the track to the village.

"Check up at the cottage anyway," he muttered. "Better not mention the hallucination—make people laugh. It's partly that damned syllabus. Anxiety complex!"

Fortunate that Ruth Watlington's cottage was so near! At the end of the track through the wood, he did not vault the stile; he took it slowly, regaining his breath, coming to terms with his panic. A hundred yards of scrub, then the cottage, built at right angles to the lane that wound its way to the village. Slowly across the scrub.

Already he could discern the wicket gate of the cottage garden. And there—a dozen feet away—were the yellow sleeves, the pale green dress, grey-white in the moonlight. He bounded forward. As he snatched her in his arms his nostrils were filled with the scent he had never perceived on any other woman—the scent of gardenia.

"Oh, my darling—thank God—had a ghastly hallucination! Thought I saw you standing up drowned—in Drunkard's Leap." Her head was resting on his shoulder. The scent of gardenia spurred him—he could have vaulted innumerable stiles. "Speak, Rita, darling!"

"But I'm *not* Rita!" cried Ruth Watlington. "What on earth is the matter with you, Herbert?"

He swung her round so that she faced the moon.

"It must be this dress," she said. "Rita wore it once and didn't like it, so I took it off her hands."

He gaped at her, his senses in a vacuum in which his one clear impression was the scent of gardenia, almost as sharp as when, but a moment ago, her head had lain on his shoulder.

"I thought the hallucination, or whatever it is, was about *me,* and you seemed hysterical, or I wouldn't have——"

"Then perhaps it wasn't hallucination!" he gasped. "Where is Rita?"

"By now she's at Lynmouth, where she is spending the night with her cousin, Fred Calder, and his wife. They've got a bungalow there. Mr. Calder rang up before Rita came in. She had just time to catch the eight-fifty bus. She asked me to phone you, which I did. Effie Cumber—one of the kitchen-maids, in case you don't know—took the message. I told her you'd be in your classroom. But I'm afraid I forgot till about nine."

"I left a little before nine. Then Rita never went near Drunkard's Leap!" He laughed at his own fear, though it wasn't a wholesome laugh. "Yet—it was horrible! I can't believe it wasn't real."

"Well, come in first and tell me all about it. I keep a bottle of brandy for emergencies. I think you have been over-working on that syllabus . . . Oh, you've cut your hand,—it's bleeding! I'll try and bind it up for you, though I'm very bad at anything to do with blood."

"It's nothing. Must have cut it when I fell down."

He followed her into the sitting-room of the cottage, stopping in the hall to hang up his mackintosh.

As is known, he stayed there for about an hour, leaving before eleven, slightly fuddled with brandy. Ruth's purpose was to delay investigation. No police system, however scientific, could be expected to solve the riddle of why she should want to create the delay. The pool was obviously useless as a permanent hiding place. Once she had made her getaway, as she had, it would not have mattered to her if the police had found the body a few minutes later.

Nor did anybody attribute any special importance to Herbert Cudden's assertion that, in mistaking Ruth for Rita, he was misled not only by Rita's dress, but also by Rita's particular perfume. Yet Ruth Watlington was convicted—thanks to Detective-Inspector Rason of the Dead Ends Department—for no other reason than that she had put on the dead girl's dress and worn her perfume.

2

After a stiff brandy, Herbert gave Ruth details of the now supposed hallucination.

"But the pool is forty feet deep!" objected Ruth. "If there had been a body under the surface it would have been at the bottom, and you couldn't have seen it without a strong searchlight."

"I know. But one doesn't think of things like that at the time."

He told her about it all over again, and then, his fear banished, they talked about Rita in general, an absorbing topic to both. This conversation has been grossly misunderstood by the commentators, who said that it revealed Ruth as an hysteric, titillating her own terror by talking about the woman she had just murdered. Her showing him her scrap-book of babies' photographs was stigmatised as the height of hypocrisy—alternatively, as indicating a depth of morbid cruelty which would almost justify a plea of insanity.

Whereas the truth is that, if Ruth had been a hypocrite, she would never have committed the murder. "The schoolmarm who beat Scotland Yard" would have had short shrift if the police had been able to grasp that, though she was capable of murder, she was not capable of insincerity, cruelty, or greed.

At the time of the murder, Ruth was thirty-seven; would have been physically mistakable for thirty if she had not affected a certain dowdiness of dress. She was trim and springy, athletic without a touch of thickness. A truth about herself that she did not know was that the right touch here and there would have converted her into a more than ordinarily attractive woman. When she was sixteen, a boy of her own age had kissed her at a party, to her own satisfaction. Three days later she overheard the boy laughing about it to another boy. There was a loutish reference to her own over-estimation of her charms.

The incident distressed her sufficiently for her to confide in her young stepmother, for whom, in defiance of tradition, she entertained a warm affection. It did not occur to her that Corinne Watlington, who was only seven years older, might be sexually jealous.

"Men are rather beastly, you know," explained Corinne Watlington. "They lure you on with flattery and then laugh at you. It's as well to be on guard, or you may find yourself humiliated where you least expect it."

Ruth did not want to be humiliated, so she went on guard—so effectively that the young men of her generation dubbed her a prude and a codfish, and left her out—which made her manner more brusque than ever.

Following Corinne's advice, Ruth concentrated on a career. She won a scholarship to Oxford, generously resigning the bursary, as her mother had left her some two hundred pounds a year. She represented the University in lacrosse, tennis, and fencing. She took honours in history and literature, doing so well that she was invited to read for a Fellowship, but declined, as she wished to teach the young. She was appointed to Mardean, which was then considered the leading school for girls who required genuine education.

When she was twenty-seven she found herself thinking too intensively about one of the classical masters. In this emotion there was no echo of the boys at the parties. Indeed, she hardly thought directly of the man himself. She thought of herself in a house, just large enough, with a very green lawn on which very young children —hers—were playing. Somewhere in the background, giving substance and security to the dream, was the classical master.

Ruth resigned her appointment. She went to Paris; not being analytical, she did not know why she spent six months as a volunteer worker in a crèche. But the babies here were vaguely unsatisfactory, and she started the new school year at Hemel Abbey, a praiseworthy but undistinguished replica of Mardean on a less ambitious scale.

Here began that rare association with Herbert Cudden which baffled the romantically minded commentators. From the first she was able to talk to Herbert without any artificial coldness. From a different angle, he found something of the same restfulness in her, for he had always been self-conscious with other women. Ruth, obviously, would never expect him to make love to her. There sprang up, hardly a deep friendship—rather an intimate palliness utterly untouched by romance.

In her first year she bought Wood Cottage. A few weeks after she had settled in she cut the first of the baby pictures from a magazine. In six months, when she had cut another dozen, she began to paste them into a scrapbook. During the years that followed, the number of pictures grew. There was nothing secret about it. She would snap village babies with her Kodak, explaining that she was fond of pictures of babies, though they were so difficult to take. All the same, she never showed the scrapbook to anybody until she showed it to Herbert on the night of the murder.

Herbert used the cottage almost as a club. He came at routine times, always to lunch on Wednesdays and Sundays. She allowed him to pay half the cost of the food and a few pence over in part payment of the village woman who prepared it. Thus nearly nine years slipped by before Rita Steevens came and changed Ruth's perspective.

One evening, when the pupils were away for the half-term weekend, Ruth met Herbert and Rita together, and was astonished by the look she surprised in Herbert's eyes. For a second she had seen him young, vigorous, commanding—definitely among 'the men'— in Corinne's sense of the word. An hour later he came to the cottage and told her, as a great secret, that he had fallen in love with Rita. Ruth expressed sincere delight. A new, inner life was opened to her.

At first, Rita was cold, almost suspicious. She accepted Ruth's offer to share the cottage with indifference, bargaining shrewdly over her share of the expenses. By the end of the term she had yielded and was accepting Ruth as mentor and general benefactor.

Ruth was determined—one might say fiercely determined—that life should give to Rita what it had denied to Ruth. She positively groomed those two for each other, and without a single back-thought of malice. In her dream life, Ruth had already elected herself an honorary auntie.

A little before six on the night of the murder, while Rita was visiting in the village, Calder had rung to ask Rita to catch the eight-fifty bus—the last—and spend the night at Lynmouth. As the bungalow had no telephone, Calder would meet the bus on the chance of Rita coming. Ruth said she would deliver the message if Rita returned in time.

But when Rita came in, shortly after seven, Ruth did not deliver the message. It was the only occasion on which she treated Rita improperly—her selfish motive being that, living by deputy in Rita, she wanted Rita to meet Herbert as arranged. Also, she had just completed her plans for the wedding present, and wanted to tell Rita, and enjoy her surprise.

"You aren't meeting Herbert until nine," she said some time later. "Let's go and sit up at the pool. It's such a lovely night, and I've heaps to talk about. I'll disappear before Herbert comes."

"Righto! This tweed suit is a bit too schoolmarmy for Herbert. D'you think the suède belt you gave me would go with it?"

"It would be just right. I hoped you would wear it."

Ruth, herself dowdy, had become the arbiter of dress. Ruth had designed the pinafore dress of pale green with the underbodice of yellow and had it made by a London-trained woman living in semi-retirement as the village dressmaker. Ruth added: "What do you think of my new jumper?"

"The collar is too high for you—and I don't like yellow!" Remembering the pinafore dress in the wardrobe upstairs, Rita hastily amended: "I mean, not that mustardy yellow! You're better at dressing me than yourself. I wonder why! Ruth—why is it?"

"I suppose because I wish I had been like you when I was your age."

Rita felt resentful without knowing why. She was absentminded as they set out together, reaching Drunkard's Leap before eight.

"Mind, darling, you'll tear your dress!" There was light enough for Ruth to notice that the iron bracket of the bench had worked loose. "The screws have rusted away. They ought to have been painted. I'll tell Miss Harboro." Ruth tugged the bracket and it came clean away, a flat iron bar three feet long with a right angle turn of three inches. She leant it against the bench so that the estate handyman would see it. They sat down, and Ruth turned the conversation in the direction of her wedding present.

"You and Herbert—your heads are in the clouds, as they ought to be. You haven't thought, for instance, where you're going to live, have you?"

"Oh, Herbert's looking round for something. He likes that sort of thing. And if he can't find anything, there are lots of furnished rooms in the village."

Though it was barely dusk, the full moon shimmered on the surface of the pool. It was a lovely spot, thought Ruth, for Herbert and Rita.

"Furnished rooms are all right when you are single—awful when you're married." Ruth paused, enjoying her moment. "You're going to have Wood Cottage."

"But—d'you mean you're leaving Hemel and want to get rid of it?"

"No, dear, I don't mean that. I mean I want you to have it. I shall take Mrs. Cumber's two rooms, and you needn't worry about me. I shall be quite comfortable."

Rita was not worrying about Ruth's comfort. She was feeling that, notwithstanding innumerable small benefits, there was rather too much Ruth in her life. Again came that undefined resentment that had welled up during their dress-talk.

"But, Ruth—of course, it's awfully kind of you to offer to sell it to us, as I know you like it, but I doubt whether Herbert could afford——"

"Darling, there's nothing to afford! It's my little wedding present. I was in Barnstaple this morning, and fixed the title deeds, and the rest of it, with a solicitor. It's all settled bar formalities. You can talk it over with Herbert tonight."

"I simply don't know what to say!" Rita's voice was sulky. "Ruth, dear, don't you see it's impossible! You're only a little bit better off than we are, and—it's accepting too much."

What did it matter how much she gave them. Their life was hers. Her life would be fulfilled in the lives that were to come.

"Darling, it's not a matter of giving a present that costs a lot of money. It's a matter of sharing happiness. You know what a lot you and Herbert mean to me. And we've got to look ahead. In a year's time there may not be only the two of you to consider."

For a moment Rita was fogged.

"Do you mean we might have a baby?"

"Of course I do!" Ruth laughed happily. Rita laughed, too, but a different kind of laugh.

"But I shan't be having any babies."

"One shouldn't say that—it might turn out to be true." It was no more than a mild reproof. Then sudden fear clutched at Ruth. "Rita—there's nothing wrong with you physically, that way, is there?"

"Certainly not!" The girl bridled. "But there's no need to have all that bother if you don't want to—and I don't want to. I'm not the type. And I loathe babies anyway—yells and mess and bother!"

Ruth had the sensation that her body had taken control of her mind. She heard her own voice from outside herself and thought it sounded shrill and venomous.

"Is it fair to Herbert—to rob your marriage of all meaning?"

"Oh, be your age, Ruth! That belongs in a tuppenny novelette. And I find it a rather disgusting topic, if you don't mind."

One may say that the twentieth-century Ruth Watlington looked on while that part of her that was a thousand ages older than history obeyed a law of its own. Without her conscious volition, her muscles stiffened and she stood up. In her arms and thighs was an odd vibration, as if the corpuscles of her blood were colliding.

She heard the iron bracket whistle through the air—then heard a thud, and another. After a timeless period she felt herself going back into her body, understanding that an iris shutter in her brain had contracted until she had been able to see only one thing—that babies were a rather disgusting topic.

The iris was expanding a little. In the reflected moonlight she could see that the bench was glistening with blood. Rita had fallen from the bench and was lying, still.

"I seem to have killed Rita!" She giggled vacuously. "I wonder what Herbert will say!" The iris expanded a little more. She became vaguely aware of an urgency of time. She looked at her wrist watch, but had to try again and again before she could concentrate enough to read that it was half-past eight. Then it was easy to remember that Herbert would be there at nine.

"I'd better put Rita in the pool. When Herbert comes to the cottage I can break it to him gently. But dead bodies float, don't they. Oh well, we'll manage something just for an hour or so!" The iron bracket was ready to her hand.

There was blood at the angle of the bracket. She shuddered with a purely physical revulsion, wiped the bracket on the grass. She worked the short end of the bracket under the suède belt, then rolled the body into the pool near the waterfall. In spite of her care, there was a smear of blood on her left hand. Struggling against nausea she washed it off. The moonlight did not reveal that there was also a smear of blood on the sleeve of her yellow jumper.

In the walk back to the cottage, something approaching normality returned, and she realised what she had done. She had no thought of concealment, once she had told Herbert. She would then tell the police that she had killed Rita, but she would not tell them why, and they could not make her.

3

As she crossed the scrub to the cottage she heard the church clock chiming nine. Perhaps Herbert had finished his work. She hurried into the cottage and rang the school. A kitchen-maid answered. "Will you please go over to Mr. Cudden's classroom, and tell him that

Miss Steevens is sorry that she cannot keep her appointment."
She turned on the reading lamp. Again came nausea as she saw a
smear of blood on the sleeve of her yellow jumper—a smear half
the size of the palm of her hand. She whipped off the jumper. She
took it to her room, dropped it in the laundry basket, and put it
out of her mind.

There was no moral shrinking from what she had done. She even
felt a certain exultation, tinged with an unease which had nothing
to do with fear of the hangman. She took it for granted that her
own life was, in effect, at an end, and this gave her an immense
freedom.

She went into Rita's room. It held a faint fragrance of unknown
flowers. In the wardrobe was the light green dress and the yellow
bodice.

"Oh, I wish had been Rita!"

She took off all her clothes, put on Rita's. Last, the yellow bodice
and the light green dress. Then a spot of Rita's scent on her hair
and the merest dab behind the ears.

"I do look nice! What a pity! It's only waste. I wonder what
was wrong with me?"

Downstairs and into the air. Her life's history floated before her.
Rita's clothes helped her to review her past from the angle of a
young woman who had no fear that men would lure her on with
flattery and then laugh at her.

She was actually thinking of the classical master when Herbert's
arms closed round her. For a moment she let her head rest on his
shoulder, then realised that he had mistaken her for Rita.

The need for personal explanation shattered the mood in which
she had wanted to break the news to him. Besides, she saw now that
it would save him so little that she was entitled to think of herself.
To-morrow, when they found the body, life for her would end.
To-night she would enjoy an hour of his soothing friendliness for
the last time.

When she had made him believe the hallucination theory, she in-
dulged in the child's game of make-believe. "Let's pretend"—that
things were as yesterday, and that she had not murdered Rita. She
nearly told him about her gift of the cottage, but it would have
meant discussion, and she wanted to ask him a question. As the
minutes passed the question became more and more important to

her. The answer, if it were the right one, would help her to face the gallows with a calm mind.

"Have another brandy."

"Just a little one, and then I must hop off. Another thing Rita wants to do when we're married——"

She shirked putting the question to him directly. To help her approach, she produced her scrapbook. The whole of the first page was taken by one ebullient baby who had advertised a milk food.

Herbert grinned and turned the pages. "Ah, I used to know one just like that—same expression and everything! And when they look like that, they grab your nose if you get too close. This is a jolly book! Why have you never shown it to me before?"

"Herbert, are you and Rita going to have babies?"

"I don't see why we shouldn't. I've got a bit in the stocking, and so has she."

"Oh, I am glad!" There was a turbulence in her that he must have sensed.

"And I'm glad you're glad. Ruth, dear, you can scream for the village policeman if you like, but I'm going to kiss you."

When he kissed her, Ruth knew what it was that had been wrong with her. She also knew that to talk of robbing a man of fatherhood did not belong in a tuppenny novelette.

"I'm only thirty-seven—there's still time!" she told herself when he had gone. Murder could never be justified, and she would never so deceive herself. But a form of atonement for having taken life seemed to be open to her.

4

On the following morning, at about seven-fifteen, Herbert Cudden's landlady took his shoes out of doors with a view to cleaning them. It was, in a sense, unfortunate for Scotland Yard that Police-Sergeant Tottle happened to amble by on his bicycle.

"Good morning, Mr. Tottle. Your George's garden is a credit to the family. *Oo!* You don't 'appen to have had a nice murder, I suppose? Look at these!"

She held up the shoes. The rim of the sole and the back of one heel was caked with dried blood.

"Don't you touch 'em until I've seen 'em," barked the sergeant.

"Don't be silly! I was only joking—it can't be *human* blood. They're Mr. Cudden's. As if——"

The sergeant took the shoes and examined them.

"Take me up to his room," he ordered.

When he had succeeded in waking Herbert Cudden, the latter's reactions were, from the police point of view, ideal.

"Oh, my God!" It was almost like a woman's scream. "I shall go mad." He leapt out of bed, thrust Wellingtons over his pyjamas. "You'd better come with me, Sergeant. Give me those shoes."

"Here, what's it all about, Mr. Cudden?"

"Oh, shut up, please! I must see Miss Watlington at once, or I tell you I shall go mad. Hang on to the shoes if you like, but come with me."

Ruth was startled into wakefulness by hearing her name called while Herbert and the sergeant were still fifty yards from the cottage. She was in her dressing-gown and at the doorway almost as soon as they were.

"That hallucination!" Herbert was out of breath. "Blood on my shoes—show them to her. Look! It wasn't hallucination, Ruth. Rita was murdered on the bank and thrown in. We must drag Drunkard's Leap."

"Will one of you kindly explain——"

"Oh, all right then! I'll tell you."

It was Herbert who poured out the tale of the previous evening's experiences, of his discussion with Ruth, and the reasons for their joint conclusion that he had suffered an hallucination.

"Then as I understand it, after what you'd seen—or what you only thought you'd seen—you came to this cottage, and—is this your mackintosh by any chance?"

The mackintosh was hanging huddled on a peg in the hall. The sergeant pulled it out fanwise. The whole of the seat and part of the back were covered with congealed blood.

"How did that blood get there? On your mackintosh and on your shoes?"

"It must be *her* blood. That must have been done when I sat on the bench."

"And what's the matter with your hand that you've got that bandage?"

"Oh, hell to these footling questions! Sergeant, for heaven's sake *do* something! Can't you see that she has been murdered?"

The sergeant had never handled murder. This was unlike any he had read about. For one thing, the suspect was positively directing the investigation.

While Tottle, at Ruth's suggestion, was ringing the Lynmouth police to find out whether Rita had spent the night at Calder's bungalow, Ruth went upstairs to dress.

On a hanger on the door was the yellow underbodice. She put it in her wardrobe. Over a chair hung the pale green sleeveless dress. As she picked it up, she caught her breath. At the back, a little above the waist-line, was a distinct blood stain. For a moment she had a sense of eeriness, as if blood would meet her everywhere. Then she remembered.

"That was done when Herbert put his arm around me before I bound up his hand."

She dropped the dress into the laundry basket—on top of the blood-stained yellow jumper. She looked down at them, trying to assess their danger to herself. Then she shrugged her shoulders, and went on dressing. She had an almost superstitious belief that if destiny intended her to atone for her crime it would protect her from the police.

By ten o'clock they had found the body in Drunkard's Leap, its position explained by the fact that the iron bracket had jammed between two outcrops of rock some eight feet below the surface. By midday the county police had occupied the village. Detailed statements were taken from Cudden and Ruth, covering everything, even including Ruth's visit to her solicitor to arrange for the conveyance of the cottage to Herbert Cudden and his wife. The police took away for microscopic analysis Herbert's mackintosh and shoes and Ruth's yellow jumper and the pale green sleeveless dress. The analysis revealed that the blood on Herbert's garments had been exposed to the air for at least half an hour before it had adhered—which bore out his statements about the times of his movements.

Analysis of the skirt and jumper showed that the blood was newly shed when it had adhered—which bore out the joint statement that Herbert mistook Ruth, outside the cottage, for Rita—and that he had touched her, after he had cut his hand by the pool. It might have been Rita's blood. But only if the joint statements of Herbert and Ruth could be shown to be false—which was deemed to be impossible.

The Coroner's jury would have censured Herbert for his over-readiness to believe he had experienced an hallucination, had not Ruth generously insisted that the blame, if any, should be wholly hers. The Court returned a verdict of murder against person or persons unknown.

5

The school term opened in a somewhat strained atmosphere. True, that only three of the hundred and fifty pupils were withdrawn on account of the scandal. But there was an unhealthy interest in the events. The head-mistress explained that poor Miss Steevens had been killed by a madman who did not know what he was doing—a theory that was helped by a Press attempt to link the case up with a maniac murder in the North of England.

Ruth let the backwash of the murder splash round her, without giving it her attention. Scotland Yard rented all available rooms in the village inn. As there were apparently no clues they used the drag-net, checking the movements of every man within twenty miles and every automobile that could have been used. They would apply to Ruth now and again, mainly for information about the dead girl's habits.

In three weeks they packed up, leaving a pall of suspicion over the whole countryside. In due course the mackintosh and the shoes, the pale green sleeveless dress and the yellow jumper, minutely documented, were sent to the Department of Dead Ends.

Herbert's visits to the cottage became more frequent. At first he would sit in silence, assured of Ruth's sympathy. In time she loosened his tongue and let him talk himself out of his melancholy.

The strong forces in her nature which had produced the brain storm at Drunkard's Leap were now concentrated upon the purpose with which she had successfully drugged her conscience. At a moment of her choosing, Herbert Cudden was overwhelmed by those forces. The moment occurred at the end of the summer term.

Again we are not concerned with the detail of the methods by which that formidable will induced a transference to Ruth of the emotion which Herbert had felt for Rita. It suffices to say that it happened according to her plan. They could write to the head-mistress after the ceremony, she said, but they need not announce their marriage until the autumn term. As they particularly wished to avoid newspaper publicity they would be married by registrar in the East End of London.

This can hardly be called a tactical blunder on Ruth's part because, as far as the police were concerned, she had exercised no tactics. She did not know that a great many persons who wish to marry more or less in secret, particularly bigamists, regularly hit on that same idea. So the East End registrars invariably supply the police with a list of those applicants who obviously do not belong to the neighbourhood.

They each took a 'suitcase address' and applied for a seven-day licence. Detective Inspector Rason received the notice on the second day.

"Oh! So it was a triangle after all!" he exclaimed, without logical justification. "And now they're getting married on the quiet. That probably means that they cooked up all the hallucination stuff together. Anything they said may have been true or may not."

He took out the yellow jumper, the pale green sleeveless dress, and the mackintosh, which, with the iron bracket, was the only real evidence he had. In the garments there was no smell of gardenia.

"But Herbert said the dress Ruth was wearing was Rita's dress and that it smelt of gardenia. Well, it doesn't! Perhaps the scent has worn off in three months. Better put a query to the Chemical Department."

He had difficulty in finding the proper form, still more difficulty in filling it up. So instead, he sought out his twenty-year-old niece.

"When you put scent on your dress, my dear, how long does the dress go on smelling of it?"

"Oh, uncle! You never put any on your dress. It isn't good for the dress and the scent goes stale—and your best friends won't tell you. You put it on your hair and behind your ears."

So if there had been a smell of gardenia it meant that Ruth had deliberately applied it—the other girl's perfume. But maybe there had been no smell of gardenia. And maybe it wasn't Rita's dress.

Presently his thought crystallised.

"If Ruth was really wearing Rita's dress and Rita's scent, Herbert is telling the truth. If not—not! Wonder how far we can check up on the dress itself."

He searched jumper and dress for a trade mark and found none. "Then the dress must have been home made. Or perhaps the village dressmaker."

Deciding to take a long shot he was in Hemel the following afternoon.

"Yes, I made that for the poor girl," said Miss Amstey. "It was a present from Miss Watlington. She designed it and the yellow underbodice to wear with it, and I must say it looked very well."

Journey from London for nothing, thought Rason. Out of mere politeness he asked: "And you made this jumper, too, to go with it?"

"No, I didn't! That's a knitted line—came out of a factory. Besides, it wasn't poor Rita's. It was Miss Watlington's. I saw her wearing it the very day of the murder. And I must say I thought it frightful. Apart from its being made of wool. The underbodice I made was silk."

"Then this jumper and this dress don't go together—they belonged to different women? But you could wear the one with the other if you wanted to, couldn't you?"

"Well, you *could*," admitted Miss Amstey, "but you'd look rather funny. For one thing, being a polo jumper, it has a high collar. For another, there's the length—particularly the length of the sleeves. With one thing and another, people would laugh to themselves, even if they didn't turn round and stare."

That left Rason with the now simple riddle of the bloodstains. The two garments worn together would produce a ridiculous effect. Yet there were bloodstains on both, deemed to have been made by Cudden's hand, *at the same time*. And Cudden had identified both dress and jumper at the inquest.

Rason took it all down and got Miss Amstey to sign it.

Ruth decided that they could without impropriety arrive at the registrar's in the same taxi—nor need they be ashamed to carry the suitcases that had established the legality of their address. In outward appearance she had changed. The talent for dress she had formerly exercised for another was now successfully applied to herself.

In the hall of the registrar's office, Rason accosted Herbert and introduced himself.

"I am sorry, Mr. Cudden, but I must ask you both to accompany me to headquarters. A serious discrepancy has been discovered in the evidence you gave in the coroner's court."

They were taken to the Chief Superintendent's room. Three others were with him. Ruth was invited to sit.

Herbert was reminded of his evidence regarding the dress. Then the pale green sleeveless dress was handed to him.

"Is that the dress?"

"To the best of my belief—yes." He turned it. "Yes—there's the bloodstain."

The yellow jumper was passed to him. After a similar examination he again answered:

"Yes."

"Miss Watlington, do you agree that these two garments, formerly belonging to the deceased, were worn by you that night?"

"Yes," said Ruth, though she could guess what had happened and knew that there could be but little hope.

The Chief Superintendent spoke next.

"You will both be detained on suspicion of being concerned in the murder of Rita Steevens."

"No!" snapped Ruth. "Mr. Cudden has told the truth throughout. He knows nothing about women's clothes except their colour. the colour of that jumper was near enough for him to think it was the same. They were passed to him separately at the inquest."

"Ruth—I can't follow this!" protested Herbert.

"Miss Watlington is making a gallant attempt to get you out of your present difficulty," said the Chief. "But I'm afraid it will be futile."

"It will not be futile," said Ruth. "Will you all remain just as you are, please, and let me go behind the Chief Superintendent's chair. And can I have that dress?"

Behind the superintendent's chair she whipped off her fashionable walking suit. Then she put on the jumper *and* the pale green sleeveless dress.

Then, looking as ridiculous as Miss Amstey had prophesied, she stood where all could see her. The officials had been awed into silence.

"Herbert, you have only to answer me naturally to clear up the whole absurd mistake. Was I, or was I not, dressed like this that night?"

"No, of course not! Your neck was bare. So were your arms. And you looked properly dressed. That thing doesn't seem to fit." Ruth turned to the Chief and his colleagues.

"You see—he is obviously innocent." She added: "You may think I am not."

THE CASE OF
THE SOCIAL CLIMBER

IN ENGLAND on the rare occasions when the present Lord Haddenham figures in the social news—and often when he does not—people will hash up the murder of the young man's father in 1935. Some will tell you that Stentoller, the wealthy banker, was really innocent—that the gold snuff-box, inscribed with the Royal cipher, was planted on an already dead body. They would have you believe that Stentoller's confession and subsequent execution were part of a plot to deceive the public.

The objective facts were few and simple. On a spring evening, Lord Haddenham was crossing the Green Park on foot. He was on a tree-lined path, some three hundred yards from Buckingham Palace, when he was stabbed in the throat. There was no robbery from the person. After a few false scents, the trail petered out.

A year later, the Department of Dead Ends stumbled on evidence which convicted Stentoller, the head of a century-old financial house of unblemished reputation. Add that Haddenham's son had become engaged to Stentoller's daughter, to the satisfaction of both parents whose friendship dated from their schooldays—and you will see why the public was puzzled.

The talk outlasted the first world war. Over drinks, the locale of the murder tended to shift ever nearer to Buckingham Palace. "Practically in the Palace Yard and almost under the very nose of the sentry who, you can be sure, had been told to see nothing!" Names of various foreign royalties were whispered. If Stentoller had defended himself in court, the war would have started in 1936 —for reasons, however, that would have astonished Hitler. And so on.

The fact that the Prosecution put forward no motive for the

murder made the public suspect that there was something behind it. And so there was, of course. Something fundamental. But there was no mystery that could have made the front page—no foreign royalties or secret women or this-that-and-the-other. Indeed, the clue to the mystery—if such it can be called—might be sought in the preamble to the American Declaration of Rights—in the passage touching the equality of man. Or in the quaint ceremony by which, at the boundary of the original City of London, the Sovereign surrenders his sword to the Lord Mayor as a reminder that the King may not enter the City under arms, save at the invitation of the citizens.

But at the tragic moment of the murder, Stentoller was thinking of a cheque for a thousand pounds which he had given Haddenham thirty years previously when they were undergraduates at Oxford.

2

Oxford, preceded by four important years at Charchester School, represented a revolutionary change in the Stentoller tradition. Stentoller I was a trusted agent of the Rothschilds at the time of the Napoleonic wars. When Rothschild accepted ennoblement, the friendship terminated, because Stentoller felt that the old City families, being a kind of aristocracy in their own right, should hold aloof from the nobility. In the eighteen-fifties, Stentoller III became Lord Mayor of London and was deeply offended when Queen Victoria offered him a baronetcy. Stentoller IV decided that this attitude was no longer tenable. In the late 'nineties, therefore, young Cuthbert Stentoller was sent to Charchester with instructions to fit himself to occupy a prominent place in what the fashion papers call Society.

In the City family tradition, in so far as it still survived, the children 'lived soft.' At thirteen, that highly intelligent but inexperienced boy left the stately eighteenth-century mansion, left his home tutors and his personal servant, for the bear-pit of a public school—which in England means a special kind of private school. The more insular types will assure you that there are only six public schools in England, two in Scotland, and none at all anywhere else in the world.

In his first year he learnt—like the other younger sons of the nobility and gentry—the rudiments of cookery, how to clean out somebody else's study, how to whiten somebody else's buckskin cricket boots, how to endure injustice without making a song about it. He was comparatively ill-fed and ill-housed. He discovered that quite a number of elder boys had authority to beat him publicly for slackness at games and whatnot. In short, though he suffered no individual bullying, the system subjected his person to an indignity which, if it had been authoritatively applied to the son of a labourer, would have provoked something akin to civil war.

He made a personal friend of Charles Hendon, his 'avunculus'— that is, a boy senior by one year, appointed to guide a new boy through his maze of duties.

"I say, Stentoller! My mater's coming down on Saturday. You can come along if you like. She'll give us a blowout at the Angel."

"Thank you, Hendon." Stentoller had not yet learnt to keep formality in its proper place. "Shall I join you and Mrs. Hendon at the Angel?"

"No. We'll both meet her at the station. And I say, mind you don't call her 'Mrs. Hendon.' My guvnor's called Lord Haddenham and she's called Lady Haddenham. Come on. We've got to help roll Lower Green before tea."

Lady Haddenham perceived that Cuthbert Stentoller was more intelligent and more sensitive than the normal young public school tough. When Stentoller temporarily absented himself she asked her son:

"I like Stentoller. Who is he?"

"I dunno, Mother. I'll ask him when he comes back."

"Don't be silly, Charles! That would be an abominable thing to do."

Stentoller had overheard. When the boys were returning together he asked:

"What did your mater mean when she asked who I was? She got my name right."

"You're not supposed to ask that sort of question," said Hendon, then relented. "She meant who was your mother before she married your father. Women are always totting up people's relations."

Stentoller was puzzled. His mother never totted up people's relations. He was an undergraduate before he understood what Lady Haddenham had really wanted to know, and he acquired the understanding with literal tears of humiliation.

In the intervening years he had learnt a good deal—notably that the fashion papers wrote of a world that anyone could enter who had conventional manners, a respectable record, and a sufficiency of money—that the power and influence of this crowd was virtually limited to the racecourse and to the tradesmen of the West End. True that it was besprinkled with high sounding titles—but he had discovered, even in Charchester days, that a title was no index of a man's position. Through his friend, Charles Hendon, he had glimpsed the existence of an inner core, and was surprised to learn that his own father knew much about it.

"Winning the Derby and that sort of thing wouldn't get you anywhere with the real people. We have been doing business with them for generations and know something about them. Now and again they enter the political Government—the Cecils, the Churchills and a few others. But mostly they confine themselves to the Administration. Their influence is paramount in the Navy, the Army, the Civil Service and the Diplomatic Corps. They trust our firm, in their own way, which is not the way of the City. That is why I think they might admit you to their circle."

His father had told him too much or too little. Possibly his father had never heard of the Radlington Club—the small social club of 'the real people'—the inner core—at Oxford. Hendon, of course, was a member. Stentoller at first hoped, and then intended, to become one. His first academic year went by without result, then his second. He was personally popular, and was well known through his rendering of the part of Laertes in the Dramatic Society. For the duelling scene he had studied fencing seriously for six months, thereby acquiring a skill which was to be the means of destroying two valuable lives.

The Radlington incident occurred in his second year, which was Hendon's third. Lord Haddenham had recently died. The eldest son had gone straight from Eton into the Army and had been killed in the South African War, so Charles Hendon inherited the earldom and estate, which was heavily encumbered with death duties.

Hendon had contrived that they should have the same tutor. One afternoon, when Stentoller entered the tutor's room, he heard Hendon saying:

"It's the death duties, of course. The Bank doesn't seem eager to let me have another thousand before things are straightened out, so I've decided I shall have to 'go down' at the end of this term.

Hullo, here's Stentoller. Don't go, old man. We've finished."

Immediately after dinner that night, Stentoller went to Hendon's rooms and found him alone.

"I heard what you said to Wallingham about your 'going down.' "

"That's all right. I don't mind in the least. Only, it's not for immediate publication. There's a Radlington dinner next Saturday, and I shall explain then that I'm going down for family reasons. It'll mean the Army for me instead of the Diplomatic—that's about all, really!"

"Hendon, let me lend you the thousand."

"I say, Stentoller!"

Stentoller was not certain how the other was taking it, felt his own heart thumping, and lurched on:

"If you're offended, you've got the wrong end of the stick. If you were to 'go down' because I hadn't the nerve to ask you to let me help——"

"I'm not *offended,* you dear old nanny-goat! You took my breath away. Sort of going to throw my arms round your neck! But I'll tell you what's sticking in my gizzard. If the Bank is shy, it probably means they know the estate won't be able to pay it back for the devil of a time."

"I don't want it paid back for the devil of a time."

"Don't you! Oh, well then it's all right, and thanks most awfully! And I needn't say anything at the Radder dinner."

Stentoller took out his cheque book. 'Pay——' he nearly wrote 'Charles Hendon'—'—*Pay Lord Haddenham One Thousand Pounds. Cuthbert Stentoller.'*

He handed the cheque to his friend.

"Thanks! The Bank'll throw a fit to-morrow and serve 'em right!"

"I say, Hendon!" In those days, young men rarely used first names unless they were related. "How does one get into the Radlington?"

"Oh, I dunno! When you come 'up,' somebody you know asks you if you'd like to be a member, and the other members know you, or your relations have told 'em to look out for you, and then the secretary sends you a chit."

Stentoller waited. But there was no more about the Radlington Club. *'Pay Lord Haddenham One Thousand Pounds——'*—for nothing at all! Relations again. Back six years. 'Women are always totting up people's relations.'

Not only women, apparently.

Back in his own rooms, Stentoller wrote to his father, asking him to instruct the Bank to honour the cheque, giving his reason. Almost as soon as he had posted the letter, a college messenger brought him a note in Haddenham's hand-writing:

> Dear Stentoller. It was wonderfully kind of you to give me that cheque, and it is impossible to tell you how deeply this act of yours has affected me. All the same, I feel on reflection that I must let events take their own course. So I am returning your cheque herewith. Yours ever, Charles Hendon.

"God, what a fool I am!" Stentoller buried his face in his hands.

In that first ghastly year at Charchester his courage had been sustained, his path smoothed, by Hendon. Hendon had been waiting with a welcome at Oxford and had opened many doors. He had given and accepted favours. The friendship was genuine beyond doubt.

'I like Stentoller. Who is he?'

Hendon was his friend. Yet sooner than propose him for membership of the Radlington, Hendon had thrown up his career.

The next morning he took a one day exeat to London to tell his father why he no longer wanted the thousand.

"That's where their strength lies," said his father. "The individual is always ready to efface himself to avoid imperilling the others."

"The peril to the others being my membership of the club?"

They were in the study, a room that could seat thirty without discomfort. On a vast chimney piece stood an ormolu clock under a glass dome. Chippendale writing table, chairs, cabinets—the selection of Stentoller I.

"Not your membership of the club, but his perception that you wanted something, in return for your loan, which touched his relationship with the others. But, my dear boy, it's a storm in a teacup. It won't even affect your friend's career. The Bank have approached us on his behalf. We have dealt with the family before, and we shall give the Bank a guarantee."

"I don't understand, Father. We aren't literal moneylenders, are we? And if the Bank won't touch it——"

"Come here, Cuthbert." He opened a showcase like a showcase in a museum and took out a gold snuff-box, inscribed with the Royal cipher on one side and the Haddenham arms on the other, with a legend in dog-Latin.

"A gift, of that profligate buffoon who was unfortunately George IV of England, to your friend's great-grandfather. Haddenham had been commanded to borrow ten thousand pounds for one of George's disreputable little troubles. 'I will not lend the King a penny, because I don't trust him,' said *your* great-grandfather, 'but I will gladly lend your lordship that amount.' 'Your words touch the edge of treason, Mr. Stentoller,' said Haddenham. But I gather there was a twinkle in his eye, because he pulled out this snuff-box and added: 'I pledge the King's honour with the King's gift.'

"Well, the King had no honour, which meant that we paid ten thousand for this snuff-box. But we had helped Haddenham out of a difficulty, and he told his crowd all about it. A year later we were commissioned to underwrite a Colonial loan of ten millions— and made a hundred thousand out of it in a few days. Ever since then, business of that kind has tended to drift to us without effort or expense on our part. We have probably made a couple of millions out of that snuff-box."

At Oxford, the following evening, Haddenham burst into Stentoller's room.

"I say, Stentoller! Perfectly splendid news! I know you'll be pleased! I needn't say anything at the Radder dinner after all. Apparently, that bank manager was getting over a thick night when he was so gloomy about those death duties. . . ."

There was a joyous fantasy on the habits of bank managers. But, again, there was nothing more about the Radlington Club.

3

Cuthbert Stentoller's marriage to the daughter of one of the youngest High Court judges neither advanced nor retarded his progress to the inner core, which did not concern itself with the judiciary. For the next ten years he absorbed himself in business and family life, while keeping his eyes open. One year, to please his wife, he was seen in the Royal enclosure at Ascot.

As his father had warned him, this was a waste of energy. The

inner core would attend Levees, Drawing-Rooms and State ceremonies, but had no interest in the fashion-paper aspect of Royalty,
which to them was purely an Office of State. Without leaders, without tangible organisation, without policy except the preservation of
Britain, they held aloof from domestic politics, ignored elections
but subtly coiled themselves round Governments in being.

He discovered that the equivalent of the Radlington was the
Terracotta Club. It was housed in a rather dingy building off White-
hall. The servants, like most of the members, were appointed
on the hereditary principle and were never discharged except for
larceny which, in effect, never occurred. The fashionable world of
spenders had scarcely heard of it and none had ever entered it,
for it admitted no guests. But the Chancelleries of Europe knew all
about it.

Stentoller intended to become a member. This time he would make
no mistakes. He reckoned that it might take him twenty years to
procure an invitation to join. Actually, it took twenty-three years
of strenuous and successful living, unobtrusively observed and as
unobtrusively approved by the inner core.

On the death of his father, he had sold the family mansion on
the fringe of the City, already surrounded by offices, and transferred
the furniture to a modern house, with a hundred acres of land,
in the Surrey Hills, some forty miles out of London. He sold a
corner of this to Weslake, a young baronet in the Guards who
was a member of the Terracotta. He also arranged for the building
of a house for him. But he did not ask how one became a member
of the Terracotta Club, because he knew.

Haddenham, who had gone into the Diplomatic Service and was
nearly always abroad, kept the friendship in being and never missed
seeing him when on leave. He had married about the same time. His
wife had enough money for them to live without anxiety, but not
enough to keep up Haddenham Castle, which was let on long lease.

"It would be an odd twist," remarked Stentoller at one of their
reunion dinners, "if your youngster and mine were to take a fancy
to each other later on."

"Yes rather! Nothing I should like better!" returned Haddenham, but Stentoller knew that he did not mean it.

Yet it happened ten years later, after the youngsters had been
thrown together during a fortnight's holiday on the Riviera. Sten-

toller had remained at home. His wife had barely told him her suspicions before Derek Hendon himself turned up.

"I say, sir! I want to marry Gwen. She said I must ask you. Is it okay?"

"For a budding diplomat, young man, your approach is somewhat direct," smiled Stentoller. "Adverting to your question, I have pleasure in announcing on behalf of her mother and myself that it is eminently—er—okay by us." A moment later he asked: "I take it you have consulted your father?"

"Consult him, sir? He won't need consulting. He'll whoop, when he gets my cable to-morrow."

Events in the life of Cuthbert Stentoller began to gallop. After dinner, his neighbour, Weslake, turned up on his way home. When Derek Hendon had been congratulated, the two elders drifted to the study.

"They've dipped in the lucky bag and pulled me out for a Foreign Office job in Turkey," said Weslake. "That means a year out there, beginning on the twelfth. There's a Levee on the tenth, so I shall go by air. Had a sort of farewell lunch at the Terracotta. A lot of fellers you know were present." He named them and became so discursive that Stentoller's pulse quickened. Twenty-three years he had waited for this moment.

"I wonder, Stentoller, if you'd care to join the Terracotta? I'd be glad to put you up, and Tharme would second you." Presently Weslake was explaining: "There's a committee meeting after the Levee on the tenth. I'm not on the committee, but Tharme is. They'll probably write you the same day."

So it was a foregone conclusion! They had talked it over and agreed to accept him. Weslake was chattering about Turkey, in no hurry to go. The Terracotta at last! His marriage had staled after five years, and he was aware that his wife had hoped for a divorce; but she knew about the Terracotta, though he had never mentioned it. God, she was a good woman! Weslake was gaping at the showcase.

"A lot of interesting things you've got here, Stentoller. I suppose they all have a history."

"I'll show you something," said Stentoller, to break his own absorption in the Terracotta. He opened the case and took out the gold snuff-box.

"Is that the Haddenham snuff-box mentioned in Kyle's *Life of George IV?*—'I pledge the King's honour on the King's gift'? But, of course, I see it is!"

"I shall celebrate Gwen's engagement by solemnly handing that to Haddenham next time I see him," said Stentoller—a flourish which, indirectly, hanged him.

Gwen was a willowy blonde, springy and vital, with her share of the Stentoller sternness behind a mask of modernity—nearly everything he had wanted her to be. He meant to say something impressive to her but funked it at the last moment.

"Rushing away from your ageing parents at the first opportunity? Nasty bit o' work, darling, aren't you!"

"It's not the first opportunity! Daddy, you do like him, don't you!"

"Very much! But d'you think you're going to like stooging around one Embassy after another?"

"I shall love it. But I'm weak in Italian and German—get me a couple of good crammers, please. And when we're in England I wonder whether you'd let us have the cottage. Mother said the other day she wished you'd get rid of it."

Here was the chance to say something impressive.

"When you're in England, I'll let you have Haddenham Castle."

"But you can't! There's a tenant there for years yet."

"I know. But I'm going to make friends with the tenant."

"But we shan't really need the Castle till he's an ambassador." She looked up at him gravely. "Daddy, you aren't going berserk, are you?"

"I've been waiting all my life to go berserk. Now run off to bed, miss! I want to talk to your mother before she turns in."

His wife had expected him and was pottering about her room— a severe room dominated by a large picture of Notre Dame.

"It's what you wanted, Cuthbert, isn't it!" Her smile was ambiguous. "I don't think he has said a word to his father. If Lady Haddenham were alive she might have made difficulties. She was very old fashioned."

They exchanged platitudes about the engagement. A stiff and pointless conversation—irritating, too, because he had not come to talk about Gwen, as there was nothing that need be said.

"Did you know, Hilda, that I—had a sort of idea once that I might join the Terracotta?"

"I've known for years." She caught her breath. "Weslake—in the study to-night? Did he——?"

"Yes. There were a lot of them there to-day and they talked it over. He's proposing, and Lord Tharme is seconding. Tharme is on the committee."

"Oh, Cuthbert, I am so glad!" He had not guessed that she would take it like that. She was holding him, and he could tell from her voice that she was crying. "Then our marriage hasn't been— such an awful failure, after all—has it!"

4

If Haddenham did not whoop, he did send a cordial cable, followed by a letter saying he would be in London for the Levee on the tenth, and that they must dine at the Varsity, to which they both belonged, as did Weslake. In those days it had massive premises in a cul-de-sac off Piccadilly giving on to a slip-gate into the Green Park.

Haddenham had aged more than Stentoller. He had become a tubby little man, bald, with a long, stringy throat. He had held ambassadorial rank for five years without being affected with pomposity, for he was as unimpressed with his own position as he was with that of any man. He had the air, typical of his caste, of amiable omnipotence, the air that could make kings and communists feel self-conscious and apologetic, ready to be flattered into obedience.

"I say, Stentoller!" He shook hands with something approaching genius. "D'you realise that, all being well, we're within measurable distance of being grandfathers! I still think of you as a rather grubby little fag trying to clean out Ellerson's study and making it a darned sight dustier than it was."

That was the keynote of their conversation during dinner. Stentoller steered from reminiscence to the dynamic present.

"I say, Hendon! Have you ever heard of your great-grandfather's snuff-box?"

"Rather! Brought up on the legend. 'Your words, Mr. Stentoller, touch the edge of treason'—By Jove, it never occurred to me that must mean you!"

"I have the snuff-box here!" said Stentoller. "As our families are to be linked, I want you to take it back. I—dammit, I've left it in my overcoat! I'll go and get it."

"Thanks most awfully! But don't bother now, old man. When we go down will do. We've got to talk about the youngsters. I can't give Derek more than the five hundred a year he's getting now."

"Don't worry. I shall make a settlement on Gwen. In the mean-time, I've bought the lease of Haddenham Castle—the tenant has contracted to vacate at three months' notice. I shall give the lease to Derek for a wedding-present."

"My dear old boy, you take my breath away! I never expected we'd be back in my lifetime. The youngsters'll probably let me have the Chichester Wing when I retire."

"It'll make a foothold for them when they're in England."

"Ah, I was coming to that! I think that, in view of the very happy change in Derek's circumstances, he would be well advised to transfer to the Foreign Office—and be employed permanently at home—drop the Diplomatic branch altogether."

Stentoller felt himself bristling, for reasons he did not yet under-stand.

"Gwen will be disappointed, Hendon. She's already cramming Italian and German—she's practically bilingual in French. She's looking forward to doing a round of the embassies. Means to make him an ambassador, like his father, eh!"

A minute twitch of the other's eyebrow reminded Stentoller that members of the inner core never acknowledge personal ambition. He had said the wrong thing.

"If she's looking forward to being the wife of a diplomat, it's because the dear girl doesn't know what she's letting herself in for. Nor does Derek, yet. The romance of it is pure nonsense. It's deadly dull for the first fifteen or twenty years. And very paro-chial. You dovetail work and play inside a very small circle, who are nearly all your relations, or your wife's relations, or relations of relations."

So that was it! Relations again! But he was no longer an under-graduate to be frightened by the implications of that word. Anger was slowly mounting—checked by the chief steward approaching Haddenham.

"Telephone message from Colonel Hallingburn, my lord. Can you spare him half an hour?"

"Thanks. Don't call me a taxi—it's quicker to slip through the Park."

Stentoller knew, as well as the chief steward, that this was a summons to report at the Palace.

"I expect They want a first hand account of that Bulgarian hullabaloo," said Haddenham, rising. "But Their half an hour means just thirty minutes. I'm coming back here to collect that snuff-box from you, if you're still here. Lord, what a day! Arrived by air at breakfast time. Reported to the Cabinet at ten: a Levee at eleven, followed by a stand-up lunch. And then a committee meeting at the Terracotta!"

Stentoller felt as if an ice block were pressing on his chest. But he managed to speak before the other had moved out of earshot.

"Did you sit at a committee meeting of the Terracotta this afternoon?"

Haddenham turned back. His face looked drawn—and sad—and he was groping for words.

"Stentoller, old man, I'm sorry—very sorry indeed—that you did not consult me before letting Weslake and Tharme propose you."

"Why, Hendon?"

"I must go—They mustn't be kept waiting. We'll talk when I come back."

Blackballed, obviously!

Control was in danger of slipping. He tried to will himself back to the moment before this moment of disaster—which his imagination was refusing to accept. He told himself that the ambition of twenty-three years had been shattered. But he was actually thinking of Hilda clinging to him, crying with happiness because her faithfulness had been rewarded with his success. He did not see how he could live that down. For the first time he experienced the suicide impulse.

Suddenly, all emotion left him. He felt as he had once felt after drinking an excessive amount of old brandy—cool, clearheaded and determined in the pursuit of some purpose which was unknown to him.

He was certain that it was Haddenham himself who had blackballed him. Because long ago at Oxford he had tried to lever himself into the Radlington, thereby proving that he lacked the self-effacement required of the inner core.

"I must keep faith with Haddenham. Give him his snuff-box before I demand a showdown." He had always thought it a little ungentlemanly of his own great-grandfather to retain that snuffbox.

That dangerous mood would have passed without doing any material harm, had not the malignant fates chosen to thrust a sword into his hand—a sword, in all preposterous literality!

He could not breathe easily in the club. He could wait for Haddenham by the slip-gate into the Park. As he approached the cloak-room he heard the voice of Weslake protesting to the attendant.

"But what the dickens am I to do with it? I'm leaving the country by air at seven to-morrow. I'll have to cable my wife to call here for it. Oh, hullo, Stentoller! Look here—I changed here for the Levee and my batman packed the sword under the straps of the Gladstone because it wouldn't go inside. And the railway people have sent it back because in law it's a lethal weapon. A dress sword a lethal weapon! It couldn't cut a loaf of bread, and the point is about as sharp as the point of an umbrella."

"Give it to me!" Stentoller spoke automatically out of the cold, white haze. "I'll take it, and give it to Lady Weslake in the morning."

While Weslake was gratefully accepting, Stentoller reclaimed his coat. In the hall, he took the sword from Weslake. The belt, in girdle form, dangled awkwardly.

"I can slip that off and roll it up," said Weslake. "I don't know whether you've room for it in your overcoat?"

There was a book in one pocket and the gold snuff-box in the other. Stentoller transferred the snuff-box to the breast pocket.

"Oh! That's the Haddenham one, isn't it?"

"Yes. But Haddenham slipped off before I could give it to him."

Farewells and good wishes, while Stentoller wondered why Gwen's relations should prevent Derek from being a diplomat. But he knew the answer.

Gripping, in mid-scabbard, the sword of the Order of St. Severell of Antioch, supplied by the tailor who made the robes, he left the club, entered the Park by the slip-gate that gave on to the narrow tree-lined path.

It was little used as a thoroughfare and there were no seats for lovers. Moonlight shone intermittently through wind-driven clouds. What a lot of nonsense his father had talked about the inner core! They hadn't been able to stop the South African war. They had failed to handle the Kaiser in 1914, and now they were cold-shouldering Churchill and letting the Premier grovel to Hitler and Mussolini, to say nothing of the Japanese. The 'real people' indeed! As if they were some special kind of human being! The Americans had taped them a hundred and fifty years ago. *'We hold these truths to be self-evident, that all men are created equal———'* Nothing there about a man's relations———

"I say, Stentoller!" Haddenham's voice broke the interlude of reverie. "Aren't you cold waiting out here?"

"I've got your snuff-box. You said you would accept it."

"Oh—thanks most awfully!" Haddenham put it in his pocket. "Shall we go back to the Club?"

"Hendon, did you blackball me at the Terracotta?"

"You're not supposed to ask that sort of question. The voting is secret."

The moonlight illumined a scowl on Haddenham's face, illumined his long, stringy throat.

5

The point of the sword might be little sharper than that of an umbrella: indeed, the police thought at first that an umbrella had been used—one of the thin, expensive kind, having a steel shaft—by a man who had been taught how to put weight behind a lunge.

When Haddenham was dead, Stentoller wiped the blade on the bordering grass and returned it to its scabbard. He strode back through the slip-gate to the car park on the other side of Piccadilly.

When he arrived home, shortly after midnight, his wife and daughter had gone to bed. He took the sword to his room. He drew the blade, noticed that it was stiff in the scabbard. He held it to the light at arm's length. It was slightly bent. Better not try to correct it—it was a wonder the blade had not snapped. These tailor's blades were made of some inferior alloy, plated over. Although it appeared to be clean, he rinsed and dried it.

"If anyone saw me, there is nothing to be done. If no one saw me there is no reason why I should be suspected."

As is characteristic of murderers who are not of the criminal classes, he took an individual view of the morality of his act. He did not pretend that the murder could be justified. But he seemed to himself more sinned against than sinning. For thirty years Haddenham had amused himself by pretending friendship with a man he despised —and despised for no ethical reason. He blamed Haddenham for the murder as a man will blame a too attractive wanton for his own debauchery.

While he was dressing on the following morning, Gwen came to his room. She thrust a paper at him—the *Record*—not trusting herself to speak. He was not taken by surprise. There was skilful restraint in his reception of the news. But the sympathy be expressed was genuine. It would mean that the wedding must be postponed. He hated Haddenham afresh for making Gwen so miserable.

When she had gone, he skimmed the account in the *Record*.

'It can be stated that robbery was not the motive. In deceased's pockets were some thirty pounds—to say nothing of a gold watch and chain and a valuable gold snuff-box.'

That snuff-box! Stentoller had forgotten all about it.

"That's all right. I shall say I gave it to him over dinner," ran his thoughts.

His eye fell on the sword of the Order of St. Severell of Antioch, standing in the corner, the coiled girdle on the floor beside it.

"Weslake saw me take the snuff-box out of my pocket. He remarked on it, and I told him that Haddenham had left the Club. Weslake will prove that I saw Haddenham after he left the Palace. And that means I shall be hanged."

Weslake was at that moment in the air. But copies of *The Times* were probably in the aircraft with him, on their way, like himself, to the Embassy.

Over breakfast he looked at *The Times*. It gave headlines but did not indulge in speculations nor wallow in the details, like the *Record*. It stated merely that there had been no robbery from the person. Papers like the *Record* did not penetrate to Embassies. That meant there was a reasonable possibility that Weslake's attention would never be directed to the snuff-box.

After breakfast, he took the sword to Lady Weslake, as he had promised.

"Yes, it's terrible about Haddenham!" he agreed. "I was dining with him at the Varsity. He was called away only a few minutes before I ran into your husband."

When he reached his office, he found waiting for him a junior detective from Scotland Yard.

"We understand, sir, that you had dinner with Lord Haddenham last night at the Varsity Club. Was anything said which you think might help us in our investigation?"

"Nothing at all, I'm afraid. Our conversation was purely personal. We had been friends since boyhood. Lord Haddenham's son and my daughter had just become engaged, and we were discussing family plans most of the time."

The young detective glanced at the list of questions he had been instructed to ask. The next was the time at which they parted company.

"Somewhere about ten-thirty—I'm not sure of the exact time," answered Stentoller. "But you can check that. He was with me until he received a telephone message from the Palace—you know all about that, of course—the Palace officials will tell you what time they telephoned the Club. The chief steward delivered the message himself. I left the Club shortly afterwards."

Everything he said was carefully written down.

"There's only one more question, Mr. Stentoller. Can you tell us definitely whether Lord Haddenham was in the habit of taking snuff?"

"I can tell you that he was not." Stentoller smiled benignly. "Then why that enormous gold snuff-box, eh? I can clear up that mystery for you. I gave it him myself over dinner, although it was already in a sense his—you'll find it has his crest on it as well as the Royal cipher." He told the story of the snuff-box in full—gave the reference to Kyle's *Life of George IV*—so that the Yard should mark it as accounted for.

Then came the newspapermen. He gave them the same account, except that he made no reference to the snuff-box, which thereafter received no publicity, as the Yard had made clear that there was nothing pinned on to it.

At home a letter was waiting for him from Lord Tharme:

'Dear Stentoller, I am very sorry. I have resigned from the Terracotta—I may say, in a state of deep mystification.'

Four days later came an air mail letter from Weslake.

'Dear Stentoller, I can't think what the devil happened at
the Terracotta. Nor can Tharme. I have, of course, resigned. Haddenham's death is a shock. I read it in *The
Times,* going over. It must have happened almost while
you and I were talking—and within a couple of hundred
yards of us. I was very sorry for Gwen and Derek, as
it will mean postponement. Yours ever, Reginald Weslake.'

That meant that Weslake had no suspicion. The chance of the
snuff-box being mentioned at the inquest or anywhere else was practically non-existent.

He received another visit from the police, who were checking on
all members of the Varsity Club. Stentoller confirmed that he had
left the Club about half-past ten, gone straight to the car park and
driven home.

The doorkeeper at the Palace had recorded that Lord Haddenham
had left at ten-forty. As Haddenham had mentioned to Colonel
Hallingburn that he was going back to the Varsity Club, the murder
could be timed at approximately a quarter to eleven. If Stentoller
had not in fact gone straight to the car park he might have committed the murder. But so might a dozen other members who left
the club about that time. As no shadow of a motive could be
found against anybody, nor any clue pointing anywhere, the Yard
had to advance the theory of a foreign political fanatic. In six
months the log of the case drifted to the Department of Dead Ends.

6

The wedding was postponed for a year, actually for fourteen months,
as Derek, now Lord Haddenham, remained in the Diplomatic Service
and had to fit it in with his leave. Gwen became virtually bi-lingual
in German and Italian, and Stentoller resumed his normal life.

He avoided the ordeal of telling Hilda that he had been blackballed. There was never any publicity or chatter about the Terracotta, so he decided that she need never know. Moreover, his orienta-
tion was now somewhat different. Under his guidance, the firm had
gained even greater strength. He was no longer concerned to be
numbered among the inner core. When the youngsters were settled,
he intended to sell out and retire. The traditions of the house of

Stentoller now seemed as hollow as the traditions of the inner core. Weslake had returned from Turkey. He had called at the first opportunity, had been very friendly but had not mentioned the Terracotta incident, nor anything else of an inconvenient nature. Hilda took over the entire arrangements for the wedding. On the following day they were going for a quiet fortnight together. "A silver honeymoon," she had called it, with generous courage.

On a bright day in June the youngsters were married from Stentoller's house, which looked over the wooded hills and green valleys of Surrey. The reception flowed from the house to the garden. The inner core was sufficiently represented, and somehow or other there was a cross-section of the fashion-paper world. Had he been a mere snob, Stentoller would have regarded that reception as the seal on a successful social career.

Gwen and her husband were receiving their congratulations in the hall at the foot of the double staircase, with Hilda and himself in support. In the dining-room, behind him on his right, the presents were laid out. He must remember to go and look at them.

"Reggie doubts whether he'll be able to make it," Lady Weslake was saying. "He simply had to go to a conference this morning. But he'll come if he can."

A pity if he didn't turn up. Gwen had made him an unofficial uncle and liked teasing him. She would miss him on her wedding day. His thoughts roved. Children, even Gwen, had no tact with their parents. If she had any regrets at leaving him she hadn't shown them. Now and again fragments of conversation in the dining-room reached his ears.

"George IV gave it to Haddenham. And the original Stentoller had something to do with it. I know the King's honour comes into it somehow—look, there's the Royal cipher!"

That snuff-box! Stentoller blinked. What on earth was it doing among the wedding presents? He slipped into the dining-room.

There it was, on a little table set apart which had a card clipped in a menu holder saying: *'Traditional Presents Originated by the Second Earl of Haddenham, A.D. 1720.'* There was a necklace, a jewelled dagger, a Bible—never mind those things!—the snuff-box had a ticket to itself: *'Gift of George IV to Fifth Earl: Mortgaged to Albert Stentoller, 1825: Restored to Eighth Earl by Cuthbert Stentoller, 1935.'*

Derek was the ninth Earl.

There was nothing to worry about. The police knew—and no doubt any other interested person—that he had given it to the 'eighth earl' over dinner. Weslake alone knew that he could not possibly have given Haddenham the snuff-box over dinner.

And Weslake might turn up later.

Obviously, Weslake had forgotten all about the snuff-box incident in the hall of the Varsity Club. But the sight of the box itself might awaken memory.

Better not risk it.

Covering his movements with a certain neatness, he removed both snuff-box and ticket. He scrunched up the ticket and put it in his trousers pocket. The snuff-box could just be concealed in his hand. He rejoined Hilda, and presently slipped the snuff-box into his tail pocket. Fresh arrivals were still queueing in the hall. Greeting them was automatic—one could make nearly the same remarks to each.

Suddenly Hilda was speaking to him in an urgent undertone:

"Cuthbert! That man with his back to us in the dining-room doorway is a detective. Scotland Yard insisted on sending them to guard the presents, though I told them it was absurd. He says someone has stolen the Haddenham snuff-box. I said he mustn't make a fuss and that you'd speak to him. Shut them up at all costs."

Shut them up at all costs. Quite! But would they consent to be shut up? He signed to the detective to follow him into the little morning-room which was not in use. He wondered uneasily whether his tail pocket bulged.

"I tell you what I think has happened," said Stentoller. "Someone has picked it up, to talk about it to someone else. It'll be back in its place again presently."

The detective was unresponsive.

"When you were at that table about ten minutes ago, Mr. Stentoller, was it there then? We can't keep our eye on every item all the time."

"I didn't notice. But I do suggest that you adopt my theory. Intrinsically, the thing is doubtfully worth a tenner. And besides, you can't very well strip everybody—and I don't see that anything short of that would be any good."

"We have ways of getting over that difficulty." To Stentoller the words sounded ominous. The detective added: "Fancy thing—the thief has taken the ticket as well, saying what its history was."

When the detective had left the room, Stentoller concealed the snuff-box behind the radiator. Then he burnt the descriptive ticket, holding it so that the ashes would drop into a bowl of flowers.

When he rejoined Hilda, he had a fresh shock.

"One of those wretched detectives," she whispered, "has gone upstairs. They must mean to search the house."

"I'll keep a tab on them," he said. He went back to the morning-room and reclaimed the snuff-box. That snuff-box must not be found until the reception was over. He went into the garden, made his way to the lily pond, stopped several times on the way to exchange pleasantries.

The lily pond, with fountain and goldfish, was part of a small Dutch garden, sunk out of sight of the house. Choosing his moment, he bent down and slithered the snuff-box under a water-lily, carefully noting the position of the lily. When he returned to the house Gwen slipped her arm through his.

"In two hours, we shall be gone. I'm terribly sorry-glad—you know that, Daddy, don't you!" Bless her heart for saying that! She prattled on: "We've had a huge telegram from Sir Reginald, saying he can't turn up, and full of such awfully good good-wishes that Derek has come over all shy."

So Weslake wasn't coming after all! Stentoller felt slightly indignant that circumstances had made a fool of him. He couldn't go and fish that snuff-box out then and there. Anyhow, it didn't matter now.

After dinner that night he went alone to the lily pond. He identified the lily, took off his dinner jacket and stripped to the waist. The pond was nearly two feet deep.

He groped and found nothing. In ten minutes he realised he was stirring up masses of mud to no purpose. The job would have to be tackled properly in daylight, with rakes and the rest of it. It could wait until after the 'silver honeymoon.' Derek, on his honeymoon, would not be worrying about his heirlooms.

7

While Stentoller was holidaying with his wife on a Swiss lake, his gardener, working on the lily pond, found the snuff-box, which he promptly handed to the housekeeper, who locked it up, pending her employer's return. That night the gardener talked about it in the village inn—which meant that the local constable got to hear about it. Two days later, by an obvious chain of events, Scotland Yard demanded temporary custody of the snuff-box.

It is characteristic of the Department of Dead Ends that Detective Inspector Rason received a carbon of the report solely because the name of Haddenham figured in it.

Whenever some incident echoed on one of his filed cases Rason would produce some fantastic wild-goose theory, but this time he was stumped.

Someone had stolen a valuable snuff-box. Subsequently fearing detection, he had dumped it. No clear line to the murder of Lord Haddenham fourteen months previously! Annoyed with himself, he re-read the log of the murder then re-read the report of the theft.

'The ticket containing an historic note was also removed.'

"Historic note! That must be the bit about the King being a crook. Wonder the old boy wasn't bow-and-arrowed at dawn! Now, there's some sense in stealing a gold snuff-box, if you're that sort. But there's no sense in stealing its ticket. Therefore the thief was crackers— which doesn't help.

"Turn it upside down, then. The thief was a wise guy. That means he stole the ticket because he didn't want people to read it. But a lot of the guests must have read it already. That means he didn't want some particular person to read it. Someone who hadn't read it already. If that's right, he was stealing the box for the same reason. Box and ticket. He didn't want someone to see either of them."

Back to the log of the murder. The snuff-box, most exasperatingly, proved nothing either way. Mr. Stentoller had given it to the deceased over dinner. It wouldn't have affected the murder if he hadn't given it to him at all.

"Never mind the thief. Try the fellow the thief had in mind. Somebody is to come into the room—a fairly late arrival—see that snuff-box, or the ticket without the box, and say: 'Ah, a snuff-box! And a gift of George IV too, by Gad! That settles it. *Now* we know who killed Haddenham.' " Rason stroked his hair. "That sort of thing always happens when I do a spot of deduction."

Half-way through lunch, he made some sense of it.

"Somebody, seeing that snuff-box on that table, would say: 'Its presence here upsets some statement made at the time of the murder about the snuff-box.'

"The only person who made any statement about the snuff-box at the time of the murder was Stentoller.

"That makes Stentoller the murderer. He's one of the thirteen who might have done it, according to the times they left the Club. He stabs Haddenham with his umbrella—then stuffs the snuff-box in his pocket—so that I can catch him out telling a lie!"

Rason was following a formula he had often found useful. Test an absurdity and you may stumble on a truth.

He went to the Varsity Club and interviewed the cloakroom attendant, to whom he handed a list of the thirteen members who had left at relevant times.

"I want you to try to remember whether any of these gentlemen was carrying an umbrella—one of those very thin ones——"

"Them very thin umbrellas again!" groaned the attendant. "I had a bellyful o' them at the time. And I'll tell you the same as I told the others, that as far as I can remember not one of the lot of 'em had an umbrella."

"In particular," pressed Rason, "was Mr. Stentoller carrying an umbrella?"

"No, he wasn't." The man sniggered. "He was carryin' a sword."

"Carrying a *what!*" gasped Rason.

"Carryin' a sword, I tell you! His friend, Sir Reginald Weslake, had been to a Levee in the morning." The details followed. "Nearly tripped over the belt as he was going out of here. I heard Sir Reginald say he'd take the belt off for him, as they went into the hall: About half-past ten that was, as near as makes no matter."

Rason temporarily forgot all about the snuff-box. A sword! A couple of hours later he was in Surrey, checking up with Weslake, who came in from the garden and interviewed him in the dining-room.

Rason asked if he might see the sword of the Order of St. Severell of Antioch.

"That is a very extraordinary request. What is your reason?"

"We suspect that that sword may have been used for a felonious purpose when it was not in your possession, Sir Reginald."

Weslake glanced again at Rason's official card, then left the room, to return with the sword.

As Rason drew the blade he noted that it was slightly bent. He examined the point—which was scarcely sharper than the point of one of those very thin umbrellas.

"Sir Reginald, at about ten-thirty on the night Lord Haddenham was murdered, did you hand this sword to Mr. Stentoller?"

"I believe I did!" Weslake had obviously forgotten the incident, but now remembered. "Yes, definitely—I did. In special circumstances not worth relating."

Then Stentoller *could* have killed Haddenham with that sword. But *did* he?

Rason decided to go away now. He had got confirmation of the cloakroom attendant's statement about the sword; but, he reflected gloomily, this in itself proved nothing.

"Well, thanks very much, Sir Reginald. I'd better give you back this sword." Rason took a couple of steps forward, fouled the sword belt. That reminded him of something else the attendant had said. No harm in checking up.

"Did Mr. Stentoller carry it like this," he asked, "with the—er—all this—dangling?"

"Oh no, not at all! I took it off and rolled it. He carried it in his pocket."

"Hm! Good pocketful, wasn't it!" remarked Rason, intending only to be amiable.

"No doubt it was troublesome," said Weslake, with laboured patience. "I happen to remember he had to make room for it, to take —something—out of his side pocket and put it into his breast pocket."

Weslake's hesitation had been due to a desire to avoid opening another field for tedious questioning. Rason jumped blindly on the hesitation.

"What did he take out of his pocket, Sir Reginald?"

"He took from his side pocket, Mr. Rason, a gold snuff-box. He had intended to present it to Lord Haddenham, but something prevented him from doing so. And if you want further information about the snuff-box——"

"I'll find it in Kyle's *Life of George IV!*" snapped Rason. Weslake glared at him. Rason had sized up this man and deemed it prudent to break the rules.

"You saw that snuff-box in Stentoller's hand at ten-thirty. It was found on Haddenham's dead body. I am afraid I must take that sword away with me. We shall want it for evidence."

"My God!" gasped Weslake. "Then Stentoller must have found out that Haddenham——"

But he did not finish the sentence. Though no longer a member of the Terracotta, he would not drag the club's name into the newspapers.

THE RUBBER TRUMPET

IF YOU were to enquire at Scotland Yard for the Department of Dead Ends you might be told, in all sincerity, that there is no such thing, because it is not called by that name nowadays. All the same, if it has no longer a room to itself, you may rest assured that its spirit hovers over the index files of which we are all so justly proud.

The Department came into existence in the spacious days of King Edward VII and it took everything that the other departments rejected. For instance, it noted and filed all those clues that had the exasperating effect of proving a palpably guilty man innocent. Its shelves were crowded with exhibits that might have been in the Black Museum—but were not. Its photographs were a perpetual irritation to all rising young detectives, who felt that they ought to have found the means of putting them in the Rogues' Gallery.

To the Department, too, were taken all those members of the public who insist on helping the police with obviously irrelevant information and preposterous theories. The one passport to the Department was a written statement by the senior officer in charge of the case that the information offered was absurd.

Judged by the standards of reason and common sense, its files were mines of misinformation. It proceeded largely by guesswork. On one occasion it hanged a murderer by accidentally punning on his name.

It was the function of the Department to connect persons and things that had no logical connection. In short, it stood for the antithesis of scientific detection. It played always for a lucky fluke—to offset the lucky fluke by which the criminal so often eludes the police. Often it muddled one crime with another and arrived at the correct answer by wrong reasoning.

As in the case of George Muncey and the rubber trumpet.

And note, please, that the rubber trumpet had nothing logically to do with George Muncey, nor the woman he murdered, nor the circumstances in which he murdered her.

2

Until the age of twenty-six George Muncey lived with his widowed mother in Chichester, the family income being derived from a chemist's shop, efficiently controlled by Mrs. Muncey with the aid of a manager and two assistants, of whom latterly George was one. Of his early youth we know only that he won a scholarship at a day-school, tenable for three years, which was cancelled at the end of a year, though not, apparently, for misconduct. He failed several times to obtain his pharmaceutical certificate, with the result that he was eventually put in charge of the fancy soaps, the hot-water bottles and the photographic accessories.

For this work he received two pounds per week. Every Saturday he handed the whole of it to his mother, who returned him fifteen shillings for pocket money. She had no need of the balance and only took it in order to nourish his self-respect. He did not notice that she bought his clothes and met all his other expenses.

George had no friends and very little of what an ordinary young man would regard as pleasure. He spent nearly all his spare time with his mother, to whom he was devoted. She was an amiable but very domineering woman and she does not seem to have noticed that her son's affection had in it a quality of childishness—that he liked her to form his opinions for him and curtail his liberties.

After his mother's death he did not resume his duties at the shop. For some eight months he mooned about Chichester. Then, the business having been sold and probate granted, he found himself in possession of some eight hundred pounds, with another two thousand pounds due to him in three months. He did not, apparently, understand this part of the transaction—for he made no application for the two thousand, and as the solicitors could not find him until his name came into the papers, the two thousand remained intact for his defence.

That he was a normal but rather backward young man is proved by the fact that the walls of his bedroom were liberally decorated with photographs of the actresses of the moment and pictures of anonymous beauties cut from the more sporting weeklies. Somewhat naïvely he bestowed this picture gallery as a parting gift on the elderly cook.

He drew the whole of the eight hundred pounds in notes and

gold, said good-bye to his home and went up to London. He stumbled on cheap and respectable lodgings in Pimlico. Then, in a gauche, small-town way, he set out to see life.

It was the year when *The Merry Widow* was setting all London a-whistling. Probably on some chance recommendation, he drifted to Daly's Theatre, where he bought himself a seat in the dress-circle.

It was the beginning of the London season and we may assume that he would have felt extremely self-conscious sitting in the circle in his ready-made lounge suit, had there not happened to be a woman also in morning dress next to him.

The woman was a Miss Hilda Callermere. She was forty-three and if she escaped positive ugliness she was certainly without any kind of physical attractiveness, though she was neat in her person and reasonably well-dressed, in an old-fashioned way.

Eventually to the Department of Dead Ends came the whole story of his strange courtship.

There is a curious quality in the manner in which these two slightly unusual human beings approached one another. They did not speak until after the show, when they were wedged together in the corridor. Their voices seem to come to us out of a fog of social shyness and vulgar gentility. And it was she who took the initiative.

"If you'll excuse me speaking to you without an introduction, we seem to be rather out of it, you and I, what with one thing and another."

His reply strikes us now as somewhat unusual.

"Yes, rather!" he said. "Are you coming here again?"

"Yes, rather! I sometimes come twice a week."

During the next fortnight they both went three times to *The Merry Widow,* but on the first two of these occasions they missed each other. On the third occasion, which was a Saturday night, Miss Callermere invited George Muncey to walk with her on the following morning in Battersea Park.

Here shyness dropped from them. They slipped quite suddenly on to an easy footing of friendship. George Muncey accepted her invitation to lunch. She took him to a comfortably furnished eight-roomed house—her own—in which she lived with an aunt whom she supported. For, in addition to the house, Miss Callermere owned an income of six hundred pounds derived from gilt-edged investments.

But these considerations weighed hardly at all with George Muncey—for he had not yet spent fifty pounds of his eight hundred, and at this stage he had certainly no thought of marriage with Miss Callermere.

3

Neither of them had any occupation, so they could meet whenever they chose. Miss Callermere undertook to show George London. Her father had been a cheery, beery jerry-builder with sporting interests and she had reacted from him into a parched severity of mind. She marched George round the Tower of London, the British Museum and the like, reading aloud extracts from a guide-book. They went neither to the theatres nor to the music-halls, for Miss Callermere thought these frivolous and empty-headed—with the exception of *The Merry Widow,* which she believed to be opera, and therefore cultural. And the extraordinary thing was that George Muncey liked it all.

There can be no doubt that this smug little spinster, some sixteen years older than himself, touched a chord of sympathy in his nature. But she was wholly unable to cater for that part of him that had plastered photographs of public beauties on the walls of his bedroom.

She never went to *The Merry Widow* again, but once or twice he would sneak off to Daly's by himself. *The Merry Widow,* in fact, provided him with a dream-life. We may infer that in his imagination he identified himself with Mr. Joseph Coyne, who nightly, in the character of Prince Dannilo, would disdain the beautiful Sonia only to have her rush the more surely to his arms in the finale. Rather a dangerous fantasy for a backward young man from the provinces who was beginning to lose his shyness!

There was, indeed, very little shyness about him when, one evening after seeing Miss Callermere home, he was startled by the sight of a young parlourmaid, who had been sent out to post a letter, some fifty yards from Miss Callermere's house. If she bore little or no likeness to Miss Lily Elsie in the role of Sonia, she certainly looked quite lovely in her white cap and the streamers that were then worn. And she was smiling and friendly and natural.

She was, of course, Ethel Fairbrass. She lingered with George Muncey for over five minutes. And then comes another of those strange little dialogues.

"Funny a girl like you being a slavey! When's your evening off?"

"Six o'clock to-morrow. But what's it got to do with you?"

"I'll meet you at the corner of this road. Promise you I will."

"Takes two to make a promise. My name's Ethel Fairbrass, if you want to know. What's yours?"

"Dannilo."

"*Coo!* Fancy calling you that! Dannilo What?"

George had not foreseen the necessity for inventing a surname and discovered that it is quite difficult. He couldn't very well say 'Smith' or 'Robinson,' so he said:

"Prince."

George, it will be observed, was not an imaginative man. When she met him the following night he could think of nowhere to take her but to *The Merry Widow*. He was even foolish enough to let her have a programme, but she did not read the names of the characters. When the curtain went up she was too entranced with Miss Lily Elsie, whom (like every pretty girl at the time) she thought she resembled, to take any notice of Mr. Joseph Coyne and his character name. If she had tumbled to the witless transposition of the names she might have become suspicious of him. In which case George Muncey might have lived to a ripe old age.

But she didn't.

4

Altogether, Ethel Fairbrass provided an extremely satisfactory substitute for the dream-woman of George's fantasy. Life was beginning to sweeten. In the daylight hours he would enjoy his friendship with Miss Callermere, the pleasure of which was in no way touched by his infatuation for the pretty parlourmaid.

In early September Ethel became entitled to her holiday. She spent the whole fortnight with George at Southend. And George wrote daily to Miss Callermere, telling her that he was filling the place of a chemist-friend of his mother's, while the latter took his holiday. He actually contrived to have the letters addressed to the care of a local chemist. The letters were addressed 'George Muncey' while at the hotel the couple were registered as 'Mr. and Mrs. D. Prince.'

Now the fictional Prince Dannilo was notoriously an open-handed and free-living fellow—and Dannilo Prince proceeded to follow in his footsteps. Ethel Fairbrass undoubtedly had the time of her life.

They occupied a suite. ("Coo! A bathroom all to our own two selves, and use it whenever we like!")

He hired a car for her, with chauffeur—which cost ten pounds a day at that time. He gave her champagne whenever he could induce her to drink it and bought her some quite expensive presents.

It is a little surprising that at the end of a fortnight of this kind of thing she went back to her occupation. But she did. There was nothing of the mercenary about Ethel.

On his return to London, George was very glad to see Miss Callermere. They resumed their interminable walks and he went almost daily to her house for lunch or dinner. A valuable arrangement, this, for the little diversion at Southend had made a sizeable hole in his eight hundred pounds.

It was a bit of a nuisance to have to leave early in order to snatch a few minutes with Ethel. After Southend, the few snatched minutes had somehow lost their charm. There were, too, Ethel's half-days and her Sundays, the latter involving him in a great many troublesome lies to Miss Callermere.

In the middle of October he started sneaking off to *The Merry Widow* again. Which was a bad sign. For it meant that he was turning back again from reality to his dream-life. The Reality, in the meantime, had lost her high spirits and was inclined to weep unreasonably and to nag more than a little.

At the beginning of November Ethel presented him with certain very valid arguments in favour of fixing the date of their wedding, a matter which had hitherto been kept vaguely in the background.

George was by now heartily sick of her and contemplated leaving her in the lurch. Strangely enough, it was her final threat to tell Miss Callermere that turned the scale and decided George to make the best of a bad job and marry her.

5

As Dannilo Prince he married her one foggy morning at the registrar's office in Henrietta Street. Mr. and Mrs. Fairbrass came up from Banbury for the wedding. They were not very nice about it, although from the social point of view the marriage might be regarded as a step-up for Ethel.

"Where are you going for your honeymoon?" asked Mrs. Fairbrass. "That is—if you're going to *have* a honeymoon."

"Southend," said the unimaginative George, and to Southend he took her for the second time. There was no need for a suite now, so they went to a small family-and-commercial hotel. Here George was unreasonably jealous of the commercial travellers, who were merely being polite to a rather forlorn bride. In wretched weather he insisted on taking her for walks, with the result that he himself caught a very bad cold. Eucalyptus and hot toddy became the dominant note in a town which was associated in the girl's mind with champagne and bath salts. But they had to stick it for the full fortnight, because George had told Miss Callermere that he was again acting as substitute for the chemist-friend of his mother's in Southend.

According to the files of the Department, they left Southend by the three-fifteen on the thirtieth of November. George had taken first-class returns. The three-fifteen was a popular non-stop, but on this occasion there were hardly a score of persons travelling to London. One of the first-class carriages was occupied by a man alone with a young baby wrapped in a red shawl. Ethel wanted to get into this compartment, perhaps having a sneaking hope that the man would require her assistance in dealing with the baby. But George did not intend to concern himself with babies one moment before he would be compelled to do so, and they went into another compartment.

Ethel, however, seems to have looked forward to her impending career with a certain pleasure. Before leaving Southend she had paid a visit to one of those shops that cater for summer visitors and miraculously remain open through the winter. She had a bulky parcel, which she opened in the rather pathetic belief that it would amuse George.

The parcel contained a large child's bucket, a disproportionately small wooden spade, a sailing-boat to the scale of the spade, a length of Southend rock and a rubber trumpet, of which the stem was wrapped with red and blue wool. It was a baby's trumpet and of rubber so that it should not hurt the baby's gums. In the mouthpiece, shielded by the rubber, was a little metal contraption that made the noise.

Ethel put the trumpet to her mouth and blew through the metal contraption.

Perhaps, in fancy, she heard her baby doing it. Perhaps, after a honeymoon of neglect and misery, she was making a desperate snatch at the spirit of gaiety, hoping he would attend to her and perhaps indulge in a little horseplay. But for the actual facts we have to depend on George's version.

"I said 'Don't make that noise, Ethel—I'm trying to read' or something like that. And she said 'I feel like a bit of music to cheer me up' and she went on blowing the trumpet. So I caught hold of it and threw it out of the window. I didn't hurt her and she didn't seem to mind much. And we didn't have another quarrel over it and I went on reading my paper until we got to London."

At Fenchurch Street they claimed their luggage and left the station. Possibly Ethel abandoned the parcel containing the other toys for they were never heard of again.

When the train was being cleaned, a dead baby was found under the seat of a first-class compartment, wrapped in a red shawl. It was subsequently ascertained that the baby had not been directly murdered but had died more or less naturally in convulsions.

But before this was known, Scotland Yard searched for the man who had been seen to enter the train with the baby, as if for a murderer. A platelayer found the rubber trumpet on the line and forwarded it. Detectives combed the shops of Southend and found that only one rubber trumpet had been sold—to a young woman whom the shopkeeper did not know. The trail ended here.

The rubber trumpet went to the Department of Dead Ends.

6

Of the eight hundred pounds there was a little over a hundred and fifty left by the time they returned from the official honeymoon at Southend. He took her to furnished rooms in Ladbroke Grove and a few days later to a tenement in the same district, which he furnished at a cost of thirty pounds.

She seems to have asked him no awkward questions about money. Every morning after breakfast he would leave the tenement, presumably in order to go to work. Actually he would loaf about the West End until it was time to meet Miss Callermere. He liked especially going to the house in Battersea for lunch on Sundays. And here, of course, the previous process reversed itself and it was Ethel who had to be told the troublesome lies that were so difficult to invent.

"You seem so different lately, George," said Miss Callermere one Sunday after lunch. "I believe you're living with a ballet girl."

George was not quite sure what a ballet girl was, but it sounded rather magnificently wicked. As he was anxious not to involve himself in further inventions, he said:

"She's not a ballet girl. She used to be a parlourmaid."

"I really only want to know one thing about her," said Miss Callermere. "And that is, whether you are fond of her?"

"No, I'm not!" said George with complete truthfulness.

"It's a pity to have that kind of thing in your life—you are dedicated to science. For your own sake, George, why not get rid of her?"

Why not? George wondered why he had not thought of it before. He had only to move, to stop calling himself by the ridiculous name of Dannilo Prince, and the thing was as good as done. He would go back at once and pack.

When he got back to the tenement, Ethel gave him an unexpectedly warm reception.

"You told me you were going to the S.D.P. Sunday Brotherhood, you did! And you never went near them, because you met that there Miss Callermere in Battersea Park, because I followed you and saw you. And then you went back to her house, which is Number Fifteen, Laurel Road, which I didn't know before. And what you can see in a dried-up old maid like that beats me. It's time she knew that she's rolling her silly sheep's eyes at another woman's husband. And I'm going to tell her before I'm a day older."

She was whipping on hat and coat and George lurched forward to stop her. His foot caught on a gas-ring, useless now that he had installed a gas-range—a piece of lumber that Ethel ought to have removed weeks ago. But she used it as a stand for the iron.

George picked up the gas-ring. If she were to go to Miss Callermere and make a brawl, he himself would probably never be able to go there again. He pushed her quickly on to the bed, then swung the gas-ring—swung it several times.

He put all the towels, every soft absorbent thing he could find, under the bed. Then he washed himself, packed a suitcase and left the tenement.

He took the suitcase to his old lodgings, announced that he had come back there to live, and then presented himself at the house in Battersea in time for supper.

"I've done what you told me," he said to Miss Callermere. "Paid her off. Shan't hear from her any more."

The Monday morning papers carried the news of the murder, for the police had been called on Sunday evening by the tenants of the flat below. The hunt was started for Dannilo Prince.

By Tuesday the dead girl's parents had been interviewed and her life-story appeared on Wednesday morning.

> "My daughter was married to Prince at the Henrietta Street registrar's office on November 16th, 1907. He took her straight away for a honeymoon at Southend, where they stayed a fortnight."

There was a small crowd at the bottom of Laurel Road to gape at the house where she had so recently worked as a parlourmaid. Fifty yards from Number Fifteen! But if Miss Callermere noticed the crowd she is not recorded as having made any comment upon it to anyone.

In a few days, Scotland Yard knew that they would never find Dannilo Prince. In fact, it had all been as simple as George had anticipated. He had just moved—and that was the end of his unlucky marriage. The addition of the murder had not complicated things, because he had left no clue behind him.

Now, as there was nothing whatever to connect George Muncey with Dannilo Prince, George's chances of arrest were limited to the chance of an accidental meeting between himself and someone who had known him as Prince. There was an hotel proprietor, a waiter and a chambermaid at Southend and an estate agent at Ladbroke Grove. And, of course, Ethel's father and mother. Of these persons only the estate agent lived in London.

A barrister, who was also a statistician, entertained himself by working out the averages. He came to the conclusion that George Muncey's chance of being caught was equal to his chance of winning the first prize in the Calcutta Sweep *twenty-three times in succession*.

But the barrister did not calculate the chances of the illogical guesswork of the Department of Dead Ends hitting the bull's-eye by mistake.

7

While the hue and cry for Dannilo Prince passed over his head, George Muncey dedicated himself to science with such energy that in a fortnight he had obtained a post with a chemist in Walham. Here he presided over a counter devoted to fancy soaps, hot-water bottles, photographic aparatus and the like—for which he received two pounds a week and a minute commission that added zest to his work.

At Easter he married Miss Callermere in church. That lady had mobilised all her late father's associates and, to their inward amusement, arrayed herself in white satin and veil for the ceremony. As it would have been unreasonable to ask George's employers for a holiday after so short a term of service, the newly married couple dispensed with a honeymoon. The aunt entered a home for indigent gentlewomen with an allowance of a hundred a year from her niece. George once again found himself in a spacious, well-run house.

During their brief married life, this oddly assorted couple seem to have been perfectly happy. The late Mr. Callermere's friends were allowed to slip back into oblivion, because they showed a tendency to giggle whenever George absent-mindedly addressed his wife as 'Miss Callermere.'

His earnings of two pounds a week may have seemed insignificant beside his wife's unearned income. But in fact it was the basis of their married happiness. Every Saturday he handed her the whole of his wages. She would retain twenty-five shillings, because they both considered it essential to his self-respect that he should pay the cost of his food. She handed him back fifteen shillings for pocket-money. She read the papers and formed his opinions for him. She seemed to allow him little of what most men would regard as pleasure, but George had no complaint on this score.

Spring passed into summer and nearly everybody had forgotten the murder of Ethel Prince in a tenement in Ladbroke Grove. It is probably true to say that, in any real sense of the word, George Muncey had forgotten it too. He had read very little and did not know that murderers were popularly supposed to be haunted by their crime and to start guiltily at every chance mention of it.

He received no reaction whatever when his employer said to him one morning:

"There's this job-line of rubber trumpets. I took half a gross. We'll mark them at one-and-a-penny. Put one on your counter with the rubber teats and try them on women with babies."

George took one of the rubber trumpets from the cardboard case containing the half gross. It had red and blue wool wound about the stem. He put it next the rubber teats and forgot about it.

8

Wilkins, the other assistant, held his pharmaceutical certificate, but he was not stand-offish on that account. One day, to beguile the boredom of the slack hour after lunch, he picked up the rubber trumpet and blew it.

Instantly George was sitting in the train with Ethel, telling her not to make that noise. When Wilkins put the trumpet down, George found himself noticing the trumpet and thought the red and blue wool very hideous. He picked it up—Ethel's had felt just like that when he had thrown it out of the window.

Now it cannot for one moment be held that George felt anything in the nature of remorse. The truth was that the rubber trumpet, by reminding him so vividly of Ethel, had stirred up dormant forces in his nature. Ethel had been very comely and jolly and playful when one was in the mood for it—as one often was, in spite of everything.

The trumpet, in short, produced little more than a sense of bewilderment. Why could not things have gone on as they began? It was only as a wife that Ethel was utterly intolerable, because she had no sense of order and did not really look after a chap. Now that he was married to Miss Callermere, if only Ethel had been available on, say, Wednesday evenings and alternate Sundays, life would have been full at once of colour and comfort. . . . He tried to sell the trumpet to a lady with a little girl and a probable baby at home, but without success.

On the next day he went as far as admitting to himself that the trumpet had got on his nerves. Between a quarter to one and a quarter past, when Wilkins was out to lunch, he picked up the trumpet and blew it. And just before closing-time he blew it again, when Wilkins was there.

George was not subtle enough to humbug himself. The trumpet stirred longings that were better suppressed. So the next day he wrote out a bill for one-and-a-penny, put one-and-a-penny of his pocket money into the cash register and stuffed the trumpet into his coat pocket. Before supper that night he put it in the hot-water furnace.

"There's a terrible smell in the house. What did you put in the furnace, George?"

"Nothing."

"Tell me the truth, dear."

"A rubber trumpet stuck on my counter. Fair got on my nerves, it did. I paid the one-and-a-penny and I burnt it."

"That was very silly, wasn't it? It'll make you short in your pocket money. And in the circumstances I don't feel inclined to make it up for you."

That would be all right, George assured her, and inwardly thought how lucky he was to have such a wife. She could keep a fellow steady and pull him up when he went one over the odds.

Three days later his employer looked through the stock.

"I see that rubber trumpet has gone. Put up another. It may be a good line."

And so the whole business began over again. George, it will be observed, for all his unimaginativeness, was a spiritually economical man. His happy contentment with his wife would, he knew, be jeopardised if he allowed himself to be reminded of that other disorderly, fascinating side of life that had been presided over by Ethel.

There were six dozen of the rubber trumpets, minus the one burnt at home, and his employer would expect one-and-a-penny for each of them. Thirteen shillings a dozen. But the dozens themselves were thirteen, which complicated the calculation, but in the end he got the sum right. He made sure of this by doing it backwards and 'proving' it. He still had twenty-three pounds left out of the eight hundred.

Mrs. Muncey had a rather nice crocodile dressing-case which she had bought for herself and quite falsely described as 'gift of the bridegroom to the bride.'

On the next day George borrowed the crocodile dressing-case on the plea that he wished to bring some goods from the shop home for Christmas. He brought it into the shop on the plea that it contained his dinner jacket and that he intended to change at the house of a friend without going home that night. As he was known to have married 'an heiress' neither Wilkins nor his employer was particularly surprised that he should possess a dinner jacket and a crocodile dressing-case in which to carry it about.

At a quarter to one, when he was again alone in the shop, he crammed half a gross (less one) of rubber trumpets into the crocodile dressing-case. When his employer came back from lunch he said:

"I've got rid of all those rubber trumpets, Mr. Arrowsmith. An old boy came in, said he was to do with an orphanage, and I talked him into buying the lot."

Mr. Arrowsmith was greatly astonished.

"Bought the lot, did you say? Didn't he ask for a discount?"

"No, Mr. Arrowsmith. I think he was a bit loopy myself."

Mr. Arrowsmith looked very hard at George and then at the cash register. Six thirteens, less one, at one-and-a-penny—four pounds, three and fivepence. It was certainly a very funny thing. But then, the freak customer appears from time to time and at the end of the day Mr. Arrowsmith had got over his surprise.

Journeying from Walham to Battersea, one goes on the Underground to Victoria Station, and continues the journey on the main line: From the fact that George Muncey that evening took the crocodile case to Victoria Station, it has been argued that he intended to take the rubber trumpets home and perhaps bury them in the garden or deal with them in some other way. But this ignores the fact that he told his wife he intended to bring home some goods for Christmas.

The point is of minor importance, because the dressing-case never reached home with him that night. At the top of the steps leading from the Underground it was snatched from him.

George's first sensation, on realising that he had been robbed, was one of relief. The rubber trumpets, he had already found, could not be burnt; they would certainly have been a very great nuisance to him. The case, he knew, cost fifteen guineas, and there was still enough left of the twenty-three pounds to buy a new one on the following day.

9

At closing-time the next day, while George and Wilkins were tidying up, Mr. Arrowsmith was reading the evening paper.

"Here, Muncey! Listen to this. 'Jake Mendel, thirty-seven, of no fixed abode, was charged before Mr. Ramsden this morning with the theft of a crocodile dressing-case from the precincts of Victoria Station. Mr. Ramsden asked the police what was inside the bag. 'A number of toy trumpets, your worship, made of rubber. There were seventy-seven of 'em all told.' Mr. Ramsden: 'Seventy-seven rubber trumpets! Well, *now* there really is no reason why the police should not have their own band.' (Laughter)." Mr. Arrowsmith laughed too and then: "Muncey, that looks like your lunatic."

"Yes, Mr. Arrowsmith," said George indifferently, then went contentedly home to receive his wife's expostulations about a new crocodile dressing-case which had been delivered during the afternoon. It was not quite the same to look at, because the original one had been made to order. But it had been bought at the same shop and the manager had obliged George by charging the same price for it.

In the meantime, the police were relying on the newspaper paragraph to produce the owner of the crocodile case. When he failed to materialise on the following morning they looked at the name of the manufacturer and took the case round to him.

The manufacturer informed them that he had made that case the previous Spring to the order of a Miss Callermere—that the lady had since married and that, only the previous day, her husband, Mr. Muncey, had ordered an exactly similar one but had accepted a substitute from stock.

"Ring up George Muncey and ask him to come up and identify the case—and take away these india-rubber trumpets!" ordered the Superintendent.

Mrs. Muncey answered the telephone and from her they obtained George's business address.

"A chemist's assistant!" said the Superintendent. "Seems to me rather rum. Those trumpets may be his employer's stock. And he may have been pinching 'em. Don't ring him up—go down. And find out if the employer has anything to say about the stock. See him before you see Muncey."

At Walham the Sergeant was taken into the dispensary where he promptly enquired whether Mr. Arrowsmith had missed seventy-seven rubber trumpets from his stock.

"I haven't missed them—but I sold them the day before yesterday —seventy-seven, that's right! Or rather, my assistant, George Muncey, did. Here, Muncey!" And as George appeared:

"You sold the rest of the stock of those rubber trumpets to a gentleman who said he was connected with an orphanage—the day before yesterday it was—didn't you?"

"Yes, Mr. Arrowsmith," said George.

"Bought the lot without asking for a discount," said Mr. Arrowsmith proudly. "Four pounds, three shillings and fivepence. I could

tell you of another case that happened years ago when a man came
into this very shop and——"

The Sergeant felt his head whirling a little. The assistant had
sold seventy-seven rubber trumpets to an eccentric gentleman. The
goods had been duly paid for and taken away—and the goods were
subsequently found in the assistant's wife's dressing-case.

"Did you happen to have a crocodile dressing-case stolen from you
at Victoria Station the day before yesterday, Mr. Muncey?" asked
the Sergeant.

George was in a quandary. If he admitted that the crocodile case
was his wife's—he would admit to Mr. Arrowsmith that he had been
lying when he had said that he had cleverly sold the whole of the
seventy-seven rubber trumpets without even having to give away
a discount. So:

"No," said George.

"Ah, I thought not! There's a mistake somewhere. I expect it's
that manufacturer put us wrong. Sorry to have troubled you, gentlemen! Good morning!"

"Wait a minute," said Mr. Arrowsmith. "You *did* have a crocodile
dressing-case here that day, Muncey, with your evening clothes in
it. And you *do* go home by Victoria. But what is that about the
trumpets, Sergeant? They couldn't have been in Mr. Muncey's case
if he sold them over the counter."

"I don't know what they've got hold of, Mr. Arrowsmith, and
that's a fact," said George. "I think I'm wanted in the shop."

George was troubled, so he got leave to go home early. He told
his wife how he had lied to the police, and confessed to her about
the trumpets. Soon she had made him tell her the real reason for his
dislike of the trumpets. The result was that when the police brought
her the original crocodile case she flatly denied that it was hers.

In law, there was no means by which the ownership of the case
could be foisted upon the Munceys against their will. Pending the
trial of Jake Mendel, the bag-snatcher, the crocodile case, with its
seventy-seven rubber trumpets, was deposited with the Department
of Dead Ends.

A few feet above it on a shelf stood the identical trumpet which
George Muncey had thrown out of the window on the three-fifteen,
non-stop Southend to Fenchurch Street, some seven months ago.

The Department took one of the trumpets from the bag and set it beside the trumpet on the shelf. There was no logical connection between them whatever. The Department simply guessed that there might be a connection.

They tried to connect Walham with Southend and drew blank. They traced the history of the seventy-seven Walham trumpets and found it simple enough until the moment when George Muncey put them in the crocodile case.

They went back to the Southend trumpet and read in their files that it had not been bought by the man with the baby but by a young woman.

Then they tried a cross-reference to young women and Southend. They found that dead end, the Ethel Fairbrass murder. They found: *'My daughter was married to Prince at the Henrietta Street registrar's office on November the sixteenth, 1907. He took her straight away for a honeymoon at Southend where they stayed a fortnight.'*

Fourteen days from November the sixteenth meant November the thirtieth, the day the rubber trumpet was found on the line.

One rubber trumpet is dropped on railway line by (possibly) a young woman. The young woman is subsequently murdered (but not with a rubber trumpet). A young man behaves in an eccentric way with seventy-seven rubber trumpets more than six months later.

The connection was wholly illogical. But the Department specialised in illogical connections. It communicated its wild guess—in the form of a guarded Minute—to Detective-Inspector Rason.

Rason went down to Banbury and brought the old Fairbrass couple to Walham.

He gave them five shillings and sent them into Arrowsmith's to buy a hot-water bottle.

A MAN AND
HIS MOTHER-IN-LAW

I

In a letter written on the eve of execution, Arthur Penfold seems to share the judge's astonishment that a man of his calibre should turn to murder to extricate himself from a domestic difficulty. A student of criminology could have told Penfold—if not the learned judge himself—that murder eventuates, not from immediate circumstance, but from an antecedent state of mind.

The murder occurred in 1935. The antecedent state of mind was created five years earlier, on an October evening when Penfold, returning from the office, found a note in his wife's handwriting on the hall table.

Penfold, an only child of very doting parents, was born in 1900. At twenty-five he inherited the family business, a wholesale agency for technical inks—almost any ink except the kind one uses with a pen. His mother had died the previous year. For three years he lived alone in the twelve-roomed house, with an acre of garden, in the overgrown village of Crosswater, some twenty miles out of London. The house was vibrant with memories of a benevolently autocratic father, whose lightest wish became his wife's instant duty—whose opinions on everything she accepted as inspired wisdom. In April 1931 Arthur Penfold married and eagerly set about modelling his life on that of his father.

Of his bride we need note only that she had been an efficient business girl, a rung or two up the ladder, that she was physically attractive and well mannered—the sort of girl his friends expected him to choose. They had been married six months to a day when he found that note in the hall—six months, he would have told you, of unalloyed happiness. A wife who—*ex officio*, as it were—liked all the things that he liked, lived for the great moment of the day when he returned home, to regale her with small talk of his achievements in business. There was not, he would have asserted, a single cloud in his matrimonial sky.

'*Arthur dear. I am terribly sorry and utterly ashamed of myself, but I can't stick it any longer. It's not your fault—I have no complaint and no excuse. I shall stay with Mother while I'm looking for a job. I don't want any money, please, and I'll agree to anything as long as you don't ask me to come back—Julie.*

P.S.—There isn't another man and I don't suppose there ever will be.'

Julie remained unattached for three years. Then she wrote Penfold begging for divorce, as she wished to remarry. Penfold chivalrously insisted that he should be the one to give cause, so that she could start again untainted with scandal. He did not hate Julie, but he did hate himself and to a somewhat dangerous degree.

He was the fourth generation of his family to live in that house. The Penfolds were of the local aristocracy and 'knew everybody,' meaning fifty or so of the more prosperous families in a largish suburb. Arthur Penfold—though no one claimed him as an intimate friend—was popular, in the sense that no one disliked him nor ever suggested excluding him. He was of medium height, with thin, sandy hair, a little ponderous in manner, self-centred but not boastful. When he was deserted, for no apparent reason, 'everybody' agreed that he had been abominably treated and was entitled to sympathy.

While Julie was with him, his own happiness had been obvious to everybody. He had taken for granted that Julie was happy too. How could you have a happy husband and an unhappy wife? But, somehow, you had!

Why had she left him? Too late, he tried to imagine her point of view. It was uphill work, because he knew nothing of her intimate personal history, her tastes, her hopes, her fears. In the sense in which married lovers explore each other's personality and impulse, he knew nothing at all about her—had desired no such knowledge. It escaped him that this might be the reason why Julie had thrown in her hand.

In the sympathy of the neighbours he saw only pity for a man who had some taint or defect, unknown to himself, which made his society intolerable to a normal woman. How could he doubt that behind a mask of friendliness, the neighbours were laughing at him!

There was a certain tragic grandeur in the idea of a man with a taint that baffled definition. In a short time, he began to believe in it.

The desertion was followed by three years of bitter self-contempt, during which every friendly greeting was held to mask a sneer. Irrelevantly, he felt a little better when the divorce was completed. In the summer he accepted an invitation to stay with a cousin who was the vicar of Helmstane. Here he met Margaret Darrington, who became his second wife.

Margaret was twenty-four and a beauty, though she seemed not to know it. Her clothes, expensive but ill-chosen, verged on dowdiness. She lacked the assurance of a girl specially gifted by nature. Her intelligence was adult, but her temperament was that of a prim young schoolgirl with a talent for obedience. At their first meeting, Arthur Penfold, perceiving the talent for obedience, wanted to marry her much more than he had ever wanted anything.

"A very grave young person," the vicar told him. "She lives with an honorary aunt, to whom she is devoted—er—excessively so!" The vicar pulled himself up. "Perhaps that was a mean remark in the special circumstances!" He told a tragic tale. In the 1914 war, when Margaret was six, her mother had been killed in an air raid on London, while the child was in Helmstane with a Mrs. Blagrove. Scarcely had Mrs. Blagrove finished breaking the news to the little girl when a War Office telegram announced that her father had been killed in action. Mrs. Blagrove cherished the orphan, adopted her and did her best to fill the role of both parents.

"With indifferent success, I fear," finished the vicar. "Margaret is a dear girl—she helps me with the parish chores, which is convenient for me but not really the sort of thing she ought to be doing. She has lost her place in her own generation and shows no desire to find it. I would guess that she is, perhaps, unadventurous—a little afraid of life."

Too afraid of life, in fact, to run away from a husband, who would stand between her and the world, which she need apprehend only through his eyes. Penfold required no further information about the girl nor her intimate personal history, nor her tastes, nor her hopes, nor her fears. For their first date, he asked her to meet him in London for lunch and a matinée.

For an instant, the schoolgirl personality vanished. The wide set eyes became the eyes of a vital young woman reaching out for her share of gaiety. But only for an instant.

"I'll ask Aunt Agnes."

Six weeks later, in a punt on the river, he told her that it was in her power to make him extremely happy. He gave instances of so many ways in which she could give him happiness that the idea of marrying him began to take the colour of a moral duty. Whether he could give her a commensurate happiness was a question which was not raised by either side.

Margaret admitted having observed that a girl was expected to marry and leave home—even when her own people were fond of her, which she thought puzzling.

"Then you *will*, Madge?"

"I'll ask Aunt Agnes."

"No, darling!" said Penfold, who had not yet discovered that she was intelligent. "We'll go back at once and I'll tell her myself."

II

Mrs. Blagrove had draped her Victorian furniture in bright chintzes, hung a nude or two on her walls and believed the result to be modern. She believed the same of herself. In the nineties she had considered herself one of the New Women—had she not smoked cigarettes and read the early works of Bernard Shaw!—though she secretly preferred the output of Miss Ella Wheeler Wilcox, whose sentimental verse was already crossing the Atlantic. She had an income sufficient for all the hobbies and good works with which she fought her dread of lonely old age.

She began by putting Penfold at his ease, which slightly offended him and spoilt his tactical approach.

"I know why you have come, Mr. Penfold." Her smile was elaborately confidential. "I'll say it for you, shall I? You have *asked* Madge, and she has referred you to me. I've felt this in the air for a fortnight. And there was no way of warning either of you."

"But, Mrs. Blagrove! You cannot mean that you refuse your consent?"

"I have no such authority—my guardianship expired when she was twenty-one."

"She would never take an important step against your wishes."

"Nor an unimportant step, either. My moral influence, I admit, is paramount. For that very reason, I shall not exercise it. I shall urge Madge to do whatever she wants to do." Before Penfold could express satisfaction, Mrs. Balgrove added: "I shall simply advise her not to think any more about it. Advice—that will be all!"

Her tone removed insult from her words. Penfold retreated to prepared ground.

"Perhaps you will allow me to give a brief account of myself." The brevity, however, was not noticeable. Mrs. Blagrove politely refrained from registering inattention.

"In short, you are extremely eligible—the vicar told me all about you." She paused before resuming, on another note. "Mr. Penfold! Have you noticed, as I have, that some women are predestined mothers—you can tell when they're little girls. And some have an obvious talent for wifehood. And some—and Madge is one of these —are predestined *daughters*—daughters in mind and temperament even when they are very old women."

"Old maids, perhaps. But when Madge is married—"

"She'll make her husband more unhappy than herself. Other men have thought they were in love with her, because she's such a pretty thing. But their man's instinct warned them that too much of her would be withheld. Haven't you noticed how she comes to me to ask permission or advice on trifling matters?—and she's twenty-four, remember. It's she who insists on that sort of thing, not I. I flatter myself I'm a modern woman. I believe in complete freedom for women, single or married."

Penfold retained only the impression that 'the old lady' intended to keep the girl to herself. He was ready to fight her, tooth and claw. But there was nothing to fight. When Margaret reported back to him, he could hardly take in her words.

"I'm so glad Aunt Agnes doesn't refuse her consent. She just advises us not to. But I think—I'm sure—it's only because she would hate to seem to be glad to get rid of me. It's not reasonable to suppose she really wants me on her hands for ever. So, if you still feel sure that you do, Arthur—"

Penfold expected at best some sulkiness on the part of his honorary mother-in-law. To his amazement, she kept her word to urge the girl to do what she wanted to do. Mrs. Blagrove was positively co-operative. Pursuing some dimly understood ideal of modernity, she turned her energies to detail, took competent advice in the purchase of a most comprehensive trousseau. Further, she forced the girl into the hands of a beautician for grooming and general instruction.

The result was that Margaret's natural beauty was brought into line with modern requirements. Julie had been ordinarily good looking—Margaret would catch the eye in any community. In Crosswater, the women would be jealous and the men would be envious. They would soon see how wrong they had been in supposing that he could not hold the interest of an attractive wife.

On the last day of their honeymoon in Cornwall, there came a letter from Mrs. Blagrove, jointly addressed and beginning '*My dears*,' announcing that she had sold her house in Helmstane, bought another for the same price in Crosswater and would shortly move in.

"That's almost too good to be true!" exclaimed Margaret. "I can run round every day while you're in London and see that she's all right."

For a few seconds, Penfold hovered on the brink of protest. So that was the game! For all her amiability—for all that really broadminded trousseau—Mrs. Blagrove was hostile and intended to wreck their marriage. She would fail. Margaret's talent for obedience, which had given him such a delightful honeymoon, would prove a two-edged sword, and—and so on!

"I hope, darling," he said, feeling extremely clever, "that Aunt Agnes will stay with us while she is moving in."

Mrs. Blagrove did not stay in their house, but she let Margaret help her with the move, taking scrupulous care that Penfold's convenience should not be jeopardised. Very shrewd of her, thought Penfold. But he too knew how to wear the velvet glove.

Her house was some half a mile away: visits were constantly exchanged. No man could have been more attentive to his mother-in-law, honorary or otherwise.

In time, they slipped into a little routine. On Wednesday evenings, the Penfolds dined at Dalehurst, Mrs. Blagrove's daily help staying after six. On Sundays, Mrs. Blagrove came for supper to Oakleigh, when Penfold would read aloud a selection from the poems of Miss Ella Wheeler Wilcox who, in Mrs. Blagrove's affections, had never had a rival.

Penfold became aware that on most days of the week Margaret

would 'run round' to Dalehurst. Many minor domestic arrangements were traceable to Mrs. Blagrove; but they were sensible arrangements, which enhanced his comfort without impinging on his authority. Margaret never quoted Aunt Agnes. It would have been unintelligent to deny that the old lady seemed to be playing no game but an unobtrusively benevolent one. He began to think highly of her, even to enjoy her company, except for the sessions of Miss Ella Wheeler Wilcox. Twice she insinuated a Mrs. Manfried, a fellow devotee. It was his sole grievance.

A year passed, during which Penfold put back the weight he had lost after the collapse of his first marriage. His dream had come true. The women were jealous of Margaret, and the men, within the framework of correct behaviour, registered an envious appreciation of her. No longer did the smile of welcome seem to mask a sneer, tempered with pity.

He could not bring himself to grudge the time his wife spent at Dalehurst, in his absence. Mrs. Blagrove's prophecy that Margaret would make her husband unhappy had been stultified by the event. His life slipped into the pattern of his father's.

The inner history of an egocentric tends to repeat itself. The other half of Mrs. Blagrove's prophecy—the half that was concerned with Margaret's happiness—had slipped from Penfold's memory. He was so happy himself that he had not felt the need to probe into the question of Margaret's happiness—to explore her personality and her impulse. She was an efficient and economical housekeeper. She was of regular, orderly habits. She was lovely to look at and she was obedient in all things. His cup was full.

III

They had been married two years and a month when Mrs. Blagrove fell down in her bedroom and put a finger out of joint. The injury was beginning to be forgotten, when she fell down in the hall, bruising herself painfully. She was not too shaken, however, to come to supper on Sunday—to be whisked back to her girlhood by Penfold, in interpretation of Miss Ella Wheeler Wilcox.

The following week, a trained nurse took up residence at Dalehurst, though Mrs. Blagrove seemed to ignore her presence and to carry on as usual. In the course of a fortnight, Margaret overcame her aunt's reluctance to reveal the facts.

"She falls down because she suddenly loses consciousness," Margaret told her husband. "It's her heart. But Dr. Delmore says her life is in no danger."

Penfold expressed relief. But there was more to come.

"The air here is too bracing, Dr. Delmore says. She will have to sell up and leave. He recommends South Devon."

Some two hundred miles from London! That, Penfold admitted to himself, could be borne with equanimity. He was, in fact, about to say as much.

"I'm sorry, Arthur dear, but I must go with her."

"Yes, darling, of course you must! I'll squeeze a week off, and we'll all go down together and settle her in."

"Doctor Delmore says—" it was as if Penfold had not spoken "—that these little attacks may be frequent. They may come at any hour of the day or night. She might fall in the fire—under the traffic—anything. She must never be alone."

Still Penfold could not see it.

"That means two nurses. Pretty hefty expense—"

"There won't be two nurses. There won't be one. She can't get on with nurses. That nice Nurse Hart has gone, and Aunt Agnes says she won't have another. I must go to her, Arthur. That's what I'm trying to tell you."

There came a moment of stark panic—a long moment in which he again ran the gauntlet of smiles that masked the universal sneer at the man who cannot hold his woman.

"She may live for twenty years or more. Do you want to end our marriage, Madge?"

"It isn't a matter of what I want," she evaded. "Remember, she isn't my aunt, really. She didn't even like me, to start with—I was the horrid child of a young couple she had met on a pleasure cruise. I've never forgotten. All my life I've wondered what I could do in return."

"I'm not belittling her. But what about me? What have I done that I should lose my wife?"

"Nothing. You speak as if I were complaining of you—I'm not—it wouldn't be fair." The unconscious echo of Julie's words made him feel faint. "But you don't *need* me, Arthur—me in particular, I mean."

"Of course I need you! To come home in the evening, with no wife to welcome me—"

"You'll soon find a quiet girl, whose looks appeal to you—you ask so little, Arthur. Then, everything will be the same for you." She spoke without a trace of bitterness. "But Aunt Agnes needs me as *me!*"

He did not understand and would not try. The sense of defeat was numbing him. He went into the dining-room and took a stiff whisky. He would put his case firmly but fairly to Aunt Agnes, with every consideration for her feelings. Velvet glove, in fact. Now he came to think of it, her birthday fell on the day after tomorrow. That could be used to help his opening.

The next day was damp and foggy, increasing his depression, so that he left the office earlier than usual, determined to see Mrs. Blagrove at once.

Now, by chance—good or ill according to one's point of view—a popular publisher had decided to stage a come-back for the poetry of Ella Wheeler Wilcox and was flooding the bookstalls with an initial anthology: *The Best of Wilcox*. There was a double pyramid at one of the bookstalls at Waterloo station, which duly caught Penfold's eye.

The very thing! It would help him to open the interview on a friendly note.

He bought a copy, decided to retain the dust jacket, which carried a design of moonbeams and cupids—'the old lady' reacted to that sort of thing when you steered her into the mood for it.

On arriving at Crosswater at five-three, he reflected that Madge would not be expecting him for another hour—she had said that she would be helping at the vicarage that afternoon. So, instead of going home first, he trudged through the rain and fog to Dalehurst. Mrs. Blagrove was drawing the curtains when he appeared in the front garden. She beckoned and unlatched the french window.

"Come in this way, if you don't mind. It's Bessie's afternoon for visiting her grandmother in hospital. She's supposed to pay me back the time on Saturday, but she always has some excuse. You're home early, aren't you?"

He agreed with enthusiasm—went into the hall to deposit his coat and hat, and returned, flourishing *The Best of Wilcox*.

"This is just out—an anthology. Thought you might like it. Sort of pre-birthday present."

"How thoughtful and kind of you, Arthur! What a perfectly lovely design! I expect I know all the selections—I hope I do!" She lowered herself to the chintz-covered settee and turned over the pages. When Penfold had finished settling himself in an armchair, Mrs. Blagrove was sitting with her hands folded in her lap. The book was not in evidence.

"You've come to talk about Madge, haven't you?"

"And about you and me, Aunt Agnes. It's sheer tragedy that you have to go and live somewhere else. We made a perfect little circle, the three of us. I can safely say that, these last two years, I have been as happy as any man can hope to be."

"Yes! . . . Yes, I've noticed that you have."

The remark seemed out of focus. Also, Aunt Agnes looked amused, instead of impressed. He reminded himself that he was to be firm as well as fair.

"I have to live near London, of course. That puts Madge in a terrible position. I would not for one moment dispute your claim to a sacrifice on her part—"

" 'Sacrifice'!" Mrs. Blagrove laughed somewhat loudly. "Let's see if I've got it the right way round. It would be a sacrifice on *her* part to leave *you* and resume her life with *me*? Sacrifice of what, Arthur?"

While he was groping for a retort, she added:

"There are some things that women cannot conceal from each other, however hard they try."

"What has Madge to conceal from you?" he blustered. "Do I stint her allowance? Do I ask too much of her in return?"

"You ask too little. So that the little you do ask becomes a soul-destroying chore!"

Within him was rising a strange kind of fear, which he did not know to be fear of himself.

"To me, that doesn't make sense. But perhaps it's my fault. Perhaps I have some blind spot—some—taint—of which I am unaware."

"It's nothing so interesting as a taint, Arthur." She was leaning forward on the settee. Her elbows were bent, quivering a little. She seemed to him like a spider about to pounce. "Poor boy!" She was smiling now. "Your egotism protects you from all unpleasant truths

—protects you, even, from the hunger for companionship and shared emotion. I'm afraid I must tell you something about yourself—something that's not a bit mystical or dramatic."

"*Don't!*"

There was an antecedent state of mind, unsuspected by the judge, which made Penfold see in her smile the sneer which he had dreaded to see on the face of his friends, the sneer at the man who cannot hold his woman.

"Your first marriage—" she was saying, though her words now were lost to him "—like your second, failed because you don't want a wife—you want a puppet that can only say 'yes.'"

He had no purpose except that of compelling her to silence, lest she shatter that little world in which he lived so happily with a wife who mirrored his picture of himself. He seized her by the throat—his grip grew in strength while his mind's eye was re-reading Julie's letter: '*I am terribly sorry and utterly ashamed of myself, but I can't stick it any longer.*' Madge would leave him, too—and again he would be pitied as the man without a woman of his own. If he had been of a different social type, he might have described his ecstasy as 'seeing red and then getting a blackout.' He certainly went through a process comparable with that of regaining consciousness, though he was unsurprised when he found that Mrs. Blagrove was dead.

He lurched into the chintz-covered armchair.

"Look what you've done to us *now*, Aunt Agnes!" He whimpered like a child. He was too profoundly shocked to feel fear for himself. This would be the biggest scandal Crosswater had ever known. There was little he could do to avert it, but that little must be done.

With his handkerchief he wiped the chintz of the armchair. In the hall he wiped the hatstand and the peg on which he had hung his coat. He put on his coat and hat—and his gloves—unlatched the front door, stepped outside and shut it behind him.

He waited a minute or more, listening. He walked down the path to the gate—.

"*The Best of Wilcox!*" he muttered. "There'll be my fingerprints on that glossy jacket."

He took off his right glove, found his penknife, opened it, then put the glove on again. With some difficulty he raised the latch of the french windows, slithered round the curtain.

He had left the light burning. In this mild-mannered suburbanite there was no emotion at sight of the woman he had killed—some seven or eight minutes ago. He was concentrated on reclaiming the book—and it was not beside the body, where he had expected it to be. It was not on the seat of the settee nor on the arms nor on the floor.

He was beginning to get flustered, but only because he was always a duffer at finding things. He went down on his knees, looked under the settee—if it had fallen, he might have kicked it there himself. He crawled round to the back of the settee. He stood up, exasperated. The book simply must be in the room somewhere! He took a couple of steps backwards, bumped against the open flap of the escritoire. He wheeled as if a hand had touched him—and stared down at the cupids dancing in the moonbeams.

While he was picking up the book, his eye measured the distance from the back of the settee to the open flap of the escritoire—a good six feet.

How did the book get there, he wondered. She had it in her hand when she sat down, and he could not remember her leaving the settee. Could someone have entered the room, while he was outside the house? He hurried into the hall, intending to search the house —then abandoned the idea as useless. Anyway, it was much more likely that she had moved while they were talking, without his noticing it. Mustn't start imagining things and giving way to nerves!

He put the book in his overcoat pocket and, leaving the light burning, again left the house by the front door, forgetting to refasten the french window. The fog was being thinned out by a rising wind: with the light rain, visibility was still very poor.

He turned up his collar and adopted a slouch—he would be safe from recognition unless he came face to face with an acquaintance. He reached the gate of Oakleigh more than half an hour before his usual time. He observed that the lights were on in the kitchen but nowhere else. Madge, evidently, was still at the vicarage. He must get in without the cook and housemaid hearing him.

He used his latchkey silently, hung up his coat and hat and crept into the drawing-room. He switched on the stove and put *The Best of Wilcox* on an occasional table where Madge would be sure to see it—it would serve as a diversion. Now and again he chuckled to himself, as if he were taking rather sly measures to prevent the club secretary from learning that a friend had broken one of the rules.

He was still alone at five to six when, straining his ears, he could hear the train coming in, then rumbling away. Dangerously soon, he heard Madge's latchkey.

"Why, Arthur! You've beaten me! You must have galloped from the station!"

"I caught the earlier train—miserable day and not much doing at the office. I was dozing off when I heard your latchkey."

She was facing the occasional table—staring at the moonbeams and cupids. She looked disappointed—held the book as if she resented its presence in the house.

"It's not for you!" he laughed. "It's a Wilcox anthology. Out today! I thought Aunt Agnes might like to have it."

"Oh, Arthur, how kind of you!" Her voice was unsteady. With unwonted impulsiveness, she threw her arms round his neck. He was unaware that this was the first time she had volunteered a caress. "Let me take it to her tomorrow morning—please—I want to tell her how you thought of it for her."

Almost reverently, she replaced the book on the little table.

"As you like, dear!" The daily help would arrive at Dalehurst about eight in the morning. The alarm would come, probably, while they were having breakfast.

After dinner Madge slipped away, to reappear in gum boots and mackintosh.

"I promised the vicar I'd take some things to Mrs. Gershaw. I shan't be long."

"It's a filthy night—let me go for you."

"No, thanks! There's a lot of explanation and—and their telephone is out of order."

As soon as his wife had left the house, Penfold became uneasy. It would be all right, he kept telling himself, provided she did not 'run round' to Dalehurst with that wretched book. Presently he remembered that she had put it back on the occasional table. He swung round in his chair. The book was no longer on the table.

Gershaw lived less than a hundred yards away. In half an hour Penfold's nerve began to fail. He had endured an hour and five minutes before Margaret returned.

"What's the matter, Madge?"

"Aunt Agnes is dead. Someone has killed her!"

"Nonsense! How d'you know? Have you been to Dalehurst?"

He had to repeat the question.

"Dr. Delmore saw me from his car and stopped. Just now!"

That was all right, then! Sympathy for a bereavement was indicated. He made a suitable exclamation, would have taken her in his arms.

"I want to be alone, Arthur."

She walked past him, up the stairs to her room. She had never behaved like that before. The house suddenly seemed stiflingly hot. He opened the front door and stood in the porch—was there when the police came.

It was soon obvious that they had found nothing that need disturb him. They did not insist on seeing Madge, were content with his account of her movements and his own. They were even chatty, told him that Dr. Delmore, passing in his car, had seen the light in the drawing-room of Dalehurst and the french window swinging in the wind and had gone in to investigate. He had telephoned the police and, on the way home, had spotted Mrs. Penfold in the road and told her. There was, Penfold assured himself, nothing to worry about.

IV

At the inquest, Dr. Delmore testified that death had taken place between five and six o'clock and was due to heart failure caused by partial asphyxia resulting from strangulation. Margaret Penfold stated that she had lunched at Dalehurst, leaving at a quarter to three to go to the vicarage. Mrs. Blagrove had seemed to be in normal health, was expecting no visitor. She was confident that deceased had no personal enemy. Arthur Penfold was not called.

Police evidence revealed that the latch of the french window had been lifted with a penknife, and so clumsily that the woodwork had been chipped. The ground had been too wet to yield footprints of any value. The Coroner was encouraged to believe that an unpractised crook had assaulted deceased intending to make her disclose the whereabouts of valuables, and had then taken fright— there had been no robbery. The jury returned the obvious verdict and expressed gratification that the local police had been prompt in asking the aid of Scotland Yard.

On taking over, Chief Inspector Karslake ordered an intensive search of the drawing-room for some personal trace of the killer. "She was on that settee when he attacked her. He must have been leaning well over. Try the folds of the upholstery—between the seat and the back."

The result was disappointing. Between the folds of the upholstery were found three thimbles, two pairs of scissors, nine handkerchiefs and a book in its dust jacket: *The Best of Wilcox*.

"That's too thick to have slipped down, sir—must've been pushed down."

Karslake examined the book. A new copy—and there was nothing to distinguish it from any other copy in the edition. He opened it in the middle.

"Poetry!" He glanced back at the moonbeams and cupids. "Love stuff. And she was 64! Didn't want to be caught at it. Check on the local booksellers—she probably bought it herself. Try those curtains."

Karslake collected relevant gossip from the local superintendent, then set about eliminating the Penfolds. Margaret was easily disposed of because her movements were checkable up to six o'clock, when the cook and housemaid heard her talking to her husband in the drawing-room.

Penfold's statement that he had arrived at Crosswater station at five three was confirmed by the ticket collector. His servants had not heard him come home, so could not deny that he might have come straight home from the station. This was a negative alibi which left the theoretical possibility that Penfold might have behaved as, in fact, he did behave, but there was no single item of evidence in support. Innocent persons, in the orbit of a murder, often had no alibi.

Moreover motive, in Penfold's case, was apparently lacking. There was no known quarrel, nor conflict of interest. The Penfolds were financially comfortable. Mrs. Blagrove's income had been derived from an annuity. To Mrs. Penfold she had left a sum in cash, her furniture and her house. But the house had been bought on mortgage and the whole estate would doubtfully yield fifteen hundred pounds.

After the inquest, the feeling of tension passed from Penfold. In so far as he thought clearly about his crime, he reasoned that the police would find evidence against him at once or not at all. For the rest, he had not planned to kill a fellow creature. He had been the unwitting instrument of fate, in whose hand he was soon able to detect a measure of poetic jusice.

Madge's general demeanour caused him no unease, though she cut short his not infrequent attempts to express condolence. She spoke hardly at all. However, ten days after the murder—on the evening of the day when Scotland Yard abandoned further work in the locality—she shook off her lethargy.

"I shall not go into mourning for Aunt Agnes," she said, in the drawing-room after dinner. "It wouldn't express anything to me."

"As you please, dear." His voice was low and a little funereal. "I think people will understand—you have been so brave!"

"Oh no! But I have woken up! The shock did it—the shock of learning that some frightened lout who wasn't even a proper criminal had killed that dear, inoffensive woman. But the worst shock was finding that I myself—that I—instead of feeling grief-stricken, I felt as if a huge weight had been lifted off my shoulders.

"The feeling of relief didn't go away after a few minutes, as I thought it would. It stayed—it grew. For a few days I thought myself a low kind of beast with no proper human feelings. Then I began to understand. I had let Aunt Agnes down for years—and—myself—by always being so terrifically grateful."

"But my dear!" protested Penfold. "That was a very charming trait in your character."

"It wasn't!" The blunt contradiction made him sure that she was still suffering from shock. She went on: "I let it turn me spiritually into a poor relation, incessantly grateful and ever so anxious to please. Something the vicar had said to me three or four years ago put me on the right track. I loved Aunt Agnes very deeply. I shall love her all my life and shall go on wishing she were alive so that I could tell her I wasn't fair to her nor to myself—nor to my husband!"

"But I have no complaint, Madge, except perhaps—"

"It started our marriage on the wrong foot. I'm ready to start again—I mean, from the beginning—if you are, Arthur. Are you?"

"My darling, how can you ask!"

No, she did not want to be kissed, just then. She was so clear on that point that he felt a little ruffled—it was so unlike her. Almost undutiful.

"We'll take each other on our merits," she said and smiled. "I start at zero—you start one up. I mean—I want to tell you that I was—*stirred*—when you bought that book for poor Aunt Agnes. You'll say it was a trifle. But it pointed in the right direction, Arthur dear."

She was talking, he thought, a little incoherently, letting her tongue run away with her. But she was overwrought, poor child, and he would let it pass without comment.

"I need a change after what's happened," she went on. "We'll have a second honeymoon, Arthur! I want us to shut up the house for a month and stay in a nice hotel in London. You can go to the office, if you have to, but in the evenings we'll have fun."

'Fun' sounded a little ominous, but this was no time to damp her spirits.

"A second honeymoon!" he echoed. "Just what we both need! I know of a quiet little place, one of the old City inns—"

"But I don't want a quiet little place! I want the Savoy or the Waldorf. I know it will cost a huge amount but—listen! I saw the solicitor the other day. He says it will be about eighteen months before probate is granted, but in the meantime his firm is lending me five hundred pounds—in a proper business way, of course. I want you to take two hundred of that. More, if it isn't enough."

He would not take her money because, in the morning, she would modify her plans and they would not go to the Savoy. But they did go to the Savoy and he did take her money, though he earmarked funds to give it back to her when her 'mad mood' had passed.

Strangely, he caught something of the mad mood himself. They were both comparatively new to theatre going. And Madge discovered that, after the theatre, you could go to a cabaret. Indeed, there were remarkably few forms of entertainment in London which she failed to discover.

Most of the time he enjoyed himself, while in her company. She could be merry or quietly companionable—provocative sometimes, but never obedient. It was as if there had been some meaning in that high-falutin nonsense she had talked about herself—as if the death of Aunt Agnes had released a coiled spring in her nature. The 'second honeymoon' joke was taking on a queer kind of reality. To him it was a revolutionary conception of the relationship of husband and wife. But the month, he reminded himself, would pass. And the coiled spring would have uncoiled itself.

When he was apart from her it seemed a very long month—and a not altogether respectable one, at that—she expected him to treat her as if he had never kissed her before. At the end of the office day, he missed his railway journey and found himself counting the days to be endured before he would slip back into the groove that had become second nature—his way of life, in the protection of which he had killed Mrs. Blagrove.

When the holiday was over they parted at the hotel, he for the office, she for their home. Sitting in the train that evening, he visualised Madge listening for his footstep on the gravel path, opening the door before he could reach it. It did not happen. He let himself in and stopped short in the hall—he smelt the new paint before his eye had taken it in.

The hall, the staircase, the dining-room, the drawing-room—new paint, new wallpaper! He wandered aghast from one room to another. The Landseers had gone from the walls of the dining-room! The Holman Hunt in the drawing-room had been replaced with a modern original! Some of the furniture had been re-upholstered, some banished, and there was a new carpet in the drawing-room.

When she came in twenty minutes later, he was still struggling with his anger.

"Well! D'you like it?" she asked eagerly. She was entreating his approval.

"My dear, I am too astonished to form any opinion. Did it not occur to you, Madge, to consult me before making sweeping alterations in my house?"

"Is it your house, Arthur—or *our* house? Of course I oughtn't to have done it on my own, but I had to take a risk! I had the feeling that everything in the house was practically as it had been when your parents married."

"It was indeed! But what was wrong with it?"

"We have to give ourselves every chance, Arthur—or we shall be slipping back into the old ways."

The last words rendered him speechless. Slipping back into the old ways was precisely what he desired. He could find no means of making her understand. They were in the dining-room. He strode to the sideboard. The tantalus was still there. He took out the whisky decanter—nearly dropped it when she spoke.

"Not whisky for me," said Madge. "Gin and orange, please."

That was another shock. Never before had she taken a drink in the home, except during a party, when she would make a glass of sherry last the whole time. He hesitated, then began to mix the gin. She had turned herself into a different kind of woman and intended to stay so. He was not angry now, only afraid.

"Let's drink to our future, Arthur."

"To our future!" And what sort of future? She no longer interpreted his wishes as her duties—she was compelling him to accept some give-and-take principle of her own. She expected her tastes to be consulted equally with his, and she demanded that he should woo her afresh for every caress.

With a sense of discovery he remembered how he had sat alone in the drawing-room that night, wondering whether she had 'run round to Dalehurst with that wretched book.' Until he had removed the doubt, there would be nothing for it but abject surrender.

"I'm afraid I've been a bit bearish over the decorations, darling. Sorry! Come and show me everything, and I'll tell you how much I like it all."

She was sweetness itself whenever he made an effort to please her—but the effort had to be successful! Not that she required to be pleased all the time—she was as ready to give as to take. It emerged, however, that the month of madness at the Savoy, shorn of its expensive indulgence, was to be the blueprint for their married life. A kind of marriage which he had never contemplated and did not want.

Most evenings, in the train, he would decide to put his foot down. But when he got out of the train—you could just see the gables of Dalehurst from the arrival platform—other considerations would arise. So he would say nothing when he found a cocktail party in progress at home—nor when Madge was absent, at some one else's party—nor when she said she was sorry but she could never understand stories about business deals.

In June, five months after the Savoy holiday, he contrived to meet Gershaw as if by chance, when the latter was leaving his office for lunch, and enticed him to a drink.

"Madge seems to have got over her bereavement, but the fact is she has had a partial lapse of memory." He brought in an anonymous psychiatrist. "Now, I do remember that she went out after dinner saying that she had a message for Mrs. Gershaw from the vicar and she must go in person, because your telephone was out of order. Can you possibly tell me, old man, how long she was with you?"

"*Phew!* That's a bit of a contract. My wife let her in—I was in the drawing-room, with the door open. I heard them chattering away in the hall and presently I butted in to ask your wife to have a drink, but she said she couldn't stay. I didn't notice the time. Call it three minutes—five, if you like. Best I can do! But I can tell you definitely she's wrong about our telephone. It was on the telephone that we heard that night about the—about Mrs. Blagrove."

That was nearly all that Penfold wanted to know.

"Was Madge carrying anything, Gershaw?"

"Don't think so—oh yes, a book, loosely wrapped in newspaper. The rain had softened the paper and I offered her a satchel. But she found she could get it into the pocket of her mack—I remember pulling the flap over it for her."

So she would have had time to go to Dalehurst and get away, with a margin of minutes, before Dr. Delmore came on the scene. Penfold felt a profound unease and wished he had not tackled Gershaw. After all, there was no proof that she had gone to Dalehurst. The book was not necessarily the Wilcox book. And she might have gone to someone else with another message from the vicar. He decided to let the whole matter drop and found that he could not. The riddle travelled home with him every evening and even intruded on the outward journey, so that his attention would wander from the morning paper.

As he could not shake it off, he tried to stare it out of countenance. Let it be granted that Madge did go to Dalehurst and did know that her aunt was dead before Dr. Delmore stopped her in the road and told her. What did it matter? Was it to be supposed that she went through the open french window and, in a very few minutes—never mind the shock!—saw something, not seen by the highly trained detectives, which told her that he had killed Aunt Agnes? Utterly absurd! Therefore he would put it out of mind.

He did put it out of mind for the better part of a fortnight's holiday in August, which they spent at Brighton. On the last day, the riddle raised its head and he promptly struck at it with a new argument. Would a woman of Madge's character—would anyone but a degraded gun-moll—live with a man whom she believed to have killed a woman who was virtually her mother? She would not! Therefore Madge had no secret weapon and he could be master in his own house.

The obsession was beginning to exist in its own right, as something separate from his desire to change Madge back into a docile and obedient wife. It had an integrity of its own, with no fear outside itself. He did not believe that, if she had proof, she would take it to the police. The terror lay in an imagined moment, in which she would say: 'I know you killed Aunt Agnes.' Being an imaginative terror, it was more consuming than a reasonable fear.

If she had known before Dr. Delmore had told her, why had she not raised the alarm herself? He could find a dozen contradictory answers. Sometimes in his sleep, and sometimes in a waking dream in the train coming home, he would play the part of Madge entering the room by the french window. 'Auntie, I've brought you *The Best of Wilcox.*' No, because she would have seen at once that her aunt was dead. In the shock of the discovery she would have forgotten all about the book, which was in the pocket of her mackintosh.

She would have brought the book home.

That night, when Madge had gone to bed, he began his search. In the house there were about a thousand books, some eight hundred of which had been bought by his parents. There were four sectional bookcases—an innovation of Madge's—dotted about the drawing-room. In the section devoted to poetry and novels there was no Wilcox anthology. It was not on the shelves in the morning-room. It had not fallen behind anything. He thought of Madge's mackintosh, which she very rarely wore, found it in the cupboard under the stairs, with the pockets empty.

He had to wait three days before he could be certain that Madge had an afternoon engagement. The strain of waiting preyed on his nerves. Then he came home by the earlier train and made a thorough search upstairs. Finally he was reduced to telling Madge that he had mislaid a technical book urgently needed and, with her able guidance, searched the whole house, without result.

Given that the book was not in his house, where was it? In a week, he was again reconstructing the scene in which Madge was deemed to have entered Dalehurst by the french window. As she walked up the gravelled path she took the book from her pocket. When she entered the room, she flung it from her. In which case it would have been stored with Mrs. Blagrove's furniture, pending probate.

He knew by experience that, for a fixed fee, the depository company would allow detailed examination of goods. On the following Monday, he went to the depository. He had equipped himself with a typewritten letter, purporting to have been signed by Margaret Penfold, which told of one or two rare editions among the comparatively valueless books forming part of the goods deposited. Would they please allow a prospective purchaser to examine? As prospective purchaser, Penfold necessarily adopted a name not his own.

The manager accepted the fee, assured him there would be no difficulty. But, unfortunately, as the goods were awaiting probate, he must obtain formal permission through the solicitor in the case. If it would be convenient to call at the same time on the following day—.

Penfold said that it would be quite convenient, and escaped, thankful that he had given a false name.

The solicitor, who was ready to swear that there were no rare editions among Mrs. Blagrove's books, rang Mrs. Penfold during the afternoon to make sure. When Madge said she had never heard of any, he said that evidently some other property was concerned, that he was sorry she had been bothered and that he hoped she was well. It seemed so trivial an incident that Madge did not mention it.

On Saturday morning, as the Penfolds were finishing breakfast, the housemaid brought a card: *Detective Inspector Rason, New Scotland Yard.*

v

The telephone conversation with Margaret Penfold made it obvious to the solicitor that the introductory letter to the depository company was a forgery. He reported the facts to Scotland Yard. The report was passed to the Department of Dead Ends, to which the Blagrove case had drifted.

The impostor had concerned himself with books, so Rason searched the Blagrove dossier for mention of books. With some difficulty he found an unpromising note at the end of a list of gruesome details concerning the settee '. . . *under seat, misc. articles including newly purchased book: title, 'The Best of Wilcox.' Checked local bookseller (Penting's). Two copies sold, morning, one to Mrs. Manfried, one to Mrs. Penfold (See Penfold, Margaret: movements of).*

While waiting at the depository for the impostor who did not turn up, Rason inspected the furniture and effects removed from Dalehurst, eventually finding the Wilcox anthology which had been taken from the folds of the settee. He replaced it without feeling any wiser for the effort he had imposed on the warehouseman.

The routine of the Department, constructed by Rason himself, had a certain simplicity. When any object was offered or mentioned, one first checked the object itself. Then one checked the object in relation to the suspects. There were no suspects in this case, unless one counted the Penfolds—so Rason counted them. From the depository, he borrowed the girl who had shown Penfold to the manager's office, and stood her near Penfold's office at lunchtime.

"That's him!" cried the girl, when Penfold came out.

"Don't be silly!" protested Rason. "It can't be. This is only routine."

The girl, however, was quite positive—which presented Rason with a teaser. The only way of squeezing in Penfold as a suspect was to assume he was lying when he said he was in his own drawing-room between five and six, the time of the murder. Nearly a year later he tries to work an elaborate deception on the depository people in order to be able to 'inspect' some books, which couldn't have been there. How could all that help him to prove he didn't commit a murder, of which no one suspected him except Rason, who had to, owing to his routine?

Better ask Penfold.

"Renbald's Depository!" he exclaimed when civilities had been exchanged in Penfold's dining-room. Penfold looked ghastly, which was not what Rason wanted. "It's all right, Mr. Penfold—it's only routine. We don't worry about the forged letter and the fake name. Told 'em you wanted to inspect some books. What did you really want? Tell me, and I can cross it off."

It was an unanswerable question. Penfold remembered the excuse he had used to induce Madge to search for the anthology.

"I did want to inspect the books, though I knew there were no first editions. The truth is, Inspector, I had lost a technical book of my own. I thought it might have got mixed up with Mrs. Blagrove's books—"

"But you could have got your wife to write you a real letter for that—and you could have used your own name?"

"I did ask her. She was unwilling, because she convinced herself that the book couldn't possibly be there."

It was such an unrehearsed, knock-kneed tale that Rason was inclined to believe it.

"Perhaps I can help you," he grinned. "I've inspected those books. Was it called *The Best of Wilcox?*"

"*No!*" The emphasis was not lost on Rason.

"*The Best of Wilcox*—" Rason was mouthing the words, "was found on the settee on which Mrs. Blagrove was killed!"—So Margaret *did* go to Dalehurst, thought Penfold.

"That does not concern me," he said. Playing for his own safety, he added: "The copy of that book which I bought never left this house, so far as I know."

"So *you* bought a copy of that book, Mr. Penfold?"

"I did. I intended to present it to Mrs. Blagrove on the following day, which was her birthday. Wilcox was favourite author."

"Where did you buy it?"

"In London." He added: "At Waterloo station, before taking the train which arrives here at five three."

Rason felt he was getting somewhere. The note in the dossier said that the book had been bought by Margaret Penfold, from the local bookseller.

"If you've no objection, I'd like to see what Mrs. Penfold has to say about this."

"Certainly! She will tell you that—at around six o'clock that night —she handled the copy I had bought and talked about it—in this house. But I won't have her bullied and frightened."

Penfold did not leave the room. He rang for the housemaid, but it was Madge herself who answered the bell.

"My dear, I'm afraid we have to talk about your poor Aunt Agnes," began Penfold. "Mr. Rason has informed me that on the settee on which she was killed, there was a copy of *The Best of Wilcox*. I have—"

"Oh!" It was a quick little cry of dismay. "I think I can see what has happened. Arthur, I would like to speak to Mr. Rason alone. Please!"

She did go to Dalehurst—Penfold was certain, now. If she had also picked up a clue to his guilt he must try to cope with it before the detective could build it up.

"I am sorry, Madge, but I really feel I have the right to be present."

"Very well, Arthur!" There was a shrug in her voice. "Mr. Rason, on the morning of that day, I bought a copy of that book locally, at Penting's. I lunched with Mrs. Blagrove and gave her the book—not as a birthday present—we were jointly giving her a more elaborate present the next day.

"In the evening I reached home at six. My husband had come home earlier than usual. He showed me a copy of *The Best of Wilcox* which he had bought in London for Aunt—for Mrs. Blagrove." She paused before adding: "I was very greatly surprised —I have to say it!—I thought that my husband was not the sort of man who—who would ever think of doing a kindly little act like that. I did him an injustice, and was ashamed. I was above all anxious not to spoil the whole thing by telling him I had forestalled him. I intended to tell Mrs. Blagrove what had happened and ask her to help me in a harmless fraud. I took the book from my husband and, of course, I had to get rid of it, as Mrs. Blagrove would not want two copies. I had to go out that night to deliver a message to a neighbour, Mrs. Gershaw. I went on to a Mrs. Manfried, who was also a Wilcox fan, and offered her the book. But she had herself bought a copy that morning. The book was published that day and I suppose all the real fans bought it at once. On the way back, Dr. Delmore told me the news and I forgot the book. I found it in my mackintosh a few days later. I dropped the book in the croquet box, under the mallets. It may be there still. If it is, I'll show it to you."

"Don't bother on my account, Mrs. Penfold. I'm glad it's all cleared up," said Rason untruthfully. He had been quite hopeful when he thought he had cornered Penfold over the books. Journey from London for nothing!

"I wish my wife had told me at the time—it wouldn't have hurt my feelings," said Penfold when Madge was out of earshot. "Is it too early for a drink, Inspector?"

"Too early for me, thanks. I—"

Madge burst in.

"Here it is!" The newspaper on which the rain had fallen was crinkled and torn. "Just as I pulled it out of the mack!"

"Well, I can put it on record that I've seen it!" said Rason, as he unwrapped the newspaper. "Cupids, eh! Same as the one I saw at the depository. *The Best of Wilcox!*" With hardly a change of tone, he went on:

"Now let's get this book business straightened out. At lunchtime, Mrs. Penfold, you gave Mrs. Blagrove a copy of this book? So the copy you gave her would still be in her possession at five-three— when Mr. Penfold arrived at the station here? Around six, Mr. Penfold shows you this copy I've now got in my hand—and you take charge of it?"

"Correct!" cut in Penfold, and was echoed by Margaret.

"Somewhere between five-three and six—" Rason turned from Margaret to her husband "—you picked up the wrong copy, Penfold. Look here!"

He opened the book and pointed: *'To dear Aunt Agnes With love from Madge.'*

THE HOUSE-IN-YOUR-HAND

The murder of Albert Henshawk, headlined as the House-In-Your-Hand Mystery, became a test case for plain-clothes constables who had put in for promotion. It is still used to emphasise that the most trivial remark of a murderer—such as a comment on a work of commercial art—may contain the raw material of a clue.

Henshawk, who specialised in financing the purchase of houses, had been running an advertisement showing, in an outstretched palm, a picturesque country cottage, with the slogan: 'A House In Your Hand is Worth Two in the Clouds.' It is noteworthy that the picture in the advertisement was a photograph of a model. The whole models, including the outstretched hand, covered an area about equal to that of a pocket handkerchief. It was kept in Henshawk's office under a glass dome, flanked by the bronze statuette with which Henshawk was battered to death. It is an ironical comment on this amiable egotist that the statuette was the work of Henshawk, and the subject—Henshawk himself.

A tubby, chubby little man in the early forties, he was naïvely proud of himself and his not inconsiderable talent as an artist. "Neat bit of work, that model, eh! Supplied the idea myself," he would say, if you were a business acquaintance. Your attention would be directed to the seventeenth-century thatched cottage, to the oaks on one side of it, to the sloping meadow in which a cow drank at a sluggish brook, to a somewhat startling confusion of farm stock in the foreground.

"And, mind you, it isn't a studio fake, except for those pigs and things. Made from a drawing. A little effort of my own." You were urged to inspect a charcoal drawing—complete with farm stock but minus the outstretched palm—hung in a somewhat elaborate frame. "Of course, I'm only an amateur, but you can see it's drawn from life."

The last statement was confirmed, after the murder, by a number of experts, consulted independently. Each said, in his own words, that if the model had been a work of fancy it would have exhibited certain essential differences. Architects, also consulted independently, passed the house as structurally and historically correct; surveyors agreed that the layout of the land contained no absurdity.

The murder took place on 16th February 1938, at about six forty-five, in Henshawk's office in Gorlay House, Westminster. After lunching at the Redmoon Restaurant, Henshawk had spent the afternoon at his club, discussing business with an official of a big investment trust, for which he was, in effect, an agent.

At a few minutes past six, when his staff had left, with the exception of his secretary, he entered his room by the private door, which opened directly on the corridor. In the wall on your right as you entered by this door was another door, now ajar, to the staff room, in which Miss Birdridge was waiting.

She heard his key, then his voice talking to a companion. Of the latter she had only an oblique view. But she was able to state that he was between forty and fifty, of medium height, regular features with an iron-grey moustache.

"I must have a word with my secretary—shan't be a minute," Henshawk was saying. "Suppose you look about and see what you see. I think you'll be pleased." He went into the staff room, leaving the communicating door open.

"Miss Birdridge, I simply must get that report off tonight. So will you go and have a meal right away, and be back here at seven sharp." Henshawk had a booming voice: the other man must have overheard him. "Oh, and you might phone Mrs. Henshawk that I shan't be home till about ten and I'll feed in Town."

There was nothing unusual in this. Miss Birdridge was a middle-aged woman with no home ties, who appreciated a restaurant dinner at the firm's expense and the extra payment for late work. Henshawk lingered in the doorway while she reported an item of minor importance, but she noticed that his attention had shifted to the other room.

"Ah! It caught your eye at once, old man. Neat bit of work, eh! Made from that drawing of mine on the wall there."

Then the other man's voice:

"But, my dear fellow, that damned cow spoils the whole thing! And why is it perched on a giant's hand? Makes it look like a cartoon."

"You're not far off. I've been using it for an advertisement display. I felt sure you wouldn't mind. After all——"

At that point the communicating door was closed. Miss Birdridge was sure that it was exactly at that point, and sure that she had reported the exact words used by each man.

She went out to dinner, returning as Big Ben was striking seven. In the meantime the communicating door had been used and was again ajar. A couple of minutes later, having equipped herself for work on the report, she went into the inner office, to find Henshawk sprawling face downwards over his chair, patently murdered. She observed no more than this before rushing back into the outer office and calling the police.

By midnight Detective Inspector Karslake had a clear outline. For about forty minutes, during which he had smoked four of Henshawk's cigarettes, the murderer had sat in the client's chair, with his back to both doors.

At about six-forty Henshawk's wife had knocked on the private door. Henshawk had opened the door but had stepped into the corridor to speak to her. He told her, she said, that he was engaged with a client, so could not take her home. He himself expected to be home late.

Over her husband's shoulder, Mrs. Henshawk had seen a man sitting in the client's chair with his back towards her. She did not take particular notice of him, because, she said, being a client he was of no interest to her. She was somewhat hurt because her husband had apparently forgotten that he had asked her to call for him at the office.

After getting rid of his wife, Henshawk had probably sat down again in his chair. But a few minutes later he had got up and turned his back, whereupon the other had struck him on the back of the head with the statuette, causing almost instant death.

At the cupboard-toilette the murderer had washed blood-stains from his hands. He had not removed blood-stains from the soap-well. He had left the statuette immersed in the basin.

Although his time was running perilously short, he had lingered in order to remove a drawing from its frame on the wall. As this drawing was the original from which the House-In-Your-Hand model was made, the incident gave emphasis to the remark, over-heard by Miss Birdridge, seeming to connect the deceased with the cottage depicted in the model.

The murderer left by the outer office, within two minutes of seven o'clock, carrying the drawing loosely wrapped in tissue paper. In the hall he asked the porter to call him a taxi. He was getting into it when Miss Birdridge returned, though she noticed no more than that a man was getting into a taxi, carrying some-thing flat and loosely wrapped in tissue paper. He told the driver to take him to the Westminster station of the Underground. Nothing further was known of his movements.

"The porter is no good, sir," said young Rawlings. "All he can do is a 'middle-aged, middle-height, middling-well-dressed gentleman with a moustache'—which of course will be shaved off by now."

"Never mind his moustache—he has practically left us his address, hasn't he!" snorted Karslake. He had recently had several important successes, and was becoming a trifle didactic.

"Yes, sir—that cottage!" said Rawlings, who had not yet learnt how to handle seniors.

"I guessed that myself," snapped Karslake. "Where is that cot-tage? What's it called?"

Rawlings slunk away and woke Miss Birdridge by calling her on the telephone.

But Miss Birdridge did not know, had always thought the cot-tage was an imaginary one until she had overheard the murderer's reference to it. Next, he rang Mrs. Henshawk, who was equally unhelpful. Her husband was a prolific amateur artist, but she knew nothing about art, and he never talked to her about his hobby.

"All right then—we'll advertise for that cottage," said Karslake. "The papers will make a news story of it, with picture. Warn all stations in the U.K. to study that picture in the press and report to us if the cottage is in their district."

In his Appreciation for the Chief, Karslake wrote:

> '*An unpremeditated murder (cigarettes) by a man on familiar terms with deceased, who was urging Henshawk to do something important enough to make the latter forget his appointment with his wife (Mrs. Henshawk's*

*admitted annoyance). Mrs. Henshawk's interruption broke
the trend of their talk. Henshawk rejected the proposition,
whereupon the other lost his temper and struck with the
nearest object, not necessarily intending to kill. The murderer owns, or has some direct or indirect interest in, the
cottage (theft of drawing: remark reported by Miss Birdridge 'I felt sure you wouldn't mind'——i.e., use of cottage
as advertisement). There should be little difficulty in tracing such a cottage.'*

Karslake had Miss Birdridge's report under his hand as he wrote.
Yet he missed the clue-value of that other remark about "that
damned cow."

2

True that the murder was, in the legal sense, unpremeditated.
But it might be argued that Harold Ledlaw had been uncon-
sciously premeditating the murder for eighteen years, though he
did not know that the victim would be Henshawk.

Ledlaw had been waiting outside Gorlay House expecting Henshawk to leave at the end of the office day. But he spotted him at
once when he stepped out of the taxi that brought him from the
club.

"Hullo, Albert! . . . Dammit, you've forgotten me!"

"I certainly have *not*—" a second's pause—"Harold Ledlaw, of
course." He was pumping the other's hand. "You've changed a lot,
old man, but I'd have known you at once anywhere. I suppose we
shall both soon be what they call middle aged. Well, I'm jiggered!
We must fix something. Are you staying long?"

"I'm not going back to Canada. It has done me proud, but I'm
back for keeps. I landed last week. Been getting acclimatised. I'm
counting on you to give me the low-down on one thing and another."

"Look here—I'm rushed off my feet, but come up to the office
for a few minutes and we'll fix something."

They ignored the lift and walked to the first floor, exchanging
the commonplaces of an almost forgotten friendship, for Ledlaw
had been in Canada for nearly eighteen years.

At the first pause, which occurred just outside Henshawk's private door, Ledlaw said:

"Whiddon Cottage! I heard some of the timber had been cut. Can you tell me anything about it?"

"It so happens I can tell you quite a lot about it—though I'm not in touch with—er—*anyone*." He unlocked the private door, said that he must speak to his secretary and, with a fatuous archness, invited the other to look about the office.

The first thing one noticed in that office was the model under its glass dome. Ledlaw stared at it, at first in confusion, then with full recognition.

"My God, what damned cheek, and what the hell does it mean!" he muttered under his breath, then warned himself that he must keep his temper. Albert Henshawk was braying at him from the doorway: he must say something in reply.

"But my dear fellow that damned cow spoils the whole thing!" Ledlaw heard his own voice making the protest, and asking what the hand meant, and Henshawk telling him it was a sort of advertisement.

"I felt sure you wouldn't mind. After all, a place like that belongs, at least in its artistic aspect—well, it belongs to England, don't you think! It symbolises the urban Englishman's dream of home. And that's my line of business now, Harold—helping the hard-up middle class to own their homes. I had to put those beastly animals in afterwards on the advice of the advertising experts. You see, the town dweller always fancies he'll do a spot of spare-time farming, the stock to look after itself and pay off the mortage."

There was a good deal of it, but Ledlaw rarely listened. He had already decided that they would not 'fix something.' He would find out the two things he had come to find out, and then he need never see Henshawk again.

"You were going to tell me about the timber, Albert."

"Ah! Wheels within wheels! I have not seen—er—Mrs. Ledlaw. But I heard last year through a mutual acquaintance—a woman you don't know—that your daughter, Harold, wants to be a doctor. Let's see, she's nearly eighteen now, isn't she? That's a seven years' course. Well—er—my informant said that you would not be asked to make any further contribution. So Mrs. Ledlaw decided to sell the timber in Swallowbath Rise. Mind you, it won't affect the look of the place, being the other side of the hill."

He had been speaking with some awkwardness which now slipped away.

"When I heard this, I thought perhaps Mrs. Ledlaw might want to sell the whole outfit, as I knew you had bought it outright for her. I went down to see her last year, but she was on holiday and the place was shut up. So I thought I'd sketch it. I wrote to her asking if it was in the market and got a reply, written in the third person, saying no. I don't suppose she remembers me. I haven't seen her since—well, *since!*"

So that was that! He had the right to see that his daughter took her medical course in comfort. Now for that other question that must be approached circuitously. Twenty past six. He would have to hurry or he might fumble the showdown he had planned— if indeed it was to be a showdown, of which he was not yet certain.

"There's another thing I want to ask you, Albert. You perhaps remember that when Ruth divorced me I withdrew the defence I had previously entered denying infidelity. I then vamoosed to Canada. I want to know whether you believed what Valerie Carmaen said—that I had been her lover?"

"Really, Harold, after all these years!" Henshawk was definitely embarrassed.

"You knew her. And you knew she was the kind of dirt I wouldn't touch if she were the only female left in the world."

"Yes, yes, Harold! Just as you say!"

"Then you believe she faked that bedroom incident—that my original pleading—which I showed you—stated the truth?"

"Of course I believe it if you say so! Didn't I tell you at the time that I believed you! I wondered why you didn't go on with the defence."

"I withdrew the defence because Ruth made it clear that, whatever was proved in court, she would believe me guilty. That broke me up, Albert. Ruth and I hadn't started too well. The first few months had been difficult. But we were just getting right. Life was going to be grand. And then this thing happened."

"But it's more than eighteen years ago, old man!"

"To me it's as if it were yesterday. I know it's an obsession and not quite sane, and all that. But all these years, when I've not been actually working, I've felt much as I felt at the time—humiliated, washed up, finished."

Henshawk was making soothing noises. He looked sympathetic, not afraid. Perhaps, thought Ledlaw, there was no reason why he should be afraid. Perhaps the information he had received about Henshawk had been incorrect. He glanced at the clock—he would know in a few minutes.

"Have you any idea why that girl picked on me? I didn't like her, but I never insulted her. She had no reason to hate me."

"No, of course not! You shouldn't let your mind dwell on it, old man. What about seeing a good psychiatrist?"

"She didn't hate me. She just used me callously because she wanted to be divorced."

He was not thinking now of Henshawk. In the grip of his obsession, he repeated the words he had been repeating for eighteen years.

"She had an income in her own right and could have fixed it with a professional co-respondent for a tenner and a little bother. That sort of thing is worse than positive cruelty, which at least has the excuse of malice or perversion. I think of that woman as the lowest moral type—a moral slug."

"You're working yourself up, Harold. It's bad for you, and it's very distressing for me—ah, excuse me!"

There had come a knock on the private door—the knock for which Ledlaw had been waiting. Both glanced at the clock. It was twenty-two minutes to seven.

Henshawk went to the door. Ledlaw remained still, his back—as Superintendent Karslake had inferred—to both doors. He would let her get well into the room before he turned and faced her. And if she were not *the* woman, he would just acknowledge the introduction and go.

"I am in conference," he heard Henshawk say.

Too late, Ledlaw turned round. Henshawk had stepped into the corridor and was speaking to her there. Ledlaw could see neither. He sprang up, intending to thrust himself into the corridor. But Henshawk had already returned alone and shut the door.

"Only an anxious client! Look here, I don't want to turn you out, old man, but I must get some work ready for my secretary, who will be back presently. What about dining with me at the club tomorrow night?"

Ledlaw saw that a simple bluff would give him the answer he must have.

" 'An anxious client,' you said, Albert. Why did you say it?"

"I don't get you, old man."

"Was it your wife, Albert? I ask, because I sent Mrs. Henshawk a wire in your name asking her to call here at six-thirty—I phoned it from the Redmoon—where you were lunching. She was a little late." He paused, decided it was safe to add: "I saw her face, Albert. I must apologise for having called *your wife* a moral slug."

Ledlaw got up, actually intending to go. The love of self-torture that accompanies such an obsession as his had something new to feed on. Fate had used him even more vilely than he had known, for Henshawk had been his friend since schooldays.

But Henshawk, the frank egotist who had delighted in making a statuette of himself, could not endure the loss of face.

"I am sorry you saw Valerie. It can only deepen the tragedy for all three of us. To know all, Harold, is to forgive all. I want you to sit down again and let me explain."

"Go ahead!" Ledlaw dropped back into the client's chair. "It might be amusing to hear why she smashed up my life to save herself a tenner. Why, surely she could have got the tenner from you! And you'd have taken all the bother off her hands."

"I didn't know what she was doing until she had done it," Henshawk began. "And I didn't know the man was you until you yourself told me. It all originated in my refusal to deceive her husband. I'm like that, as you know—I can't bear anything underhand. Well, I went to Carmaen and asked him to divorce her and let us marry. If ever there was a dog-in-the-manger it was Carmaen. He refused. But, being a beast, he gave Valerie to understand that if it was anybody but myself he would gladly divorce her. I happened to mention that I had recommended that hotel when you had to run down to Fensmouth for the night, and Valerie ran down too—but without my knowledge."

"But what about your knowledge when I showed you the writ and my defence? You didn't believe that I had been her lover?"

"No, of course not! Naturally, I put it to Valerie. And she refused to budge an inch. Said it was entirely her affair and that I could take what attitude I pleased. What could I do? Telling you about it wouldn't have made any difference."

"Yet you married her! Built your marriage on the ruin of mine!"

"Ruin of my grandmother's aunt!" exploded Henshawk. Both were standing, glaring at each other across the table. "Can't you see you're pulling your own leg? Ever asked yourself why Ruth didn't believe you? Of *course* she believed you! Your marriage had crashed. D'you think I didn't know that much? Ruth couldn't stick you any longer, and she jumped at the chance of release which Valerie had given her."

To Ledlaw the words brought horrifying self-suspicion, the glimpse of an utterly unbearable truth. As Henshawk turned his back, Ledlaw snatched up the object nearest his hand and struck. He struck at the image of a self-pitying poltroon, at himself posing and strutting for eighteen years in order to hide from himself the truth that his wife had been unable to endure his affection—that she had been driven to a mean escape.

But what he had actually done was to kill Henshawk.

Returning clarity brought not remorse but renewed self-pity.

"Just my luck! I lost my head for half a second and now I shall be hanged."

Not death, but the dreadful ritual of trial and execution awakened self-preservation. He remembered the danger of fingerprints. When he had washed his hands, he refilled the basin and put the statuette in it. With Henshawk's sponge he wiped the ashtray and the arms of the chair.

"That secretary may have heard him blithering to me about the cottage. I shall be hanged! Steady! I shall just have to bet she didn't hear—or that he hasn't told anybody where it is."

He stood over the model, wondering whether there would be any safety in smashing it.

"That damned cow!" Taut nerves and muscles suddenly relaxed, and he giggled like a schoolgirl. A moment later he had sobered and turned to the charcoal drawing on the wall.

"It looks more realistic without the hand. And the damned cow isn't so pronounced." About to pass on, he turned back on impulse, dipped his hands in the basin and removed the drawing from its frame.

"The outer office would be better—more people turn the handles." With hands still wet he opened the communicating door. In the outer office he caught up a piece of tissue paper and wrapped it loosely round the drawing.

Downstairs the porter was loafing about the hall. If he were to try to slink past, the fellow might think he had stolen the drawing. What was the most ordinary and natural thing to do?

"Get me a taxi, please."

In the taxi he checked his first impulse to leave the drawing under the mat. That drawing must be burnt—the mill-board was too stiff to be torn in small pieces. He re-wrapped it in the tissue paper.

At Westminster he travelled by Underground to Earl's Court. He was staying at the Teneriffe Hotel, near the station. He emptied a dispatch-case and put the drawing in it. He would take it out to the countryside and burn it tomorrow. He had the illusion of forgetting Henshawk and his own peril. Active thought was suspended. He dined in the hotel, and afterwards went back to the West End to a music-hall.

The next morning the later London editions carried the photograph of the model. When Ledlaw opened a paper over breakfast he instantly accepted failure.

With a certain coolness he worked out how arrest would come. Ruth would see the picture and the police appeal. As a respectable citizen, she would write to Scotland Yard. A detective would call, would learn from her that she had passed her childhood in the cottage, that her father had been compelled to sell it, that some years later, on her marriage, her husband had bought it and made it over to her, that they had lived in it for a short time. Then the divorce and his departure to Canada. They would hardly need to trace him through the bank. The shipping lists would show that he had arrived six days ago and put up at the Teneriffe Hotel.

At a guess, he would have about forty-eight hours—at worst twenty-four, unless Ruth telephoned, which was improbable.

Before he died he wanted to see his daughter. Even more than that, he wanted to know whether Henshawk's taunt had any foundation. In short, he would go at once to the cottage and see Ruth, whether she wanted to see him or not.

In his baggage were some things he had left her in his will—a photograph album of snaps he had taken during their first year, a packet of her letters to him before marriage, a rare edition of *Canterbury Tales* which her father had given him. In half an hour he had sorted them out. He put them in the dispatch-case on top of the drawing, which no longer had any importance. In his sense of defeat, he thought only that he had been a fool for his pains in bringing it away. He had forgotten that Ruth would be sure to recognise the photograph of the model at once. And she would remember Henshawk's name. He would take no further precautions against arrest. He would not even shave his moustache.

By the middle of the morning he was in the train for Hallery-on-Thames. There was no taxi at the little station and no car to be hired in the village, so he had to walk the half-mile along the towpath and then tackle the stiff climb up the hillside.

He was hot when he arrived at Whiddon Cottage, stopped to rest a minute by the oaks. While he was getting his breath, he reflected, with the self-conscious wistfulness of one who believes that his days are numbered, that the beauty of Whiddon was even greater than his memory of it. Set high on a hill on the edge of the Berkshire Downs, there was a clear view of undulating country for fifteen miles. To the rear of the cottage, the downland sloped half a mile in a green carpet to the Thames. And now for Ruth.

She opened the door to him. She was a tall woman who had once been pretty and was now handsome, but with an air of masterfulness that was not romantically attractive. Yet at sight of him, he thought, she had looked afraid.

"Harold! Why have you come?" Her tone was reproachful, but not unfriendly.

"I want to see Aileen. I imagine you will not raise objections."

"Of course not! But she's away for a few days with friends."

"I also wanted to see you. May I?"

It was ridiculously formal, not in the least as he had planned. It chilled them both into small talk. She offered him lunch, and he said he had already lunched, which was untrue. They chattered about Canada and London. He congratulated her on her success as an author.

"Well, of course, only students read my books and only a few of those, though I get good reviews—Harold, is that man who has been murdered the Henshawk you used to know?"

"Yes. You've seen the paper, I gather. I rather took it for granted that you had already notified Scotland Yard. I knew you must recognise the picture, in spite of the pigs and hens and that preposterous cow."

"*Harold?*"

"Yes, Ruth—I killed him." She had guessed before he said it. He added: "Did you know that he married Valerie Carmaen?"

She winced at the name. "No. But that was no reason for killing him."

"As he knew that that woman bore false witness against me, I accused him of building his marriage on the ruin of mine. And I lost my temper when he said that you, too, knew it was false— that you had jumped at the chance of getting rid of me. Did you, Ruth?"

She was long in answering. His own tension had vanished. It was as if he were no longer interested in her answer.

"I believed her evidence at the time. But after a few years I began to suspect I was wrong. It would be meaningless to say that I am sorry. As young lovers—we were not successful, Harold. In our maturity, I can feel deep friendship as well as gratitude for your generosity."

"Well, my dear, that's that! This case"—he placed the dispatch-case by the side of the huge open hearth—"contains a few purely personal knicknacks you might like to keep. I'll leave it." He got up to go.

"Will you be caught, Harold?"

"Yes, I think so. Someone will bring them to this cottage, and then they're bound to find me. I wish I could have seen Aileen."

"If they come here I shall do everything I can to put them off. You may say you do not wish me to make sacrifices on your behalf. I am thinking of Aileen and—frankly—my public, small though it is. If you are tried—and if you give your reason for—doing what you did—the scandal will hurt us both. I want to do everything we can both do—to ensure your escape."

Three-quarters of a mile away the village police sergeant was advising Scotland Yard of the existence of the seventeenth-century cottage, known as Whiddon Cottage, identical in appearance with that in the published picture.

3

There are more seventeenth-century cottages in England than many Englishmen would believe. By midday, local police had reported eighty, of which thirty-three were 'possibles'. By the end of the week the grand total for all Britain stood at one hundred and seventy-three 'possibles'.

In sorting, three features beside the cottage itself were deemed essential: oaks on left of cottage; contiguous, sloping meadow; brook from which it would be possible for an animal, such as a cow, to drink. True that barely sixty contained these essentials. But the balance included cottages of the correct period and dimensions, whose oaks had been felled, whose meadow had been built over, whose brook had been diverted.

Within a week the sixty 'probables' had been inspected, without noteworthy result. In another fortnight the balance of 'possibles' had been eliminated. Detective Inspector Karslake felt that he had been handed a raw deal.

Within twenty-four hours identification of the cottage had become the solitary line of investigation. The comb had been run through all Henshawk's business and social acquaintances. The telegram to Mrs. Henshawk had been telephoned from a call-box at the Redmoon Restaurant. This started new hope—until a client reported that he had lunched there with Henshawk, who had excused himself for a few minutes before lunch in order to telephone.

At the end of a month the press, somewhat grudgingly, complied with the request to reprint the photograph of the model and the police appeal. They helped its news-value and at the same time got their own back by writing up the absurdity of such a cottage being untraceable. The comic artists were allowed free play. There was a rather unkind picture of a cow goggling at a model of Scotland Yard on an outstretched palm.

In short, Karslake was unable to advance in any direction. At the end of April the case was allowed to drift into the Department of Dead Ends.

By its very nature, it was impossible for the Department to originate any investigation. Cases sent there were, in effect, put into cold storage against the chance of some other case accidentally

criss-crossing, the chance of some unrelated circumstance happening
to throw a side-light.

A day or so after the statuette of Henshawk, the model under its
glass dome and the empty picture-frame had been sent to Detective
Inspector Rason, Karslake made a perfunctory inquiry and received a somewhat voluble answer.

"Well, sir, since you ask me, I think that instead of looking for
the cottage we ought to have looked for that cow."

It was a dangerous moment, for there had been a comic picture
in the *Daily Record* rather in that sense.

"I mean, I think there's something funny about this case—something psychological, if you understand me."

"I don't," said Karslake.

"There's that remark in the girl's statement about what he calls
'that damned cow'. Why was it a 'damned' cow? And why should
it spoil the whole thing? A cow is just what you'd look for in those
surroundings. You'd miss it if it wasn't there. Now, suppose that
man had been frightened by a cow when he was very little—too
young to remember? All his life, though he doesn't know why——"

"Now look here, Rason, if you talk to the press with a tale of a
man frightened of cows, there'll be trouble good and hot and all of
it for you."

"I was thinking of the mental hospitals——"

"So was I—only I don't mean what you mean. It's facts we want,
Rason. And if you're lucky enough to find any, we'll fix 'em up
with a theory as soon as we've time."

Lucky enough! Rason's past successes in linking apparently un-
connected events, in perceiving method in that which seemed blind
chance, had never earned him a pat on the back for anything but
his 'luck'. Even when he found Harold Ledlaw, Karslake ungener-
ously asserted that success was thrown into his lap solely because
he chanced to go to a particular picture theatre on a particular
night with his sister-in-law.

He had invited his niece, whom he regarded, since his brother's
death, as an honorary daughter; but her mother had come instead.

They had arrived too early and were afflicted with a 'short', advertising a breakfast food, in which a spirit voice whispered to a young
wife that her husband could not do a hard day's work on tea or

coffee. What, therefore, should she put in his cup, held in a slender
be-jewelled hand? Trick photography then showed a huge ox gal-
loping into the picture and leaping into the breakfast-cup.

"Sorry, Meg," said Rason. "I've got to go."

"Why, George, what is it?"

"That damned cow!" chuckled Rason, and left her.

That was not luck, in Karslake's sense. The whole of Scotland
Yard might have seen that film without learning anything from its
apparent irrelevance. But it was lucky that Ledlaw happened to be
at Whiddon Cottage when Rason took Karslake there—though they
would have caught him just the same if he had been elsewhere.

4

The day after his visit to Whiddon, Ledlaw had met his daughter.
They had met as strangers and had approved of each other.
When a month had gone by and the chances of his escape now
seemed overwhelming, Mrs. Ledlaw consented to another meeting.

After the failure of the second press campaign, Ledlaw was convinced that the trail was utterly lost, and Mrs. Ledlaw concurred.
He reasoned that if the police ever succeeded in finding the cottage
they would inevitably reach him through Mrs. Ledlaw. Therefore
he risked nothing by taking his daughter home—which he did one
evening in June. The efficient domesticity he witnessed awakened
dormant longings.

"I have been thinking, Ruth," he said at the end of June, "that if
anything were to happen—not that we need fear it now—but if it
were to happen, you would be in a dangerous position for having
shielded me. You would certainly go to prison. But if we were
married, you could successfully plead that you acted under my
domination—absurd, my dear, though it may sound."

On the understanding that it was to be a marriage of companionship only and on the further understanding that he would take steps
to pursue his profession of engineering, Mrs. Ledlaw re-married
him on 11th July.

By this time he had long lost all sense of peril. Indeed his crime,
when he thought of it, seemed no more than a bad dream, of which
the details were already blurred.

In August there was a strike at the engineering works, leaving
nothing for the supervising engineer to do. So Ledlaw was pottering

in the garden when the car containing the detectives arrived towards the end of the morning. Mrs. Ledlaw, hearing the car, came out of the cottage.

Rason, carrying a largish bag, was in nominal charge. As they got out of the car Karslake muttered: "It's not the place. It's not a bit like it, except for the cottage itself. It's no different from sixty others."

"Mr. Ledlaw?" asked Rason, having learnt the name at the local police station. "We are from Scotland Yard. I believe you knew Albert Henshawk?"

"The fellow who was murdered? We wondered." He turned to his wife. "This is Mrs. Ledlaw. We knew an Albert Henshawk slightly some twenty years ago. But we lost touch. Anyhow, what did you want to ask us about him?"

"I want to know when you last saw Albert Henshawk, Mr. Ledlaw."

"But you aren't connecting my husband with the murder," boomed Mrs. Ledlaw, "because we live in a seventeenth-century cottage? The local sergeant told me he had reported this cottage at the time, and it was inspected by a Scotland Yard man."

"It isn't very like the one in the picture, you know," said Ledlaw tolerantly. "True, there are somewhat similar oaks. But there——" He waved his hand at the half mile of hillside sloping down to the Thames.

Karslake maintained a glum silence, wondering how they would explain Rason's ineptitude. Rason opened his bag, took out the original model of the cottage and laid it on the ground.

"I admit it's not a bit like it," he said.

Ledlaw smiled, while Karslake looked glummer than ever. Rason continued:

"But that is because—*that damned cow spoils the whole thing*, Mr. Ledlaw."

Ledlaw's face was expressionless.

"I can't follow that," said Mrs. Ledlaw.

"Funny thing, Mrs. Ledlaw. I went to the pictures last night. Saw a film where a whopping big cow—or was it an ox?—appears to jump into a tea cup. Clever bit of photography—messing about with perspective. Made me think of this cow. So I thought—well, look here!"

The last was addressed mainly to Karslake. As Rason spoke, he plucked the figure of the cow from the model.

"Good Lord!" muttered Karslake, gaping from the model to the landscape and back again at the model.

With the removal of the figure of the cow, the meadow had vanished. It became, in fact, a half-mile of sloping hillside, while the 'brook' was instantly recognisable as the Thames, half a mile away in the valley below.

"No deception in this trick, ladies and gentlemen!" chirped Rason, and fitted the peg back into its socket—restoring the meadow, with a brook from which a cow was drinking.

"It's messing about with perspective! Got the idea from that ox jumping into the teacup!" he told them all over again.

"That's what you meant when you told Henshawk the damned cow spoilt the whole thing, wasn't it, Mr. Ledlaw! I suppose you can account for your movements on the evening of 16th February?"

"I can, if he can't," said Mrs. Ledlaw. "He was here. I remember the date, because he was asking me to marry him."

"*Last* February, madam!" cut in Karslake. "We are informed that you have a grown-up daughter. And that she's known as 'Miss Ledlaw'."

"Yes, but it's all quite simple, really," said Mrs. Ledlaw. "You see, we were divorced some years ago. And then we thought better of it—you look as if you didn't believe me."

"It's of no great importance at the moment, Mrs. Ledlaw——"

"It is of great importance to me," retorted Mrs. Ledlaw. "I insist on your inspecting my marriage certificate. I will not keep you a couple of minutes."

When she had gone, Karslake spoke to Ledlaw.

"If you deny that you saw Henshawk that day, Mr. Ledlaw, are you willing to come back with us to London and let us see if Henshawk's secretary and the porter recognise you?"

"Certainly not. You've no case against me. You can darned well bring them down here if you're so keen to waste your time."

Mrs. Ledlaw was coming from the house carrying his dispatch-case, which had become hers.

With horror he suddenly remembered.

"The certificate is not in there, dear. I took it out last week. Don't you remember, Ruth?"

"Oh, of course! How stupid of me!"

But there had been altogether too much anxiety in Ledlaw's voice. Karslake strode forward.

"I'll have that opened, please, Mrs. Ledlaw."

"Oh, very well, if you wish!" Mrs. Ledlaw did not know why her husband had shouted that nonsense about removing the certificate. It surely couldn't matter much when they re-married.

Inside the case were: a packet of Mrs. Ledlaw's letters; a photograph album; a rare edition of *Canterbury Tales;* the marriage certificate, a few other oddments and—Henshawk's drawing of the cottage, loosely wrapped in tissue paper.

LITTLE THINGS LIKE THAT

Peter Curwen was every bit as sane as we are. No repressions: no unmentionable cravings. If you were looking for faults, you might have said that he lacked repose. He was one of those men who can never really sit still and are generally fidgeting with something. But you couldn't have made a grievance of it, as his wife did.

Most wives would have taken no notice—that is, most sensible, give-and-take wives such as Marion. Her enemies, if she had any, could hardly have picked on a flaw in her character worth mentioning. Nor could Peter—though he might have admitted to himself that, after three years of marriage, the sweetness of her nature had mellowed along lines he could not have predicted. True that she still took pains to delight his eye at all hours and that he still paid her dress bills with gratitude. Their flat in Kensington was tasteful and homelike. She had a sufficiency of the domestic virtues. But she did make a grievance of his little foible.

Of course, there was more in it than fidgeting and not sitting still. About one night in five he would get out of bed in the small hours to make sure he had turned off the light in the sitting-room. He would find pins on floors. Halfway to a theatre, he would wriggle and mutter that he was making sure he hadn't forgotten the tickets. Multiply that sort of thing to cover most of the small activities in which there is a chance of forgetting or mishandling something.

Crisis came—unrecognised as such—at breakfast on the first Tuesday in March, which was an extremely windy day. Even the well set windows of the Kensington flat rattled now and then. Marion, like any other woman who dresses constructively, did not like windy days.

As Peter finished his coffee, he put the coffee spoon on the plate that contained the débris of his toast and marmalade. Marion had first noticed that little trick on their honeymoon—which meant that she had noticed it at about a thousand breakfasts.

"Peter! Why do you always put your coffee spoon on your plate like that?"

"I dunno, dear. I suppose I do it to make sure it isn't mistaken for a clean spoon."

"I think you ought to see a psychiatrist. I mean it, old boy. There are so many little things like that. The bath taps, for instance—the stoppers of the whisky bottles—all that ritual when you park the car. I have sung my little song about it—quite often, frankly—but I suppose you've forgotten. Forgetting is one of the symptoms."

"Symptoms of what?"

"I can't remember the name for it. Something that means excessive anxiety about trifles—when it wouldn't matter if they went wrong. But they never do go wrong. The light always has been turned off. The stoppers are always air-tight. The taps never drip. The thing is growing on you, Peter."

"There isn't a 'thing' to grow. Part of it is habit. But the main idea is deliberate. There's a system in it. I started it as a result of something that happened when I was in the Navy—"

"Darling, you really *have* told me how the signaling officer's braces fused something and sank—or was it burned?—the corvette. But that's a long time ago. And if you took another corvette and some more braces, you couldn't make it happen again. It was a freak accident. And, I mean, if you're like this at thirty-four, what will you be like at fifty?"

"My system has paid off in business—"

"People are beginning to notice, and that's not very nice for me. People laugh at people who are fussy. Why, you can't even help me into an evening cloak without feeling the hem, to make sure my heel won't catch in it."

"I didn't know you had noticed. I oughtn't to let it touch—us. I'm sorry, Marion."

"Peter! I didn't altogether mean to say that—it was beastly of me!" She would have burst into tears of contrition, but this was unnecessary because, at this period, he was a good tempered man who readily forgave almost anybody for almost anything.

"The charge of fussiness stands," he said, while he was kissing her. "I promise I'll overhaul the system right away."

"You'll never remember, darling, but it's sweet of you to want to."

Outside the flat, he was about to shake the door, to make sure that the Yale lock was in order, when he cut his hand away. Salute to Marion! Three years of married life and still monstrously attractive at breakfast time! Wriggling a little as he made sure that he had not forgotten his latchkey, his note case and his fountain pen, he entered the lift.

If a prowling cracksman—he reflected on the way down—were to test the door and find it insecurely fastened, he would enter the flat, sandbag Marion, gag her clumsily and perhaps suffocate her. It wouldn't take a minute to get back into the lift and make sure the door was locked.

In a couple of seconds he had decided against going back. He had promised to overhaul the system. A pity, because it was a good system. Admittedly, the risk of disaster in any given case was minute. But why take even a minute risk of disaster when you need not? Still, in marriage, each side has to make concessions of principle. As he stepped into the street he removed his hat and carried it, to make sure it would not be blown away.

The system, even if he overworked it a little, had contributed to his success. He had made a niche for himself as a shipping agent, specialising in art objects and merchandise of a costly and fragile nature. By his own methods he had reduced loss and damage to a minimum, with the result that the insurance companies wafted business in his direction. In five years he had twice moved to larger premises.

It so happened on this windy and vexatious morning that he received a claim for damage which he believed to be fraudulent. He rang his lawyers and by eleven was walking the few hundred yards to their office in Hedgecutter Street. The lawyers occupied two floors in Sebastopol House, a dingy Victorian building, with a wastefully large entrance hall of unredeemable dinginess. The partners communicated with each other by means of a number of speaking tubes, the forerunner of the house telephone. But their fees were high and their efficiency had been a catchword for three generations.

He was delighted when they advised him to fight. In the hall, on the way out, he lobbed a half finished cigarette into a huge brass coal vase, placed there for the purpose. He had walked a dozen paces into the wind before the system stopped him short.

He had thrown the cigarette into the vase, but had not actually seen it land. Lots of fires—some fires, anyhow—were caused by half finished cigarettes thrown carelessly away. Suppose he had missed the coal vase? Suppose the half finished cigarette had rolled along the floor, slipped through a chink in the boards? On a windy day like this, that old-fashioned building would burn like matchboard. He flashed up a pageant of disaster. The traffic cordoned off, the police holding back the crowd of morbid sightseers. He could hear the fire gongs, the cries of the doomed in the upper floors. Why not slip back and make sure about that cigarette?

"I have no reason to believe that I missed the coal vase—a damned great vat like that! It's simply that I don't want to alter the system. And I promised Marion I would. Got to begin somewhere!"

It was not the wind alone that made walking back to his office a trudging labour. The slight feeling of guilt stayed with him until he went out for lunch. His way took him past the corner of Hedgecutter Street. No fire gongs. No police. No morbid sightseers.

He let out a long breath.

"I mustn't get worked up like that again! The system cut out all worry. Better watch my step, or I shall get nervy."

Having thus warned himself, he was free to enjoy lunch with a director of the insurance company whose support he secured in resisting the claim for damage.

On the way back after lunch his eye travelled over a display in one of Hoffmeister's windows, came to rest on a purse-comb in tortoiseshell. It would be fun to give it to Marion, in token that their little misunderstanding at breakfast time had been rubbed out. He gave his name and business address. If they would send the comb during the afternoon he would pay the messenger in currency. The manager insisted on his taking the comb and sending a cheque at convenience. Curwen thanked him and placed the comb—unwrapped—in his breast pocket—inside his note case, to make sure it would not be crushed.

Approaching Hedgecutter Street, he caught the unmistakable echo of a fire gong. At the corner, the traffic was cordoned off. The fire brigade was in action and the police were holding back the crowd of sightseers. Sebastopol House was in flames.

In the first confusion, Peter Curwen had the sense of being cheated—as if he had been promised that there would be no fire. While he gaped, his eye took in detail. Above the flames, seen intermittently through the smoke, a man was standing on a window sill on the top floor, steadying himself with one hand on the gable. The escape ladder was swaying towards him. When it reached the edge of the window sill the man loosened his hold on the gable, stooped for the ladder and overbalanced. Curwen shut his eyes. His mind stepped back some three hours. He saw himself standing in the wind a dozen yards from Sebastopol House, hesitating.

"If I had gone back, that man would be alive now."

In the office, he steadied himself. He was as able to distinguish fact from phantasy as anybody else. It would be hysterical to jump to the conclusion that he had caused the fire. That long sequence about the half finished cigarette falling through a chink in the floorboards, and the rest of it, had been phantasy. The mathematical chances against all that having happened were enormous. Admittedly, he had suspected that the cigarette might have missed the coal vase, but that did not mean that it had in fact done so. His suspicion had been created by the system. As Marion had pointed out, these systematic suspicions were uneconomical. The light always had been turned off. The taps never did leak. Judgment, therefore, could be suspended.

The afternoon editions weakened the mathematical part of the argument by stating that the fire was believed to have started between the hall and the basement.

Now and again, there came sharp mental images of Marion. Of Marion at breakfast, complaining about the system. Of himself giving way, against his better judgment. Of himself hesitating on the wind-swept pavement. Better go back and make sure about that cigarette. I promised Marion. Got to begin somewhere. Begin—oh God!—begin with the fire gong. Steady! Mathematical chances.

He decided to say nothing to Marion about the fire. He was not thinking about her feelings—Marion wouldn't have any feelings about someone else's fire. Intuition warned him that it would be better for himself if the fire were never discussed with her.

"Sebastopol House has been gutted! There's a whole column

about it," said Marion as soon as he came in. "But I expect you know, as it's so near the office."

"I saw it when I came back from lunch." As long as he kept close to the newspaper reports, there should be no danger. "I was there when that man fell."

"Poor darling! How upsetting for you! No wonder you look limp. Go and sit down and I'll bring you a drink."

The hall lounge was warm and cosy. He sat down, under inward protest. He must be very careful about drink, now—never allow himself to get the very slightest degree fuddled.

"We've nothing on tonight," Marion was saying, "so you can have a good rest."

Normally, he enjoyed a quiet evening at home. Tonight, he felt an undefined reluctance to be alone with Marion. He drank the whisky at a gulp.

"I'm not tired. I was going to suggest that we look in at the Parnassus after dinner."

In his dressing-room he took out his notecase, stared at the tortoiseshell purse-comb, until he remembered buying it, to placate Marion. Why did that now seem so contemptible? He glanced at the communicating door, then furtively slipped the comb into a drawer, under a pile of handkerchiefs.

The spiritual vulgarity of his action shocked him into momentary suspicion of himself. He was, he reminded himself, a free agent. If he wished, say, to turn back a dozen yards or so, for any purpose whatever, no one could prevent him. If he did not wish to turn back, the choice was exclusively his own, for which he would bear exclusive responsibility. Further discussion of this subject would be unnecessary.

The inquest, as far as Peter Curwen was concerned, was far from satisfactory. The deceased, Henry Morprill, was a clerk, in the middle thirties, employed by a manufacturer's agent occupying the top floor. The manner in which he had met his death was not in dispute. The police did not suggest incendiarism, nor was there any evidence that anyone had been culpably careless.

"It seems to have been one of those fires that have no detectable cause," said the Coroner. "It was a very windy day. A live cigarette end, or a spark from a distant chimney, might have been blown through a ventilator and carried to the space between the ground floor and the ceiling of the basement. It seems that we shall never know for certain. You are not, however, concerned with the fire, as such."

Peter Curwen had attended the court with something approaching confidence that the fire would be attributed to a half-finished cigarette falling outside the coal vase. The protracted doubt was attacking the flank of his defences.

Direct inquiry of the experts would be impossible because he had sustained no financial loss in the fire. Using his connection with the insurance companies, he contrived a drink with the fire assessor concerned.

"An incendiary generally leaves something for us to work on," said the assessor. "But a straight fire—I should say about a third of 'em have to be left to inspired guesswork. A man may do something slightly dangerous every day for twenty years, and suddenly it starts a fire!"

"In the hall—"

"The wind may be blowing at an angle it's never blown at before. Freak combination of small factors. This is a case in point."

"In the hall," said Curwen, "there was a large coal vase. People would lob half-finished cigarettes into it as they passed. Now, suppose a cigarette missed the coal vase, rolled through a chink in the floorboards—"

"Could be! It's as likely as anything else. That's what I meant by inspired guess. Let's have another drink."

The doubt was now securely entrenched. When he had parted from the assessor, Curwen pinched a cigarette in half. He lobbed one half at a litter bin, and missed.

That night they were booked for a dinner party. When he opened the drawer for a handkerchief, he remembered that under the pile lay the tortoiseshell comb. He felt unable to cope with the complicated vibrations set up by that comb. He lifted a handkerchief as if he feared to disturb the pile. It could lie buried until he had focused the death of that clerk.

That it was a poor hiding place did not occur to him. Like many a man in his circumstances he put his soiled linen in a basket and was incurious as to the processes by which it eventually reappeared in a chest of drawers.

He kept his end up at the dinner party. Afterwards, Marion

was quieter than usual. She had perceived that the climate of their marriage had changed.

The coroner's jury had expressed sympathy with the widow and had felt the better for it. The widow—the half-finished cigarette—sympathy! The doubt was a haunting abstraction, but the widow was an inescapable actuality. He wrote to her, on office paper bearing his name. He asserted that he was under a moral obligation to her late husband—the nature of which he was not at liberty to divulge—that he proposed to call on her on the following day to inquire whether he could be of any service to her.

He was glad they had another dinner engagement that night. It was as if he were afraid of being alone with Marion. The pile of handkerchiefs in his drawer was considerably higher. He did not know that Marion always placed incoming handkerchiefs at the bottom of the pile.

At breakfast the next morning, he stopped with the coffee spoon halfway to his plate. He put it back in the saucer, then stole a glance at Marion.

"I'm so glad you're trying," she said. "It'll come easier after a while."

He felt fury so sudden and so intense that he left the room and did not return. Before leaving the flat, he went to his dressing-room, took the tortoiseshell comb from under the pile of handkerchiefs and later put it into storage in the office safe.

By lunch time his calm had returned. Indeed, he was on the verge of good spirits as his thoughts dwelt on his coming interview with Mrs. Morprill. A clerk's widow would be faded and poor—or at least shabby-genteel—faced with a hundred financial anxieties. It would be balm to his lacerated conscience to smooth her path through life. His success in business would acquire an added sweetness.

Gormer's Green, where the widow lived, was some twelve miles out, a part of London unknown to him. He left the office shortly after four. On emerging from the underground, he groped his way in a maze of five-roomed semi-detached houses of identical pattern.

At first glance, Mrs. Morprill was fairly close to his mental picture of her, except that she was tall and did not droop. Faded she certainly was, but her make-up was passable. She had shape, too, which survived the dowdiness of her dress. Her eyes were calm and friendly.

"It was so kind of you to write, Mr. Curwen. Do please come in. I expect you could do with a cup of tea, after that long walk from the station."

Her voice was soft and her speech free from affectation. She showed him into the parlour-dining-room and left him while she prepared tea. The furniture was mass produced: the carpet was garish and the pictures he thought awful. But a home-made bookcase gave a pleasing touch of individuality.

Mrs. Morprill was not parading her grief. She made some conventional remarks to which he did his best to respond, waiting to get in with his little speech.

"Mrs. Morprill, you know why I have come here. In your bereavement, you are called upon to face a number of practical difficulties. I earnestly hope you will allow me to help."

"I'm sure I don't know how to thank you for offering, Mr. Curwen." She was unembarrassed, took his words at their face value. "But we've been living in a quite simple way, and I don't think there's really anything that isn't being taken care of, one way and another. There's less practical sort of bother than you'd think."

For Curwen, it was the wrong answer. This woman was courageous, but she was feminine and would yield to the right kind of pressure.

"I'm sure you'll let me speak openly, Mrs. Morprill. Let's look squarely at the facts. To begin with, your income has been cut off."

"Oh! I didn't know you meant money help!"

"You're not offended? Please don't say you are."

"Why, of course not! I couldn't be offended at such a very kind thought. But, you see, I don't think I need any money help, thanking you most gratefully all the same.

"It isn't as though Henry had left me in the lurch," she explained. "He was a thoughtful man—clever too, though not what I'd call pushful. He paid a bit extra to the building society on the instalments, and now this house becomes ours—mine, I should say. And besides that, he was insured for a thousand pounds. And Maggie —that's our daughter—she'll be twelve next month—she's at the Grammar school I'm pleased to say, and she seems to have all the clothes and things she needs."

Curwen was losing his nerve.

"The interest on that thousand will be less than forty pounds a year."

"I shall go back to work. I was a typist before we married. I shall take a refresher course as soon as I've straightened my mind a bit. As to the next few weeks, they're paying his salary till the end of the month. And there's the holiday money we've saved, which we shan't be wanting now—for holidays I mean."

Curwen groped vainly for a new line of appeal. This faded woman, with her soft, monotonous voice and her homely idiom, was crushing his spirit. Telling him he was a nice kind man, and would he please stop talking about money.

"Mr. Curwen, I'd like it if you would tell me something about Henry. Nothing private, I mean. Just little things. It won't upset me —I promise!"

"I will tell you this about him." He faltered, feeling now that his presence in her house was a loutish intrusion. "If you would let me make you an allowance equal to his salary, I would still be in debt to your husband. And you would make me very happy indeed."

She ought to accept, or kick him out. But her eyes showed only a mild wonder.

"Your debt to him wasn't a money debt, so it can't be repaid in money," she said, forming the thought as she spoke. "I'm sorry you're unhappy about it, Mr. Curwen. I feel a bit like that about him myself. He was much kinder to me than I was to him. I'm sort of in debt to him, too."

Walking back to the underground, missing his way again, Curwen realised that his fruitless visit had substantially damaged him. He had thought of a woman deprived of a breadwinner. He had understated the case so grossly that the Doubt was beginning to lose its essential character. It was no longer of primary importance to know whether his half lighted cigarette had in fact rolled under a chink in the floorboards and caused the fire. What if it had? The law and public opinion would pronounce it an accident—a trivial act of carelessness with an unforeseeably tragic sequel.

All very reasonable—until he remembered that he himself had set up the postulate that an act of carelessness of that kind need never and ought never to occur. That was the essence of the system, thoughtfully based on the so-called freak accident to the corvette.

Like a muddled child he had rushed to the widow, begging to be allowed to buy back that moment of self-betrayal in Hedgecutter Street.

He reached home an hour later than usual. Marion, in a dinner dress, was waiting in the hall.

"Peter, have you forgotten that we're taking Mother to the theatre tonight and that she's due at any minute?"

He had forgotten. He tried to break out of his pre-occupation. "Sorry, dear! I'll hurry."

"I have the tickets," said Marion. "I will hand them to you at the theatre. You will remember that, won't you? And not keep feeling in all your pockets before we get there? Mother notices everything."

Again her words awoke that queer kind of anger that was new to him. It was something apart from ill-temper, indefinable and alarming.

Marion kept back dinner until he was ready. Mrs. Lardner was excessively polite about it. Service sent up a new maid, who was very slow. They reached the theatre a full minute after the curtain had risen. There were two intervals, in each of which he had two double whiskies, which was a lot, for a man of his habits.

"Mother wasn't on her best behaviour," remarked Marion, after Mrs. Lardner had gone. "We started off on the wrong foot."

"My fault for being late." He was pouring himself a stiff one. "I stayed to clear up some arrears and didn't notice the time."

"Yes, Peter. I thought you might forget, so I rang you about four. Miss Aspland said you had left the office and would not return."

She was making a point of his white lie. Doubtless, she was expecting further evasions. She darned well wouldn't get any.

"I was at Gormer's Green. I went to see the widow of the man who was killed in the Sebastopol House fire."

"Really? Then, you knew her before? What an extraordinary coincidence!"

"I had never heard of her until the inquest. I sought her out because it is possible—I repeat, possible—that I was the indirect cause of her husband's death."

He could see that she was startled to the point of confusion. Serve her right!

"I haven't got there yet, Peter. A man you've never heard of before falls from the top floor—"

"Stop guessing and listen!" He told her of his call on the lawyers, told her in detail of his lobbing the half-finished cigarette and his uncertainty whether it had gone into the coal vase. He paused to drain his glass—and remembered that he had taken several whiskies at the theatre. Instantly, he sprang on guard.

"Yes—well—what next?" she prompted.

Deep, intuitive fear of himself—fear that some words, spoken out loud, might unleash something—saved him from telling her what happened next. He resented his fear and wanted to defy it. Wanted to play with fire. Play with the Sebastopol House fire. Nothing in the fire, as such. Nothing in the half-finished cigarette, as such. Nothing in the widow.

"The fire broke out between the ground floor and the basement." The formula for safety was to speak as if to a person other than Marion. "If my cigarette fell on the floor it is possible that I caused that fire."

Marion was at a loss. The fire story, however true in itself, did not account for that tortoiseshell comb which she had found under his handkerchiefs, when she was distributing the laundry yesterday. She had examined it—found the Hoffmeister mark, which meant that it was as costly as it looked. This morning the comb was no longer there.

"I wish you had mentioned all this at the time—if it's the fire and nothing else that's worrying you. I can tell you positively that you did not cause that fire."

"That, my dear, is an extremely silly remark. You cannot conceively know anything about it."

"Can't you see it, Peter? It's the corvette-and-braces story all over again. That's why you simply must consult a psychiatrist. After all, if you'd been wounded and the wound was giving you trouble now, you'd at least ask an ordinary doctor if he could do something about it."

"So my anxiety for the widow and the child seems to you a mental disease which could be cured by an expert!"

Marion shrugged and left him. He chuckled with self-satisfaction. He had talked about the fire in such a way that nothing had happened except that she had gone off to bed in a huff, which she would have forgotten by morning. He had shown that he could trust himself. There would be no harm in a nightcap.

That night, after he had got into bed and turned out the light, he resisted the impulse to get up and take a last look round the flat. He must play fair with Marion. For as long as they lived under the same roof he would keep his word to her.

The next morning he found that the reading lamp in the sitting-room had been left burning. So Marion was wrong! It *did* happen, sometimes. He felt excitement creeping over him, giving the illusion that he could feel the blood moving in his veins.

With a glance in the direction of Marion's room, he shut himself in the sitting-room and locked the door. He stood with his back pressed against the door, contemplating the faint glow from the reading lamp. Net result, waste of a few pence. Net result, Sebastopol House gutted and a mild-eyed widow whose image could never be banished. Generically, the two events were identical.

He crossed the room on tip-toe and switched off the lamp. He walked back to the door and turned the handle, without result. He blinked, turned the handle a second time. Then his eye fell on the key. He turned it and opened the door.

"Now, why in heaven's name did I lock myself in this room?"

He could not remember why he had entered the room—could not remember what he had done after he locked the door. He had a slight headache. Too much whisky overnight—which, he decided, explained the whole thing.

He resumed his morning routine, as if nothing had happened.

At the end of a month he again journeyed to Gormer's Green and again drank tea with Mrs. Morprill. He made the acquaintance of her daughter, who was, he thought, too shy for her age. He succeeded in drawing her into an enthusiastic account of a fortunate neighbour's television set. The next day he sent the child a set. To her mother he wrote: '*I respect your decision, though I regret it. A toy is not "help" in the sense of our conversation. I hope you will allow Maggie to keep the set. Children can love but they cannot mourn as we do.*'

The month after that, he secured Mrs. Morprill's permission to provide Maggie with a bicycle. Through the child he was hoping to weaken the resistance of the mother. He would rake over their small talk for fragments with which to build up a picture of their life without Morprill.

His home life, seen in outline only, would have suggested that the curtain had fallen on the first Act of their marriage. In the interval, they were stretching a little, looking about and doing their best to entertain each other.

Marion was frankly competing with the shadowy rival whose existence she had inferred from the tortoiseshell comb. That expensive trifle, she decided, was not connected with the nonsense he had talked about the fire. Whoever the girl might be, she was not making much progress. Peter was spending nearly as much time in home activities as before.

For his part, Peter believed that he had fallen out of love with her for no reason that could be summoned to his consciousness. Something had taken the place of his feelings as a husband. Some strong but indefinable attachment made him hurry home in the evenings, as if he could not bear to be without her.

In a sense, he had turned her into a stranger—a woman of whom he knew little except that she had a repertory of pretty tricks. She would chatter breezily about their friends and the trifles of their very comfortable existence. She dressed brilliantly. With colour and line tempered to occasion she could draw his eye and renew his sense of discovery of her. He incited her to deploy her attractions. He was fascinated by his own sensitiveness to her charms—a fascination tinged with guilt, as if he had no right to be charmed by his wife.

The smoothness of this somewhat dangerous relationship was imperilled when he suddenly produced the tortoiseshell comb. It was an evening in July, the day before her birthday. The comb was in its sheath, unwrapped, exactly as she had seen it under his handkerchiefs. He dropped it into her lap.

So the shadowy rival had sent it back!

"What—what is it?" Her tone might have meant anything.

"A comb for your purse—it swivels out of that sheath."

She gazed at the comb without touching it.

"It's not the birthday present proper—that's why you're getting it tonight." Her restraint made him suspect that he had bungled somehow. "As a matter o' fact, I bought that for you some months ago. I actually brought it home—then took it back to the office, for some reason." He frowned. "I can't think why."

"*Peter!* Was it at the time you were so worried about that fire?"

"Yes, it was." The fire and his own concern with it were crystal clear and always would be. He remembered coming home—taking the comb out of his note-case—

"Darling, it's exactly what I wanted!" The shadowy rival was proved to be but a shadow. She enlarged on the theme of the profound usefulness of a tortoiseshell purse-comb. Her sudden enthusiasm surprised without interesting him.

Why had he not given her the comb at the time? The fire was irrelevant. While she prattled, he tried hard to remember why he had put the comb in the office safe. He had lost the intuitive fear that, in certain circumstances, he might not be able to hold his own demons on the leash.

The leash was torn from his hand by the comparatively trivial accident of his car being stolen—more accurately 'temporarily removed from the possession of its owner', as it was found abandoned and undamaged after a couple of hours.

The next morning brought perfect summer weather. It was traditional that he should make a holiday of her birthday—traditional also that they should bathe in the sea at Honsworth Wood. They set off in the car after breakfast, packing a picnic basket.

Shortly before midday he was running the car off the coastal road on to the strip of grass that gave on to the 'wood'—a score or so of stunted trees at the cliff head, a landmark on a bleak coastline. The 'ritual' of parking, of which she had so often complained, consisted of altering the leads from the distributor so that the engine could not fire a complete cycle. He was about to lift the bonnet, but abandoned his intention when he heard her laugh.

"I'm getting better, aren't I?" His good temper was genuine because he had forgotten that he had ever resented her objection to the system.

"You've practically cured yourself and I think you're marvellous."

They undressed in the car, put on sand-shoes, passed through the trees. At the head of the cliff, which was not sheer, was a wooden bench which had probably never been sat on. A rough track led to the beach.

"I'm bound to get cold before you do, Peter."

"No shirking. Button that cap up properly."

It all seemed very natural and jolly. On their honeymoon he had insisted on her swimming instead of pottering. Tradition was observed, but in five minutes she was out of breath, and left the water. He saw her climbing the track, watched her disappear through the trees. Some five minutes later she was sitting on the bench, still in her swimming suit, combing her hair. By this time, he was getting cold himself.

When he reached the cliff-head, she patted the bench.

"Let's sit here for a bit!"

"Not without my beer. I've been doing some work."

"Then bring the basket back with you and let's have lunch here, just as we are. I'm frightf'ly hungry."

"Rightho!" he answered over his shoulder. Idly she watched him, admiring the youthfulness of his form—he moved like an athlete of twenty. Minutes passed. When he came back through the trees, the springiness had gone out of him. And he was empty handed.

"You've forgotten the lunch basket," she shouted when he was some thirty feet away. He made no answer and did not quicken his pace.

"I thought we were going to have lunch here," she said, as he reached the bench.

He stared down at her.

"The car has been stolen," he said.

"What! It can't have been! I went to it when I left you, because I got my hair wet—there was no one about then." When her imagination had grasped the fact, she wailed: "With our clothes and everything! What on earth are we going to do?"

She wondered why he did not answer. He was usually calm and helpful when anything went wrong. His eyes were still on hers, but they were not focusing her.

"You can't stand there mooning about it," she grumbled. "You must do something."

His eyes came into focus, looked at her as if with sudden recognition.

"Now, you know! It *does* happen—sometimes. What you don't know is that the lamp in the sitting-room *has* been left burning—sometimes."

"Peter!" she screamed. "Snap out of it, Peter! Let go of me!"

"The corvette *was* sunk. The fire—"

The fire-gong sounded in his brain. He was conscious enough to know that he was in ecstasy and that he was killing Marion, whom he hated.

"Before we have it fair copied, Mr. Curwen, I'll run over the main points. When you last saw your wife alive, you were in the water and she was at the cliff head, proceeding in the direction of the car?"

"Correct!" Curwen was sitting at county headquarters, a police overcoat covering his swimming suit. "She had been in the water with me for about five minutes, when she said she had had enough."

"About ten minutes later," continued the superintendent, "you left the water and followed the course taken by your wife, expecting to find her waiting for you in the car? Your car was missing? You caught sight of the body of your wife lying close to where the car had been parked and partly concealed by a clump of ferns? You perceived that your wife was dead, and noticed marks on her throat suggesting to you that she had been strangled? You carried the body into the so-called wood and partly covered it with ferns, after which you waited in the road and, after a short lapse of time, stopped a motor cyclist and asked him to call the police? It is your belief that deceased was killed by the person or persons who stole the car?"

"I don't quite like 'belief,' Superintendent. I think I said 'guess.' What about making it 'inference'?"

Presently his car was brought in by the Brighton police, who had found it in a side street. The police handed him his clothes and the note-case—which, as he had explained, was concealed on a special little shelf under the dash—but would not allow him to touch the car.

Beyond this, the police made no restrictions. There were no signs that the murder had been planned. The theory that a husband is the first suspect when a wife has been murdered was weakened by the theft of the car, which could not have been anticipated. Curwen took an afternoon train to London.

Curwen assessed his position much as a speculator might assess his own crash on the Stock Exchange. On a different Exchange, Curwen had crashed and now adjudged himself a moral bankrupt —a conception that held a ray of hope. A bankrupt could qualify for discharge and rebuild his credit. He would so live that, at the end of his life, he would have caused more happiness than unhappiness. He assumed, with honest indifference to his own peril, that it would be impossible to convict him. In London, he took the underground to Gormer's Green.

He told Mrs. Morprill that his wife had been murdered, giving her the version he had given the police. He spoke in tragic terms, without hypocrisy, because he saw the death of Morprill and the death of Marion as a single tragedy.

"There is a certain sameness in the way you and I have been treated by life," he said. "In a little while, I hope you will feel as I do—that is, I hope we shall be seeing each other more frequently."

The mild eyes looked troubled, as if they understood too much.

"I don't really know what to say to that, Mr. Curwen." For the first time since he had known her, she was groping for words. "I think—I'm sure—I ought to confess that I haven't been quite straightforward with you. About my husband, I mean."

He was badly startled.

"I simply can't imagine your being anything but straightforward," he said.

"It was your kindness and all the things you've done for Maggie that sort of tied my hands. First, it was you never saying anything about Henry when I tried to coax you. Then, the last time you were here, I spoke about him being a tall man, and before you left, I spoke about him being a short man. And you won't mind my saying it now, Mr. Curwen, but I don't believe you know which he was. I don't believe you ever knew him."

"Then you'll have to think up some reason why I should seek you out and tell you lies about my having a moral obligation to him."

"Well, it couldn't have been anything Henry did for you, could it! And I never thought you were telling lies, Mr. Curwen." She paused, then forced herself to continue: "When Maggie was thanking you for the bicycle, I watched you looking at her. And then I sort of caught you looking at me in the same way. It's because we stand for the same thing to you."

"And you know why?"

When she answered she avoided his eye.

"I only want to say that I shall always think of you as a *good* man, Mr. Curwen. It's little enough to say, but I do hope it will be a help to you. And, please, we don't want you to give us any more things. I promise that, if I'm ever unable to look after Maggie, I'll ask your help, for Henry's sake. And—we'd better not see each other, though I do hope you won't think it's because I'm ungrateful or—or anything like that."

In the underground, he tried to re-shape the theory of working for a discharge from moral bankruptcy. What could one do if one's mild-eyed creditors refused payment? He was still seeking the answer when he reached his flat, to find the local superintendent waiting outside the front door.

"On the back seat of your car," said the superintendent, when they were inside the flat, "was a lady's swimming cap, wet on the inside, and a towel, part of which was damp. Analysis returns sea water in both cases. Do you agree that this points to deceased having entered the car before she was attacked?"

Curwen nodded. "Presumably, she was dragged from the car."

From a brief case the superintendent produced two envelopes. The first contained a cracked purse-mirror, which he replaced as being unidentifiable. The second envelope contained a tortoiseshell comb, with sheath.

"Did you buy this comb at Hoffmeister's on the fourth of March last? And did you give it to your wife?"

"Yes, to both questions."

"That comb was found close to the bench at the cliff-head, approximately one hundred and twenty yards from the spot where you told us you found the body. Don't say anything, please, until I've finished. We think that your wife went to the car, removed her swimming cap, towelled herself a little, then took that comb and mirror to the bench, no one molesting her. While she was on the bench waiting for you, the car was stolen—which she didn't know, unless you told her before you strangled her."

"Good enough, Superintendent." Curwen spoke absently. He was thinking, 'I can beat that widow and child by making a will in their favour. If I don't die morally solvent, I shall at least have paid something into court.'

Before they started, the superintendent accepted a drink. On the way to the police station the two men became quite friendly. Curwen admitted that he had expected to escape detection.

"Speaking off the record," said the superintendent, "your plan was okay, but you're not the right type. The man who stands the best chance on a job like this is the fussy sort, with an eye for small details that might cause trouble. You know? The chap who thumps the doors of a car to make sure they're properly shut. The chap who turns back to make sure he's switched the stove off—which he always has. Checks and double-checks everything. Gets on people's nerves.

"Take your case f'rinstance. We could never have charged you if you'd thought of going back to that bench to check—to *make sure* she hadn't dropped something that might give you away. See what I mean? Little things like that!"

KILL ME, KILL MY DOG

"Acting on information received"—the cliché which means that a copper's nark, or other informer, has pulled Scotland Yard out of a difficulty—the police located the corpse of Arthur Crouch, some six months after the murder. It was, from the police point of view, a nice, tidy murder, with no loose ends. Locate the corpse and you had located the murderer.

Oddly enough, it was not the murder but the cliché which caused the scandal, the questions in Parliament, the public hullabaloo. *How* had the information been received? The circumstances of the crime excluded the possibility of a witness at any stage. Something, it seemed, was being covered up.

Nobody suggested that Stretton might be innocent of the murder: his guilt was obvious. Nobody wanted to know the name and address of the informer. But nearly everybody wanted to be assured that, in this case, the cliché was true—that a person or persons existed who had told Scotland Yard where the body was to be found.

It was the Animal Lovers League that set the snowball rolling —due to the fact that Crouch happened to have a dog with him when he was murdered. And the dog happened to be a mastiff! The legendary dog of England, now as rare a spectacle as a carriage and pair! A huge, fierce animal, looking even fiercer than it is—in appearance suggesting a bull-dog the size of a Great Dane.

The breed of the dog swelled the publicity. The public was reminded that mastiffs used to board the Spanish galleons with Drake's men—that Nelson had been afraid of them, and had banished them from the Navy.

And here, in 1937, was a mastiff turning up in a murder mystery —but in the strange role of informer. Indeed, there were those who believed that this dog was able to reason that its master had been murdered; that it understood that it must therefore communicate with the police; that it had persisted in its efforts for more than six months—only to be shot by Scotland Yard when it had nobly done its duty.

This sob-story of the Martyred Mastiff—with a near human mentality—was even accepted by many who were not dog-minded, because it was the simplest way of dodging a logical dilemma.

Crouch, who lived in Hampstead, came out of his house, leading the mastiff, in the late afternoon of 23rd July, his car being parked nearby. A schoolboy of fifteen, who stopped to gape at the mastiff, testified that Crouch shouted to a man who had just strolled past the house, apparently a friend. The boy's interest was on the dog, so he had observed only that the other man was 'big' and that Crouch was 'little.'

On one essential point the boy was positive. Crouch, the victim, had persuaded the big man—presumed to be the murderer—to enter the car. "Be generous and use my car," Crouch had said. The words had stuck in the boy's memory because he had thought it a funny way to talk about giving a man a lift.

At dawn the car had been found in central London. But the man and the dog—which was taller, on its hind legs, than the man, and substantially heavier—had disappeared, leaving no traces whatever. Nothing relevant was discovered in six months. Then—*hey presto!*—the whole case was cleaned up in a few hours.

2

The tall man who had been persuaded to enter the car was Dennis Stretton. He was an engineer, of some minor distinction, in the early forties. He and Crouch had been fellow students and close friends. Stretton had graduated with a First; Crouch, who had taken only a Fourth, subsequently specialised in the finance of engineering. Their friendship had never been formally broken, but they had not seen each other for seven years.

A news paragraph had misinformed Stretton that Crouch was away on holiday with his wife—his second wife—or Stretton would not have been loitering outside Crouch's house in Hampstead.

He had come solely to indulge his own morbid melancholy. He wanted to gloat over the house in which Crouch lived—more precisely, the house in which Crouch had lived with the late Mrs. Crouch, who had died some eighteen months previously. The late Mrs. Crouch—a wistful, attractive Belgian—had been engaged to Stretton before she married Crouch seven years ago.

The car was parked some dozen yards up the road, so Stretton missed its significance. Crouch, coming out suddenly with the mastiff, had spotted him before he had gone three full paces.

"Dennis!" he called.

It would have been ridiculous to walk on as if he had not heard. Stretton turned round, startled into speechlessness as much by the bull-head of the mastiff, flush with Crouch's hip, as by the awkwardness of the meeting.

"I say, Dennis, we don't have to cut each other, do we?" Crouch added: "I've missed you like the devil!"

"It's very civil of you to say that, Arthur!" He did not believe that Crouch had missed him. "The *Journal* said you were in Sussex, or I——"

"Driving down this evening. I'm on my way to park poor old Oscar with the vet. For ten days." Pointless conversation, which showed that Crouch, too, felt the strain, though he could, Stretton reminded himself, talk his way out of anything. "Look here, Dennis—let's be frank with each other, as we used to be. I know there's a certain atmosphere which nothing I can say will dispel. All the same, I'm going to ask you a favour."

"By all means!" When you felt as Stretton felt, no satisfaction could be obtained from mere discourtesy.

"I'm having a ghastly job with the Belgian Probate people to wind up poor Léonie's estate. Red tape about identification—and I wondered if you would be good enough to help?"

"Me! How could I possibly help?"

"Léonie told me once that you never returned her passport."

"*Didn't* I?" Stretton was trying to remember.

Crouch went on: "As we were married in Belgium, we used mine —endorsed with her married name, of course. Her original passport is about the only means of convincing them that Léonie Crouch was once Léonie de Ripert."

"If I still have it, I know where it must be. I'll send it to you." This was not what Crouch wanted.

"Could I come with you and collect it now, Dennis? The thing is becoming a nightmare. Marion—my present wife—keeps worrying me to get it all settled."

"But I've given up my flat. I'm living in a remote cottage in Essex—by the marshes. Open-air life. Doctor's orders. It's fifteen miles the other side of London. With the traffic, it'll take you more than an hour and a half to get there."

"It doesn't matter what time I turn up at my father-in-law's place. I can have dinner on the way down." He added: "Be generous, and let's use my car."

Crouch could put an infernal persuasiveness into his voice. Again and again in the past Stretton had let himself be talked into agreement.

"Very well! But we may find that I haven't got the passport." He looked at the mastiff with misgiving. "D'you want to park the dog first?"

"No. Two sides of a triangle. Quicker to drop him after I leave you."

He opened the rear door of the car. The mastiff ambled in and bestowed himself on the floor.

"Make for the other side of dockland—near Tilbury—and then I'll pilot you," said Stretton as he got in beside Crouch. "I'm right in the wilds, on the north bank of the river."

Crouch skirted north London, driving eastwards. Now and again they exchanged commonplace remarks—thrown, as it were, over the wall of hatred between them.

In a long traffic block, Crouch leant over and patted the mastiff. The dog yawned. Crouch glanced from the huge jaws to Stretton's throat. For it was Crouch, the victim, who had the psychology of a murderer—the kind of murderer who kills slowly and without tangible weapons.

As students they had been normal young men of more than average promise, normal in their friendship, with a touch of honest, unconcealed jealousy on Crouch's part.

In the 1914 war they were in the same technical company. On their way out the troopship had been torpedoed, when Crouch's nerve had failed rather lamentably and Stretton, at some risk of his own life, had saved him from drowning.

It may be doubted whether any man can feel unalloyed gratitude to another for saving his life. He is apt to regard his rescuer as a moral creditor who can never be paid off. In the special circumstances—notably the circumstance of Crouch's panic—Stretton had incidentally committed the offence of revealing a definite superiority. Thereafter their relationship had changed, but so subtly that Stretton had been unaware of it. Crouch persuaded himself that he detected patronage in the other's manner. He hid his resentment, used it as fuel to the inner fire which burned steadily for the rest of his life.

For ten years following return to civil life, Stretton did not know that Crouch had become his enemy: once or twice he had his suspicions, but Crouch talked his way out. It was not until Crouch actually married Léonie that the truth flashed upon Stretton. Even then, he did not understand why. Stretton had, almost literally, forgotten the life-saving episode.

The first outstanding incident occurred when Stretton was given a favourable opportunity to acquire a junior partnership. While he was completing arrangements with his bank manager, he was informed that the opportunity had been snapped up by another—who turned out to be Crouch. But Crouch had explained that away.

Later, Stretton leased patent rights in an invention of his own —a valuable adaptation of the steam turbine—to Harmoddle Limited, who intended to put the engine into immediate production. A few weeks later Crouch became chairman of Harmoddle's. The patent rights were retained: the penalties for non-production were paid quarterly. But Stretton's engine was kept off the market. Crouch explained that away, too.

In the course of professional visits to Brussels, Stretton met and eventually proposed marriage to Léonie. Owing to the strict religious views of her family, they had decided to marry without religious ceremony in England. During some slight routine delay which he encountered in connection with her passport she wrote breaking off the engagement and begging him not to see her again.

Stretton did not grieve very much at the time. Her harsh and arbitrary rejection of him even inclined him to the view that he had had a lucky escape, notwithstanding her very considerable physical attractiveness.

Six months later Crouch, having converted himself to the religious views of her family, married her ceremonially in Belgium.
Instantly the frustrations of the last ten years were floodlit.
Stretton derided himself as a credulous fool who had let Crouch
climb on his shoulders to steal or to spoil the prizes.

There was no showdown, no harsh words, nothing in the nature
of a quarrel. It was as if their friendship had merely lapsed. Stretton
settled down to the kind of passive, well-mannered hatred that
rarely harms its object but acts as slow poison in the brain of the
hater.

He stood well in his profession, but his career had its ups and
downs: when the slow poison got to work he debited all the downs
to Crouch. Léonie became the symbol of his blighted life. The
memory of her physical beauty began to torture his imagination,
shutting out the possibility of his seeking other women. In the
background of this obsession was some kind of belief that she
would one day come to him. When he learnt of her death, he
had a nervous breakdown.

After some weeks in a nursing home he was advised to knock
off work for a year and live a simple muscular life in the open
air. He bought the cottage in Essex, standing by itself on the
fringe of the marsh, where he dug and re-dug the garden, occasionally shooting duck and occasionally sailing in the Thames estuary.

Within a year of Léonie's death he learnt from the personal
column of an engineering journal that Crouch had married again.
The same column misinformed him that Crouch had joined his wife
for a short vacation at her father's house in Sussex.

His physical health had been greatly improved, but the vision
of Léonie persisted, finally driving him to look at the outside of
the house in which another had enjoyed her charms.

3

Sunk in his own thoughts, Stretton forgot to function as pilot
when they reached and passed Tilbury. Within half a mile of the
cottage, it dawned on him that Crouch had taken the correct
route off the main road, through the lanes.

He had not given Crouch the name of the cottage. Even with

that information, a stranger would have to enquire, or to put in some close work with an ordnance map.

They were now in a very lonely spot. Linked with the realisation of Crouch's odd behaviour was acute consciousness of the mastiff lying on the floor behind, separated only by the back of the bucket seat. Stretton felt a prickling in his spine. He would have concealed his feeling, but for a mischance of the road.

The whole incident was over in a few seconds. A shaggy white-coated sheepdog burst through the hedge almost under the wheels of the car. Crouch braked hard. The mastiff sprang up with a whine. A sound like a muffled scream broke from Stretton.

"Sorry!" exclaimed Crouch. "Couldn't help it." From the other's tone, Stretton felt sure he had betrayed himself.

Ahead, the lane dipped into a stream some ten feet wide.

"Can I get through, Dennis?"

He knew he could get through, thought Stretton, because he had been here before. But he answered:

"You'll be all right if you take it very slowly. It's only a cattle-ford."

To himself his voice had sounded wobbly. The mastiff was sitting on it haunches, looking through the windscreen, its head between those of the two men. Stretton was nauseated by the creature's breath. He was still unsure of his voice, felt he must put it to the test.

"Don't let your megatherium jump out of the window and eat that sheepdog," he said, as Crouch slowed to walking pace for the ford, "or the farmers will smoke me out."

"Oscar would never fight until I told him to," laughed Crouch. "And then he'd fight anything."

The laugh rasped Stretton's nerve. No unarmed man would stand a chance againt that animal. And Crouch was putting on an act of some sort.

"They're a fighting breed, you know," prattled Crouch. "That is, they hold their bite until they can land on a vital spot. They've rather outlived their day—there are less than a dozen in the whole country."

They cleared the ford, and at the next bend came to the cottage.

"You'll have to drive right in, or you'll block the lane. Not that anybody ever comes out this way."

He found himself wishing he had not made the last remark. Then common sense steadied him. If Crouch were to set the mastiff on him, it would be murder. Crouch might get away, but the police would know that a mastiff had been used; and as there were less than a dozen in the country they would soon pick them out, and Crouch would be hanged.

"You can park at the side of the cottage—then it will be easy to back and turn."

As Crouch stepped out of the car the mastiff put its head through the open window. With something between a slither and a leap it landed in the garden, stretched, sniffed the air.

"Oscar had better stay in the car," said Crouch, and opened the rear door. "Oscar—guard!"

Instead of obeying, the mastiff cringed and whined.

"Why, what's the matter, old boy!" He patted the dog and talked nonsense to it. But when he again ordered it into the car it circled round him, fawning and whimpering, in canine apology for disobeying an order.

"Something's upsetting him!" Crouch was puzzled. "Dennis, d'you mind if I touch you! I want to show him we're friends." Crouch put his hands on Stretton's shoulders. "There, there! Dear Dennis! Nice Dennis!" In his preposterous pantomine of affection, Crouch stood on tiptoe and went through the motions of administering a kiss.

The mastiff ignored the whole performance. Only when Crouch bellowed at him did he slink back into the car.

Crouch slammed the door—but he did not, Stretton noticed, shut the window. The dog would come if Crouch were to call him.

"Those scientific tests of the dog's intelligence are damned unscientific!" exclaimed Crouch. "They're tests for elementary human intelligence. Dogs haven't got any. Take Oscar. He only understands seven words, and he thinks all policemen are sugar-daddies, because a constable petted him when he was a puppy. All the same, they understand the devil of a lot in their own way. I believe they have a thought-pattern which we can't analyse."

"Afraid I've never had any feeling for animals," returned Stretton, his fear subsiding. "Shall we go in?"

4

It was a spacious little five-roomed cottage, incongruously furnished with items from Stretton's London flat. The front window
of the parlour looked over marshland to the Thames. From the side
window, when Crouch's car was not blocking the view, could
be seen only a meagre wood, which screened the nearest neighbour,
half a mile away.

"Only fifteen miles from London and not a human habitation
in sight!" Crouch, lounging in a very urban armchair, was making
conversation. "You're pretty snug here, Dennis. D'you do your
own housework?"

Stretton had taken a deed-box from what was once a cocktail
cabinet. He had already produced whisky. Quarrel with Crouch or
treat him as an ordinary guest—there could be no middle course.

"A woman comes on a push-bike three days a week to clean
up and cook me a joint."

Stretton unlocked the deed-box, untied the string of a small
parcel marked with an initial. 'L' for Léonie.

Crouch raised his glass.

"Whatever may be wrong with your health, old man—may it
soon pass!"

"Thanks!" With his back to Crouch, he opened out the small
parcel—and saw that Léonie had been right about the passport.
Folded in were her birth certificate and similar documents. It
would be petty to pretend he had found nothing.

"That's what you want, Arthur."

"I'm enormously obliged, Dennis!" If Crouch had put the passport in his pocket he would probably have departed unharmed.
But he flourished it and talked about it.

"Thundering good likeness for a passport photo!" Crouch turned
the pages. "Ah, this is what we want: *'Léonie Thérèse de Ripert:
Parents: Alphonse Maria de Ripert*——' "

It was the fluttering of the pages that stirred the chord of
memory. Stretton had supplied all those details, in triplicate,
to British and to Belgian authorities. Obviously, a Belgian lawyer
could settle the whole thing from the files.

"Arthur, why did you really want to come here?" Stretton's

voice was steady; so was his hand when he took up his whisky. "The passport story is punk."

"My dear fellow!"

"You've been around here before, in my absence."

"How can you possibly suggest that?"

"You forgot to ask me the route."

It would take him some time to talk that away, thought Stretton, but again he was wrong.

"You win, Dennis. I plead guilty to a pious fraud." He drained his glass. "I told you I had missed you like the devil. I couldn't approach you while Léonie was alive. After her death I heard you were ill—and I guessed what had pulled you down. I had to find out how things were with you."

The same old technique, an explanation that could be neither proved nor disproved. In reality, Crouch had probably come to gloat over his handiwork.

"And now that you have found out?"

"I want to know whether I can be of any help to you, Dennis— in any way whatever?"

"Thanks, Arthur, you can!" At the expression in the other's eyes Stretton's last doubt vanished. He laughed offensively. "It's not going to be a request for a loan. It's going to be a request for the truth. It will help me to straighten things in my own mind if you will tell me the truth about Léonie."

Crouch shrugged as if with embarrassment. To lengthen the silence he poured himself another drink. So Léonie had hurt—could perhaps be made to hurt a little more! Even by telling the truth.

"The truth, I'm afraid, was well known to most of our acquaintances. There are no lurid details. We just bored each other beyond bearing. Unfortunately for us both, her religious principles put divorce out of reach."

Stretton was aware of a thudding in his ears. The suppression of his invention—all the disappointments, real and imaginary, in which he had seen the hand of Crouch—were concentrated in the now tragic figure of Léonie.

"So you spoilt her life without even getting any pleasure yourself in doing so!"

"That's very bitter, old man! And it's exaggerated. It wasn't all gloom. There was the honeymoon era——"

"*Stop!*" The word cracked like a whiplash. Crouch was beginning to be alarmed by the extent of his own success.

"I think I'd better go now, Dennis. We ought not to have talked about her. But you demanded the truth."

"I'm still demanding it, Arthur. What filthy lie about me did you tell her to make her throw me down as if I had been a moral leper?"

Crouch set down his glass unfinished and got up.

"I told no lies about you. I did not approach her until after she had jilted you."

Stretton cut off his line to the door.

"What filthy lie did you tell her about me?" It was as if he had been repeating that question for seven years. "Answer that and you can get out of here and we need never see each other again."

"I have already explained——"

"You dirty little rat, you'll tell me if I have to choke it out of you!" He gripped Crouch by the throat, thrust him back into the armchair and, with his knees on the other's thighs, bent his head back over the arm of the chair. "It must have been a *filthy* lie, or she would have asked for a showdown. You wanted her solely in order to take her away from me and debauch her. Answer—d'you hear! or I'll choke you. Speak, you little fool! *Speak!*"

He had not choked Crouch but broken his neck.

Part of him was bewildered, still waiting for Crouch's confession, wondering why he did not say something. But another part of him knew that he had intended to kill Crouch for saying that Léonie was a bore—except on the honeymoon.

He stood back, getting his breath, staring at the wreckage in the armchair.

"My God! I'd forgotten his damned dog!"

No unarmed man would stand a chance against that animal. There came a different kind of thudding in his ears now, which might have been made by the pads of the mastiff in the hallway of the cottage. Had the front door been left open? He couldn't remember.

"It will see Arthur through the window—then jump through the glass."

He caught up a rug and flung it over what had been Crouch.

He looked through the front window—from one side then the other, to widen his angle—and saw nothing. He crossed to the side window, stepping over the feet of the corpse.

"I can see into the car."

The brute was not sitting, or it would have been visible. By standing on a couple of books he was able to see part of the floor of the car.

"It's not there. Then it must be prowling round the cottage looking for its master. Or in the hall, waiting for him to come out of this room."

The thudding in his ears produced the illusion of any sound that panic conjured up. Wherever he feared the dog might be, there he heard it. In the garden—scratching on the wall—padding about upstairs.

The gun, with which he occasionally shot wild duck, was upstairs in the bedroom.

He knelt and peered through the keyhole, without result. Was the beast crouching, to spring as soon as the door was opened?

"It can't know what has happened, or it would bark, or something." Also, he remembered, Crouch had had no chance to call it. "Have to risk it!"

He opened the door, found nothing in the hallway. But the front door was open. If he could get upstairs he would be safe. He shut the parlour door behind him, then rushed the stairs.

He slammed the bedroom door and stood, panting, for some seconds. There was a box of cartridges under the bed. When he had loaded, panic passed, leaving him free to face the fact that it was not in self-defence that he had killed Crouch. Nor would anyone believe that it had been accidental—he didn't altogether believe it himself.

He was cool now, even self-possessed. Crouch had been on his way to Sussex: had changed his plans after he came out of his house. Therefore no one knew where Crouch had gone.

"Better locate that dog and let him have both barrels."

Holding the gun like an infantryman mopping-up, he skirted the cottage, then the garden, then looked again in the car, to make sure.

"Where are you? Come out, you brute, and fight."

With the gun in his hand he no longer feared the teeth of the mastiff. Yet in some way the animal was dominating him, mocking both his scientific training and his common sense. He was aware that his hands were sweating while his spine was cold and prickling. He was fighting the eerie feeling that the dog had gone to summon the police.

He forced a laugh, but the idea refused to seem as absurd as it ought to seem. Crouch had said something about a thought-pattern, different from human intelligence.

And something about this particular dog being specially fond of policemen.

5

In a quarter of an hour the scientific training and the common sense had prevailed, and he was able to make rational arrangements.

The marsh, he knew, would be useless as a hiding place for the body. A few hours of rain and the whole waste became a network of rivulets, all swirling into the highway of the Thames. It would have to be the garden, the potato bed. The earth there was deep and soft.

It was nearly seven when he started digging, the loaded shotgun within arm's reach. The moon would rise at ten fifty-seven. He must fill the grave before then. Not that he feared observation. But he would prefer to bury Crouch with as little light as possible, for the sake of his own nerve.

In this, he was successful. When he had finished digging there was just enough light for his purpose.

He returned to the cottage, gritted his teeth, and set about his task. In his preoccupation with the corpse, he had forgotten the risk of the mastiff appearing and taking him by surprise.

The grave was some fifteen feet from the large shed that served him as a garage. On the return journey, with his burden, he had to pass near the tail of Crouch's car, parked between the cottage and the garage. That reminded him that he had left the shotgun at the grave side.

For a moment he stood still, paralysed by physical fear of the mastiff. Then, hampered as he was, he ran. An hysterical sob broke from him as he found the shotgun. He turned at bay, his finger round the triggers. As the minutes lengthened he recovered his breath.

"I lost my head then. If I lose it again, I shan't make the grade."

The moon was rising as he finished filling in the grave. Panic was far behind. Even if the mastiff were to return, it would not know what had happened, and it would not attack him unprovoked. He carried the shotgun comfortably under his arm as he returned the spade to the shed.

Back in the cottage he shut the front door. In the kitchen, he heated water on the oil stove, then stripped naked and washed in the zinc footbath. When he had dressed, he prepared supper. He poured a small whisky, then put the bottle away. He would have to drive Crouch's car into London and leave it in a side street.

He did not bother to wash Crouch's glass. That kind of precaution was a waste of energy. His plan was based on the assumption that he could prevent suspicion from reaching him.

Shortly after midnight he was rested and ready to start. He took a light overcoat, knowing that he could not return until the day buses were running—even then he would have a four-mile walk.

Moonlight was bathing the marsh, glistening on the distant Thames, when he stepped out of the cottage. He shut the door behind him. There was no need to lock your doors in those parts.

At the same spot—by the tail of Crouch's car—came the same panic. He had stolen an oblique glance to the left, where the grave lay.

This time, he saw the mastiff.

It was by the grave, sitting motionless on its haunches, guarding it as if it were guarding the car. The moonlight caught its eyes, which gleamed green.

Ignorant of the ways of a dog, Stretton thought it was unaware of his presence. He backed slowly, holding his breath, out of the line of vision. Then he bolted into the cottage for the shotgun and spare cartridges.

The sporting gun, he knew, would be useless except at a range of a few feet. He would have to walk right up to the brute—or hold his fire to the last half second if it attacked him. He crept out, telling himself that in less than a minute it would be all over—one way or the other.

The mastiff was in the same position. The same green glint came from the eyes. Within ten feet of it, Stretton stopped. The mastiff took no notice of him. The luminous eyes were not looking at him. They were looking in the direction of the lane, as if expectantly.

Stretton advanced. The mastiff gave a low, indifferent growl—a protest rather than a menace. And still it would not look at him. It was positively ignoring him. Following a thought-pattern of its own?

But the mastiff's thought-pattern, if any, had never envisaged the nature of a gun.

The job of burying it would be even more laborious than that of burying its master. It would have to wait until he had rested. He managed to lever the carcase into a wheelbarrow and lurch with it into the garage. Then he had to go back to the cottage for another wash.

By half-past two he had dumped the car in Central London. He spent the rest of the night in a Turkish bath.

The next afternoon he buried the mastiff close to Crouch.

6

At midnight Mrs. Crouch, alarmed by the non-arrival of her husband at her father's house in Sussex, began to telephone inquiries as to road accidents. After ringing the vet, and her own servants in Hampstead, she made a full report to Scotland Yard.

In the next few days the mastiff received its first instalment of publicity—but only on the reasonable ground that it intensified the mystery of Crouch's disappearance.

No man taking an illicit holiday with a fair companion would burden himself with a mastiff. Nor could he lose his memory and disappear without being quickly identified by the presence of such a rare and such a noticeable animal. Any crook could shoot a mastiff: but to dispose of the carcase in a secret manner would be as difficult as to dispose of a corpse. The case became a murder mystery with, as it were, a double corpse.

For a week Stretton read the newspapers with anxiety. The schoolboy who had seen him getting into the car with Crouch had given a description which would fit tens of thousands. There were appeals to this 'unknown friend' to communicate with the police. The lack of response created suspicion of the 'big' man, but provided no clue to identity. No one east of London claimed to have seen a mastiff in a car. In a few days it became clear that there was nothing to lead the police to examine Stretton's garden.

Yet there were periods of depression and uncertainty, and some moments in which his scientific training and his common sense would again fail him. He felt no moral guilt, gave never a thought to Crouch as a person. But now and again his imagination was haunted by the luminous eyes of the mastiff staring expectantly in the direction of the lane—the mastiff that had a special affection for the police. There was that thought-pattern nonsense! Of course, some of the social insects—bees, ants and whatnot—could achieve a sort of collective thinking——

"If dogs do have a thought-pattern of their own, they obviously can't communicate their conclusions to humanity—so what the hell does it matter if they have!" Thus he would laugh it off: but he could never wholly forget it.

In a month of hard work the police failed to pick up any clue to the identity of the murderer or the whereabouts of the corpse, and the case was passed to the Department of Dead Ends. Except when he lapsed into mysticism about the dog, Stretton lost the sense of peril.

The vision of Léonie's beauty no longer tormented him, so his nervous health improved. It was as if he were starting his life afresh, the past expiated and forgotten. In a couple of months he began preparations for a professional comeback.

He decided that he would have to live on in the cottage for a while. The potato patch bulged over the two graves. He finicked with a spade, breaking the outline. The soil might take a year or more to subside, he supposed, but while he remained at the cottage he was safe. The woman who did his housework had an elementary, incurious mind.

The woman came about eleven on Tuesdays, Thursdays and Saturdays. By January he was driving to London on Mondays, Wednesdays and Fridays to re-establish contacts in his practice as a consultant.

To put it in the absurd terms of Stretton's own mysticism, the mastiff spoke from the grave in the first week of February—some six months after the murder.

7

It was a little after ten on the Thursday morning. Stretton was rising late after a heavy evening on theory, and had just finished dressing, when he saw a car draw up in the lane. Behind it was another—a third and a fourth. At leisure, a dozen or more men emerged from the cars, some in police uniform.

Stretton hurried downstairs and opened the front door.

"Good Lord, sir, there he is!" exclaimed Detective Inspector Rason. "I thought he'd be in London by now. Cor! He'll ask us a lot o' questions before we've dug up the answers."

"Your show!" said Chief Inspector Karslake grimly. As usual, he was in grave doubt as to the legality of Rason's position.

"Good morning, Mr. Stretton." Rason introduced himself and Karslake. "We have received certain information—that is—well, to cut it short, we'd like to do a spot o' digging in your garden. Any objection?"

Stretton knew, of course, that he was done for, though there might still be some faint chance of stalling.

"That's a curious request," he said evenly. "I think I'm entitled to ask what sort of information?"

He expected them to say that they were looking for the body of Arthur Crouch. If they had said it, he would have kept his head.

"P'r'aps I oughtn't to 've said 'information', Mr. Stretton," Rason amended. "The fact is, we got a tip from that mastiff——"

"My God!" gasped Stretton. As before, his hands sweated with superstitious terror, while his spine felt cold.

Rason reacted quickly.

"Do I make myself clear, Mr. Stretton, or don't I?" he chirped. "I see that I do. Perhaps we can go inside and swap yarns while the men get busy. They won't be long. I was here yesterday with one of those young scientific farmers—you know, B.Sc. and all that! *And* farming as well, mindjer! He spotted a patch over there, where the earth had been dug up to a depth of several feet. Some time during the last year, he said. Wonderful how they can tell all that by looking over your hedge!"

Stretton led them into the parlour. In half an hour, he supposed, the men would uncover the body. It would serve no purpose to pretend someone else had put it there. In those few steps, hope vanished. Dignity alone remained.

"I think you know already that your men will find the body of Arthur Crouch——"

"Half a mo'!" protested Rason. "Wait till I've warned you that anything you say may be used——"

"Unnecessary, thanks!" Stretton was taking it very well; but he lost some composure as he went on: "You implied that Crouch's mastiff is still alive. Either I'm partly mad, or your men will also dig up the carcase of that mastiff."

Rason gave him a long, noncommittal look.

"Shouldn't wonder!" he agreed. "But maybe Arthur Crouch's mastiff sent for us, just the same."

Stretton's nerve gave. He gaped at the detective, then collapsed into the armchair.

"Are you telling me it was someone else's mastiff I killed?" The words came from the heart of a broken man.

"I've no statement to make." Rason was almost apologetic. "You see, everything I say is used against me, too." He glanced at his superior officer, and added: "I'm sorry, Mr. Stretton, but you'll have to work it out for yourself."

"It must have a natural explanation!" cried Stretton. "I *can* work it out. A second mastiff strayed into the garden. On that particular night! The million to one chance turned up!"

"And double the odds for luck!" guffawed Rason.

"Even then, that thought-pattern rot turns out to be true!" Stretton's voice was slipping out of control. "Thought-pattern or not, how the hell could that animal bring you here? It travelled on the floor of the car—six months ago! It's against reason, I tell you."

"Quite right!" said Rason, soothingly. "Only, you can't expect a mastiff to work according to reason. Thought-pattern, you said. And that's about as near it as a dog can get."

8

A couple of hours later Rason was alone in a police car with Chief Inspector Karslake on their way back to the Yard. Stretton had been taken away an hour previously in charge of a sergeant. Both smoked in silence until they were running into East London.

"Your case, and a good job o' work too, Rason!" Karslake's tone was aggrieved. "You've produced your evidence, and you don't have to tell me how you got it if you don't want to."

Rason did not rise. Karslake continued: "Couldn't follow what he meant by a 'thought-pattern'. But he was right about that second mastiff being a million to one chance. It's the sort of thing that's turned up in your favour before."

"Yes, sir, only it didn't, this time," said Rason. "There's only one mastiff in this case. Matter o' fact, there are only nine of 'em now in the whole country. And, d'you know, sir—" he paused for effect—"d' you know that not one of the nine has ever set foot in the county of Essex? Makes you think, doesn't it!"

"No, it doesn't!" snapped Karslake. "You told me last night, all formal and correct, that you had entered his cottage in his absence and taken finger-prints which corresponded to one set of the prints found in Crouch's car. Also that you had taken along a soil expert, et cetera. Of course, if you don't want to tell how you found the cottage in the first place?"

"Oh, luck as usual!" Rason was inclined to be bitter on this point. But he relented at the other's disappointment. "You see, sir, my niece likes to do a bit o' shop-gazing——"

"Damn your niece!" exploded Karslake. "I'm sorry that slipped out, Rason. Nothing personal, of course! But it's not the first time you've stalled me with a winkle-an'-whale about that young lady. Can't we leave her out of it?"

"Okay!" grinned Rason. "Try it the other end up—have you ever seen a mastiff?"

"Y-yes. Of course I have! Must have! Awful-looking brutes. Don't tell me your niece breeds 'em, or I shall cry."

"No, she'd never seen one before, any more than you have, sir!" Rason was following his own train of thought. "And she was so tickled by what she *did* see that she went in to ask the price." He leant forward and spoke to the driver. "George, you can take us back via the Strand—and stop at No. 968."

The car stopped outside a shop which, in fancy lettering, proclaimed itself to be 'The Dogs' Club'. The windows were partitioned into alcoves. In each alcove dogs were lounging.

Rason glanced at the windows.

"It's gone!" he exclaimed ruefully. "Maybe it's inside."

In the shop, Rason nodded to an assistant and pressed on to the proprietor's office at her rear.

"Mr. Braddell, this is my senior, Chief Inspector Karslake. Could you show him what you showed my niece—and tell him what you told me?"

"Certainly. We've had an offer for the dog, and he'll probably be gone tomorrow—unless the Yard wants him?"

"No thanks! He's done his job for us."

Mr. Braddell took them into a long room tiered with cages containing dogs of almost every known and conceivable breed, with variations.

"There you are, Mr. Karslake!"

"Where?" asked Karslake. He was looking for a mastiff.

Rason pointed to a medium-sized dog with a white shaggy coat and a somewhat astonishing head.

"What is that animal?" asked Karslake.

"Pure cross-bred—sheepdog and mastiff," answered Mr. Braddell.

"You see, sir?" cut in Rason. "Sheepdog—mastiff! Mastiff—sheepdog! That's the thought-pattern *you* want!"

"The puppies," said Mr. Braddell, "were brought to us by a small peasant farmer in Essex, near the marshes. He didn't know what they were. Nor did we—until the mastiff head began to develop."

"My niece," said Rason, "saw two of 'em in the window. Happened to mention it over tea."

THE NINE-POUND MURDER

Some superstitions die hard, particularly the superstition that a man can possess "hypnotic eyes," capable of compelling others to do his will—with special reference to women of property. This was said of Joseph Smith, who drowned various brides in their bath; more recently of Heath, who savagely murdered two women within a month.

It was said in the mid-nineteen-thirties of James Gleddy, an ill-mannered little bounder who explained his sex appeal. The hypnotic nonsense was dragged in to explain his success in marrying a girl of distinguished family, who apparently thought he was of her own class.

In their honeymoon there was a gap of six months while the bridegroom purged his offence in the matter of a worthless cheque. But his minor knaveries need not detain us. We can best contact the couple in the third year of their marriage—on a Saturday morning in May 1934, in the offices of the Domestic Animals Charitable Association, of which Margaret Gleddy was the president's secretary: for by this time Gleddy had run through her money and she was supporting the home.

The association rented a basement suite in one of the best blocks off Parliament Square. On Saturday the staff were not required to work, with the exception of the president and his secretary. The president would leave at eleven-thirty during the summer for his week-end cottage in Dorsetshire. Margaret would generally work on until one, when the porter would enter to sign on the cleaners.

On this particular Saturday, when the porter entered the suite he smelt chloroform. He ran into the secretary's office, where he found Margaret lying on the floor near the big safe, which was shut. A duster hung over the door of the little wall safe, which was open and empty. Over the girl's face was another duster, tied in a simple knot at the back. The porter untied the duster and whipped it away—with it a wad of cotton wool on which chloroform had been poured. There was a cut on her chin, from which a trickle of blood had stained her jumper.

The porter shouted to a constable on point duty at the corner. Margaret was carried on a stretcher the hundred-odd yards to Westminster Hospital. In half an hour she recovered consciousness, to be dimly aware of a police sergeant at her bedside. The cut on her chin had been dressed; bruises on her arms and shoulders were not serious enough to need attention.

Soon she was able to talk, though a little wildly.

"Police! That's a good thing!" she exclaimed. "It was my fault, really. I ought to have known it would happen. I ought to have taken special precautions on Saturdays."

"Jest so, Miss! Can you remember anything of what happened?"

"Everything. Until he bumped my face on the back of the chair, and then I passed out. I feel awful. You might call a nurse, will you."

Some ten minutes later the conversation was resumed with greater coherence.

"It must have been a little after half-past twelve when it happened. I made the mistake of threatening to scream, instead of screaming at once. He collared me from behind and put his hand over my mouth. He's much stronger than you'd think. I'd have bitten his hand if I could, but he had my chin squashed up. I landed a good back-kick with my heel, and I think that toppled him on to the back of the chair—with my face underneath. Ugh! Speaking hurts all over."

She began to laugh.

"If he had come six weeks ago," she explained, "he would have found about a hundred and fifty in that little safe. This morning it was empty—I was dusting it when he came in."

"The little safe?" echoed the sergeant. "What about the big safe?"

"It's only used as a cupboard. There's nothing in it but photographs and gramophone records deposited by animal fans."

"We shall want to open it, so as to make a complete checkup."

After a long wait, the sergeant added: "Would the key of that big safe be in your possession, Miss?"

"You'll find it in my desk—the one with the typewriter—top right-hand drawer. But you'll only waste your time."

"Matter o' routine, Miss. You always open everything after a robbery, to make sure."

"On my desk," said Margaret, "there were nine pounds in notes, clipped together, and a four-shilling postal order. And he won't even be able to keep that!" She frowned in sudden doubt. "You have caught him, haven't you?"

"Not yet. Who is he, Miss? I can see you know."

"Yes, I know who he is!" She sighed with vast weariness. "He is my husband—James Gleddy. He has been to prison before. He will spend the rest of his life in and out of prison. I've done my best and I've failed. I'm giving evidence against him—turning on him, betraying him—what's the word crooks use?—ratting on him."

"What's your home address, please?"

She gave it and added: "If you wait until about four, you'll find him lying on his bed in a drunken sleep. Oh God, I'm all in! Don't think me rude, sergeant, but please go away."

The sergeant went back to the suite to report to the local superintendent who had taken charge.

"The key of the big safe isn't in her drawer, where she said it was, sir."

"No hurry about that!" grunted the superintendent. "It's awkward dealing with a half-doped typist. Who runs this place?"

He rang for the porter, who gave the president's London address. "Did any stranger enter the block about twelve-thirty?"

"Nope. I started doin' me brasses about twelve-fifteen—takes half an hour. No stranger, in or out. There's very little going on here on a Saturday morning. Half a mo'! There's a door in the wall here."

He drew the superintendent to the window. The latter slipped over the sill and examined the door in the wall, which was used only to give access to the control chamber of the hydraulic lift.

"Locked on the inside!" exclaimed the superintendent. "He didn't use this. You must have missed him when he came and when he left."

"Not me!" said the porter confidently. "I was right across them steps from twelve-fifteen to a couple o' minutes of it striking one. As I was finishing my brasses, a passing gent spotted my medal ribbons: turned out I'd served under his uncle." He added: "No stranger came in or out o' this building from twelve-fifteen to one."

Half an hour after he had left Margaret's bedside, the sergeant returned. The president of the association, he said, was apparently out of Town.

She gave the address of his week-end cottage and the telephone number.

"But it's no use ringing up until about four, because he won't have arrived."

"To come back to the matter of that big safe," said the sergeant, "the key isn't in the drawer. And we took the liberty of looking in your bag, and it wasn't there either. Was the door of that safe open or shut when your—er—when the intruder entered the office?"

"Shut," said Margaret. "I opened it and shut it again about twenty minutes before he came. I kept the key in my hand while I went to the safe, and I remember putting it back in the drawer. Have you arrested my husband yet?"

"We've got a couple o' men at your house, but he hasn't come back yet. By the way, how did he get into your room?"

Margaret appeared to be puzzled. "Like anybody else," she answered. "That is, through the outer office."

The sergeant reported back to the superintendent.

"Well, the porter missed him, that's all! As to the key, the crook must have taken it out of the drawer after he had doped her and then walked off with it," said the superintendent. "Phew! How that beastly smell does hang about!"

"Rather funny, isn't it, sir—husband doping his wife when he knew she knew who he was?"

"Not so funny as you think. I've been talking to the Yard on the phone. He was a crook and she was a society girl—daughter of a judge—who fell for him. If he hadn't doped her she wouldn't have let him carry on. And he reckoned that when she came to she wouldn't give him away. But she did. Anyway, you wouldn't get a put-up job for nine quid. If it *is* only nine quid, of course!"

At four o'clock, when they contacted the president by telephone, he agreed that there had been no more than some such sum in the office.

The superintendent talked about the key to the big safe.

"Well, if you really want to check up, phone Renson's. They'll open it without doing any damage. I'll pay their charges, as I don't want to come back for what appears to be a very small matter. If any of the gramophone records are damaged, you might ring me again."

The sergeant rang Renson's, the makers, who said they would send a mechanic within an hour.

2

Margaret Demster was the daughter of a High Court judge who had made a comfortable fortune at the Bar. He had a Town house in Kensington and a country house in Oxfordshire, where his daughter was hostess.

Lady Demster had left her money to her husband, but had bequeathed to her daughter a little present of four thousand pounds. In a lakeside hotel in Switzerland, James Gleddy had overheard a friend of the family referring to this modest legacy. It is a tragic circumstance that he misheard 'four thousand' as 'forty thousand', to discover his mistake a few hours after the marriage ceremony. Thus Margaret was a very great disappointment to him, though he was for a time genuinely attracted.

She was indeed a rather exceptionally attractive young woman, though not photogenic. Her few photographs in the sporting and fashionable papers suggest a demure young miss, which she never was. A vital, springy brunette with quick, perceptive eyes and full red lips, she combined a radiant chastity with an intelligent worldliness—a shrewd scale of values with a spiritual generosity.

She had her own way in pretty nearly everything, but she chose to live hard. Two years before her disastrous marriage, her father became Master of Foxhounds. Margaret took over most of the work. She won the admiration of the veterinary surgeon by administering chloroform for him in an emergency operation on a valuable hunter.

At twenty-three she became engaged to Gerald Ramburn, a shipping broker whose ancestors had provided seven of the ships which met the Spanish Armada. It was a romance based on companionship. Oddly, she never varied in her feeling for Gerald—held it to the end of her life, though it proved powerless to protect her from Gleddy.

Margaret was staying with her aunt at the hotel in Switzerland, while her father was deer-stalking in Scotland. No one introduced Gleddy. He accosted her with the technique which such men acquire, and between dances made an immediate impression.

It is not true that she thought he was of her own class, though she probably did think there was no reason why he should not be. One would reasonably suppose that a girl like Margaret Demster would be the last of all social types to fall for the palpable cheapjackery of a man like Gleddy, who was not even good looking. Discarding the hypnotic-eye theory, one is bound to assume that such men have a natural talent for appealing to the maternal instinct under the guise of romanticism.

Poor Margaret followed in the beaten track. To a point, she made a better job of it than most women. She married him in London within three weeks of their meeting. She wrote as honourable a letter as it was possible to write to Gerald Ramburn. Her father was still in Scotland when he received her telegram.

She made the first draft on her four thousand for the honeymoon. The two detectives, astonished at the sight of Margaret, whose type they recognised, allowed Gleddy to make the usual bluster that the charge against him was a ridiculous mistake. But they took him back to London. When the magistrate refused bail, Margaret rushed home to invoke the powerful aid of her father.

She arrived in the late afternoon. At the door of his study, where the judge was sitting alone, her assurance vanished. Her faith in James Gleddy seemed to glow only when she was in his presence.

"Come in, Margaret." Her father's voice was gentle. "I am very, very glad to see you."

"Oh, Daddy!" She was a child again, climbing on his knee. "D'you think it rotten of me—doing it like that?"

"Not rotten, my dear—impulsive. Such things do happen. Your mother and I got married like a flash of lightning." Presently he asked: "Is your husband here?"

She moved away.

"A perfectly preposterous thing has happened!" She gave the details. "I thought perhaps you could order that fool of a magistrate to grant him bail."

The judge shook his head.

"You say he is charged with obtaining only seventeen pounds. You have made restitution, and you have offered bail in three thousand pounds. The police opposed bail. That means they have a record of at least one previous conviction."

"Then it must be mistaken identity! Why it's utterly absurd! James is a barrister himself, but he couldn't practise because his father died suddenly, leaving no money."

The judge rose heavily, went to his bookcase and consulted a reference book.

"If your husband told you he was a barrister, I am afraid he was not telling the truth." Their eyes met in mutual commiseration. "Between ourselves, dearest girl, what sort of man is he?"

"I don't know, Daddy." The confession was a salute to his success as a father. "But I know what sort of man he is going to be—the sort you would not be ashamed to welcome to this house."

Gallant words of a gallant woman. But gallantry was not enough to save James Gleddy—nor herself.

3

Margaret had never even seen a typewriter in action. The business college gave her many surprises and one or two shocks, which her wit and courage turned to profit.

When her husband was discharged she was able to welcome him to a small house, bought on mortgage, which she had furnished tastefully and, in the circumstances, a little extravagantly. With her own maintenance and one thing and another, her reserve was reduced to approximately three thousand pounds.

But they spent the first three days of his liberty at a West End hotel, to cheer him up. Not that he was in the least depressed. He had the air of a man returning from a successful business trip. They danced in London, but not as they had danced in Switzerland. She was consciously entertaining him, as part of her programme of reconstruction, and he was dimly aware that he had lost glamour in her eyes. That he had gained in affection and tenderness was no compensation.

It was a long journey in the Underground to the outer suburb, and nearly ten minutes' walk when they emerged. While he carried their suitcases she could feel his spirits sinking. But he was intelligent enough to make appreciative noises when she showed him over the 'four-roomed semi-detached, with garden'.

"It's a fine little hide-out, darling," he concluded. "But what a ghastly neighbourhood! I mean, what do we do in the evening?"

"We shall probably be too tired to go out much, even when we can afford it," she answered. "I have another two months' grind before I get my certificate, which means I shall have to read for at least five evenings a week."

"But, my sweet, why all this strenuousness? Don't tell me you've blown the whole four thousand while I've been away."

"Of course not! There's a bit over three thousand left, but it's all we have in the world. We mustn't spend a penny on luxuries. I thought I'd better be trained so that I could earn something in emergencies."

"Surely your people would help in an emergency!"

"We shall never ask them!" He looked shocked. "We can pull it off together, James, you and I. Make good and earn our own fun."

Without knowing it, she gave him a pep talk, full of kindliness and confidence, which shocked him again, though he barely listened.

"On Monday you must order all the clothes you'll need. That'll help us to work out what it'll cost to get you decently started."

"Started on what?" he asked.

"Earning a living first, James—then a career."

To James Gleddy it seemed sheer lunacy to talk like that when you had three thousand pounds in the bank. The problem, of course, was to detach as much as possible of the three thousand.

He smiled carefully. He had a good smile. A smallish man with a large head and a large face, he could use the smile to suggest that things had somehow gone wrong with him, through no fault of his own.

"That's what I've wanted all my life, Margie! A chance to work. And someone to believe in me. You're giving me both. By God, I'll prove I'm worth it!"

Margaret swallowed it whole and was happy for the first time since his arrest. In the first six months he detached six hundred pounds, clear of living expenses.

4

Beginning as an almost unteachable student, Margaret passed out of the college with a first-class certificate, just short of the star class. She obtained immediate employment at a salary which covered bare living expenses and the wages of a charwoman.

A couple of months after her appointment she met Gerald Ramburn in the street—by chance, as she thought.

Ramburn had enjoyed all the advantages which Gleddy had lacked. He had made good use of them. Physically, he was a large bony athlete; culturally, he had wide interests.

"Do you know of any reason," he asked, "why you should not have lunch with me?" When she could produce none he carried her off. He settled their relationship by subtly pushing her backwards in time—to the period preceding their formal engagement. He asked no questions, but babbled welcome news of friends, things and places.

On parting he gave no invitation; but a month later he was at the same spot and again took her to lunch. She told her husband, but he evinced no interest. Thereafter, their meetings became regular.

In the first phase of detaching the money, Gleddy used the 'golden business opportunity' which in due course comes unexpectedly to grief. Margaret believed the first tale and bullied herself into believing the substance of the second, though she detected falsities of detail. Alarm for their rapidly shrinking reserve made her refuse to finance any further 'operations'. There followed an intermediate phase in which he contented himself with small sponging and by obtaining local credit. Margaret had a dread of bills and always paid at once.

One day he turned up at the office to 'borrow' a couple of pounds. She gave it him at once to get rid of him. He repeated the trick, raising the ransom to ten pounds; to avoid argument he had previously drunk himself into a state of noisiness.

"I am leaving the office," she told him that night. "And as you don't seem to be having any luck, I shall look for another job."

She added no word of reproach. For her lack of progress in the reconstruction of her husband she blamed herself. Her job compelled her to leave him too much alone, so that he fell in with bad companions. She began to envisage the possibility of ultimate failure.

She was saved from complete exhaustion by the regular lunches with Gerald Ramburn. His rambling conversations acquired a certain continuity—through them she began to live imaginatively the kind of life that might have been hers. When she told him she had resigned from her job for a formal reason, he registered flat disbelief.

"That man turned up drunk at the office so that you should buy him off the premises. Let me buy him off altogether—and marry me after the divorce."

If she had taken offence he would merely have told her not to be silly. So she answered from her heart.

"I don't think it would work out as we'd want it to, Gerald. He is a sort of moral cripple. You and I would always remember that I had left him to stagger into the ditch in order to be happy myself."

"You're pulling your own leg," he told her. "He is in the ditch —always has been, and you haven't dragged him an inch out of it. Eventually, he will drag you in. Think it over. Meantime, if you want another job there's one waiting for you with Domestic Animals Charitable Association."

She had not intended to say anything to her husband, but suddenly she said it.

"You seem very unhappy, James. Would you like a divorce?"

"My dear, what a dreadful thing to say! Divorce is immoral—it's against my principles. And I'm not unhappy with you, beloved. I'm unhappy because it looks as if I shall go to prison again. And I don't think I shall survive it, this time. I didn't talk much about it before, but——"

"James!" She was terrified. "What have you been doing?"

"Nothing whatever. I backed a bill to help a friend out of a hole. The friend let me down. The bill turned out to be a forgery of some sort—I don't even now understand what happened. We've got to pay up in three days or face the music. And he has bolted."

"How much have you to pay?"

Gleddy had decided on a Napoleonic coup, for the story of the bill to help a friend would not work twice.

"Eight hundred pounds!" As she gasped, he hurried on: "What's the use of talking! You've done enough for me. And you work yourself to the limit. You need a holiday from me—and it'll be for five years or so, this time."

The eight hundred pounds brought the reserve below a thousand. His habits steadily pushed the cost of living above her salary. For the first time the protective instinct weakened and she began to think of herself.

The end was in sight, but as yet she had no idea of what form the end would take. For the immediate present she saw only the need to hold down her new job, in spite of its unpleasant features.

The association held itself at the disposal of any who maintained any living thing for pleasure, and would perform almost any service from paying a pauper's dog licence to photographing a pet cobra. It would make gramophone records of a lion's roar or a cage bird's cheep. The president, though honest and capable in his administration, was a fatuous man with immature tastes and affectations.

He engaged Margaret on the spot.

"And now come and meet your new companions!" He patted her hand, drew her arm through his and held it there while he introduced her to the staff. In a month the hand-patting advanced to knee-patting.

One morning when she had stepped inside the big fireproof safe to file a record he shut the door and imprisoned her for a second or so.

"There now! I've saved your life, my dear! Isn't that worth a kiss?"

Margaret took the kiss, imparting to it a degree of indifference that was definitely embarrassing.

"Ah! Now I think you realise, Mrs. Gleddy, that this was just my little joke to impress on you how dangerous it is to step into that safe without first stepping on this automatic stop. Anything might chance to shut the door on you—that very nice skirt might catch it—and within an hour you would be asphyxiated. Remember that, though you need a key to unlock it, it locks on its own spring."

Her conscious mind forgot the incident—she did not even use the automatic stop. But the president's warning was, in a sense, filed away in her subconsciousness.

In January 1934 the reserve had sunk to four hundred, though she had bluffed James that only a hundred remained. She bluffed and lied quite a lot, these days. In accepting the patting and the

silly, snatched kisses at the office, she had accepted a lowering of
her own standards. There were moods in which she realised that
the reconstruction problem had become a farce.

One evening in February James interrupted one of his own
windy dissertations on bad luck.

"We can't go on like this. We must have money!" he proclaimed.
"That means I shall have to sell the shares I've been telling you
about." A slight hesitation and then: "I wonder if your friend Ramburn would like to buy them."

"I wouldn't care to ask him a favour," she protested.

"Favour! Sweet child, the favour is the other way round. This
time next year, those shares will be worth a thousand pounds—
easily. Because he's your friend I'll let him have them for what I
paid for 'em—that is, two-fifty. No profit to me—only to him."

She was still a little doubtful. He went on:

"Listen darling!" He made it all as clear as noon-day while he
stroked her hair. "If he doesn't jump at it when you have lunch
with him tomorrow I know a round dozen of men who will—at
that knockout price!"

He began to repeat it all with variations: and Margaret, notwithstanding all the other golden opportunities and ground-floor
chances, began to believe him.

The share certificates were in her bag when she met Gerald for
lunch. They would stay there until coffee, which was the time, she
had heard, when men discussed their business.

Before she had been with Gerald five minutes she flushed with
sudden understanding that she was about to perpetrate an insolent
fraud, relying on his personal feeling for her to provide the money
and avert the consequences.

After lunch she parted from him at the restaurant. She felt as if
she had snatched herself from the brink of a precipice. Before going
back to the office she turned into the park. In dumb misery she
faced the fact that she had stultified her womanhood by marrying
James Gleddy.

She took out the share certificates, tore them and dropped them
into a waste bin. Then she went to the bank and drew two hundred
and fifty pounds from the meagre reserve. It did not matter now.
The end was so very near.

5

"That's quick work!" approved Gleddy when she gave him the cash. "You clever, wonderful girl!"

"Yes, aren't I! Spend some of that on me, please James. I'd like a dinner and a show."

"Darling, you're waking up at last! We'll have a gorgeous time." This was a short-lived, intermediate phase, which brought her a certain distraction—the dipsomaniac's final fling. Almost nightly he took her out. He delighted in her company when she encouraged him in idiotic extravagance—was bored and querulous when she behaved as a conscientious housekeeper and breadwinner. It was her fault that, until now, he had spent none of her money on her.

By the end of March the cash was giving out. She had not the funds for any more imaginary transactions, and he apparently could not even lay hands on another parcel of phoney shares.

He began to talk about the subscriptions that flowed into Domestic Animals Charitable Association on Saturday mornings and remained in the office, as the banks closed so early.

"That animal slop is a wicked waste of money that ought to be stopped by law," he asserted. "It's maddening to think of it, when human beings like ourselves are so terribly hard up."

Soon he was unfolding a plan by which he should come to the office and remove the cash. She would then tidy up, and it would be assumed that the office had been burgled while it was deserted for the week-end.

She listened with cold fear—of herself. Very soon, she knew, she would let him talk her over. She would make herself believe his shoddy nonsense about their having a better claim to the money than had the animals. She might even help him in the burglary.

At the next office kiss, she told the president she wanted to ask a favour.

"After you've gone on Saturdays, I get frightened—alone with all that money. If I come up an hour earlier I can get it all listed before you leave—and you can bank it on your way to the station."

When he consented, after making her plead a little, she took another lonely walk in the park. She was even more desperately miserable than on the previous occasion—and again she came to a pivotal conclusion.

In asking for the cash to be banked, she had taken an artificial precaution against her own weakness. She accepted this as the final degradation—the admission that she could not resist James Gleddy. For this she did not blame him. The dipsomaniac does not blame the bottle—but he sometimes smashes it.

"I've worked it out, James," she told him that night, "and I find I couldn't cover the traces. I have a safer plan." When she had secured his attention, she explained: "There's an outside door in the basement giving on to an alley. I'll unlock it and you can come in through the window, and we'll pretend a hold-up man has over-powered me."

"No good, darling! The police always rumble a job like that by the way the knots are tied and so on——"

"Listen! I'm going to be found genuinely unconscious. I learnt a lot about chloroform from a vet. I know how to take just enough for unconsciousness without risk to life. And I know how to make out a chit so that the chemist will sell it to you. And I'll tell you where to buy it."

At twelve-twenty on the morning of Saturday, 6th May 1934, Margaret slithered out of the window and unlocked the outer door that gave on to the alley. At twelve-forty precisely James Gleddy came through the door, wearing thin rubber gloves, and entered the office by the window.

"Splendid, James!" she applauded. "You're bang on time!"

Acting on previous instructions he took from his pockets a stop-pered bottle of chloroform and a handful of cotton wool, which he placed on her desk, and a screw driver, which he retained. He picked up a wad of nine one-pound notes pinned together and a four-shilling postal order and put them in his pocket.

She led him to the big safe, the door of which was ajar.

"Mind you don't upset any of the records," she warned. "The cash is in one of those two little drawers at the top—I don't know which, but it's generally the end one. I'll stand clear and listen."

"I doubt whether the screwdriver will do it from inside the safe," he muttered. "Ought to have brought a tyre lever."

When she heard him scrabbling with the screwdriver, she removed the stopper from the bottle, carefully poured a small quantity of chloroform on to the cotton wool, which she wrapped in a duster.

She glanced at the safe at floor level. The automatic stop was not in action. She crept towards the safe. With her gloved thumb she loosened the stopper and lobbed the bottle inside the safe. Almost before it struck the floor she had slammed the door of the safe. She felt neither horror nor fear, nor any acute desire to escape the consequence of her act. Her main preoccupation was to prevent that door from being opened before James Gleddy was dead. The key was inside the safe, on the floor, where she had placed it before he arrived.

Back through the window to relock the door giving on to the alley. Next she picked up an upright chair, pressed the wooden back of it to her face then dropped herself forward. The wood cut her flesh round the jaw, and the blow dazed her.

In a few minutes she was able to continue her programme. Holding her breath, she tied the duster round her head, after placing the chair sideways on the floor as if she had toppled over while sitting on it.

She removed her gloves, then lay down and inhaled the chloroform. Perhaps she had used too much and it would kill her before she was discovered. She did not care.

Thus the porter found her. In trying to render first aid before rushing to the hospital, he destroyed any evidence which Margaret might have left for Scotland Yard.

At about five o'clock the house surgeon told Margaret that he need do no more for her, and suggested that she was now sufficiently recovered to go home.

A hundred yards away, in the office, the mechanic from Renson's was opening the big safe.

"He's dead—don't touch anything!" shouted the superintendent. He hurried the mechanic from the office while the smell of chloroform mounted. To the sergeant he said:

"Society girl married to a crook! And then this little how d'ye do and the funny business with the key of the safe. I'm going to pass the buck straight to the Yard."

6

Medical evidence but faintly illumined the obvious. Even if the chloroform had been released at once, the deceased could still have

made himself heard by tapping on the wall of the safe with the
screw driver. In his struggles to attract notice the chloroform bottle
might have fallen out of his pocket, its contents greatly accelerating
his death.

The key was found on the floor of the safe, leaving the possibility
that Gleddy, after drugging his wife, had taken the key from the
drawer, opened the safe, removed the key and dropped it when the
door shut on him.

As to how the door had been shut, there was the possibility that
the unconscious woman had fallen against it when she toppled
from the chair. Or Gleddy, through carelessness or alarm, might
have shut the door on himself. 'Misadventure' covered all these
possibilities, singly or in combination.

The contribution of Scotland Yard was limited to the discovery
of unidentified finger-prints on both sides of the door in the basement giving on to the alley, though not on the key which remained
permanently in the lock. The coroner was uninterested in the door,
preferring to believe that Gleddy had slipped by the porter, probably while the latter was dilating on his military service to an unknown passer-by.

Margaret added nothing to the account she had originally given
to the sergeant. Her last vague memory, she said, was of the smell of
chloroform. As to the preceding circumstances, she admitted that she
had described the routine of the office to her husband several
months previously. The president's evidence on the banking of the
cash eliminated suspicion of collusion in the attempted robbery.
Further, the house surgeon testified that she was unconscious when
admitted to the hospital.

"You have told us that deceased came into your room from the
outer office. Did he assault you the moment he came in?"

"No. He said he had come to 'clean up', meaning to steal. He
said I could leave everything tidy and I would never be suspected.
I thought at first he was joking. When he picked up the nine pounds
and the postal order and I threatened to scream, he seized me from
behind. He said, 'I'll make everything quite safe for you—all you
have to do is forget it was me. I know you'll never give me away
once it's done'. Then I kicked him."

It sounded very straightforward. Anyone might guess that Margaret had slammed the door of the safe on a husband who had

wrecked her life—whom she loved so little that she was ready to hand him over to the police. But it remained a guess. There was no means of proving that she had in fact slammed that door. The police, after tracing Gleddy's purchase of the chloroform and the cotton wool, completed their investigations, with negative result. The finger-prints on the door giving on to the alley remained unidentified.

After the inquest, Margaret declined her father's invitation to come straight back to his house. Leaving instructions for the sale of the furniture and her interest in the 'semi-detached with garden', she spent several weeks in a cottage in Kent, the paying guest of a Miss Prinfold, who had been her mother's governess.

This may be called the decontamination period, during which her former scale of values returned. When the Long Vacation came, her father took her to Norway, then to his home in Oxfordshire. The nightmare of her marriage was beginning to grow dim. The murder she put completely out of her mind, until Gerald Ramburn turned up in early September and took her for a walk in the woods.

"How soon shall we get married?" he asked.

As he spoke, she realised that, in four months, she had come to believe that the version she had given police and coroner was the true one, when it was not.

"I don't think we can get married at all, Gerald. I'd like to, but I've changed, without your knowing it. You said something once about James being in the ditch. Well, I fell into the ditch myself. And I feel that—if we were married—it would *show*—if you understand what I mean."

"Of course I understand! You're giving me a hint that you scuppered that feller. You ought to have let me buy him off. No good going into that, now it's all over. How soon shall we get married?"

She put her hand on his arm.

"Are we both quite sane, dear?" she asked. "Do you *really* want to marry me if you *really* think that?"

"*You* were never quite sane, dear. As to me, I turned up that Saturday hoping to collect you for lunch. While I was hanging about, I spotted Gleddy. Saw him turn up that alley and go through that door. Went to see what he was up to. Opened the door myself. It was unlocked. Found myself in that sort of hole-place. Heard you say: 'Splendid, James, you're bang on time.'

Went round to the front to see if one or other of you would come
out. Chatted with the porter for a few minutes, then buzzed off."
He added: "I read the reports."

"But Gerald! For the first time I feel guilty. I think I'd better
go and confess."

"Haven't you made enough mess as it is! Why not tell me it's my
duty as a citizen to denounce you—for doing what I would have
done myself if I could have seen my way clear! Alternatively, how
soon shall we get married?"

Together they had not even the sense of sharing a guilty secret.
The impact of James Gleddy on their joint lives had been a sordid
irrelevance, something so contrary to the current of their thoughts
that it had little place, even in their memory.

They bought a house within a mile of the judge's, where they
lived a normal and happy life—until Margaret won the Ladies' Point-
to-Point challenge cup. When they moved back to their flat in
Bloomsbury, they took the cup with them, and Margaret had her
name added to those of the other winners.

One evening, returning to the flat after seeing Gerald off to
Manchester for a business conference, she noticed that the challenge cup had been moved from its usual place—then that the flat
had been burgled.

She called the police, who asked all the usual questions and took
finger-prints, eliminating those of Margaret and a service maid.
There was one unidentified set, identified the following afternoon
as Gerald Ramburn's. Thus there were no prints at all of the burglar.

The police held out little hope of success. Because it would be
extremely embarrassing to Margaret to be unable to return the
challenge cup, she offered a reward of one hundred pounds. As
metal, the cup was worth barely five.

The reward merely scared the burglar. In two months, during
which no clue had emerged, the case was passed to the Department of Dead Ends. A month later, a railway company's official,
opening a suitcase abandoned in a cloakroom, found what proved
to be the articles burgled from the Ramburns' flat.

Detective-Inspector Rason examined the items. He was reflecting that there was not much chance of obtaining a finger-print
after three months—when a perfect print leapt to his eye, as

visible as if it had been made in plasticine. It was made, in fact, on a clot of shaving-soap on a gold razor case.

"Cor! Happened to put his thumb down bang in the middle of that lovely bit o' soap!" exclaimed Rason. "That's what I call coincidence."

Rason sent the razor case for examination and was duly informed that the print had been matched with an unidentified print found on a basement door adjoining the offices of the Domestic Animals Charitable Association eighteen months previously—which was not in itself helpful.

Following routine, he turned up the dossier of the Gleddy case. The main facts were familiar, but there was something new in a postscript.

'*Margaret Gleddy re-married 15 October 1934, to Gerald Ramburn.*'

"Looks as if that crook follows the girl around!" mused Rason. "He's close at hand when Hubby One is getting his. Then he boots Hubby Two. That's what I call coincid—*hullo!*—two fat coincidences in one case!"

After writing to Gerald Ramburn asking him to call and identify his property, Rason looked up the report of the burglary, to see if he could find any more coincidences.

'*Unidentified print found in dressing room,*' he read. And, in the next line: '*Later identified as print of Gerald Ramburn, owner.*' The photographs of the print were enclosed in the dossier—believed to be of no significance, they had not been passed to the register. There was a final, summarising note.

'*Prints of owner, owner's wife and service maid only.*'

"I'd like to meet this bloke. He doesn't wear gloves the first time—leaves a print on that basement door. When he robs the flat he does wear gloves and he leaves no print. But he suddenly goes haywire, takes off his glove and puts his thumb on that clot of soap—so as to tell me he is the same bloke who went through that basement door." Rason ran his hand through his hair. "That's the worst of being logical—always leads to something damn silly. Meaning to say, the soap print is *not* the print of the burglar."

He picked up the photograph of the print found in the dressing room, identified as that of Gerald Ramburn, and sent it for identification. He was informed that the print was the same as the one

on the razor case, which was the same as the one on the door giving
on to the alley. So he hurried round to see the porter who had been
discussing his medals with a stranger at the relevant time on 6th
May 1934.

Margaret accompanied Gerald to Scotland Yard and was delighted to regain possession of the challenge cup. On their way
through the corridor to Rason's room, the porter had identified
Gerald.

"That settles the burglary," chirped Rason. "And now we can
discuss the murder. Sorry! I mean, I want you both to carry your
minds back to the day when James Gleddy lost his life."

Margaret gasped. Gerald gave no sign.

"At the time when Gleddy was making all the noise he could
inside that safe, you, Mr. Ramburn, were talking to the porter—
about his medals, I think. So the porter heard nothing. As to how
Gleddy got inside that safe—and as to how he got the door shut
on him, with the chloroform and all——"

Rason paused, for again Margaret had registered alarm.

"The door in the basement giving on to the alley," resumed
Rason, "was found by the district police to be locked—at about
one-fifteen. At some time previous to one-fifteen it was unlocked.
You, Mr. Ramburn, entered the well by that door. And you left
the well by that door——"

"I neither admit nor deny anything," cut in Gerald. "I'll talk
to you through a lawyer."

It was one thing to forgive oneself for murdering James Gleddy
—quite another thing to involve Gerald Ramburn.

"My husband," said Margaret, "need neither admit nor deny
anything about that door. I unlocked it to admit Gleddy by arrangement. And I locked it again after I had shut him in the safe."

MARION, COME BACK

The murder of Marion Pinnaker ("Mrs. Pin" in the headlines) was a popular mystery, though the Press hated it. Time was an active factor—the mystery grew more mysterious every week merely because the week had passed. After the first fine flare-up, the papers could neither feed it nor kill it.

The mystery had the added charm of simplicity. There was only one popular suspect—her husband. After a preliminary examination, however, the police showed exasperatingly little interest in him. He had the means and the opportunity and it was simple enough to equip him with most of the traditional motives. His peccadilloes could easily be viewed as depravities. On the other hand, his virtues made it easy to see him as the unfortunate victim of slander.

The Pinnakers lived in a detached, six-room house with garden and garage—named "Hillfoot," by grace of a modest slope—in the dormitory suburb of Honshom, which is thirty-two miles out of London. Nearly all the houses are of the same kind and so are the residents—that is, they present a united front of respectability, neighborliness, and adequacy of income.

In such a neighborhood people tend to know each other's affairs, as well as each other's movements. No one had seen Marion leave home at a relevant time. Within forty-eight hours there were whispers that she had not left the house at all and would shortly be found under the floorboards.

Tom Pinnaker, armed with a degree in commerce, had entered Bettinson's to begin at the bottom. In the furniture department he learned upholstery; in the catering department he acquired knowledge of wines and cold storage. He was in a straight line for managerial rank when his father died and he took over a small but steady house agency in central London specializing in the renting of small office suites.

The Pinnakers were a little better off than most of their neighbors because, in the second year of their marriage, Marion inherited twenty thousand pounds. She had placed half with her husband for investment. Although this money loomed large in the case there was never anything wrong with Tom Pinnaker's accounts. His losses were due strictly to bungling.

The legacy had come as a surprise—at least, to Tom. It had been a marriage of mutual attraction—which is itself a bit of a mystery because their temperaments were so different. Marion was no glamour girl, to stampede a man's judgment. Among the millions who saw her photograph on television, opinion seemed to be divided—which means that she was attractive to some and not to others. Her face suggested a grave young woman who could be gay, but with the gaiety of a family gathering. A domesticated woman, one would say —remembering that domesticity is highly esteemed by men of many different kinds.

Pinnaker loved his home. He also loved his wife, in his fashion, and was proud of her rigid code of morals: after five years of marriage he would not have changed her for any other kind of woman. Not that he despised all the other kinds. One's character, he told himself, had many facets. There was the facet that had enjoyed fun and games with a business girl in London—doing no harm, he convinced himself, to anybody. And at Honshom there had been—and still was—Freda Culham.

Except for occasional nights in London and sometimes a weekend—attributed to the social demands of clients—his habits were regular: he would never leave home earlier than nine, nor return earlier than six thirty.

Routine was broken on the afternoon of Tuesday, January 5, 1954, when he arrived home a few minutes before three. The official police narrative begins with his entering his house at three. But we can profitably go back one hour—to two o'clock, when Mrs. Harker, the domestic help, entered the sitting room to report that she had finished her work and was going home.

Mrs. Pinnaker, she said, was not dressed—meaning that she was wearing an overall over skirt and sweater, and house shoes. She was sitting at the writing table handling "funny looking papers" (which turned out to be Bearer Bonds) which she was placing one by one in a small attaché case.

Mrs. Harker was conscientiously rude to anyone in a higher income bracket than her own. When she eventually appeared on television she snapped and snarled at the interviewer, expressed her feelings freely without regard to her briefing, and was a huge success. She had a deep regard for Marion.

"You only picked at that grilled sole and I know it was done just as you like it," she grumbled. "To say nothing of the veal cutlets yesterday! And you're thinner than looks healthy. It's not my business, dear, but why don't you see a doctor?"

"There's nothing wrong with me, Mrs. Harker." Marion rarely used first names and never called anybody "dear." "I've been advised to —well, to take a sort of holiday."

"Good advice, too! Take it. I'll manage here all right." She noticed a sealed envelope on the television set. "D'you want that letter posted?"

"No, thanks. It's—"

"Then, if there's nothing else, I'll be off."

"Just a minute, Mrs. Harker." From a drawer in the writing table Marion took out a small jeweler's case, opened it, and displayed a diamond brooch. "On your daughter's wedding day—next Saturday isn't it?—I want you to give her this. That is, if you think she'd like it."

Mrs. Harker protested at the munificence of the gift.

"Don't think about it like that. But if you feel you must, just remind yourself that you've done much more for us than you were paid for. And now you must hurry or you'll miss your bus."

That incident could be interpreted as a kind of farewell; but the important point is that the bus touched its stopping point on schedule, at two twelve, and that Mrs. Harker caught it.

A few minutes later Freda Culham turned up. Instead of leaving her car on the street, as would be usual, she drove in. A postman happened to notice the car—satisfactorily identified—standing between the kitchen door and the garage, within five minutes of half-past two.

Freda provided a triangle motive for those who felt that the mystery would be incomplete without it—though there is evidence that

Tom Pinnaker had no ambition to make Freda his wife. She was the daughter of a professor and the widow of a test pilot who, between them, had left her enough to live by herself in her own house in Honshom. A lively brunette in her middle twenties, with no occupation.

She records that she came in a friendly spirit to admit that she had fallen in love with Tom Pinnaker, to apologize for causing scandal, and to express the hope that she had not given Marion any pain. She may have dressed it up like that, but it is unlikely. She was untroubled with anything resembling a social conscience. To her, marriage meant little more than a formal announcement that you intended to live with somebody until further notice.

The conversation took place in the hall, both women standing. Freda towered over Marion but otherwise was at a disadvantage. Indeed her friendliness, if any, was wasted on Mrs. Pinnaker.

"I think, Mrs. Culham, you are about to suggest that we should arrange a divorce. I am sorry that I cannot agree. For reasons which you would not appreciate I would in no circumstances whatever divorce my husband."

There were arguments by Freda, unanswered by Marion, but our present concern is that Freda had left the house before Tom Pinnaker arrived at three o'clock.

His account of his movements on entering the house has an unusual crispness. He did not claim a mental "blackout" nor any clouding of memory. He said that he entered the house by the kitchen door, shouted that he had come home. Receiving no answer, he went into the sitting room where his eye was caught by an envelope, propped up on the television set. It was addressed *Tom*, in Marion's handwriting. This made him quite certain that Marion had left him. He put the note, unopened, in his pocket. This was not absent-mindedness. He was positive, he said, that he knew the substance of what his wife had written.

At ten past three he was speaking on the telephone to his bank manager in London. That morning he had asked for the loan of one thousand pounds, promising that his wife would provide the necessary collateral.

"Infernal luck—my wife has been called away to a sick relation. I want you to ring James Roden, manager of the branch here. He's secretary of our tennis club and a personal friend—he will confirm my statement to you that my wife has securities of her own to the value of at least ten thousand pounds. Deposited with him."

At three forty the local bank manager, Roden, rang Hillfoot. He first asked for Marion, and was told about the sick relation.

"Look, Pin. I've just had a call from your branch in London. I'm sorry, but I can't help at all."

"That's all right, Jim. I know you can't talk about clients' affairs. But you did not deny that you hold securities of Marion's?"

"I did deny it—I had to! Marion closed her account here yesterday."

These two conversations on the telephone were much quoted as indicating that Pinnaker must have been telling the truth when he asserted that Marion had left the house before three. But those who preferred The Floorboards Theory suggested that, as soon as he came in, he asked her to provide securities, that when she refused he lost his temper and killed her, probably without intending to, and that the telephone talks were a blind.

When Mrs. Harker brought his breakfast tray on the following morning she ignored his greeting and glared at him.

"Is she coming back today?"

"If you mean Mrs. Pinnaker—no. I expect her to be away for at least a fortnight." He sat down and opened the newspaper. "You might get her room done this morning, then we can lock it up until she comes back."

"And another thing, Mr. Pinnaker! You let the furnace out last night. D'you want me to light it?"

"No, thanks. There's no sense in keeping the house heated night and day—I shall be home very little. I'll use the stoves. You can keep warm in the kitchen, can't you?"

Pinnaker had reached the marmalade stage when Mrs. Harker returned.

"Where has she gone?"

"At the moment, I don't know. She didn't leave word. I expect she'll telephone during the day. What's upsetting you, Mrs. Harker?"

"Her luggage, Mr. Pinnaker! She didn't take any. You can't count that little attaché case that wouldn't hold any clothes. Her suitcases are in the glory-hole under the stairs. *All* her clothes are in her room. She must have gone out on that bitter day in just an overall and jumper. No furs. No coat. Wearing those blue house shoes with soles like paper."

Pinnaker was unable to suggest an explanation.

"I know what might have happened, Mr. Pinnaker—but I won't say I believe it did."

"Let's have it, Mrs. Harker—straight from the shoulder."

"That old Buick you've been trying to sell. If somebody brought it back again yesterday afternoon she might have got straight in and driven herself away without thinking what she was doing. And small wonder after all she's been through!"

"No good! I sold the Buick on Monday. That reminds me—I must send a receipt and the log—"

"Never mind that now!" Mrs. Harker nerved herself to ask the crucial question. Her words crept out in a near whisper.

"What've you done to her?"

"A great deal that I ought not to have done, Mrs. Harker, and I'm ashamed." He was playing for sympathy and getting it. "Most of it was through thoughtlessness, but that's no excuse. As a result, she has left me. I didn't want anybody to know because I hoped she would return in a week or two. I still hope she will. I didn't want you to know, so I tried to dodge your questions. For that I apologize."

"You haven't done *me* any harm. But you must have upset her extra special and driven the poor girl off her head. People must have turned round and stared at her—going out in an overall in January! She may have caught pneumonia and that's why she hasn't telephoned for her clothes. Or had an accident. Or lost her wits. What about asking the police to ask the hospitals?"

With some reluctance Pinnaker consented, provided Mrs. Harker would come with him.

"I want you to back me up. Tell them everything you know—especially that bit about her not taking any of her clothes. Between us we must convince the police that it's not a case of a wife walking off with a lover. They'll pay more attention to you than to me."

The nearest police station was in the town of Kingbiton, four miles Londonward. Pinnaker gave a brief outline to the superintendent—not mentioning the clothes—then left Mrs. Harker with him and drove on to his office.

Mrs. Harker returned by bus and put in a couple of hours work at Hillfoot. In that time she thoroughly cleaned and tidied Marion's bedroom. Before she left at two o'clock she had answered one caller in person and four inquiries by telephone. In sum, she told the neighborhood that she did not know where Mrs. Pinnaker had gone, how long she would be away, nor when she had left. These statements met and clashed with the bank manager's information about a sick relation.

In the early evening there were more inquiries, some containing a trap, in which Pinnaker was invariably caught.

Kingbiton had forwarded a report to Missing Persons, Scotland Yard. By midday on Thursday they had picked up the local gossip which tended to feature Freda Culham. But it was the sudden closing of Marion's banking account that brought Chief Inspector Karslake to Hillfoot on Friday morning. Adding Mrs. Harker's testimony of Marion Pinnaker leaving home in an overall and house shoes, Karslake was ready to explore the possibilities of The Floorboards Theory.

2

Karslake was invited to the most comfortable chair, nearest the electric stove. He was using his frank approach which was so often successful, perhaps because the frankness was genuine.

"It all adds up to what my missis would call queer goings-on. You've given contradictory explanations to different persons. We don't care tuppence about that. At this minute we're starting from scratch. Your wife disappeared on the afternoon of Tuesday the fifth. Will you begin there?"

"I'll have to start a bit further back." Pinnaker was rising to the occasion. "My wife and I had differences, but I did not want to break up. Let it be granted—I don't admit it, you understand—but let it be granted that I had given her cause to divorce me. She was very upset about it. Her religious views prevent her from entertaining the idea of divorce. In a nutshell, she said that she intended to desert me for the statutory three years. At the end of that time I could divorce her if I wished. If I preferred to resume our married life she would have had the three years in which to decide whether she would wish to do so."

"Plenty of others have done that," commented Karslake. "But she didn't have to run away and hide. It's legal desertion if she simply refuses to live under the same roof."

"She knew all that—she's a very knowledgeable woman. She insisted that it must be a genuine desertion, not a mere legal formula. She said she would go away in such a manner that I would not be able to find her. Her angle is that she has an inner need to change her way of living—sort of go into cold storage for three years. I knew it would be very awkward for me. For one thing, our financial arrangements are interlocked—"

"But why did she have to sneak out of the house? Without a change of clothes. Without even an overcoat."

"I just can't make it sound sensible!" Pinnaker was being frank, too.

"Any witnesses to the desertion story?"

"N-no—unless you count Marion herself as a witness." From his pocket case he produced the envelope addressed *Tom*. "I found it on the TV set when I came home that afternoon."

"The flap is stuck down," snapped Karslake.

"Yes—yes, it is!" Pinnaker was apologetic. "I may seem rather callous, but the fact is I had other things to attend to at the time and it slipped my memory. Perhaps you would prefer to open it yourself?"

Slipped his memory! A bit off-beat thought Karslake, as he thumbed the envelope open.

" 'Dear Tom,' " he read aloud. " 'At your request, I hereby put on record that I intend to desert you, in the moral as well as the legal sense, for the statutory period of three years. During that time I shall not communicate with you and shall make it impossible for you to communicate with me.' "

Karslake looked up. "That confirms her intention to desert you," he admitted.

"The next bit is more important, at the moment," said Pinnaker.

" 'I cannot take seriously,' " read Karslake, " 'your suggestion that you might be accused of murdering me. If such a fantastic thing were to happen, I would be certain to hear of it and you cannot believe that I would remain in seclusion and allow you to be convicted. Marion Pinnaker.' "

Karslake asked the obvious question:

"Did you dictate this letter?"

"I didn't actually dictate it. I wrote out the first paragraph for her, but I only made a note about the murder stuff. As a matter of fact, I added a bit about there being no ill-feeling on either side. I wish she had put that in."

Karslake blinked. Here was a frankness of heroic proportions. He studied the handwriting. It might be genuine. Pinnaker's tale might be true. In fact—a few hours later—the science department reported that the letter had not been forged.

"This letter," said Karslake, "answers all the questions before I've asked 'em. And tidies up all the loose ends—why she put all her money into Bearer Bonds, why she slipped away without anyone seeing her, why she took no clothes, not wanting to be traced through her luggage."

"Yes," said Pinnaker reflectively. "I think it does cover everything."

"Everything *except*—" Karslake reached for the ashtray "—when and how she left this house."

"Is that so important, Inspector?"

"Between you and me, Mr. Pinnaker, I don't suppose it matters a damn!" Karslake laughed and Pinnaker laughed too. "But as you probably know, we work by formula in these cases. Missing Wife. First thing: Has the husband salted her away under the floorboards? Yes—No. See what I mean?"

"Exactly!" chortled Pinnaker. "That's why I got her to write that letter." He was opening the door. "This house has an attic—you don't want to go up there, do you?"

"It's in the book," grinned Karslake. "Work downwards from roof to foundations."

The attics were a feature of these houses, as they were often required as extra rooms. On the upper landing Pinnaker stopped at a cupboard-like structure.

"Good lord, it's cold up here!" Pinnaker shivered. "I'm not sure I know how to work this thing. I've only been up there once—the week we moved in. We use the attic only for storage."

Karslake found the lever which opened the cupboard, whereupon a fanciful stepladder changed into position. Pinnaker went up and opened the trapdoor. Karslake followed. Conspicuous among a litter of household articles were two cabin trunks and three old suitcases, which proved to be empty.

Back on the upper landing, they contemplated five doors.

"The bathroom. The etcetera. And this is the guest room."

Karslake's eye was drawn to the bed by a gaudy coverlet barely covering the mattress which was evidently too big for it. When he went to the curtained recess he noticed an electric cord leading from an outlet in the wall to the mattress itself.

"The Allwhen mattress," exclaimed Pinnaker, the house-proud husband. "See that flex? It heats the mattress in winter. Nothing new in that. But look at this switch. Turn it to 'C' and a thermal unit draws out the air between the springs. Ventilates it: uses heat to make you cooler."

He whipped off the coverlet, laid himself full length on the bed, and would have expounded the hygienics of sleep if Karslake had been willing to listen.

The next room was smaller.

"Dressing room," said Pinnaker. "I'm sleeping in it now."

Pinnaker produced a bedroom key and unlocked the next door. "This is—was—our—her room."

Karslake noted twin beds stripped of bedclothes. Each was equipped with an Allwhen mattress, wired to a double outlet between the beds. He examined a wardrobe, a built-in cupboard, and a curtained corner, all containing clothes. As he flicked the curtain back, the draught dislodged a folded sheet of paper which had been lying flush with the skirting board.

"Looks like a bill," said Pinnaker.

"It's a railway ticket—bought on January second from an agent in Kingbiton—from Honshom to York, via London, first class. Journey dated for January fifth—last Tuesday. What d'you make of that, Mr. Pinnaker?"

"That she had planned beforehand to leave here on the Tuesday," answered Pinnaker. "But she cannot have planned to start at Honshom station in an overall and house shoes. Something went wrong with her plans. I can't understand it."

"I don't have to understand it—yet," said Karslake. "Anyway, she didn't go near Honshom station—we've checked."

Pinnaker re-locked the door before following the Inspector down the stairs.

"The sitting room you've seen. This is the dining room. The other is what we call my study. And there's the kitchen and scullery."

Karslake took the two living rooms first. In the kitchen he

opened the cupboards, looked about, hesitated, then went through the scullery to the outhouse. The garden had been examined in Pinnaker's absence.

Back in the kitchen, Karslake pointed at the floor in the direction of the window:

"What's that?"

"I can't see what you're pointing at."

Karslake strode forward, then folded back the linoleum which was loose.

"Dammit, Inspector!" Pinnaker laughed grimly. "When you talked about putting wives under floorboards I thought you were joking."

"So did I!" said Karslake. "I didn't know then that these boards had been taken up. Look at that nail there—and this one."

"Oh, yes, I remember now!" exclaimed Pinnaker. "A little while ago we had a scare about dry rot."

"Good enough," said Karslake. "We'll check on the dry rot."

He went to the front door and whistled. Three men got out of the police car, one carrying a tool bag and the other a pick and spade.

Very shortly, Karslake joined Pinnaker in the sitting room.

"Found anything, Inspector?"

"It'll take them about half an hour. While we're waiting, you and I can pick up the loose ends."

Again the two men sat amicably by the stove. Karslake put a number of routine questions, watching Pinnaker for signs of strain. The answers were satisfactory, although Pinnaker invariably was unable to offer a witness.

"After you found your wife gone on Tuesday afternoon, did you leave the house before Wednesday morning?"

"Yes. And here at last I happen to have a witness—or rather, collateral evidence." Pinnaker passed an official-looking paper. "I found this waiting when I got home this evening. Summons for parking without lights at ten thirty that night—Tuesday, January fifth—at Shoreham. The Association will represent me and pay the fine."

"Shoreham-*on-Sea*?" said Karslake. "What might you have been doing at the seaside in the middle of a cold winter's night?"

"I don't know. I think I went there with the idea of—of drowning myself—"

He broke off as one of Karslake's men knocked and entered.
"No dry rot, sir. And nothing else. The whole area is undisturbed. Washout!"

"If I may butt in, Inspector," said Pinnaker, "would your staff be kind enough to put everything back? Mrs. Harker is a prickly customer."

"That's all right—we're all house-trained." When they were alone Karslake added, "You were telling me what you did at Shoreham-on-Sea.

Pinnaker looked unhappy.

"Forgive me, Inspector, but this does strike me as rather nightmarish. Floorboards are out of it, so we jump into my car and drive into a jungle of revolting possibilities. Did I dump my unhappy wife in the sea? If so the currents will probably bring her back, though we can't be certain about it, can we? In the hours of darkness I could have covered a large slice of country. The Sussex Downs, for instance—there are lots of dull corners no one ever visits. In Surrey, in the unbuilt parts of the Wey valley, there are innumerable, meaningless little ponds. Hampshire and Bucks are pockmarked with abandoned gravel pits. There are probably at least a hundred disused wells within fifty miles of this house—any one of which I might have used. I mean, your checking technique can hardly cover all that territory, can it?"

"Give the poor old technique a chance," Karslake was genuinely amused. "You tell me where you went in your car that night and I'll do my best to check it."

Pinnaker shook his head.

"Sorry, Inspector! I sincerely thank you for doing an unpleasant job in a thoroughly pleasant way. But, honestly, I've had enough of it. I propose to settle the whole matter myself by getting in touch with my wife."

"That certainly would settle it," admitted Karslake. "You think you can find her without our help?"

"*With* the help you've already given," corrected Pinnaker. "I'm sure I could interest a newspaper in this garish incident of the floorboards. And all that checking. And my journey after dark in the car. It will be clear to Marion that I am under suspicion and I am confident she will keep her word and come forward."

3

This chronicle can give no more than the barest outline of the publicity campaign, which stands by itself in the history of crime reportage and commentary. Its uniqueness lies in the fact that a man, suspected of murder, voluntarily discarded the protection afforded him by the law. Pinnaker told a conference of reporters that he wanted his wife to know that he was suspected of having murdered her. So he authorized them to work up all the facts in his disfavor and color them with the strong suggestion of guilt. He co-operated generously, refusing payment for his services.

In an open letter to Marion—front page, center—Pinnaker wrote:

"After the police had torn up the floorboards in the kitchen and searched the foundations to see if I had buried you in the manner of Crippen, they asked me—very fairly—to account for a 'journey' in the car during the hours of darkness. It was no journey, Marion. It was a melancholy escape from the loneliness of what had been our home. I can remember only that I drove to the sea—I hardly know why. Everything else is a blank. There are many who believe that I threw your dead body into the sea, or disposed of it somewhere in the countryside."

That may be taken as typical of the directly personal appeal he made in print and on the air. There was always just a touch of resentment in references to the floorboards incident. The rest was extremely fair-minded. The journey by night was the main feature. The sea would be dragged in, rather vaguely, without mention of Shoreham—emphasis being on the gravel pits and the disused wells. And always the moral was rubbed in—that there was such a strong *prima facie* case against Pinnaker that it was Marion's duty to come forward—alternatively the duty of anyone who had seen her to report to the police.

On Sunday the first sightseers came to gape at Hillfoot and wander into the garden, whereupon Pinnaker was given a police guard. The only personal friend to seek admittance was Freda Culham.

"This is wonderful of you—I shall never forget it!" exclaimed Pinnaker. "But I wish you had thought of yourself for once. The scandalmongers will make the most of your coming here."

"Darling! I'm in the scandal up to my neck. I'm The Other Woman in the Case—didn't you know? So let's be scandalous in comfort!"

"For one thing," persisted Pinnaker, "we should both feel rather awkward if Marion were to walk in while you're here."

There was a long silence before Freda said:

"Tom! On that Tuesday afternoon I was in this house with Marion until about a quarter to three."

"Good *lord!*" It was the first Pinnaker had heard of it. "She must have rushed out of the house as soon as you had left. Do the police know you were here?"

"I don't think anyone knows. I drove in and parked beside the garage." She then described her talk with Marion.

"A quarter to three!" exclaimed Pinnaker. "And yet you stand by me! Just like you—you refuse to believe that I killed her!"

She came close, put her hands on his shoulders. Perhaps at this moment it occurred to him that Freda was one of those women who make excellent mistresses but impossible wives.

"It would be all the same if I did believe you had killed her. She was playing dog-in-the-manger and deserved it. I hated her."

"You don't mean that, Freda! Not if I killed Marion!"

"Of course I mean it, silly boy! I don't know how soon we can get married, and it doesn't matter. When all this police business has blown over—"

"If you don't stop, I shall be sick." He pushed her away. "It's a perfectly revolting idea!"

The quarrel developed on conventional lines, leading to the conventional threat.

"It's the first time I've been thrown down, Tom, and it hurts. Aren't you afraid I might hit back?"

"No, darling!" He laughed. "Tell the police you were alone in the house with Marion—that she refused your demand for divorce and made you angry—a big strong woman like you who could tuck *her* under your arm. Tell them your car was parked next to the kitchen door. Tell them you left a few minutes before I entered the empty house."

She was so frightened that he had to water it down.

"I am only warning you that people may think you took her away in *your* car. It fits the facts. I am not suggesting you killed her—it's not your style. Besides, Marion is sure to come forward—probably tomorrow, certainly during the week."

But Marion did not come forward during the week—nor the week after.

Pinnaker, the home-lover, adapted his habits to circumstance. His attempt to economize on fuel had been abandoned after three days and the house was nearly as comfortable as ever, thanks to Mrs. Harker.

In the third week the publicity simmered down. Uninvited, he called on Karslake at Scotland Yard.

Karslake was not very genial.

"The ballyhoo has not produced your wife, Mr. Pinnaker."

"It has been a disappointment," confessed Pinnaker, "a humiliation! Some of my neighbors are cutting me. I shall have to resign from the committee of the tennis club. But I shall have one more try—on my own."

Karslake showed no curiosity.

"The newspapers," continued Pinnaker, "have written themselves dry—they have no new facts. Marion has not responded to facts. But she may respond to—sentiment. It was suggested to me that I should write a book—a history of our marriage and an appeal to Marion to return. Under the title *Marion, Come Back*. What do you think of the idea?"

"Nothing!" said Karslake. "The only advice I can give you, Mr. Pinnaker, is this: if you think of changing your address, be sure to let us know well in advance."

"There won't be any change of address. I shall have to stay in Honshom and live down the feeling against me—for the full period of three years. After all, my wife promised to come forward if I were in danger of *conviction*. Subject, of course, to your correction, Inspector—I am *not* in danger of conviction."

He was in no danger of conviction on the facts possessed by the police. In the next couple of months no new facts emerged, and the files subsided into the Department of Dead Ends. . . .

4

The Department of Dead Ends could reopen a case only at a tangent—when a ripple from one crime intersected the ripple from another. In May 1955—sixteen months after Marion Pinnaker's disappearance—Detective Inspector Rason was investigating a case of suspected arson in which, among many other things, an old Buick car had been burned out. The car's log had been burned too, but he was informed that the car had been bought second-hand from a Mr. Bellamy, who lived at Shoreham-on-Sea.

Mr. Bellamy confirmed the sale and added, "I myself bought it second-hand—from a man named Pinnaker. The man who was supposed to have murdered his wife. You remember? Just about the time it all happened, too."

That, thought Rason, was the sort of remark that often led to business. He went through the files of the Pinnaker case. The car sequence showed Pinnaker's admission of the drive by night—to Shoreham-on-Sea. Checked by Karslake on the summons for parking. Checked that the number of the car on the summons was that of a Buick car owned by Pinnaker. That tidied that up. What a pity!

Rason was putting the file away when he remembered to check the license numbers himself.

Number of the Buick car checked by Karslake: PGP421. Number of the burned out Buick: PGP421. The same car!

Nothing in that, thought Rason gloomily. Coincidence that Pinnaker should have happened to drive to Shoreham-on-Sea. Perhaps to clinch the sale of the car to Bellamy? In which case Bellamy might be able to throw some light on Pinnaker's movements that night. Just worth a ring on the chance of showing Chief Inspector Karslake he had missed something.

"Mr. Bellamy, sorry to trouble you again. On the night of Tuesday, January fifth, 1954, did Mr. Pinnaker drive in that Buick to see you at Shoreham?"

"No. I don't think he knows I live here—I dealt with him at his office. Anyhow, he couldn't have driven anywhere in that car on the Tuesday because he delivered it to me the previous day—Monday, the fourth."

Rason perceived only that there had been a tangle of dates.

"One more question if you don't mind, Mr. Bellamy. Did you have any trouble with the police over parking without lights that Tuesday night?—the fifth of January."

"It's funny you should ask. I did park without lights. And when I was going home I saw a chit fixed on the wiper, warning me that I would be reported. But I never got the summons. It just occurs to me, Mr. Rason, that Pinnaker may have got that summons. He delivered the car on Monday but I didn't receive the log from him

until the Thursday, so the registration was still in his name."
Rason thanked him effusively. Already he was making wild
guesses, all pivoting on his mental pictures of Freda Culham, Mrs.
Harker, and Pinnaker himself, none of whom he had ever seen. He
called at Pinnaker's office, posing as a prospective client. He was
disappointed when he visited Freda Culham, who didn't seem to
believe that he had once studied under her late father. And Mrs.
Harker was very rude to him but unwittingly propped up the juiciest
of his guesses.

The next step was to obtain Chief Inspector Karslake's consent to
go ahead—usually a tricky business.

"You've got something there!" said Karslake, when Rason had
told him the tale of the "two" cars. "But not very much!" he added in
his most deflating style. "Pinnaker lied about the night ride. Maybe
he didn't leave the house at all that night. That doesn't make him a
killer."

"Let's try it the other way round," Rason was holding himself in.
"You get a tip-off that Pinnaker may have scuppered his wife and
buried her at home. You search the house and you find no stiff.
O-kay! You're all smiles and apologies for troubling him. How does
he react?"

"He didn't."

"Just so! When you tell Pinnaker he's in the clear, does he say
'cheers!'—like anybody else? No! He says, 'Mr. Karslake, don't be
too sure I haven't murdered my wife, just because you found nothing under the floorboards! I went out for a long drive as soon as it
was dark. How d'you know I didn't take the body along and dump
it? He didn't use those words but that's what it adds up to. And now
we know the midnight ride was a lie!"

"But not necessarily a killer's lie!"

"What's more," persisted Rason, ignoring the interruption, "Pinnaker flashed that parking summons to fake evidence that he had
driven to the *sea!*"

"It doesn't surprise me as much as you'd think," said Karslake.
"Take that letter the wife was supposed to have left behind for him.
She wrote it herself, all right. But it was a darned funny letter. And
that business about the way she was dressed—going out in winter in
her indoor rig—that was darned funny too!"

"Which is the funny bit?" asked Rason.

"That book of his. Story of his married life—might have been almost anybody's married life. Yet it sold a half a million copies. And one of the Sunday papers printed about half of it in bits each week. Must have brought him thousands of pounds. He talks soft, but he's no softie."

Rason had missed the cash angle on the book. It took most of the wind out of his sails.

"Anything else?" asked Karslake.

"Mrs. Harker, for instance," said Rason with his customary irrelevance. "She's what I call a tower of strength. D'you know she nearly sacked herself because Pinnaker wouldn't let her use the furnace to keep the place warm? That was about the time when you made your examination of the house—sir!"

"Furnace? There was nothing in the furnace."

"Just so!" chirped Rason. "There was nothing in the furnace— when there ought to've been—*if* you understand me."

"I don't!" snapped Karslake. "One thing at a time! Tie him down on that car story of his and we'll charge him with creating a public mischief by misleading the police."

Pinnaker was making a very good job of living down the scandal. True, he could not appear at the tennis club, but a minority were ready to pass the time of day at a chance meeting. The police had left him unmolested. He had never been seen with Freda Culham and it was obvious that their friendship had ended. Mrs. Harker stood by him. Some believed that Marion would reappear at the end of the three-year period. His habits were as regular as ever except that he was frequently away from home on week-ends. There were two sides to every question—and so on.

Pinnaker showed no recognition of Rason when the latter gave his name, but he greeted Karslake as an old acquaintance.

The police rarely have a personal animosity against a suspect unless he gives them personal cause. They accepted his offer of a drink. A little small talk passed. Then Rason opened—and in a manner that shocked his superior.

"A few days ago, Mr. Pinnaker, I talked to a Mr. Bellamy—the man who bought your old Buick. The short of it is we know now that your tale about going out after dark to Shoreham-on-Sea is all punk. You never left the house that night."

Karslake registered unease. Rason rippled on:

"That drive by night! Corpse in the car or *not,* according to taste! What was the idea, Mr. Pinnaker?"

"There was no idea—I acted on the spur of the moment. A childish impulse. And this is where I lose face." He made an appealing gesture which had no effect.

"Listen, please! It was obvious that Mr. Karslake believed me to be innocent of any criminal act. So when he started to search the house I did not take it seriously. To me, it was like a parlor game—I'll be the Murderer and you be the Detective! Without any effort, I began to identify myself with all the men who had murdered their wives and hidden their bodies. I tingled with fear. I felt guilty—in the sense that an actor can feel guilty while he is playing a murderer. I got a tremendous thrill out of it."

"Yes, but what about that car story?" pressed Rason.

"Wait! Mr. Karslake and I came downstairs. The whole experience was ending rather tamely—when Mr. Karslake spotted that the floorboards in the kitchen had been taken up recently. I told him about the dry rot—and he did not believe me! Quite suddenly, he saw me as a murderer who had concealed his wife's body under the floorboards. Floorboards, by heaven! Crippen! *Me!* It was wonderful! I had never felt so stimulated in my life. We sat in this room. Mr. Karslake asked me some questions to help him 'build up the case'—which I knew would be shattered in half an hour when the men found no body.

"Like a dope addict, I wanted more—and at once. I remembered that summons for parking—I knew it was intended for Bellamy—but I couldn't resist the temptation. With the summons to back up a car story I could go on playing the role of suspected man—living under a hanging sword that could never possibly fall. To you no doubt it sounds silly—perhaps even contemptible. I do not defend myself—and I suppose it's no good apologizing now."

Both Karslake and Rason had dealt with psychopaths who try to get themselves suspected for the sake of the thrill. Their silence encouraged Pinnaker to keep talking.

"My wife disappeared on the Tuesday afternoon, if you remember. By midday on Wednesday, Mrs. Harker's well-meant chatter had alerted half the neighborhood. If there had been a corpse in the house I couldn't possibly have moved it later than Wednesday morn-

ing—I couldn't have moved a dead rabbit without everybody knowing. Therefore I had to create suspicion of my actions on the Tuesday evening."

"So it was just a jolly prank!" exclaimed Rason. "Was Mrs. Pinnaker playing, too? That letter she wrote about coming forward if
you were in danger? Was that part of the prank?"

"Certainly not!"

"We needn't go into that now," snapped Karslake.

"My superior officer," said Rason, nodding at Karslake, "is more
interested in how and when Mrs. Pinnaker left this house. He
won't tie you to that tale about her going away dressed in house
clothes and nothing else but ten thousand quid in a brief case."

"To the best of my belief that is what she did."

"Come. Mr. Pinnaker! If she was excited or absent-minded she'd
have been pulled up by the cold before she reached the gate. And
if she was out of her mind and started walking away to nowhere,
how far would she get in this suburb where pretty nearly everybody
knows her? Dressed like that in January, she'd have been as
conspicuous as if she'd been got up as a fan dancer. Yet no one saw
her."

"I have nothing to add," said Pinnaker.

"Then I'll add a bit," retorted Rason. "Your wife did *not* leave
the house that Tuesday. Something went wrong with your plans.
And she didn't leave that Wednesday nor that Thursday nor that
Friday. Your wife was in this house when my superior officer
searched it!"

"You needn't answer that, Mr. Pinnaker," said Karslake. "It's
ridiculous!"

Rason grinned at his senior. "Did you look under the beds—sir?"

Both men stared at him.

"Under the beds!" Rason repeated. "All those jokes about burglars
under the bed—as if any burglar would be such a fool! It's such a
damn silly place to hide anyone—living or dead—that when you
come to think of it, it's rather a good place."

For a moment Karslake was doubtful.

"I was looking for a corpse—"

"And the corpse had to be under the floorboards!" cut in Rason.

"—I wasn't looking for a living woman. Come to that, she could have stayed in the attic while Mrs. Harker was here in the mornings. And dodged about while I was searching the house—"

"Could she? Let's try it—if Mr. Pinnaker doesn't mind."

Again they began with the attic. On the top landing, the built-in ladder clanged into position and clanged back again when Karslake decided that no woman, however slight, could have remained hidden in the attic.

"She couldn't have dodged from one room while I was in another and slipped up to the attic, because I would have heard that ladder." Glaring at Rason, he added, "If she *was* in this house when I searched it, she must have been in one of the rooms on this landing."

He opened the nearest door, which was that of the guest room.

"There you are! I didn't look under that bed because I can see under it from the doorway."

"Quite right!" agreed Rason, himself stepping into the room and examining the bed. "So this is the Allwhen mattress!" He observed the flex running from the mattress to an outlet in the wall. "Hot and cold laid on. Mrs. Harker told me about 'em—said they were unhealthy because—"

He was talking to himself. The others had inspected the smaller room and he joined them in the corridor.

"This is the big room," Pinnaker was saying. "It was—our room. It has not been in use since she left." The hint was not taken by Karslake. So Pinnaker produced a single key on a pocket chain, then opened the door.

The windows were shut and the room had a disagreeable mustiness. The twin beds were as Karslake had last seen them except for a slight film of dust. Pinnaker was chattering like an anxious host. He observed that Rason's eye was on one of the mattresses.

"That's the Allwhen mattress. By means of an insulated—"

"Yes, I've been told how they work," interrupted Rason and turned to Karslake.

"You've heard me speak of my niece—"

"Tell Mr. Pinnaker some other time," scowled Karslake.

"She's a fair-sized young woman. I measured her yesterday. Not for roundness—for thickness. Meaning the highest point of her when she's lying flat on the sitting-room floor. A shade over nine inches, she made."

He strode to the nearer bed, unfolded a pocket rule, and measured the sides of the Allwhen mattress.

"Ten inches thick," he announced. He folded the pocket rule. "Mrs. Pinnaker was a small woman, wasn't she?"

"Five foot three—and slender," answered Pinnaker.

"Small enough to fit easily inside one of these mattresses—in which case Mr. Karslake would probably have missed it, having his mind on floorboards."

"I don't think a skilled eye could be deceived—nor even an unskilled one," said Pinnaker indulgently. "If you remove the springs and the insulation and the cold air conduit, you have little more than a canvas bag. The silhouette of a human being—"

"There'd be no silhouette if she'd been packed in nicely by a skilled upholsterer. When you were a youngster at Bettinson's, Mr. Pinnaker, you learned upholstery, didn't you?"

"True!" answered Pinnaker. "But the most skilled upholsterer in the world could not prevent a corpse enclosed in such a mattress from declaring its presence after a day or two."

"That's right!" cried Karslake. "If there had been a corpse in one of the mattresses that evening, I couldn't have helped knowing it. But I'll own up I'd have missed a *living* woman!"

"A living woman sewn up in a mattress?" asked Pinnaker.

"Sewn up or buttoned up by a skilled upholsterer an hour before I arrived. That mattress has about a dozen air vents—and you could have prepared it weeks beforehand."

Pinnaker looked thoughtful

"Physically possible, I suppose," he conceded. "But what on earth *for!* What would be the purpose of such a trick—which, as you say, must have been planned beforehand?"

Karslake answered the question with another.

"How many thousands did you make on that book of yours, Mr. Pinnaker—*Marion, Come Back?*"

Pinnaker caught his breath.

"You used Mrs. Harker pretty smartly," continued Karslake. "You two did some conjuring tricks with those clothes. You gave Mrs. Harker faked evidence. So she told us in good faith that tale about your wife going away in her house clothes—which made it

dead certain the police would come here and search the house for
a corpse. You played up the newspapers and the TV, as you played
up Mrs. Harker. And now you're going to tell me that as a result of
all that advertisement no one was more surprised than yourself
when half a million suckers bought that book!"

"Suckers!" echoed Pinnaker. He flushed and his voice revealed
an unsuspected aggressiveness. "Let me tell you something! That
book may have had its faults from a literary angle. But the public
liked it. They bought it—they passed it from hand to hand—and
they talked about it. And you have the damned effrontery to call
them *suckers!*"

Rason stepped between them. Karslake regarded Pinnaker with
some surprise.

"I apologize for saying 'suckers'," he said coldly. "But you admit
that the two of you hoaxed us—as well as the newspapers?"

"Absolute rot!" stormed Pinnaker. Then with sudden calm he
continued, as if repeating a prepared statement: "I admit only that
I personally misled the police with that car story. I expect to be
prosecuted for having 'created a mischief.' I deny that my wife
helped me in any way whatever. Alternatively, if she did help me,
she did so 'under the domination of her husband.' You can't touch
her."

"Good enough!" snapped Karslake. "It's your case, Rason. You
can take his statement."

When Karslake had left the house Rason rejoined Pinnaker in the
sitting room.

"This statement will take some time, won't it?" suggested Pinnaker, producing a portable typewriter. "Let's have another drink
before we start?"

"Not for me, thanks!" Rason's tone carried a reminder of duty
to be done. "Never mind the typewriter. What about that furnace
of yours? The one that heats the house."

Pinnaker smoothed the hair from his forehead.

"Your senior got my goat, Mr. Rason. I'm finding it hard to concentrate. If you won't join me, d'you mind if I have a drink by
myself?"

He opened the cocktail cabinet. His back was toward Rason but
his face was reflected in a glass panel of the bookcase.

"At the time, Mr. Pinnaker, you were hard pressed for a thousand pounds. Saving a trifle on house fuel wouldn't have helped you. You let the fire out on that Tuesday night. You kept it out during Wednesday and Thursday. But on Friday—after the house had been searched for the dead body of your wife—you lit the fire again and heated the house."

"In a crisis one's small acts are sometimes idiotic." Pinnaker's face showed indifference but Rason was watching his hands, reflected almost as clearly as if the glass panel had been a mirror.

A second later Rason crept up like a cat and snatched the half-filled tumbler of whisky.

"What's that you dropped in the glass?"

"Only a sedative. I told you Karslake had rattled me."

"Then it wouldn't do me any harm." Rason raised the glass to his lips.

"If you drink that it will kill you," said Pinnaker calmly. "I don't think you intend to drink it, but I daren't take the risk."

"Good boy!" said Rason. There was a long silence while he opened his bag, poured the contents of the glass into a small bottle, then shut the bag. "There's not much of the murderer about you, Mr. Pinnaker. When she wouldn't let you have that thousand you lost your temper and dotted her one. Didn't you? I'm just guessing."

"You are! All you've got is that I tried to kill myself," said Pinnaker. "How much do you *know?*"

"Enough to go on guessing," chirped Rason. "After you had given her that unlucky wallop on Tuesday afternoon, you put her in the attic, out of Mrs. Harker's way. You kept the house close to freezing for obvious reasons. You had plenty of time to doctor that mattress and get her sewn up inside before the Chief Inspector came on Friday evening. And you messed about with the floorboards, so's he'd be certain to have 'em up. Then everybody would be sure that there was no corpse in the house. Am I right?"

"As there are no witnesses present—yes, you are substantially right." Pinnaker thrust his hands into his pockets as if he did not trust them. "But you still have no evidence. After that Friday, I was able to use my other car without anyone suspecting that it might contain a corpse—and so was able to hide it in the countryside—"

"No good, laddie!" interrupted Rason. "The safest place in the world to hide that corpse was the one place where Chief Inspector Karslake had reported that there was no corpse!"

Under the floorboards, deeply buried, the police found the body of Marion Pinnaker, clothed in sweater, skirt, and overall—beside the body a pair of thin blue house shoes and an attaché case containing ten thousand pounds in Bearer Bonds.

THE PARROT'S BEAK

It is impossible to measure the skill of a criminal until he has been caught. Pure chance has saved many a bungler from the gallows. Similarly, pure chance has hanged many a murderer who has successfully outwitted the organized intellect and resources of society. And the Department of Dead Ends was really nothing else than a device for allowing pure chance to operate.

Florence Hornby was, in sporting parlance, another fox who had got away from hounds. No amount of cleverness on the part of the detectives, no amount of thoroughness of police organization, could have convicted her of the murder of her husband.

Her case has another unusual feature in that she, like the Marchioness of Roucester and Jarrow, was another of the very few women murderers in England to use firearms.

Further, like so many male murderers, she made her victim help to set the stage—to put himself just where she wanted him to be found by the police.

Percy Hornby was the son of a timber merchant of Barking. His mother died when he was fourteen. The family had lived on a very modest scale, although the father was making a small fortune. Percy had attended the board school (as it was in those days) and had been considered a very backward pupil.

A year after his mother's death his father suddenly dropped the habits of a lifetime and bought a large house at Richmond-on-Thames, with a garden of three acres that ran down to the river. It was a home singularly ill-suited to their requirements. An elderly, slatternly woman, their general servant, migrated with them from Barking. No further attempt was made to educate Percy, who seems to have spent the next four years idling in the garden, depending for companionship upon errand boys who came to the back door.

When he was eighteen his father died, leaving his son an estate valued at £ 80,000, unprotected by anything in the nature of a trust. A guardian had been appointed who seems to have been content to leave Percy in the charge of the elderly slattern.

At twenty-one Percy came into his property, which merely meant that every time he went to the solicitor, who had been his guardian, to ask for money, it was given without question.

Percy did not, as might be supposed, "paint the town red." He was probably too undeveloped for that, having the tastes and mental outlook of a boy of twelve. He merely led a disorderly life— in the literal sense of the word—that is, a life without any kind of order.

He would feed when the elderly slattern, now a confirmed drunkard, happened to think of getting a meal ready. He would sleep when he felt sleepy, rarely going to bed for the purpose. He would keep a number of gold sovereigns in a drawer in the dining room and when money was wanted, there it was. If it was not there, it would merely mean that he must get the slattern to tidy him up and then go to ask his solicitor for more.

At any hour of the day or night a casual stranger might have come upon him in the big dining room, stacked with the heavy furniture that had been bought with the house from the previous owner. Grouped about him would be a dozen or more of the young wastrels of the town. On the long mahogany table would be a vast litter of dirty and broken plates. On the mantel-piece, the sideboard, the chairs were innumerable glasses, and on the floor, countless empty bottles.

As a matter of fact, a casual stranger—a woman—did come upon such a scene as this—at three o'clock in the afternoon. She was a canvasser for an insurance company; she had heard about him and had called in the hope of selling him insurance.

For the rest, she was thirty-five, rather more than moderately good-looking, her somewhat stern face softened by big, hazel eyes. She might even have been considered a bit of a beauty, but for the fact that when you looked at her again you saw that the white of her left eye was speckled with pigment.

She stood in the huge French window, a little confused, while the hobbledehoys guffawed. But the confusion did not last long. She must have grasped the full situation almost at a glance and with it came an iron determination to seize her chance.

The iron determination was so effective that in six weeks she had married Percy Hornby.

She did not find it necessary to deceive Percy at the outset. She told him truthfully that her name was Florence Hornbeck (an odd echo of the name she was about to assume), that she was a widow and that she had lived in America for some years.

Nor did Percy deceive her. He gave a truthful, if muddled, account of himself and his fortune, insofar as he understood either, which was not far. Of course, the facts about himself did not matter. As to the facts about the fortune, Florence seems to have been unaccountably careless. She did no more than verify the story of his inheritance by inspecting the will at Somerset House.

She did not interview his solicitor until the day after the wedding. (They seem to have dispensed with the formality of a honeymoon.) Then she learned that the fortune of £80,000 had shrunk, by a process she imperfectly understood, to an approximate value of £7000, yielding an income for the two of them about the size of that which Florence had earned as an insurance agent.

She promptly asked her late manager to recommend a solicitor whom she could trust to investigate the conduct of her husband's affairs. The inquiry resulted in a report to the effect that there had been no fraud. Two companies had gone bankrupt, two or three parcels of shares had proved valueless—and so on. There was, in short, no hope.

At this stage, ignoring subsequent events, she presents a picture of a brave woman making the best of a bad job. She dismissed the elderly slattern and set to work to make her husband and his house presentable.

Among many little improvements in the house was the installation of a telephone in the hall, with an extension to the "best bedroom" —which latter Florence does not seem to have regarded as an extravagance.

Under the régime of the elderly slattern Percy's health had deteriorated. Florence took him to Harley Street to be overhauled and devoted the next three months to the task of building him up.

She made him take rowing lessons and saw to it that he put in regular practice. She encouraged him in other manly sports. She bought him a shotgun and cartidges and urged him to practise in the garden—also a target pistol, but in these directions Percy showed no ambition.

At the end of three months she decided that it was time to resume consideration of their financial affairs.

From the first she had taken control of expenditure—we are given to understand at his request. True, he signed the checks, but she kept the check book.

It was his wish, we are told, that they should each make a will in the other's favor. After all, he still had the remnant of a fortune (now very little more than £6000) and the freehold of his house. Florence, for her part, had vaguely "a little property."

The next step in financial prudence was to insure his life for £15,000. This presented no difficulty. Thanks to his wife's care he was now bronzed and in excellent condition and passed easily as a first-class risk.

Florence developed a positive enthusiasm for insurance. She insured, as it were, everything she could lay hands on—in particular, a collection of old miniature portraits that had been acquired with the furniture. We find correspondence with two leading insurance companies each of which declared that the miniatures were artistically valueless. Finally, she insured them with a small company for £400—against fire and theft.

And here it must be admitted that Florence was no financial genius. Out of a gross income of £300 she was spending £225 on insurance alone.

It is difficult to draw any clear impression of their brief married life—the woman of thirty-five and the half-idiot boy of twenty-one, alone in that great white elephant of a house except for the intermittent presence of one general servant.

One incident only stands out during the next four months. Percy contracted a mild form of pneumonia and Florence nursed him. Suddenly the doctor, for no stated reason, refused to go on with the case and made it clear that unless the patient were taken at once to a hospital, there might well be trouble.

What the doctor saw we do not know. We can be reasonably certain that he could prove nothing from the fact that he did not try to do so. But we may guess that he suspected her of helping the disease.

Within a fortnight Percy was home again and in a week or so
regained his normal health. Then it was that Florence broke it to
him that they were desperately poor. They could no longer afford to
keep even the one general servant, who must be given immediate
notice.

Percy did not mind—until he was made to realize that he would
have to do the housework. Florence did such cooking as there was—
Percy did everything else. Florence, he discovered, was very particular. She wanted the whole house to be kept clean.

For six weeks he endured a state of virtual slavery. It did not
occur to his feeble intelligence that his work had not previously
been done by the general servant—nor by anyone else. Just as he
approached breaking point, Florence propounded her scheme.

"Percy. These miniatures are insured for £400. If burglars were
to steal them we should get the £400—and then we could have a
servant and you wouldn't have to do any more housework."

"I wish a burglar would steal them."

"I see what you mean—you mean we might *pretend* the place has
been burgled. We could burgle it ourselves—and throw the stuff in
the river—and get the money."

"Cor, Florence, that's a good 'un! Let's do it tonight as soon as it's
dark."

"Not tonight—but soon. It will have to be done very, very carefully. If you want me to help you with this clever idea of yours,
Percy, you must promise to do everything I tell you."

On the chosen night, Florence, wearing a pair of Percy's boots,
stole a boat from its moorings by Richmond Bridge, rowed until she
was in line with the house, then tied up.

Percy was waiting for her in hiding near the water's edge. He
gave her a sack containing the miniatures and numerous other small
articles "stolen" from the little safe in the dining room.

She put the sack in the boat, whereupon he walked back to the
house, entering it by the dining room window. In Percy's simple
mind the sack was already at the bottom of the river by the time he
arrived—for that was a part of what he believed to be the program.

Actually the sack was carried by Florence to the middle of the
lawn and left there—to suggest, on the following morning, booty
dropped by burglars in their haste to escape. Florence, you see, had
no real intention of taking all this trouble for the paltry £400 insurance of the miniatures.

She had worn Percy's boots in order to provide man-size foot-prints. When she rejoined her husband she took off her boots; then, without bustle or flurry, she proceeded to clean and polish them.

Then, leaving the door of the safe open, they went upstairs, undressed, and got into bed. Almost as soon as they had done this, Florence reached for the telephone and put an urgent call through to the Richmond police station, some mile and a quarter distant.

"Is that the police?" she cried. "Oh I think burglars are in our house downstairs! Wait a minute! My husband will speak to you."

"I'm sure I hear burglars," said Percy, carefully repeating the lines in which she had rehearsed him. "I'm going down to see. I have a pistol to protect myself, but will you please come along at once?"

Percy then put on his dressing gown (one of the many little refinements in his personal life introduced by Florence), took up the target pistol, previously loaded and placed ready to his hand, and went downstairs.

"Wait till I come and give the word," cautioned Florence.

As soon as he had left the room, she slipped on a pair of gloves and dragged from under the bed an old cabin trunk that had been hers long before she had met Percy. From the trunk she took an old double-barreled shotgun—not, be it noted, the shotgun she had bought for Percy, which was in its place behind the cupboard in the "morning room."

Then she hurried downstairs.

Percy was waiting for her in the dining room, a candle in one hand, the target pistol in the other.

"Now!"

Percy, as previously arranged, fired the target pistol at the wall near the safe—as if he had aimed at a burglar and missed. As soon as he had done this, Florence slipped in front of him, let go the two barrels of the shotgun, and blew his brains out.

Then she extracted the cartridge cases, dropped the gun on the floor near the safe, and hurried back to her bedroom. She locked the door, removed the key and put it, with the empty cartridge cases, in her dressing gown pocket. It was a duplicate key. The other key had been previously placed in Percy's dressing gown pocket.

Finally, in a well-simulated state of hysteria, she rang the police station again, told them that she had heard guns being fired down-stairs and feared the worst, that she could not get out of her bed-room because her husband had locked her in for safety. Would the police, in pity's name, hurry up?

From the first, the case was watertight. When the police arrived they released Florence with the key taken from the dead man's pocket. They did not know, that night, that the deceased was heavily insured in his wife's favor. By the time they heard this, Florence, we know, had contrived to get rid of the duplicate key and the spent cartridge cases.

If the police ever held the theory of her guilt they were compelled to drop it as there was not the tiniest particle of evidence against her. Florence had staged a burglary and had had the good sense to "act" it so that it was complete in all its objective traces.

Every new line, in fact, brought them back to the burglary. The safe had not been forced, but opened with a key. How had the burglars obtained a key? Investigation showed that some three weeks previously Percy had lost his bunch of keys. But as the prudent Florence had insured them, they had been returned by the insurance company. While they had been lying about, a burglar might have taken an impression.

The shotgun was the most valuable piece of evidence. Trace the shotgun and you have traced the murderer. And at first sight the shotgun seemed remarkably easy to trace.

It was about thirty years old and, when new, had been very expensive. It bore the name of a well-known London gunsmith—and a number. Further, on the stock there was a deep jagged scratch making the rough outline of a parrot's beak. Further still, on the butt end were the engraved initials "R. O."

The makers were able to say that it had been supplied to a West Country landowner. Following this up, the police learned that, shortly after the purchase, the landowner had given it to his game-keeper. The gun was next heard of as being sold by an itinerant market dealer in Exeter to a farmer named Odlum who sold it back to the same dealer a year later. It was bought again on the same day by a man unknown to the dealer. This last transaction was twenty years old and after that the gun became untraceable.

Had it been bought by a man who kept it for twenty years and then himself turned burglar? A shotgun was not part of the normal burglar's outfit. Further, the burglar-murderer knew that the gun was untraceable, but feared that the cartridges might not be—for he had had the clearheadedness to take the empty cases with him. . . .

A nice little logical tangle that led nowhere.

Organization did its best. A description of the gun was circulated in all the papers, but without result. And so, in due course, the dossier and the shotgun were sent to the Department of Dead Ends.

Florence collected the insurance and when probate had been granted, sold the house at Richmond. With one thing and another she came out of her brief marriage some £20,000 the richer.

She went to live in a residential hotel in Kensington while, to occupy her leisure, she opened a one-room office in the city as an independent insurance broker—an enterprise she did not take too seriously. But the business brought her in touch with a fairly wealthy broker who came to live in the same hotel. He seems to have shown a certain resistance to Florence's charms for, a year after he had installed himself at the hotel, they were still spoken of merely as friends.

Whether she would eventually have brought him to the point of marriage can never be known. The ceremony had certainly not taken place when they went to Harrogate together—where the detectives came to arrest her for the murder of her husband two years previously.

It is no reflection on Florence's skill as a murderess to say that she failed to guess that, some twenty months after her crime, Mr. John Wodderspoon, an American citizen, staying with English friends at Sevenoaks in Kent, might himself become mixed up in a burglary.

Mr. Wodderspoon, in defense of his host's property, had rushed upon a couple of burglars and had been knocked unconscious for his pains. And in a rather unusual manner. For they had begun by menacing him with a shotgun. And when he had refused to be menaced, they had clubbed him with the butt, giving him a very bad concussion.

He was not permanently injured: but nearly four months had passed before the doctor allowed him to make the short journey to London at the request of the officials of Scotland Yard.

Burglars—shotgun! A most unusual combination. And the combination had occurred twice within two years. Tarrant, however, assumed a logical connection and promptly assumed that the burglars who had assaulted Wodderspoon were the burglars who had killed Percy Hornby.

To Tarrant Mr. Wodderspoon described them as "hoboes," which was not in itself very helpful. He was, in fact, of no use at all, but Tarrant was too polite to tell him so. He was, too, inattentive, obviously seeing Scotland Yard as a tourist, and thoroughly enjoying it. His eye kept straying to the shotgun. As it had been in that room for nearly two years before Wodderspoon had even landed in England, Tarrant did not expect him to be able to throw any light on it.

But here Tarrant was wrong. Here, in short, he was presented with a victory he had done nothing to earn.

"Say, that's remarkable, officer! I guess I've seen that gun before. There's the parrot's beak on the stock that was made by my own mule when my friend dropped it. Look in the butt end and you'll find the initials 'R. O.' If the regulations permit, I'd like to ask you what that gun is doing here."

We have, of course, no exact record of the actual words used, but the conversation must have flowed somewhat on these lines.

"You know the owner of this gun, Mr. Wodderspoon?"

"Sure! He was my friend—Ralph Hornbeck of Milton, Ohio. He bought the gun from a secondhand store when he was touring in Britain. The poor fellow thought the world of that gun."

"Do you know ——?"

"You'll excuse me, officer, but it's a painful subject. My friend shot himself with that gun. He tied string round the trigger and took both barrels. I'm not saying it was done on account of his wife, mind. She was of British birth—and I dare say she had no fault, bar that of being twenty years younger than her husband. Anyway, she wasn't too popular. She collected the $20,000 insurance and moved on."

Inevitably, in some form or another, Tarrant must have asked:

"Did any suspicion fall on the wife?"

"No. It was suicide right enough. He locked his wife in the bedroom before he did it. She heard the gun go off and rang the sheriff from the telephone at her bedside. The sheriff had to take the key out of the dead man's pocket to let her out of the bedroom."

Then, of course:

"Could you identify that woman if you were to see her now, Mr. Wodderspoon?"

"I guess so. But it's a good many years ago—wait, she had little specks of color in the white of her left eye."

A FOOL AND HER MONEY

I

In the reports of a trial for murder, the defendant and the victim
are generally seen as cardboard figures against the background of
the crime. By tradition, the cardboard woman is coloured brightly
and the cardboard man darkly.

Thus, in the Cosy Nook murder, Hedda Felbert fitted neatly into
the *cliché* of the woman scorned, and William Surbrook into that of
the money-seeking male who overreaches himself. Legally, it is irrelevant that Hedda did not know she had been scorned, and that
Surbrook never moved a finger to possess himself of her money.

The money sequence was short and clear-cut. It began in Surbrook's office in Throgmorton Street on a morning in February
1929, two days after Henry Fauburg—the Fauburg who tried to
corner quinine—had shot himself. Surbrook was a thoroughly respectable member of the Stock Exchange with a small but steady
clientèle, of whom Fauburg has been the wealthiest. The suicide
meant that Surbrook must conjure twenty thousand pounds out of
the void within five days, or be hammered.

It ought not to have been possible for Surbrook to be involved.
But no sane broker would be starchy about Stock Exchange rules
with an apparently gilt-edged client like Fauburg—and that was the
limit of Surbrook's adventurousness. As to his position, you could
have added or subtracted a nought, for all the chance he had of
raising the money.

Surbrook's reputation was spotless. A hammering was so rare and
universally detested that he very nearly cherished the hope that the
bank might waive the matter of securities and come to his rescue
out of sheer public spirit. That, or a miracle, would save him.

We need not dwell upon his mental torture. It reached its highest point at the moment when he decided that he must go out to lunch, to·keep up appearances, even if it choked him. It was then that the miracle appeared to happen—only he didn't believe it was a miraacle. The message from the bank was no more than a form, stating that twenty thousand pounds had been credited to his account by a well known firm of financial agents.

There was no violence in his relief—he was calm as a reprieved murderer. Some minutes had passed before he made a constructive attempt to cheer up—with very qualified success. He must behave decorously. During the lunch hour, he sipped a coffee, then rang the financial agents.

He was interrupted almost as soon as he had announced his name.

"Our commission was to make the payment. We have no further instructions."

He replaced the receiver without surprise, and made no further attempt. For five days he tried to humbug himself with one absurd explanation after another. Then, his reputation saved by the twenty thousand, he went in search of Hedda Felbert, whom he had not seen for some seven years—not since the day, to be precise, on which he had married Myra.

There was no difficulty in tracing her to Beringham, thirty miles out, in the Surrey hills. He checked with a local directory—*Felbert, H. Miss, Cosy Nook.*

Cosy Nook! His laugh held a touch of brutality. The moment she had a house of her own, she would inevitably call it Cosy Nook, even if it were a mansion. She had not changed. Some girls never changed—only became, as it were, more so.

With some difficulty he found it on the outskirts of the town. It was not a mansion, but a small, brick-built bungalow. There was nothing about it to suggest the home of a woman who could throw away twenty thousand pounds on the basis of a single courtesy kiss, bestowed more than seven years ago.

II

His mother had started what he and Myra had called the Hedda Felbert saga. It was in the summer following his demobilisation after the Kaiser's war. As part of the programme of resettling him in civil life, his mother had given a series of tennis parties.

"I want you to make sure that Miss Felbert enjoys herself, Willie.

I met them during the war. Her father is a builder or something, and he was splendid at the Red Cross, but he's a bit—stiff. Hedda acts as his secretary and I'm told she's very clever. But I don't think they go about much."

In 1919 Hedda was thirty, three years older than himself. She was of medium height, with a figure which inclined to lumpiness, but would have yielded to treatment. She had a mass of brown, unruly hair and brown eyes, a shade too prominent. Her mouth was firm and her nose well formed. Though she could never have attained an insistent appeal, she could certainly have turned herself into a reasonably handsome woman, had she but perceived her need to assist nature.

Surbrook partnered her in a mixed double, when it became painfully clear that someone ought to have advised her to say that she did not play tennis. The game became a face-saving contest, in which their opponents co-operated. Surbrook felt more than a little annoyed with his mother. But the feeling passed at the end of the set, when he glanced at Hedda. She was very hot, and the unruly hair was in open rebellion, but her eyes were the eyes of a happy child. She had enjoyed every minute of it, had no suspicion that there had been any face-saving.

Later, when there was some danger of her being involved in another four, he detached her and gave her a lesson in clock-golf. She paid profound attention to his instructions, which she could understand but could not implement. Perseverance was among her qualities; but she failed to observe that she was keeping him from his guests for an unpardonably long time.

"I must try again," she would say, and, with dreadful archness: "I mean to make you thoroughly proud of your pupil!"

It was not possible to squirm—it was only possible to pity. She was not stupid, but imperceptive. It might even be true that she was clever at her work. But as a woman she was a lout, a predestined spinster.

His interest in her had been noticed and misunderstood. Thereafter, when people invited him, they tended to invite her also. Her existence became a mild nuisance to him, but he could not bring himself to the point of snubbing her. Her social life, he foresaw, would be a pageant of snubs.

He did not actively dislike her—he looked upon her as some sort of relation whom one had to treat kindly, because she was a little backward. He neither encouraged nor repelled her. He did not, in the phrase of today, make a date with her. True that he gave her a box of chocolates—by a regrettable coincidence, the decoration was a coloured photograph of Miss Mary Pickford playing clock-golf—but this was only by way of apology for spilling coffee on her stockings.

His conduct was blameless, except in the matter of the courtesy kiss—which was a mistake, made in the utmost good faith.

They had been fellow guests at a birthday dance and there was no one but Surbrook to drive her home. Drawing up at her father's house, he was seized with a doubt—suppose she had found out that men generally kiss girls when they drive them home after a dance? Some girls have a pretty grim time—and some old maids have pretty grim memories, when you come to think of it.

He touched cold, bewildered lips, wondered whether he had made a fool of himself—went on wondering on the drive home, certain only that she had not been offended. Poor kid! She just couldn't get the hang of things. At least, she would now be able to brag to herself that a man had kissed her.

He did not guess that sexual charity is a virtue of which Nature does not approve. Surbrook, in fact, had grossly underestimated the extent to which Hedda failed to 'get the hang of things.' In matters of organisation and finance she was practical, efficient, and even talented. Except for a brief period at a kindergarten, she had been educated by her father, who had given her a view of human relationships which her budding womanhood was bound to reject. Accordingly, she had retreated into a world of her own of which she herself was the hub—a world of friendly women and gallant men.

Surbrook, of course, was wrong on the point of such a woman's memories. Even at twenty-five, Hedda had begun to 'remember' more than one handsome young man who had deliberately con-trived his own death in battle for lack of her kisses. Another group, equally handsome but inclined to wistfulness, had refrained from declaring their passion lest they be suspected of fortune hunt-ing. Here was a touch of realism—for the practical Hedda had satisfied herself that her portion would eventually be about one hundred thousand pounds. And so the courtesy kiss, rather disap-pointing in itself, was shaped and fortified, until it became the keystone of her bridge to a reconstructed Valhalla.

There were no immediate repercussions. For some weeks Surbrook and Hedda chanced not to meet. Then he received an invitation to come to dinner and meet her father. As Mrs. Surbrook had frequently entertained Hedda, it was impossible to refuse.

Mr. Felbert turned out to be very much as Surbrook had expected —a social recluse forcing himself to be sociable. No one else had been invited. At dinner, the conversation took its tone from the furniture, which had been fashionable in the 1880's. After dinner, Hedda, at a nod from her father, 'left the gentlemen to their port' —a good port but wasted on Surbrook, whose suspicions had been aroused.

Mr. Felbert offered a summary of Hedda's life, her mother's premature death and his own attempt to take her place. This was welded into a brief account of the growth of his business. Mr. Felbert, in short, was on the brink of expressing himself delighted to welcome Surbrook as a son-in-law.

Surbrook was sufficiently adroit to escape without making a scene. Thinking about it the next day, he inaccurately concluded that it was Mr. Felbert who had forced the pace—even Hedda would surely have sense enough to tell him not to talk like that to the first man who had made a point of not avoiding her—for that, he assured himself was all his own part amounted to.

A few days later he met Myra, who drove from him the consciousness and almost the memory of Hedda. In a month, their engagement was announced in the local paper. Among the letters of congratulation was one from Hedda. It was conventional throughout, except for the last paragraph: '*I quite understand! Believe that, in all sincerity. I wish you every happiness.*'

Surbrook assumed that it was no more than a clumsily phrased attempt to show friendliness. He next saw her on his wedding day —over the heads of a small crowd of idlers, when he was coming out of church. She was standing alone on the opposite pathway. She had accepted an invitation but had not turned up.

On his first wedding anniversary he received a letter from her, which gave him his first twinge of unease. It was an inoffensive meander, but its atmosphere was intimate, as if the writer were a close companion. After passing it to Myra, he decided not to answer.

There had been one such letter for each of his five anniversaries. Some eighteen months ago she had written a personal letter of condolence when Myra and his mother were killed in an air crash.

III

Before he could knock at the door of Cosy Nook, Hedda herself opened it. In seven years she had not even changed physically. There was the same unruly brown hair, the same suggestion of unnecessary lumpiness. Her face was unwrinkled, but, incredibly, she had taken to lipstick—possibly for the first time. The lipstick, too, tended to lumpiness.

She spoke as if they had parted, not seven years ago, but the previous day.

"You see—I was waiting for you! You did not have to knock."

"Good lord!" He was disconcerted. "How did you know I was coming?"

She smiled.

"I knew."

Of course she knew he was coming—to talk about that twenty thousand! But he had an uneasy feeling that this was not what she meant.

She had wafted him into the bungalow, chattering as she had always chattered.

"I built this very soon after father's death. I always wanted a cosy little nook of my own—where I could *wait*, all by myself. I still go to the office, but you'll find I've become ever so domesticated. I manage with a half-daily woman. Say it's clever of me!"

While she prepared tea, he waited in the sitting-room. Not a sitting-room, he decided, but a drawing-room, more formal than comfortable. The furniture was modern and new as the house, but the room itself contrived to look old-fashioned. There was something indefinitely wrong with it—it exuded a spiritual lefthandedness.

On a doubtfully serviceable escritoire was a large silver-framed photograph—of himself. She must have bought it from the photographer. Beside it was a very small one, cut out of a group, also of himself. He could not escape the truth that she believed herself to be in love with him. He would make every effort to avoid wounding her.

When she came in with the tray he noticed her dress, a pleasing green, well cut in a low 'v'. There was nothing wrong about the dress, though there seemed to be.

There followed the ritual of tea, which he had always disliked and now endured with foreboding. She had not changed, but she had indeed become 'more so.' The gaucherie remained, and the fatuous little mannerisms. But her personality had been intensified, so that their former roles were reversed and it was she who was taking charge of him.

Hedda, in fact, had acquired strength through her unshakeable belief in her own ideals. When Surbrook's engagement was announced she had kept her sanity by adapting her dream-life to the new facts. She identified herself with the great women, of so many legends, who wait for their wayward lovers, the waywardness being a test of faith. In a short time she became convinced that Surbrook would 'return' to her. The air crash that removed Myra was therefore seen as the hand of fate.

Supporting the fantasy was a certain emotional shrewdness. She valued her man above her fortune, which was meaningless without him.

He let her prattle on about her cakes and her garden and her house until he reached breaking point.

"Hedda! That twenty thousand! Why did you do it?"

"Willie! What a question!"

She got up, turned on the light and drew the curtains. He waited until she stopped fidgeting.

"Look at the facts!" he exclaimed. "No sane business man would have lent me a thousand. I was due to be hammered. After that, I couldn't have got a job. I would have been knocking at doors, asking housewives to buy stockings, or something—"

"I know. I happened to see a man doing just that—and I got panic."

"But—*why?* I never gave you any reason—"

"I won't be bullied by a big, strong man like you!" She pouted with inexorable archness. "And why do you go on asking that silly question? You haven't any proof at all that the money came from me." She paused and added: "And yet you *know!* Ask yourself how you know."

She was not making it easy for him to be kind, he told himself—

as a mouse might have grumbled that there was no opportunity to be kind to the cat.

"We have to discuss what can be done about it," he said stubbornly. "It will take me a lifetime to repay—"

"Did you think I was looking for an investment?"

He got up, tried to pace the little room, but had to sit down again.

"Don't you see, Hedda, that the most dishonourable thing I could do—the most damnable insult I could offer you—would be to make love to you in return for the twenty thousand?"

He had taken the gloves off and struck, but she only laughed at him.

"Oh, my poor Willie! How you men deceive yourselves with words! We women are much more realistic. I wrote you—at the time—that I understood. I still understand. Just think it over, while I get rid of the tea things."

Surbrook did *not* understand—was, in fact, struggling to sustain himself in a state of non-understanding, an effort which failed when she returned.

"My father was purse-proud. He thought people esteemed him for his money. He thought the same must apply to his daughter. While he was talking to you after dinner that night, I—was crying! I knew that your self-respect would be affronted—that you would never seek me out again nor permit yourself to think of me. I *understood!*"

"But—my dear girl! I fell in love with someone else!"

"Of course you did!" Her smile made him feel that her 'understanding' would suffocate him. "I have learnt a little about human nature—I know how such things happen. They cannot affect one's destiny."

That gave him the clue to the existence of the fantasy—revealed that she believed he had been in love with her and had married Myra in the hope of forgetting. No reasoning could shake that kind of belief.

If he were to marry her, it would not be for her money—she had made neither promise nor threat. It would be from pity. And. of course, gratitude. Lots of reasonably happy marriages must have been founded on much less.

"Hedda, you have saved me from the gutter. So far, I haven't uttered a single word of gratitude to you, because I—"

"Because you feel that you're under a terrible obligation!" she interrupted. "Please, dear Willie, do let's be sensible about the money. Listen!" She sat on a pouffe close to his chair, put her hand on his. "I never made father's mistake. From the first—d'you remember when you taught me to play clock golf?—I knew you were not drawn to me by the fact of my being an heiress—you did not even know I was, until father told you. The other day, I had to butt in with that money because, if you had been hammered, I would have suffered more than you—wondering whether you would do what Fauburg did."

Again he felt that dangerous sense of superiority that permitted him to pity her.

"You have given me so much, Hedda, and I can give you so very little!"

"Don't think about it like that! Give me only what you can't help giving me. I demand nothing, Willie."

She was telling him he was free—free to say thank-you for the twenty thousand, walk out of her house and dodge her in future.

He looked down at her. At close view, the lipstick wasn't really lumpy—it was desperately pathetic. And she had saved him from the gutter. It wasn't as though she were ugly, or physically defective. Surely, with a little imaginative effort on his part—

He lifted her from the pouffe.

While he was holding her, he faced the stark truth that this woman could never attract him, never elicit the faintest response from his nervous system. The muddled kindliness that had prompted him to kiss her—with histrionic emphasis—gave place to resentment.

"Hedda! That was a wrong-headed attempt to say thank-you for that money."

She laughed happily. In her fantasy, the kiss always marked the end of cross-purpose.

"You *understand!* . . . Or you couldn't have made that joke!" Her voice was ecstatic. "We have waited so long, Willie, and now we have our reward. We can be married just as soon as you like."

IV

Presently she was sitting beside him on a settee. She had said that she demanded nothing. That was romantic jargon, even if she

thought it was true. She would soon discover it was not true. Before
the period of the honeymoon was over, the forlorn little butterfly
would turn into a spider. Now and again, her prattle penetrated
to his consciousness.

"There are some lovely houses in Surrey, almost in the country.
Not really far out. You could be at your office almost within an
hour."

And when he got to the office he would know that he was operat-
ing by virtue of her money. As a sub-species of gigolo, lacking the
gigolo's adaptability, but taking the gigolo's fee. And at five every
day he would have to go home to the spider—even if the spider
were only the symbol of his own self-contempt in the knowledge
that he must perpetually fail her. The feeling of suffocation was
coming back.

"I shall sell my interest in the business and give all my time to
making our home as you like it."

No!

He had made no sound, but had the illusion that he had shouted.
The superiority had been stripped from him—the arrogance that had
betrayed him into pitying this woman—leaving his egotism naked. He
was as a frightened animal about to fight for his life.

"And the rooms must be large, Willie. It will be lovely entertaining your friends."

Her chatter strengthened his will. His life would still be worth
living, even with a secret he could share with neither man nor
woman. He was cool-headed now—could see exactly how it must be
done.

He would tell the police that he had proposed marriage.

"Darling," he said, "I had no idea this would happen to us—so
suddenly—I've come unprepared." He drew from his hand the signet
ring which had belonged to his grandfather. "Will you wear this
until I can get you a proper engagement ring?" He took her left hand
and placed the ring correctly. "I'm afraid it's too big for comfort!"

"No, it isn't! I shall love to wear it."

Next, he must make sure that there was something in the bungalow that would tempt a thief.

"Hedda! Have you any jewellery?"

"How funny you should ask!" She seemed irrationally pleased.
"I have a little. I bought it myself. For a *reason!*" As he did not

inquire the reason she added: "Would you like to see it?"

"Very much!"

She left the room, returning with a decorated cardboard box: a faded ribbon panelled a coloured photograph of Miss Mary Pickford playing clock golf.

"D'you remember sending me chocolates, Willie?"

"And d'you remember when I drove you home, after the Walbrook dance?"

Inside the chocolate box were three pieces. A star pendant, in diamonds, on a thin gold chain; a bracelet in rubies and diamonds; and a brooch in diamonds. The brooch was a ponderous affair—a monogram, *WH*—her initial and his—intertwined.

The audacity of that monogram acted as a spur.

"This is a secret, isn't it?" As she nodded: "No one knows that you have it."

"No one but you!"

Then no crook could have marked it down. But there were a lot of men on the prowl nowadays. If she were wearing it when one of them came to the door—

"Let's see it on you . . . I can fix the bracelet."

"Oh, no, Willie! Please, no! It would spoil so much. I didn't really want to tell you, but you can guess. Can't you?" She lowered her eyes. "I look at it every night when I go to bed—just for a minute. I bought it for our wedding day."

When it came to telling the police that she had been wearing the jewellery, he must not trip over detail.

"The pendant—that hangs on this little chain just below your throat, doesn't it? If you were wearing the brooch—with that dress, for instance—where would it go?"

"Here!" She placed her finger at the base of the 'v' of her blouse.

She put the chocolate box on the pouffe and began to put the pieces back in the box. He moved near enough to the door to be able to reach the light switch when he wanted it.

"I'll have to be going now." He lowered his voice. "Come and say goodbye to me, Hedda."

She obeyed, without waiting to put the lid on the box. He studied her mouth. Even though it was a large mouth, it was yet small enough to be completely covered by the palm of his hand. When she came close, infatuated, he playfully took her wrists, drew them down until her hands rested on her hips. He had remembered the danger of her fingernails marking his face. With swift concerted movements he switched off the light, slipped behind her and pinioned her arms. With the base of his left hand on her chin, he forced her mouth shut, her head pressing against her shoulder, his own back steadied against the wall.

His imagination had suggested that she was suffocating him, but it was he who, in all literality, suffocated her.

She had been dead for many minutes before he was aware of muscular strain. He had shifted his position and could not reach the switch. In the dark, he lifted the body, carried it to the settee. On the way, he nearly stumbled over the pouffe. He heard the jewellery fall to the floor. His right foot touched one of the three pieces. That did not matter. He lowered his burden and sprawled it on the settee.

He stretched, pinched and massaged his left arm. As he turned on the light, he spoke aloud.

"The financial agent will tell the police about that twenty thousand as soon as he's read his paper. The police will ask me for my alibi. Incidentally, my car has been parked outside all the time I've been here." He laughed, to whip up his courage. "All right—no alibi! In case the nerve falters, we'll remove temptation to pretend there is."

He opened the flap of the escritoire. On the blotting pad he wrote in pencil the telephone number of his flat and added: '*If out, try club: Embankment 7210.*' The technique of the crook would be worse than useless to him. Invert it. Give 'em fingerprints galore. He picked up and fingered the large photograph of himself, touched the top of the escritoire.

"Steady, now!" He glanced at the clock—eight minutes to seven. "Get the narrative right. I proposed to her, asked her to wear my signet ring. I left before seven, but I'll say I didn't notice the time. She was alone—wearing the jewellery—when she answered the door to a prowler who forced her in here, smothered her and removed the jewellery.

"Footprints! The police can trace 'em even if there's no mud on your shoes."

He went to his car, put on the rubbers he carried for emergency, and re-entered the bungalow.

The jewellery was lying near the pouffe. The box itself was intact, the lid on the pouffe, the tray upside down on the floor. He left the box untouched. He picked up the pendant, the bracelet—lodged in the monogram of the brooch was his signet ring. Obviously, it had fallen off the finger while he was carrying the body to the settee.

He dislodged the ring, and examined it. The hoop was uninjured, but the matrix had been scratched and a small piece had been cut clean out. Evidently, his foot had forced it against one of the diamonds. Better dump it, when he dumped the jewellery.

There would then be nothing to support his statement that he had proposed marriage.

"It's all right. Check up. She was wearing the jewellery. The ring could have been forced against the brooch while she was struggling with the prowler."

He went to the settee and replaced the ring on the finger.

"She was wearing the jewellery." It was becoming a chant. "A prowler wouldn't remove it as if he were a ladies' maid."

He picked up the pendant and wrenched at the thin gold chain. By luck, it snapped at two points. A length of about a couple of inches fell to the floor.

"That bit might have dropped down under her dress."

He dropped it under the dress, at the back of the neck. He noticed that the blouse was hardly disarranged. He disarranged it.

On the bracelet was a safety device—a short length of gold chain much thinner than that of the pendant. He wrenched the chain free and dropped it on the floor, near the settee.

That was all, for the bungalow.

As he approached Beringham, his headlights picked out The Barley Mow, a tiny one-time inn that was now little more than a beerhouse. He stopped, entered the empty bar and beamed on the landlord as if they were old friends.

"Got any champagne?"

"Champagne! No, sir, I can't say as I 'ave."

"Then I'll have a brandy. And you have one too. I'm not mad, you know. A little light-headed, perhaps. Have a heart, landlord! One doesn't get engaged every day."

He bought a packet of cigarettes. With a question or two about how long it would take him to get to his club, he induced the land-lord to note that the time was three minutes past seven.

He drove back to London via Thadham. On Thadham bridge, which is not bordered with a footpath, he kept close to the parapet. Assured that there was no one else on the bridge, he flung the jew-ellery into the Thames, knowing that it would sink in the mud some thirty feet below the surface. The rubbers, too, would sink, provided there was no air pocket—he slit them close to the soles and flung them after the jewellery.

Then he drove on to his club, reflecting that, in order to hang him, the police would have to prove that Hedda had been mur-dered before seven. As the body was not found until the half-daily woman arrived on the following morning, the police were unable to do so.

v

Whether Surbrook actually got the better of Chief Inspector Karslake may be doubted. But it is indisputable that he avoided all the pitfalls and walked out of the traps. The respectable stock-bro-ker, the man of mild tastes and rather kindly disposition, had turned into a hard-headed egotist. He consistently inverted the crook's formula. From the first, he flourished all the facts unfavourable to himself and left the police to discover those that favoured him.

When the preliminary courtesies had been exhausted and Sur-brook's fingerprints had been taken, Karslake began at what he be-lieved to be the beginning.

"How long have you been engaged to the deceased?"

"No time at all! Until yesterday afternoon, I hadn't seen her for seven years." At Karslake's expression, he said: "I see I must give details. It's very awkward for me, Inspector. The fact is—five days ago, to be exact—Miss Felbert lent me twenty thousand pounds."

Karslake was startled and looked it. He repeated the figure with awe. "And deceased lent you all that before you were even en-gaged?"

"I'm putting it badly," apologised Surbrook, and weighed in with the tale of Fauburg's suicide and his own impending ruin. "The loan to me wasn't quite such an act of eccentric philanthropy as it sounds. I am a widower. I married, very suddenly, seven years ago. Before that happened, it was thought—that is, Miss Felbert and I —we thought it was she and I who were going to be married.

"I need not trouble you with any more about that. But please let me say this, Inspector, in fairness to Miss Felbert and myself. When I called at that bungalow I did not know that I would propose marriage. It happened of its own accord—as these things do." He stared vacuously at his own left hand and added, as if to himself: "I gave her my signet ring."

Surbrook was gaining ground. There were those photographs in the sitting-room, and two more in the bedroom, bearing out his general statement. Karslake produced the signet ring.

"We took this from her finger. Do you recognise it?"

"Yes. It's mine, all right. But—what's happened to it?"

"Our expert's report says that cut was made by a diamond. We found the chip on the floor. The ring could have been crushed against one of the pieces of jewellery, while he was attacking her."

"Horrible!" ejaculated Surbrook, and wisely left it at that.

"Was the deceased wearing her jewellery while you were with her?"

"Yes. Rather a lot of it for the afternoon, but this was an occasion. The jewellery had belonged to her mother—it had been locked in her father's safe during his lifetime. She was glad of a chance to wear it."

"Describe it, please, Mr. Surbrook."

"I haven't much eye for that sort of thing, but I'll try. A bracelet —rubies and small diamonds. A thing on a chain at her throat—a pendant. And a brooch—about *here*—joining the folds of the blouse. It was in diamonds and it was large—but don't infer Miss Felbert was an ostentatious woman—"

Karslake pressed for a detailed description of the brooch.

"Sorry, Inspector! To me it was just a brooch."

Surbrook was treading carefully. To admit that it was a monogram of their initials would clash with his statement that the jewellery had been her mother's.

"Can you give me the names of a few friends who might be able to describe it?"

Surbrook obliged, knowing that no friend had ever been allowed to see it. He had cleared an awkward little obstacle and his nerve was the steadier when Karslake asked what time he had left the deceased.

"I didn't happen to notice the time. I can remember that nine struck when I went into the dining-room at the club. So I suppose I must have left the bungalow about a couple of hours before that."

"Can you produce any witnesses?"

"Not a soul!" sighed Surbrook. "Unless some men I nodded to at the club could help."

Surbrook had made a thoroughly good impression. The landlord of The Barley Mow had already talked to the local police, quoting the time as five past seven.

At the inquest, Surbrook gave evidence as to his physical movements and as to the deceased having worn jewellery. The medical witness was unable to state that death must have taken place before seven in the evening. In short, the jury adopted Surbrook's theory of a prowling crook knocking at the door intending a preliminary investigation and seizing his chance to take the jewellery from the person of an unprotected woman.

In six months the case, with its items of real evidence, was passed to the Department of Dead Ends.

"You'll need more luck than usual for this, Rason," said Karslake. "There's nothing sticking out but the jewellery—and that'll be broken up by now." He added: "If Surbrook scuppered her himself, he'll have dumped it. Not much to work on, there. Everything Surbrook said stands up."

Everything Surbrook had said stood up. Fear receded to vanishing point, taking with it the sharp consciousness of his crime. By Hedda's will he benefited by a further thirty thousand pounds. He moved into a larger flat in Bayswater. He did not cut himself off from the society of women. After one or two transient intimacies, he was considering a marriage of convenience to a wealthy widow, when he received a call from Detective Inspector Rason.

VI

The streak of boyishness in Detective Inspector Rason—the ability to take a silly thing seriously—had never in itself brought him success, but it sometimes gave him a new approach to an old problem. It was a piece of boyish foolery with some jewellery—in no way connected with the Cosy Nook murder—which turned his attention to Surbrook.

He had spent an unprofitable morning in Hatton Garden, trying to identify some stolen jewellery, which included a star pendant in diamonds. Instead of going straight back to the Yard, he dropped into his sister-in-law's flat in Bloomsbury, and asked himself to lunch. He showed the jewellery to his niece, who admired it. She was having a fortnight's holiday at home and was going to an afternoon party.

"Pity I can't lend you this little lot—that star would look a treat in your hair. Try it, and see!"

"It isn't for the hair, Uncle, it's for the throat. And anyway, no woman would wear a diamond pendant in the afternoon."

"You don't know everything, miss! As a matter of fact, that rich girl, Miss Felbert, was wearing one very like this on the afternoon she was murdered."

"I don't believe it," said his niece, whom he encouraged to be cheeky. "You've got the evidence wrong again, Uncle."

He remembered her impudence some fortnight later, after a prolonged bout of desk work, which always depressed him. It was when he was in such moods that he would chase his wildest geese.

"Suppose the kid was right!" Rason urged himself. "Suppose the Felbert wasn't wearing a pendant, why did Surbrook say she was? Because he's a liar. Or because he mistook it for the brooch? No, he mentioned the brooch separately."

He opened the locker containing the real evidence of the Cosy Nook murder. He took out the green blouse. And two small pieces of gold chain, with cards attached:

'Found next skin, small of back: believed fragment of chain securing pendant.'

"Small of the back!" repeated Rason. "Then she must have been wearing the pendant at the back of her neck. Hm! You've got the evidence wrong again, Uncle. Where's that blouse?"

He arranged the blouse on his desk, trying to visualise the position of the pendant. "Must have been about here—no, that'd be under her chin. Much lower down. That makes it right on top o' the brooch."

He consulted the open dossier.

Brooch secured 'v' junction of blouse.

"Where's the 'v' junction of the blouse? No buttons. Can't tell. Find the pinholes made by the brooch . . . Must be in front somewhere."

But they were not in front—nor behind, for that matter. In a couple of minutes, though aided by a magnifying glass, he had failed to find the pinholes. With commendable caution and remembering the lapse of time, he sent the blouse for microscopic examination. He received a report stating that there had never been any pinholes in the blouse.

"She may have been wearing a pendant, but she was *not* wearing a brooch!"

His discovery set him lurching and tottering along a trail which better detectives had already seen and rejected as futile.

"He said she was wearing a brooch, when she wasn't. Ten to. one she wasn't wearing any jewellery at all." An odds-on chance, however, was rarely accepted by the legal department as evidence. He returned his attention to the dossier. "That signet ring was crushed against a diamond, so there was jewellery there, even if she wasn't wearing it. What was she doing with it? Just showing it to him? Then why couldn't he describe it properly—especially the brooch she was *not* wearing?"

There was something funny about that jewellery. None of the girl's friends had ever seen it, nor the servants employed by her father, though it was supposed to come from her mother.

"Women who own jewellery and don't wear it keep it at a safe deposit. She never· wore hers. But she kept it at that bungalow, which was often empty and unguarded. Wonder where she *did* get it? Come to that, she might have bought it herself. Girls do, sometimes, when a man doesn't give her any."

The dossier told him where Hedda had kept her private account. Rason astonished the bank manager by asking permission to inspect Miss Felbert's account for the last seven years.

"But the account closed with Miss Felbert's death. We have not the record," he told Rason. Eventually, the manager was persuaded to send for an elderly clerk who had been in charge of the account.

"I would probably have noticed a payment to a jeweller, as such." The clerk held out no hope. "Poor Miss Felbert would draw the same amounts month by month, almost to a pound—year in year out. The only largish cheque I can think of—why, it must be six or seven years ago, now!—was for three hundred and fifty pounds. It was to a Mr. Maenmawr—a Welsh name—I remember, because I happen to be Welsh myself. But I don't know that he was a jeweller."

He was a jeweller. He turned up the record.

"This is what you want, Mr. Rason. It was a special order. A pendant star and a bracelet from stock and a monogram in diamonds in brooch form—*HW*, intertwined. You can see from this illustration the sort of thing it was."

Hedda—William! Rason came within an ace of slapping the back of the very dignified jeweller.

"Can you make us one like it? We'll pay for the work, of course, but we'll only rent the diamonds."

VII

On the way to Surbrook's flat, Chief Inspector Karslake felt all his usual mistrust of Rason's slapdash.

"It's your case, Rason. I only hope, for your own sake, that you've worked out a proper line?"

"Shan't want one, sir," chirped Rason. "I reckon he'll give one shriek, then throw in his hand. You might watch him, if you don't mind, for cyanide."

On the Stock Exchange a man learns a great deal more than stockbroking—among other things, to keep his head in an emergency.

In the dining-room of the flat which the real estate agent had classified as 'extremely commodious,' the two detectives sat, with Surbrook at the head of the table. Karslake had coldly declined the offer of drinks.

"Ever seen this before, Mr. Surbrook?" On the table Rason put a large diamond brooch—in monogram form—*HW* intertwined.

Surbrook caught his breath. But Surbrook knew that a catch of the breath cannot be produced as evidence.

"Damn!" exclaimed Surbrook with elaborate embarrassment. "I've been dreading this moment. I'm extremely sorry, Mr. Karslake. I funked telling you about the monogram because it would have revealed that Miss Felbert had it made—unknown to me—while I was married to another woman. It was undignified behaviour on her part—which I could not have explained away. And as it could not affect your investigation—"

"You can't know that!" snapped Karslake. "Misleading the police is a public mischief for which you can be heavily fined or imprisoned, or both." But his ill temper was directed at Rason who was looking as if it were he who intended to throw in his hand.

"My superior officer," said Rason, rallying, "is a bit sore about your telling him that the poor lady was wearing her jewellery. In particular, you mentioned the brooch—you said it was pinned on at the *v* junction of the blouse. Look at the size of the pin on that brooch!" From his bag, he produced the green blouse. "There you are! You find the pinholes—unless you like to take my word for it that our miscroscope boys swear there never has been a pinhole of any size—anywhere—in that blouse. As to the pendant—d'you want me to go on, Mr. Surbrook?"

Surbrook wondered how much they were keeping up their sleeve. Bad as things were, there must be a fighting chance left, or they would have arrested him without talk.

"One lie was the father of the other, Mr. Rason. After I'd proposed to her, she fetched that chocolate box, showed me the jewellery, telling me she had bought it, to wear—to wear on our wedding day. She had always had a superstitious belief that my first marriage would come to an early end—it would break the charm, or something, if she were to wear it before then. So she put it back in that chocolate box in which she kept it—also for sentimental reasons—I gave her the chocolates years ago." Surbrook added: "It's the sort of thing one shrinks from telling a public official."

To Karslake's indignation, Rason was positively oozing sympathy.

"Well, I suppose we're all human, Mr. Surbrook. We accept your explanation—on the understanding that you will hold nothing back in future." Rason's graciousness was profound. As Surbrook relaxed, Rason went on: "It's agreed that the jewellery was not on her person when she was murdered. As we have your full cooperation now, Mr. Surbrook—perhaps you can give us a slant on this?"

He produced the signet ring.

"This scratch and cut, here! Made by pressing up against a diamond. Our miscroscope boys again! As there weren't any diamonds on her person, the ring could not have been on her person when it was pressed up against the diamond. It must have fallen off her finger, while she was being murdered. See what I mean?"

There was a long pause before Rason added:

"Who put the ring back on the dead woman's finger, Surbrook?"

THE MAN WHO
MURDERED IN PUBLIC

HOW little do you know about a man if you only know that he has committed four murders! That is all the public of his day knew of George Macartney. The papers handed out the usual thoughtless nonsense about a 'human monster,' and reminded the public that he was the son of Henry Macartney, the fraudulent financier—and that he therefore had a tainted heredity.

Now it is impossible to inherit a tendency to falsify balance sheets (not that George ever did anything of the kind). And as to the human monster stuff, with its suggestion of morbid bloodlust, it may be remarked that George netted by his murders a little over twenty-two thousand pounds. Further, it is the essence of anything to do with morbidity that the act should be secret. George Macartney is perhaps unique amongst murderers in that each of his four murders was eye-witnessed by anything from a dozen to several hundred persons, including a policeman or two.

All the same, the fact that Henry Macartney, his father, actually received fourteen years' penal servitude, is the key to the queer psychology of George himself. It was, however, not a matter of heredity but of objective circumstance—being the direct cause of young George receiving his first thrashing.

George was a late-grower both physically and mentally. Eventually he grew into a hefty man with plenty of pluck and intelligence. But at fifteen he was about the physical size of a boy of eleven, with much the same mental range. And a pretty dreadful little boy, too!

His mother was a very good sort but she had died when he was three. His father in his private life was amiable and undisciplined. There had been two or three schools which he had allowed the boy to leave, and two or three governesses who had been allowed to give up in despair. Unsuspected by his father, George had become a horrid little snob and a bully.

The story of the murders really starts with this boy sitting down to lunch at home in the big dining-room of their Surrey house on the last day of his father's trial. Akehurst, the butler, and the parlour-maid, are both in the environs of the Old Bailey waiting for the verdict which is expected at any time. Elsie Natley, the first house-maid, is waiting on George and thoroughly detesting him. In fact, her fingers are itching to get at him—and she is a very muscular girl of twenty.

"You've got to stand behind my chair when you wait on me. If you don't I shan't tell father—I shall jolly well tell Akehurst and he'll make you cry. I've seen him do it."

"All right, Master George! I'll stand behind your chair when I come back."

She ran out of the house because she had seen a telegraph-boy coming up the drive.

"Guilty. Fourteen years. Akehurst."

The other servants had not seen the telegraph-boy coming, so they could wait. She put the telegram down on the hall table, and from a little cupboard in an elaborate fitment surmounted by a stag's head, she took a galosh.

"Now, Master George!" she said. She whipped his coat over his head and dragged him on to the table, smashing the crockery. It is doubtful whether she was consciously avenging the three governesses and all that the butler and a succession of parlourmaids had endured, but there is no doubt that she laid it well in with the sole of the galosh.

We may assume that the pain to his person was no more than salutary. Nevertheless, damage was done of a more subtle nature. He knew that she was only twenty. And she was a girl. And he was fifteen and a boy. And for all his budding manhood he had been un-able to offer effective resistance.

The girl cannot be blamed. She was behaving naturally, as others ought to have behaved before—with no cruelty and with no more violence than she would have used towards a young brother if she had had one. It was beyond her imagination that she could have in-flicted a deep hurt that would take years to heal.

2

After the home was broken up George did not see Elsie again until he was twenty-one and she was twenty-six, when he met her by chance at Ilfracombe.

In the meantime a sister of his mother's had taken him over and sent him to an expensive private school run on public-school lines. He was there until he was nearly nineteen. They gave him a rudimentary education, taught him manners of a kind, but finally expelled him in spite of the fact that he had been instrumental in winning a swimming-cup for the school.

She sent him up to Cambridge but he did not last there a full term. His aunt did not turn him out—he just drifted off and eventually joined a theatrical touring company, where he was quite a useful man provided he were cast to type.

Elsie had kept herself very well and had scarcely changed at all. To George she no longer looked so dreadfully muscular—she looked rather pink-and-white and nice. He took off his hat to her and smiled, but he had to speak before she answered:

"Well, Master George! Oh, do excuse me calling you that when I ought to say 'Mr. Macartney.' Who *would* have thought of meeting you like this!"

The conversation followed standard lines. Elsie was having a holiday in a boarding-house selected by her late mistress who had departed for America, after which she intended to look round again for another job. George gave an account of himself, truthful except for a little romantic colour. He presented her with a stall for that night's performance, and the next afternoon hired a boat and took her for a row.

(*"I wasn't thinking about what she did to me all that time ago. Or if I was, I only thought I would wait for a chance to kiss her and sort of get even that way, like any young fellow might, as she was a good-looking girl and full of fun."*)

A muscular girl, too, and full of physical energy. George, in spite of some philandering experience, was perhaps a bit slow in making the running. For when they were about a mile off shore she became bored and suggested that she should take a turn at rowing.

Anything to please her, thought George, just like any other young man.

"Here, I may knock this. Put it in your pocket for me, George, and don't forget to let me have it afterwards whatever you do!"

She detached a bracelet, liberally set with big red stones. George affected to think it valuable. He put it in his pocket-case for her and she began to row. She had never rowed a sea-boat before and the inevitable happened. She lost an oar and made a grab for it. He made a grab, too, and the boat capsized.

George, as we have noted, was a crack swimmer, so here was a chance to play the hero in real life to a maiden in distress. But Elsie had not had time to consider George in the role of hero.

"Leggo, you brute, you'll drown me!" she cried, and landed him a useful blow on the nose.

(*"I swear I had no thought except to rescue her, like anyone else would. But when she hit me, somehow it all came back. I let her swim a couple of strokes to the boat, which was between us and the shore, and then before I knew what I was doing I collared her by the head from behind and put her under."*)

Fifty or sixty holiday-makers had seen the accident from the Capstan Hill. But there were no motor-boats in those days and it was some little time before a boat rowed by two seamen reached them. George was clinging to the upturned boat with one hand and with the other supporting Elsie.

But Elsie was in a vertical position, and her lungs had been full of water for something like a quarter of an hour.

At the inquest George admitted that she had been a housemaid in his father's house and that they had met by chance. He described the incident truthfully and then:

"I came up under the upturned boat and when I got out it was on the other side. I looked round for Elsie and couldn't see her, for she was on the sea side. Then I wriggled round the boat and after a bit I saw her hand come up. And then I caught hold of one of the oars which was floating and splashed up to where I'd seen her and after a bit I got her. I can't remember much about how I got her back to the boat because I'd swallowed a lot of water myself."

He took the risk of implying that he could hardly swim at all and no one in the theatrical company could deny it. The Coroner gave him a lecture on the folly of standing up in a small boat, opined that he had had a terrible lesson which would stay with him for the rest of his life and then, like everybody else, forgot about him. There are a certain number of boating and bathing fatalities every year, and this was one of them.

The company had moved on to Plymouth before George discovered that he was still in possession of the bracelet which Elsie had asked him to hold. He had not the slightest intention of stealing it but he did not want to stir things up. So he kept the bracelet and a little later gave it to Polly, a small-part girl in the company. When they quarrelled she gave it back to him, when something she said revealed to him that it was worth about eighty pounds. He was delighted, for he intended to pawn it at once.

Then he reflected that if it was worth all that money Elsie had almost certainly stolen it—which might lead to complications. It would be safer to get rid of it or keep it out of sight for a few years. More or less out of inadvertence, he kept it.

3

The theatre held no future for him. At the end of the tour he went back to sponge on his aunt for the few remaining months of her life. She was an annuitant with a negligible capital, but she left him some two thousand pounds with which he established himself as a motor-car agent.

Selling motor-cars in 1903 was a slow and heart-breaking process. It is incredible nowadays, but on the rare occasions when you booked a customer, some eight months would pass before you could redeem the car from the coach-builder's and collect your cheque.

The two thousand did not last very long. Soon a more balanced concern took over the agency and employed George as part clerk, part salesman. His new employer had been one of his father's victims but very generously felt only sympathy for George. He suggested that the name was an unfair handicap and himself paid the expenses of George changing his name by Deed Poll. Between them they constructed the name of 'Carshaw' as a good omen for business.

George was living fairly contentedly in lodgings in Richmond. We have no clue to his inmost thoughts at this time, but we may deduce that at the back of his thoughts was the consciousness that he had committed murder and got away with it. What fools, we imagine him reasoning, are murderers to be caught! To mess about with poison and guns and knives, which always leave clues! Whereas, if you have an accident which lots of people can witness it does not matter if you contradict yourself a bit. You are expected to be flurried. And unless they can prove that you deliberately upset the boat there is no possibility of their proving anything at all.

His evenings tended to be lonely, for he was not a very sociable young man and had no friends of his own sex. Indeed his earnings did not give him scope for much in the way of social activities, and he was already inclined to believe that the motor-car trade held no prospects.

Spring came with its insistent urge to be up and doing. If he could have Aunt Maud's two thousand over again he would know better what to do. On Sunday afternoons he began to loaf around the more prosperous residential streets of Richmond. The connection between this activity and the thought of two thousand pounds will not be immediately obvious to you. But it is almost certain that it was not immediately obvious to George.

Violet Laystall was a house-parlourmaid, whom he picked up one Sunday afternoon. She was reasonably good-looking and of quiet manners; and George, though he thought of himself as a gentleman, had been cured of snobbery and class-consciousness. On May 5th, 1904, he married her, a notable gift from the bridegroom to the bride being the ruby bracelet which had once belonged to Elsie.

He took her to live in his rooms, for his holiday was not yet due. On May 9th, he insured her life for £2,000. He proposed his own life for a similar amount, but the proposal was rejected by the Insurance Company on account of certain medical information he felt obliged to give the doctor about himself. And, of course, they made wills in each other's favour.

Their deferred honeymoon took place in the middle fortnight of August. He took her to Bognor. On the first three days the sea was choppy. On the afternoon of the fourth day he hired a small rowing-boat. When they were about a mile from the shore he suggested that she might like to try her hand at rowing.

She was a docile little woman and obediently took her place on the thwart. She pulled a few strokes while he manipulated the boat broadside to the shore. There were several pleasure boats dotted about, but none of them too close for his purpose and the nearest was that of the attendant on the fringe of the bathers.

He waited for her to lose an oar but, as time was valuable, he leant forward and bumped the sea-side oar out of the row-lock. Then he stood up and capsized the boat.

The little play had already been rehearsed, and he had only to repeat his lines. Even the Coroner made very much the same little speech about its being a lesson to him for the rest of his life. When he was leaving the Court, in a suitable state of collapse, an official handed him the ruby bracelet that had been taken from the dead woman's wrist.

<h1 style="text-align:center">4</h1>

Even with two thousand pounds in the bank, George Carshaw, as he now was, did not lose his head. Go slow and look round, was his motto. The motor trade, it seemed, was improving of its own accord; so without any extra effort George was soon more than equalling his salary in commission. He decided to stay on, a course which presented no embarrassment. His employer did not even know that he had married; and, as George was an unsociable man, he had not confided in any of his colleagues where he had intended to go for his holiday.

There being no immediate opening for capital, George thought a fellow might as well do himself comfortably for a bit. He began to spend his evenings in the West End. Shortly before Christmas he ran across the girl with whom he had had a flirtation in the touring company. She had a one-line part in pantomime, and was now glad to be taken out to supper. Before the pantomime was actually put on she resigned and joined forces with him, without benefit of clergy, in a flat in Baker Street.

She could not be described as mercenary, but she helped to make a very large dent in the two thousand. He grudged her nothing, for she fascinated him. She was known as 'Little Polly Flinders,' lived as Miss Flinders and would never tell him her real name. She certainly did not grab, and it was certainly he who tumbled on the original idea of replenishing their dwindling capital on the race-course. By June she discovered that she was not good for him and left him for his own sake. She may even have meant it, for they remained friends and from time to time renewed their association.

In September he married Madge Turnham, another muscular girl, a quick-witted, suspicious Cockney. But there was nothing very much to be suspicious about. He gave her the ruby bracelet and she promptly sneaked off and had it valued. When she learnt its worth she opened her eyes. When she had assured herself that he really was employed by a respectable motor agency she thanked her stars for a mug and eagerly married him.

At this stage George was undoubtedly planning everything very carefully. He insured her life for £100 only. Again he proposed a similar policy for his own life, and again got it turned down on the 'confession' he made to the doctor.

Life Insurance at best is a troublesome matter; but Accident Insurance is very simple. He took out an Accident policy on both their lives for ten thousand pounds each. The policy covered death by any kind of accident—including, of course, the accident of drowning.

5

Of his three wives Madge, who was the second, was the only really bad one. She was slovenly and quarrelsome. Her ill-nature, indeed, came near to imperilling George's plan. For she soon became known as a termagant—the kind of woman that nearly every kind of man would very soon come to hate. They lived in the upper part of a jerry-built house in Harringay and all the neighbours knew that occasionally they came to blows, after which she would be docile and well-behaved for nearly a week.

It is probable that her detestable temperament made George speed up the programme. They had a scrap on the Thursday before Whitsun 1906. George lost his temper this time and very nearly had to call a doctor for her afterwards. After the thumping she was extra docile, and perhaps George saw his last chance of staging a reconciliation. He took her to Paignton, a growing seaside resort on the south coast of Devon.

She said that the sea made her sick and she wouldn't go on it. But George, of course, was much more intelligent than his wife. He put up a convincing little pantomime with a five-pound note concealed at the back of his pocket-book against a rainy day—teased her and said that she should have the fiver if she could stay in a small rowing-boat with him for an hour without being seasick. And the greedy fool succumbed.

We imagine that George put to sea with a certain confidence. He had found a method of murder that was clue-proof. But on this occasion he was very nearly tripped by the element of time. For artificial respiration was applied in the boat that picked them up, and the heart was actually re-started, though it beat for a few seconds only.

But this was the only little contretemps—except that George caught a very bad cold. The inquest went off without a hitch. For neither the Coroner nor the local police kept indexed news cuttings of other boating and bathing fatalities in other years and other places.

But Dead Ends, which kept a large number of more or less useless records, used to file a cross-index of every death by violence in any form. They found that, within the space of two years, George Carshaw had lost two wives in precisely the same circumstances, detail for detail. In each case the boat had capsized about the same distance from shore. In each case he had prevented the body from sinking but not from drowning.

Then there was the cross-index (*'Fatality—Sea—Boat'*). In ten minutes a clerk had found that a similar accident, detail for detail, had happened at Ilfracombe in 1903 with Elsie Natley and George Macartney.

Detective-Sergeant Martleplug, an energetic officer attached to Dead Ends, dug out the Deed Poll and identified George Carshaw with George Macartney. He found that the two wives had been insured, that Elsie Natley was not his wife and was not insured—which puzzled him.

He found George arranging for a sale of his furniture and effects in Harringay. This was a fortnight later. George had drawn the insurance, and their few sticks were not worth preserving. The only joint possession of any value was the ruby bracelet, which he had again recovered.

The detective opened in a friendly manner and George responded. Martleplug revealed his knowledge of Violet, but was keeping Elsie up his sleeve.

"It fairly beats me, Mr. Martleplug, and that's a fact!" said George. "You'd think that when a thing like that's happened once, it couldn't possibly happen again. It used to haunt me—and that's why poor Madge persuaded me to go out again. And that—but why talk about it?"

"I've come here to talk about it," said Martleplug. "And I want to ask you a few questions."

"I am sorry," said George, who did not make the ignorant mistake of confusing a detective with a judge, "but the subject is very painful to me and I cannot discuss it. If you don't like that, why don't you arrest me for murder? I'll tell you why you don't—because you haven't got any evidence and can't get it."

George, as you will know, was quite right. The Public Prosecutor informed Martleplug that he quite agreed with George.

Of course, as far as commonsense goes, they were quite sure that George had murdered Madge. But George was saved by a very simple point in legal procedure. The only ground for assuming that he had forcibly drowned Madge was that he had taken part in two exactly similar 'accidents' before. Neither of these two earlier accidents could be put in as evidence in regard to the third accident, since there was no connection between them except the assumed connection in George's mind.

6

Ten thousand pounds enabled George to throw up his employment and start an independent agency once again himself. This time he could do it in style. He was able to buy two cars for demonstration purposes. He had a decent showroom with a well-equipped workshop in Tottenham Court Road.

One of his first customers was little Polly Flinders who came in on the arm of a prosperous broker from Newcastle. She was astonished to see him and rather pleased. In the course of the trial run he persuaded her to drop the broker. It meant losing a customer, but Polly was worth it, and he had more than half the ten thousand in reserve.

They took a flat on the unfashionable side of Regent's Park, which was conveniently near the office. This time Polly was determined to be good for him. She put her foot very firmly down on horse-racing, and after the first week or two refused to let him give her expensive dresses—except just a few, which, she said, would be economical in the end. He must, she said, learn to be sensible with his money. He must not speculate—he must invest. And if you invested money sensibly you could get as big a return as if you had speculated with it. There was, for example, The Theatre, of which

George already had too much practical knowledge to be fooled, as he had been fooled by racing tipsters.

She had, it transpired, heard of a play only the other day which contained great possibilities of profit. By the instrumentality of one of the economical-expensive frocks she obtained the script from the author. When she read the part which she would play if George should decide to go into production as a side-line, he agreed that it sounded fine.

George paid for the play to be put on and, by running a small mortgage on the agency, managed to prop it up for six weeks at one of the minor West End theatres. He had just enough left to send it on tour in the provinces—with Polly in her part. So he lost both his money and his girl—though she continued to write him most affectionate letters from the provinces until the tour collapsed.

George did quite well with the agency. He had a liking for motor-cars and put in plenty of work. But he was handling one of the smaller makes that has since perished. There was the slack first quarter of the new year in which the rent and wages of the workshop staff became a problem. He pulled up a bit in the summer but not quite enough. If the agency were to live it must have new capital.

He found May Toler outside a servants' registry office in Piccadilly. She was thirty-two and the only one of his wives who was definitely pretty, with beautiful long hands, which she had been able to preserve; for it was more than ten years since she had been anything but a very good-class parlourmaid.

With her he had to exert all his resources and his rather crude charm. And there were several set-backs. Her family, who lived at Willesden, did not like him at first. But their hostility was killed by his gift of the ruby bracelet which they recognised to be valuable.

She married him, against her better judgment, in February 1908. He had persuaded her to cut out the still querulous family and more or less make an elopement of it. For the ceremony was performed with paid witnesses before the registrar at Camden Town.

Possibly he thought that in this way he was preventing the police from learning of his marriage. On the other hand we can be quite certain that, at this stage, his attitude to the police was one of open defiance. He was aware that they believed him to be a murderer. Well, he had invented the perfect murder that could even, as it were, be performed in public. And here we must reluctantly concede a small point to the fanatics of heredity—for his father had behaved just like this, faking his balance sheet with a system of his own when he knew the police accountants were looking for the fake.

They took out a joint-life assurance for £500. The joint-life element can hardly have been a serious attempt to throw dust into anyone's eyes, for he used it subsequently as a means of raising a small loan for his business. They made wills in each other's favour—and he sent her on her own to take out an Accident Policy with a different company for £10,000 against death by accident.

Their circumstances during the summer were easy enough, but the winter was a bit of a pinch. They had taken a small, noisy flat off Theobald's Road. The very superior parlourmaid proved a very indifferent cook and a hopeless manager. Personally, too, she went to pieces very soon after the wedding. He seems to have been kind enough to her and she herself was not quarrelsome. But she missed her occupation and she would whine a good deal and drop into melancholy and latterly there is evidence that she took to drink.

It became doubtful whether George would have enough capital to take full advantage of next summer's business. So between Easter and Whitsun he took her to Colwyn Bay in North Wales.

This time the only variation in the programme was that he rowed her farther out from shore. There was no question of her being alive when they were picked up.

He got his shock this time in the Coroner's Court. He had just repeated his little speech as to how it had all happened when a barrister got up, representing the police.

Now the Rules of Evidence in a High Court are many and varied. But the rules of evidence in a Coroner's Court are just exactly what the Coroner likes. It may be a legal anomaly that the man who is often an amateur is given more discretion than a judge—but there it is! And George had to make the best of it.

"Was your wife insured, Mr. Carshaw?"

"We had a joint policy for five hundred pounds, in mortgage for my business."

"Any other insurance?"

"I don't know. She may have."

"You don't know. Was your last wife insured against death by accident for ten thousand pounds?"

"Yes."

"Did she on June 15th, 1906, meet with an exactly similar accident at Paignton? I mean, had you rowed her out and did the boat capsize in—er—the precise manner in which you have just described in respect of your—er—latest wife?"

Point by point he brought out the details of the drowning of Madge, then of the drowning of Violet and, point by point, matched them with the drowning of May.

Three was good enough. He could not make the insurance point in respect of Elsie, so he left it alone.

It is open to the critical to take the view that this cross-examination was a definite 'wangle' on the part of the police. They could bring the facts out in the Coroner's Court, though not in the High Court. But by the time the Coroner's case was reported, every man in the country who was likely to sit on the jury would have been certain to read the facts. So the jury would know.

But the Coroner's Court carried them a bit further than they meant to go. The jury brought in a verdict of wilful murder against George Carshaw and he was committed for trial on the Coroner's warrant.

The Crown felt that it must go on with the case. George was brought up for trial in the following June.

In the meantime, Martleplug had traced George back to the private school where he had been instrumental in winning a swimming-cup. They had got against him now that he was a powerful swimmer, and that his thrice-repeated tale of floundering about with an oar was all nonsense.

But even so George got away with it.

7

It was a rising young lawyer, now well known as Sir Ernest Quilter, K.C., who saved George Carshaw from his reasonably certain fate of being hanged as the murderer of his wife, May.

Counsel for the Prosecution opened by describing in minute detail the circumstancees in which May had met her death. He then paused and looked at the judge—an action which was very close indeed to being a prearranged signal. But as this was done by arrangement with the defence there could be no objection. The judge promptly ordered the jury to retire and then listened to arguments on both sides as to the admissibility of evidence of the two previously drowned wives. Owing to the absence of the money-element the Crown had come to the conclusion that the first drowning, of Elsie Natley, was a genuine accident which had given George the idea for the subsequent murders.

The Prosecution claimed admissibility of the previous accidents and quoted precedent. But Quilter scotched him.

"In all the precedents which my learned friend has quoted, there has invariably been the *prima facie* assumption of guilt. In this case I submit that there is no *prima facie* assumption of guilt whatever. There is the overwhelming assumption of an accident—which can only be upset by consideration of the previous cases."

A bold line—for it admitted by implication that George was a murderer.

The judge agreed and ruled that the evidence of the previous drownings was inadmissible until the Prosecution had established a reasonably strong *prima facie* assumption of guilt in respect of May. Each counsel seemed extremely pleased with this ruling.

At an early stage the Treasury man called George's old school-master, together with one of the staff and two men who had been pupils with George. These men proved George's swimming prowess. The Prosecution was triumphant.

"My lord, the deceased was drowned admittedly within a dozen or so yards of the upturned boat. Is it to be believed that the prisoner, who was a very able swimmer, was powerless to effect her rescue, as he stated? I submit that a *prima facie* case has been made out of the prisoner's guilt. I shall therefore ask your lordship's leave to intro-duce—other evidence."

Mr. Quilter had been waiting for this.

"I object, my lord. It is no part of my case to deny that my client *could* have saved his wife from drowning had he wished to do so."

Daring again! Sailing right into the wind! There was what the newspapers insist upon calling a sensation in Court. And Quilter went on:

"My learned friend has forgotten more law than I ever knew, so he will not object to my reminding him of the principle enshrined in the doggerel:

> *'Thou shalt not kill, but needst not strive*
> *Officiously to keep alive.'*

"I admit that Carshaw *did not strive* to keep his wife alive. I am
not here to defend his moral character, nor his conscience. I am still
waiting for my friend to show that any action of Carshaw's betrays
evidence of felonious intent."

Quilter scored again.

Once those two persons were in the water, the most that could be
proved against George was that he had deliberately refrained from
rescuing his wife. Again, the law may be at variance with the public
conscience, but the law remains. And the law lays it down that you
need never rescue anybody from anything if you don't want to.

That limited the Prosecution to proving that the boat had been feloniously capsized by George—which in the nature of things was un-
provable. At the judge's direction the jury found George Carshaw
'not guilty.'

After escaping under police escort from the mob around the Court,
George showed his gratitude to Mr. Quilter by briefing him to re-
cover the ten thousand pounds from the Accident Insurance Company in respect of May's death. And again Quilter won.

Fortunately for George, he had given his agency a fancy name
and was able to resume business, equipped now with ample capital.
He got in touch with Polly Flinders, but this time she shrieked when
he came near her and he had to run for it.

There was, it would be safe to say, no one in the country who
doubted George's guilt. He had to take an assumed name, without
Deed Poll this time. But whatever inconvenience he may have suffered in this way was compensated for by his egomaniac delight in
the fact that the police knew him to be a multiple murderer and
could not touch him.

8

In the following October there arrived at a West End Hotel a Mr.
and Mrs. Huystefan. Mrs. Huystefan was an Englishwoman who had
married an American. One evening, while she was dressing for dinner, she was assaulted in her bedroom and robbed of her jewellery.
She was too shaken to be of much use to the police that night. But
her husband, who was a methodical man, gave them an old typewritten list of the items of his wife's jewellery.

His name, he contrived to explain, was that of an old Southern
family who had arrived before the *Mayflower,* and on all the gold

pieces the family crest, a lion couchant, would be found.

The Yard had not very much hope. A hotel job would mean crooks in a good way of business. But they sent out the drag-net and were rather surprised to get a response from a pawnbroker in Holborn, who produced a ruby bracelet with the crest stamped inside the gold mount.

"How long have you had this?"

"Pawned with me last February by a Mrs. Carshaw. There's the address—Theobald's Road——"

"Then you're all right, because it's not what we want. But you might leave it with us for a couple of days."

On account of the name and address, the bracelet went to Dead Ends as a matter of routine. No purely logical detective would have wasted a moment over that bracelet. Mrs. Huystefan had been in England a week and this had been pawned in London last February. And it wasn't as though the crest were in any way an unusual design.

But a ruby bracelet was listed amongst the stolen jewellery. So Detective Inspector Rason requested Mrs. Huystefan, now restored to health, to call at the Yard and identify it.

She identified it at once as her bracelet, and then became profusely apologetic.

"I'm so sorry you've had this trouble with the bracelet," she said. "I forgot it was on that old list my husband gave you, or I would have notified you at once. I gave it away as a present when I was in England six years ago. I'm very sorry she had to pawn it. If you are in touch with her, I would be so glad if you would give me her address, as I would like to help her again."

"Help *who,* Mrs. Huystefan?"

"The girl I gave it to. Elsie Natley. She was one of my maids in Town here just after I married Mr. Huystefan. We took a bungalow that year at Croyde, near Ilfracombe in North Devon, and she came with us as cook-general, for we were roughing it, you know. You don't want the whole story, but I gave it to her because she saved my life. It wasn't the sort of thing you could give a money tip for, was it? If she's in trouble I would so like to know her address."

"Do you mind telling me how she saved your life, Mrs. Huystefan?"

"It was at bathing—yes, bathing! The currents round there are simply dreadful and I didn't know it. I swam out and couldn't get in again. It was a bit choppy and my strength was going. My husband rushed in after me, but he was a poor swimmer. Elsie spotted my trouble from the bungalow. She came rushing out, whipping off her skirt as she ran, then her shoes. She outstripped my husband and got to me just in time and brought me in. She was a magnificent swimmer—her father used to be a waterman on the River Lee."

"Thank you, Mrs. Huystefan. You don't think of leaving England for a few weeks?"

"No, we're over for six months."

Rason thanked her again, then looked up the dossier of Elsie Natley. Elsie had died, as had the other women, of asphyxia resulting from drowning. Not of anything else.

Rason told his tale to the Chief, and soon was telling it again to a junior lawyer from the Public Prosecutor's office.

Rason, of course, was privileged and he received the young man with a smile.

"If you had been able to prove that Carshaw's wife, May, had been a very strong swimmer, you'd have got a conviction, wouldn't you?"

"Of course we would! We could have used it to prove, what every one knows, that he held her under! Also, it would have established a *prima facie* case and we could have brought in the other cases."

"Well, there's a Mrs. Huystefan to prove that Elsie Natley was a strong swimmer. And you've still got the two other cases left— Madge and Violet. And as they wouldn't let you use them the other day you can use 'em now."

George was hanged on Dec. 7th, 1909, for the murder of Elsie Natley.

A CATALOGUE OF
SELECTED DOVER BOOKS
IN ALL FIELDS OF INTEREST

A CATALOGUE OF SELECTED DOVER
BOOKS IN ALL FIELDS OF INTEREST

RACKHAM'S COLOR ILLUSTRATIONS FOR WAGNER'S RING. Rackham's finest mature work—all 64 full-color watercolors in a faithful and lush interpretation of the *Ring*. Full-sized plates on coated stock of the paintings used by opera companies for authentic staging of Wagner. Captions aid in following complete Ring cycle. Introduction. 64 illustrations plus vignettes. 72pp. 8⅝ x 11¼.   23779-6 Pa. $6.00

CONTEMPORARY POLISH POSTERS IN FULL COLOR, edited by Joseph Czestochowski. 46 full-color examples of brilliant school of Polish graphic design, selected from world's first museum (near Warsaw) dedicated to poster art. Posters on circuses, films, plays, concerts all show cosmopolitan influences, free imagination. Introduction. 48pp. 9⅜ x 12¼.
23780-X Pa. $6.00

GRAPHIC WORKS OF EDVARD MUNCH, Edvard Munch. 90 haunting, evocative prints by first major Expressionist artist and one of the greatest graphic artists of his time: *The Scream, Anxiety, Death Chamber, The Kiss, Madonna,* etc. Introduction by Alfred Werner. 90pp. 9 x 12.
23765-6 Pa. $5.00

THE GOLDEN AGE OF THE POSTER, Hayward and Blanche Cirker. 70 extraordinary posters in full colors, from Maitres de l'Affiche, Mucha, Lautrec, Bradley, Cheret, Beardsley, many others. Total of 78pp. 9⅜ x 12¼.   22753-7 Pa. $5.95

THE NOTEBOOKS OF LEONARDO DA VINCI, edited by J. P. Richter. Extracts from manuscripts reveal great genius; on painting, sculpture, anatomy, sciences, geography, etc. Both Italian and English. 186 ms. pages reproduced, plus 500 additional drawings, including studies for *Last Supper,* Sforza monument, etc. 860pp. 7⅞ x 10¾. (Available in U.S. only)
22572-0, 22573-9 Pa., Two-vol. set $15.90

THE CODEX NUTTALL, as first edited by Zelia Nuttall. Only inexpensive edition, in full color, of a pre-Columbian Mexican (Mixtec) book. 88 color plates show kings, gods, heroes, temples, sacrifices. New explanatory, historical introduction by Arthur G. Miller. 96pp. 11⅜ x 8½. (Available in U.S. only)   23168-2 Pa. $7.95

UNE SEMAINE DE BONTÉ, A SURREALISTIC NOVEL IN COLLAGE, Max Ernst. Masterpiece created out of 19th-century periodical illustrations, explores worlds of terror and surprise. Some consider this Ernst's greatest work. 208pp. 8⅛ x 11.   23252-2 Pa. $6.00

CATALOGUE OF DOVER BOOKS

DRAWINGS OF WILLIAM BLAKE, William Blake. 92 plates from Book of Job, *Divine Comedy, Paradise Lost,* visionary heads, mythological figures, Laocoon, etc. Selection, introduction, commentary by Sir Geoffrey Keynes. 178pp. 8⅛ x 11. 22303-5 Pa. $4.00

ENGRAVINGS OF HOGARTH, William Hogarth. 101 of Hogarth's greatest works: *Rake's Progress, Harlot's Progress, Illustrations for Hudibras, Before and After, Beer Street and Gin Lane,* many more. Full commentary. 256pp. 11 x 13¾. 22479-1 Pa. $12.95

DAUMIER: 120 GREAT LITHOGRAPHS, Honore Daumier. Wide-ranging collection of lithographs by the greatest caricaturist of the 19th century. Concentrates on eternally popular series on lawyers, on married life, on liberated women, etc. Selection, introduction, and notes on plates by Charles F. Ramus. Total of 158pp. 9⅜ x 12¼. 23512-2 Pa. $6.00

DRAWINGS OF MUCHA, Alphonse Maria Mucha. Work reveals draftsman of highest caliber: studies for famous posters and paintings, renderings for book illustrations and ads, etc. 70 works, 9 in color; including 6 items not drawings. Introduction. List of illustrations. 72pp. 9⅜ x 12¼. (Available in U.S. only) 23672-2 Pa. $4.00

GIOVANNI BATTISTA PIRANESI: DRAWINGS IN THE PIERPONT MORGAN LIBRARY, Giovanni Battista Piranesi. For first time ever all of Morgan Library's collection, world's largest. 167 illustrations of rare Piranesi drawings—archeological, architectural, decorative and visionary. Essay, detailed list of drawings, chronology, captions. Edited by Felice Stampfle. 144pp. 9⅜ x 12¼. 23714-1 Pa. $7.50

NEW YORK ETCHINGS (1905-1949), John Sloan. All of important American artist's N.Y. life etchings. 67 works include some of his best art; also lively historical record—Greenwich Village, tenement scenes. Edited by Sloan's widow. Introduction and captions. 79pp. 8⅜ x 11¼. 23651-X Pa. $4.00

CHINESE PAINTING AND CALLIGRAPHY: A PICTORIAL SURVEY, Wan-go Weng. 69 fine examples from John M. Crawford's matchless private collection: landscapes, birds, flowers, human figures, etc., plus calligraphy. Every basic form included: hanging scrolls, handscrolls, album leaves, fans, etc. 109 illustrations. Introduction. Captions. 192pp. 8⅞ x 11¾. 23707-9 Pa. $7.95

DRAWINGS OF REMBRANDT, edited by Seymour Slive. Updated Lippmann, Hofstede de Groot edition, with definitive scholarly apparatus. All portraits, biblical sketches, landscapes, nudes, Oriental figures, classical studies, together with selection of work by followers. 550 illustrations. Total of 630pp. 9⅛ x 12¼. 21485-0, 21486-9 Pa., Two-vol. set $15.00

THE DISASTERS OF WAR, Francisco Goya. 83 etchings record horrors of Napoleonic wars in Spain and war in general. Reprint of 1st edition, plus 3 additional plates. Introduction by Philip Hofer. 97pp. 9⅜ x 8¼. 21872-4 Pa. $4.00

THE EARLY WORK OF AUBREY BEARDSLEY, Aubrey Beardsley. 157 plates, 2 in color: *Manon Lescaut, Madame Bovary, Morte Darthur, Salome,* other. Introduction by H. Marillier. 182pp. 8⅛ x 11. 21816-3 Pa. $4.50

THE LATER WORK OF AUBREY BEARDSLEY, Aubrey Beardsley. Exotic masterpieces of full maturity: *Venus and Tannhauser, Lysistrata, Rape of the Lock, Volpone,* Savoy material, etc. 174 plates, 2 in color. 186pp. 8⅛ x 11. 21817-1 Pa. $5.95

THOMAS NAST'S CHRISTMAS DRAWINGS, Thomas Nast. Almost all Christmas drawings by creator of image of Santa Claus as we know it, and one of America's foremost illustrators and political cartoonists. 66 illustrations. 3 illustrations in color on covers. 96pp. 8⅜ x 11¼. 23660-9 Pa. $3.50

THE DORÉ ILLUSTRATIONS FOR DANTE'S DIVINE COMEDY, Gustave Doré. All 135 plates from Inferno, Purgatory, Paradise; fantastic tortures, infernal landscapes, celestial wonders. Each plate with appropriate (translated) verses. 141pp. 9 x 12. 23231-X Pa. $4.50

DORÉ'S ILLUSTRATIONS FOR RABELAIS, Gustave Doré. 252 striking illustrations of *Gargantua and Pantagruel* books by foremost 19th-century illustrator. Including 60 plates, 192 delightful smaller illustrations. 153pp. 9 x 12. 23656-0 Pa. $5.00

LONDON: A PILGRIMAGE, Gustave Doré, Blanchard Jerrold. Squalor, riches, misery, beauty of mid-Victorian metropolis; 55 wonderful plates, 125 other illustrations, full social, cultural text by Jerrold. 191pp. of text. 9⅜ x 12¼. 22306-X Pa. $7.00

THE RIME OF THE ANCIENT MARINER, Gustave Doré, S. T. Coleridge. Dore's finest work, 34 plates capture moods, subtleties of poem. Full text. Introduction by Millicent Rose. 77pp. 9¼ x 12. 22305-1 Pa. $3.50

THE DORE BIBLE ILLUSTRATIONS, Gustave Doré. All wonderful, detailed plates: Adam and Eve, Flood, Babylon, Life of Jesus, etc. Brief King James text with each plate. Introduction by Millicent Rose. 241 plates. 241pp. 9 x 12. 23004-X Pa. $6.00

THE COMPLETE ENGRAVINGS, ETCHINGS AND DRYPOINTS OF ALBRECHT DURER. "Knight, Death and Devil"; "Melencolia," and more—all Dürer's known works in all three media, including 6 works formerly attributed to him. 120 plates. 235pp. 8⅜ x 11¼. 22851-7 Pa. $6.50

MECHANICK EXERCISES ON THE WHOLE ART OF PRINTING, Joseph Moxon. First complete book (1683-4) ever written about typography, a compendium of everything known about printing at the latter part of 17th century. Reprint of 2nd (1962) Oxford Univ. Press edition. 74 illustrations. Total of 550pp. 6⅛ x 9¼. 23617-X Pa. $7.95

THE COMPLETE WOODCUTS OF ALBRECHT DURER, edited by Dr. W. Kurth. 346 in all: "Old Testament," "St. Jerome," "Passion," "Life of Virgin," Apocalypse," many others. Introduction by Campbell Dodgson. 285pp. 8½ x 12¼.   21097-9 Pa. $7.50

DRAWINGS OF ALBRECHT DURER, edited by Heinrich Wolfflin. 81 plates show development from youth to full style. Many favorites; many new. Introduction by Alfred Werner. 96pp. 8⅛ x 11.   22352-3 Pa. $5.00

THE HUMAN FIGURE, Albrecht Dürer. Experiments in various techniques—stereometric, progressive proportional, and others. Also life studies that rank among finest ever done. Complete reprinting of *Dresden Sketchbook*. 170 plates. 355pp. 8⅜ x 11¼.   21042-1 Pa. $7.95

OF THE JUST SHAPING OF LETTERS, Albrecht Dürer. Renaissance artist explains design of Roman majuscules by geometry, also Gothic lower and capitals. Grolier Club edition. 43pp. 7⅞ x 10¾   21306-4 Pa. $3.00

TEN BOOKS ON ARCHITECTURE, Vitruvius. The most important book ever written on architecture. Early Roman aesthetics, technology, classical orders, site selection, all other aspects. Stands behind everything since. Morgan translation. 331pp. 5⅜ x 8½.   20645-9 Pa. $4.50

THE FOUR BOOKS OF ARCHITECTURE, Andrea Palladio. 16th-century classic responsible for Palladian movement and style. Covers classical architectural remains, Renaissance revivals, classical orders, etc. 1738 Ware English edition. Introduction by A. Placzek. 216 plates. 110pp. of text. 9½ x 12¾.   21308-0 Pa. $10.00

HORIZONS, Norman Bel Geddes. Great industrialist stage designer, "father of streamlining," on application of aesthetics to transportation, amusement, architecture, etc. 1932 prophetic account; function, theory, specific projects. 222 illustrations. 312pp. 7⅞ x 10¾.   23514-9 Pa. $6.95

FRANK LLOYD WRIGHT'S FALLINGWATER, Donald Hoffmann. Full, illustrated story of conception and building of Wright's masterwork at Bear Run, Pa. 100 photographs of site, construction, and details of completed structure. 112pp. 9¼ x 10.   23671-4 Pa. $5.50

THE ELEMENTS OF DRAWING, John Ruskin. Timeless classic by great Viltorian; starts with basic ideas, works through more difficult. Many practical exercises. 48 illustrations. Introduction by Lawrence Campbell. 228pp. 5⅜ x 8½.   22730-8 Pa. $3.75

GIST OF ART, John Sloan. Greatest modern American teacher, Art Students League, offers innumerable hints, instructions, guided comments to help you in painting. Not a formal course. 46 illustrations. Introduction by Helen Sloan. 200pp. 5⅜ x 8½.   23435-5 Pa. $4.00

THE ANATOMY OF THE HORSE, George Stubbs. Often considered the great masterpiece of animal anatomy. Full reproduction of 1766 edition, plus prospectus; original text and modernized text. 36 plates. Introduction by Eleanor Garvey. 121pp. 11 x 14¾. 23402-9 Pa. $6.00

BRIDGMAN'S LIFE DRAWING, George B. Bridgman. More than 500 illustrative drawings and text teach you to abstract the body into its major masses, use light and shade, proportion; as well as specific areas of anatomy, of which Bridgman is master. 192pp. 6½ x 9¼. (Available in U.S. only) 22710-3 Pa. $3.50

ART NOUVEAU DESIGNS IN COLOR, Alphonse Mucha, Maurice Verneuil, Georges Auriol. Full-color reproduction of *Combinaisons ornementales* (c. 1900) by Art Nouveau masters. Floral, animal, geometric, interlacings, swashes—borders, frames, spots—all incredibly beautiful. 60 plates, hundreds of designs. 9⅜ x 8-1/16. 22885-1 Pa. $4.00

FULL-COLOR FLORAL DESIGNS IN THE ART NOUVEAU STYLE, E. A. Seguy. 166 motifs, on 40 plates, from *Les fleurs et leurs applications decoratives* (1902): borders, circular designs, repeats, allovers, "spots." All in authentic Art Nouveau colors. 48pp. 9⅜ x 12¼. 23439-8 Pa. $5.00

A DIDEROT PICTORIAL ENCYCLOPEDIA OF TRADES AND INDUSTRY, edited by Charles C. Gillispie. 485 most interesting plates from the great French Encyclopedia of the 18th century show hundreds of working figures, artifacts, process, land and cityscapes; glassmaking, papermaking, metal extraction, construction, weaving, making furniture, clothing, wigs, dozens of other activities. Plates fully explained. 920pp. 9 x 12. 22284-5, 22285-3 Clothbd., Two-vol. set $40.00

HANDBOOK OF EARLY ADVERTISING ART, Clarence P. Hornung. Largest collection of copyright-free early and antique advertising art ever compiled. Over 6,000 illustrations, from Franklin's time to the 1890's for special effects, novelty. Valuable source, almost inexhaustible.
Pictorial Volume. Agriculture, the zodiac, animals, autos, birds, Christmas, fire engines, flowers, trees, musical instruments, ships, games and sports, much more. Arranged by subject matter and use. 237 plates. 288pp. 9 x 12. 20122-8 Clothbd. $14.50

Typographical Volume. Roman and Gothic faces ranging from 10 point to 300 point, "Barnum," German and Old English faces, script, logotypes, scrolls and flourishes, 1115 ornamental initials, 67 complete alphabets, more. 310 plates. 320pp. 9 x 12. 20123-6 Clothbd. $15.00

CALLIGRAPHY (CALLIGRAPHIA LATINA), J. G. Schwandner. High point of 18th-century ornamental calligraphy. Very ornate initials, scrolls, borders, cherubs, birds, lettered examples. 172pp. 9 x 13. 20475-8 Pa. $7.00

CATALOGUE OF DOVER BOOKS

ART FORMS IN NATURE, Ernst Haeckel. Multitude of strangely beautiful natural forms: Radiolaria, Foraminifera, jellyfishes, fungi, turtles, bats, etc. All 100 plates of the 19th-century evolutionist's *Kunstformen der Natur* (1904). 100pp. 9⅜ x 12¼. 22987-4 Pa. $5.00

CHILDREN: A PICTORIAL ARCHIVE FROM NINETEENTH-CENTURY SOURCES, edited by Carol Belanger Grafton. 242 rare, copyright-free wood engravings for artists and designers. Widest such selection available. All illustrations in line. 119pp. 8⅜ x 11¼.
23694-3 Pa. $4.00

WOMEN: A PICTORIAL ARCHIVE FROM NINETEENTH-CENTURY SOURCES, edited by Jim Harter. 391 copyright-free wood engravings for artists and designers selected from rare periodicals. Most extensive such collection available. All illustrations in line. 128pp. 9 x 12.
23703-6 Pa. $4.50

ARABIC ART IN COLOR, Prisse d'Avennes. From the greatest ornamentalists of all time—50 plates in color, rarely seen outside the Near East, rich in suggestion and stimulus. Includes 4 plates on covers. 46pp. 9⅜ x 12¼. 23658-7 Pa. $6.00

AUTHENTIC ALGERIAN CARPET DESIGNS AND MOTIFS, edited by June Beveridge. Algerian carpets are world famous. Dozens of geometrical motifs are charted on grids, color-coded, for weavers, needleworkers, craftsmen, designers. 53 illustrations plus 4 in color. 48pp. 8¼ x 11. (Available in U.S. only) 23650-1 Pa. $1.75

DICTIONARY OF AMERICAN PORTRAITS, edited by Hayward and Blanche Cirker. 4000 important Americans, earliest times to 1905, mostly in clear line. Politicians, writers, soldiers, scientists, inventors, industrialists, Indians, Blacks, women, outlaws, etc. Identificatory information. 756pp. 9¼ x 12¾. 21823-6 Clothbd. $40.00

HOW THE OTHER HALF LIVES, Jacob A. Riis. Journalistic record of filth, degradation, upward drive in New York immigrant slums, shops, around 1900. New edition includes 100 original Riis photos, monuments of early photography. 233pp. 10 x 7⅞. 22012-5 Pa. $7.00

NEW YORK IN THE THIRTIES, Berenice Abbott. Noted photographer's fascinating study of city shows new buildings that have become famous and old sights that have disappeared forever. Insightful commentary. 97 photographs. 97pp. 11⅜ x 10. 22967-X Pa. $5.00

MEN AT WORK, Lewis W. Hine. Famous photographic studies of construction workers, railroad men, factory workers and coal miners. New supplement of 18 photos on Empire State building construction. New introduction by Jonathan L. Doherty. Total of 69 photos. 63pp. 8 x 10¾.
23475-4 Pa. $3.00

THE DEPRESSION YEARS AS PHOTOGRAPHED BY ARTHUR ROTH-
STEIN, Arthur Rothstein. First collection devoted entirely to the work of
outstanding 1930s photographer: famous dust storm photo, ragged children,
unemployed, etc. 120 photographs. Captions. 119pp. 9¼ x 10¾.
23590-4 Pa. $5.00

CAMERA WORK: A PICTORIAL GUIDE, Alfred Stieglitz. All 559 illustrations and plates from the most important periodical in the history of
art photography, *Camera Work* (1903-17). Presented four to a page, reduced in size but still clear, in strict chronological order, with complete
captions. Three indexes. Glossary. Bibliography. 176pp. 8⅜ x 11¼.
23591-2 Pa. $6.95

ALVIN LANGDON COBURN, PHOTOGRAPHER, Alvin L. Coburn. Revealing autobiography by one of greatest photographers of 20th century
gives insider's version of Photo-Secession, plus comments on his own work.
77 photographs by Coburn. Edited by Helmut and Alison Gernsheim.
160pp. 8⅛ x 11. 23685-4 Pa. $6.00

NEW YORK IN THE FORTIES, Andreas Feininger. 162 brilliant photographs by the well-known photographer, formerly with *Life* magazine, show
commuters, shoppers, Times Square at night, Harlem nightclub, Lower
East Side, etc. Introduction and full captions by John von Hartz. 181pp.
9¼ x 10¾. 23585-8 Pa. $6.95

GREAT NEWS PHOTOS AND THE STORIES BEHIND THEM, John
Faber. Dramatic volume of 140 great news photos, 1855 through 1976,
and revealing stories behind them, with both historical and technical information. Hindenburg disaster, shooting of Oswald, nomination of Jimmy
Carter, etc. 160pp. 8¼ x 11. 23667-6 Pa. $5.00

THE ART OF THE CINEMATOGRAPHER, Leonard Maltin. Survey of
American cinematography history and anecdotal interviews with 5 masters—
Arthur Miller, Hal Mohr, Hal Rosson, Lucien Ballard, and Conrad Hall.
Very large selection of behind-the-scenes production photos. 105 photo-
graphs. Filmographies. Index. Originally *Behind the Camera.* 144pp.
8¼ x 11. 23686-2 Pa. $5.00

DESIGNS FOR THE THREE-CORNERED HAT (LE TRICORNE),
Pablo Picasso. 32 fabulously rare drawings—including 31 color illustrations
of costumes and accessories—for 1919 production of famous ballet. Edited
by Parmenia Migel, who has written new introduction. 48pp. 9⅜ x 12¼.
(Available in U.S. only) 23709-5 Pa. $5.00

NOTES OF A FILM DIRECTOR, Sergei Eisenstein. Greatest Russian
filmmaker explains montage, making of *Alexander Nevsky,* aesthetics; comments on self, associates, great rivals (Chaplin), similar material. 78 illustrations. 240pp. 5⅜ x 8½. 22392-2 Pa. $4.50

HOLLYWOOD GLAMOUR PORTRAITS, edited by John Kobal. 145 photos capture the stars from 1926-49, the high point in portrait photography. Gable, Harlow, Bogart, Bacall, Hedy Lamarr, Marlene Dietrich, Robert Montgomery, Marlon Brando, Veronica Lake; 94 stars in all. Full background on photographers, technical aspects, much more. Total of 160pp. 8⅜ x 11¼.   23352-9 Pa. $6.00

THE NEW YORK STAGE: FAMOUS PRODUCTIONS IN PHOTOGRAPHS, edited by Stanley Appelbaum. 148 photographs from Museum of City of New York show 142 plays, 1883-1939. *Peter Pan, The Front Page, Dead End, Our Town*, O'Neill, hundreds of actors and actresses, etc. Full indexes. 154pp. 9½ x 10.   23241-7 Pa. $6.00

DIALOGUES CONCERNING TWO NEW SCIENCES, Galileo Galilei. Encompassing 30 years of experiment and thought, these dialogues deal with geometric demonstrations of fracture of solid bodies, cohesion, leverage, speed of light and sound, pendulums, falling bodies, accelerated motion, etc. 300pp. 5⅜ x 8½.   60099-8 Pa. $4.00

THE GREAT OPERA STARS IN HISTORIC PHOTOGRAPHS, edited by James Camner. 343 portraits from the 1850s to the 1940s: Tamburini, Mario, Caliapin, Jeritza, Melchior, Melba, Patti, Pinza, Schipa, Caruso, Farrar, Steber, Gobbi, and many more—270 performers in all. Index. 199pp. 8⅜ x 11¼.   23575-0 Pa. $7.50

J. S. BACH, Albert Schweitzer. Great full-length study of Bach, life, background to music, music, by foremost modern scholar. Ernest Newman translation. 650 musical examples. Total of 928pp. 5⅜ x 8½. (Available in U.S. only)   21631-4, 21632-2 Pa., Two-vol. set $11.00

COMPLETE PIANO SONATAS, Ludwig van Beethoven. All sonatas in the fine Schenker edition, with fingering, analytical material. One of best modern editions. Total of 615pp. 9 x 12. (Available in U.S. only)
                                    23134-8, 23135-6 Pa., Two-vol. set $15.50

KEYBOARD MUSIC, J. S. Bach. Bach-Gesellschaft edition. For harpsichord, piano, other keyboard instruments. English Suites, French Suites, Six Partitas, Goldberg Variations, Two-Part Inventions, Three-Part Sinfonias. 312pp. 8⅛ x 11. (Available in U.S. only)   22360-4 Pa. $6.95

FOUR SYMPHONIES IN FULL SCORE, Franz Schubert. Schubert's four most popular symphonies: No. 4 in C Minor ("Tragic"); No. 5 in B-flat Major; No. 8 in B Minor ("Unfinished"); No. 9 in C Major ("Great"). Breitkopf & Hartel edition. Study score. 261pp. 9⅜ x 12¼.
                                                         23681-1 Pa. $6.50

THE AUTHENTIC GILBERT & SULLIVAN SONGBOOK, W. S. Gilbert, A. S. Sullivan. Largest selection available; 92 songs, uncut, original keys, in piano rendering approved by Sullivan. Favorites and lesser-known fine numbers. Edited with plot synopses by James Spero. 3 illustrations. 399pp. 9 x 12.   23482-7 Pa. $9.95

PRINCIPLES OF ORCHESTRATION, Nikolay Rimsky-Korsakov. Great classical orchestrator provides fundamentals of tonal resonance, progression of parts, voice and orchestra, tutti effects, much else in major document. 330pp. of musical excerpts. 489pp. 6½ x 9¼.   21266-1 Pa. $7.50

TRISTAN UND ISOLDE, Richard Wagner. Full orchestral score with complete instrumentation. Do not confuse with piano reduction. Commentary by Felix Mottl, great Wagnerian conductor and scholar. Study score. 655pp. 8⅛ x 11.   22915-7 Pa. $13.95

REQUIEM IN FULL SCORE, Giuseppe Verdi. Immensely popular with choral groups and music lovers. Republication of edition published by C. F. Peters, Leipzig, n. d. German frontmaker in English translation. Glossary. Text in Latin. Study score. 204pp. 9⅜ x 12¼.
                    23682-X Pa. $6.00

COMPLETE CHAMBER MUSIC FOR STRINGS, Felix Mendelssohn. All of Mendelssohn's chamber music: Octet, 2 Quintets, 6 Quartets, and Four Pieces for String Quartet. (Nothing with piano is included). Complete works edition (1874-7). Study score. 283 pp. 9⅜ x 12¼.
                    23679-X Pa. $7.50

POPULAR SONGS OF NINETEENTH-CENTURY AMERICA, edited by Richard Jackson. 64 most important songs: "Old Oaken Bucket," "Arkansas Traveler," "Yellow Rose of Texas," etc. Authentic original sheet music, full introduction and commentaries. 290pp. 9 x 12.   23270-0 Pa. $7.95

COLLECTED PIANO WORKS, Scott Joplin. Edited by Vera Brodsky Lawrence. Practically all of Joplin's piano works—rags, two-steps, marches, waltzes, etc., 51 works in all. Extensive introduction by Rudi Blesh. Total of 345pp. 9 x 12.   23106-2 Pa. $14.95

BASIC PRINCIPLES OF CLASSICAL BALLET, Agrippina Vaganova. Great Russian theoretician, teacher explains methods for teaching classical ballet; incorporates best from French, Italian, Russian schools. 118 illustrations. 175pp. 5⅜ x 8½.   22036-2 Pa. $2.50

CHINESE CHARACTERS, L. Wieger. Rich analysis of 2300 characters according to traditional systems into primitives. Historical-semantic analysis to phonetics (Classical Mandarin) and radicals. 820pp. 6⅛ x 9¼.
                    21321-8 Pa. $10.00

EGYPTIAN LANGUAGE: EASY LESSONS IN EGYPTIAN HIERO-GLYPHICS, E. A. Wallis Budge. Foremost Egyptologist offers Egyptian grammar, explanation of hieroglyphics, many reading texts, dictionary of symbols. 246pp. 5 x 7½. (Available in U.S. only)
                    21394-3 Clothbd. $7.50

AN ETYMOLOGICAL DICTIONARY OF MODERN ENGLISH, Ernest Weekley. Richest, fullest work, by foremost British lexicographer. Detailed word histories. Inexhaustible. Do not confuse this with Concise Etymological Dictionary, which is abridged. Total of 856pp. 6½ x 9¼.
                    21873-2, 21874-0 Pa., Two-vol. set $12.00

A MAYA GRAMMAR, Alfred M. Tozzer. Practical, useful English-language grammar by the Harvard anthropologist who was one of the three greatest American scholars in the area of Maya culture. Phonetics, grammatical processes, syntax, more. 301pp. 5⅜ x 8½. 23465-7 Pa. $4.00

THE JOURNAL OF HENRY D. THOREAU, edited by Bradford Torrey, F. H. Allen. Complete reprinting of 14 volumes, 1837-61, over two million words; the sourcebooks for *Walden*, etc. Definitive. All original sketches, plus 75 photographs. Introduction by Walter Harding. Total of 1804pp. 8½ x 12¼. 20312-3, 20313-1 Clothbd., Two-vol. set $70.00

CLASSIC GHOST STORIES, Charles Dickens and others. 18 wonderful stories you've wanted to reread: "The Monkey's Paw," "The House and the Brain," "The Upper Berth," "The Signalman," "Dracula's Guest," "The Tapestried Chamber," etc. Dickens, Scott, Mary Shelley, Stoker, etc. 330pp. 5⅜ x 8½. 20735-8 Pa. $4.50

SEVEN SCIENCE FICTION NOVELS, H. G. Wells. Full novels. *First Men in the Moon, Island of Dr. Moreau, War of the Worlds, Food of the Gods, Invisible Man, Time Machine, In the Days of the Comet.* A basic science-fiction library. 1015pp. 5⅜ x 8½. (Available in U.S. only) 20264-X Clothbd. $8.95

ARMADALE, Wilkie Collins. Third great mystery novel by the author of *The Woman in White* and *The Moonstone.* Ingeniously plotted narrative shows an exceptional command of character, incident and mood. Original magazine version with 40 illustrations. 597pp. 5⅜ x 8½. 23429-0 Pa. $6.00

MASTERS OF MYSTERY, H. Douglas Thomson. The first book in English (1931) devoted to history and aesthetics of detective story. Poe, Doyle, LeFanu, Dickens, many others, up to 1930. New introduction and notes by E. F. Bleiler. 288pp. 5⅜ x 8½. (Available in U.S. only) 23606-4 Pa. $4.00

FLATLAND, E. A. Abbott. Science-fiction classic explores life of 2-D being in 3-D world. Read also as introduction to thought about hyperspace. Introduction by Banesh Hoffmann. 16 illustrations. 103pp. 5⅜ x 8½. 20001-9 Pa. $2.00

THREE SUPERNATURAL NOVELS OF THE VICTORIAN PERIOD, edited, with an introduction, by E. F. Bleiler. Reprinted complete and unabridged, three great classics of the supernatural: *The Haunted Hotel* by Wilkie Collins, *The Haunted House at Latchford* by Mrs. J. H. Riddell, and *The Lost Stradivarious* by J. Meade Falkner. 325pp. 5⅜ x 8½. 22571-2 Pa. $4.00

AYESHA: THE RETURN OF "SHE," H. Rider Haggard. Virtuoso sequel featuring the great mythic creation, Ayesha, in an adventure that is fully as good as the first book, *She.* Original magazine version, with 47 original illustrations by Maurice Greiffenhagen. 189pp. 6½ x 9¼. 23649-8 Pa. $3.50

UNCLE SILAS, J. Sheridan LeFanu. Victorian Gothic mystery novel, considered by many best of period, even better than Collins or Dickens. Wonderful psychological terror. Introduction by Frederick Shroyer. 436pp. 5⅜ x 8½.   21715-9 Pa. $6.00

JURGEN, James Branch Cabell. The great erotic fantasy of the 1920's that delighted thousands, shocked thousands more. Full final text, Lane edition with 13 plates by Frank Pape. 346pp. 5⅜ x 8½.
23507-6 Pa. $4.50

THE CLAVERINGS, Anthony Trollope. Major novel, chronicling aspects of British Victorian society, personalities. Reprint of Cornhill serialization, 16 plates by M. Edwards; first reprint of full text. Introduction by Norman Donaldson. 412pp. 5⅜ x 8½.   23464-9 Pa. $5.00

KEPT IN THE DARK, Anthony Trollope. Unusual short novel about Victorian morality and abnormal psychology by the great English author. Probably the first American publication. Frontispiece by Sir John Millais. 92pp. 6½ x 9¼.   23609-9 Pa. $2.50

RALPH THE HEIR, Anthony Trollope. Forgotten tale of illegitimacy, inheritance. Master novel of Trollope's later years. Victorian country estates, clubs, Parliament, fox hunting, world of fully realized characters. Reprint of 1871 edition. 12 illustrations by F. A. Faser. 434pp. of text. 5⅜ x 8½.   23642-0 Pa. $5.00

YEKL and THE IMPORTED BRIDEGROOM AND OTHER STORIES OF THE NEW YORK GHETTO, Abraham Cahan. Film *Hester Street* based on *Yekl* (1896). Novel, other stories among first about Jewish immigrants of N.Y.'s East Side. Highly praised by W. D. Howells—Cahan "a new star of realism." New introduction by Bernard G. Richards. 240pp. 5⅜ x 8½.   22427-9 Pa. $3.50

THE HIGH PLACE, James Branch Cabell. Great fantasy writer's enchanting comedy of disenchantment set in 18th-century France. Considered by some critics to be even better than his famous *Jurgen*. 10 illustrations and numerous vignettes by noted fantasy artist Frank C. Pape. 320pp. 5⅜ x 8½.   23670-6 Pa. $4.00

ALICE'S ADVENTURES UNDER GROUND, Lewis Carroll. Facsimile of ms. Carroll gave Alice Liddell in 1864. Different in many ways from final Alice. Handlettered, illustrated by Carroll. Introduction by Martin Gardner. 128pp. 5⅜ x 8½.   21482-6 Pa. $2.50

FAVORITE ANDREW LANG FAIRY TALE BOOKS IN MANY COLORS, Andrew Lang. The four Lang favorites in a boxed set—the complete *Red*, *Green*, *Yellow* and *Blue* Fairy Books. 164 stories; 439 illustrations by Lancelot Speed, Henry Ford and G. P. Jacomb Hood. Total of about 1500pp. 5⅜ x 8½.   23407-X Boxed set, Pa. $15.95

HOUSEHOLD STORIES BY THE BROTHERS GRIMM. All the great Grimm stories: "Rumpelstiltskin," "Snow White," "Hansel and Gretel," etc., with 114 illustrations by Walter Crane. 269pp. 5⅜ x 8½.
21080-4 Pa. $3.50

SLEEPING BEAUTY, illustrated by Arthur Rackham. Perhaps the fullest, most delightful version ever, told by C. S. Evans. Rackham's best work. 49 illustrations. 110pp. 7⅞ x 10¾. 22756-1 Pa. $2.50

AMERICAN FAIRY TALES, L. Frank Baum. Young cowboy lassoes Father Time; dummy in Mr. Floman's department store window comes to life; and 10 other fairy tales. 41 illustrations by N. P. Hall, Harry Kennedy, Ike Morgan, and Ralph Gardner. 209pp. 5⅜ x 8½. 23643-9 Pa. $3.00

THE WONDERFUL WIZARD OF OZ, L. Frank Baum. Facsimile in full color of America's finest children's classic. Introduction by Martin Gardner. 143 illustrations by W. W. Denslow. 267pp. 5⅜ x 8½.
20691-2 Pa. $3.50

THE TALE OF PETER RABBIT, Beatrix Potter. The inimitable Peter's terrifying adventure in Mr. McGregor's garden, with all 27 wonderful, full-color Potter illustrations. 55pp. 4¼ x 5½. (Available in U.S. only)
22827-4 Pa. $1.25

THE STORY OF KING ARTHUR AND HIS KNIGHTS, Howard Pyle. Finest children's version of life of King Arthur. 48 illustrations by Pyle. 131pp. 6⅛ x 9¼. 21445-1 Pa. $4.95

CARUSO'S CARICATURES, Enrico Caruso. Great tenor's remarkable caricatures of self, fellow musicians, composers, others. Toscanini, Puccini, Farrar, etc. Impish, cutting, insightful. 473 illustrations. Preface by M. Sisca. 217pp. 8⅜ x 11¼. 23528-9 Pa. $6.95

PERSONAL NARRATIVE OF A PILGRIMAGE TO ALMADINAH AND MECCAH, Richard Burton. Great travel classic by remarkably colorful personality. Burton, disguised as a Moroccan, visited sacred shrines of Islam, narrowly escaping death. Wonderful observations of Islamic life, customs, personalities. 47 illustrations. Total of 959pp. 5⅜ x 8½.
21217-3, 21218-1 Pa., Two-vol. set $12.00

INCIDENTS OF TRAVEL IN YUCATAN, John L. Stephens. Classic (1843) exploration of jungles of Yucatan, looking for evidences of Maya civilization. Travel adventures, Mexican and Indian culture, etc. Total of 669pp. 5⅜ x 8½. 20926-1, 20927-X Pa., Two-vol. set $7.90

AMERICAN LITERARY AUTOGRAPHS FROM WASHINGTON IRVING TO HENRY JAMES, Herbert Cahoon, et al. Letters, poems, manuscripts of Hawthorne, Thoreau, Twain, Alcott, Whitman, 67 other prominent American authors. Reproductions, full transcripts and commentary. Plus checklist of all American Literary Autographs in The Pierpont Morgan Library. Printed on exceptionally high-quality paper. 136 illustrations. 212pp. 9⅛ x 12¼. 23548-3 Pa. $12.50

AN AUTOBIOGRAPHY, Margaret Sanger. Exciting personal account of hard-fought battle for woman's right to birth control, against prejudice, church, law. Foremost feminist document. 504pp. 5⅜ x 8½.
20470-7 Pa. $5.50

MY BONDAGE AND MY FREEDOM, Frederick Douglass. Born as a slave, Douglass became outspoken force in antislavery movement. The best of Douglass's autobiographies. Graphic description of slave life. Introduction by P. Foner. 464pp. 5⅜ x 8½.
22457-0 Pa. $5.50

LIVING MY LIFE, Emma Goldman. Candid, no holds barred account by foremost American anarchist: her own life, anarchist movement, famous contemporaries, ideas and their impact. Struggles and confrontations in America, plus deportation to U.S.S.R. Shocking inside account of persecution of anarchists under Lenin. 13 plates. Total of 944pp. 5⅜ x 8½.
22543-7, 22544-5 Pa., Two-vol. set $12.00

LETTERS AND NOTES ON THE MANNERS, CUSTOMS AND CONDITIONS OF THE NORTH AMERICAN INDIANS, George Catlin. Classic account of life among Plains Indians: ceremonies, hunt, warfare, etc. Dover edition reproduces for first time all original paintings. 312 plates. 572pp. of text. 6⅛ x 9¼.
22118-0, 22119-9 Pa.. Two-vol. set $12.00

THE MAYA AND THEIR NEIGHBORS, edited by Clarence L. Hay, others. Synoptic view of Maya civilization in broadest sense, together with Northern, Southern neighbors. Integrates much background, valuable detail not elsewhere. Prepared by greatest scholars: Kroeber, Morley, Thompson, Spinden, Vaillant, many others. Sometimes called Tozzer Memorial Volume. 60 illustrations, linguistic map. 634pp. 5⅜ x 8½.
23510-6 Pa. $10.00

HANDBOOK OF THE INDIANS OF CALIFORNIA, A. L. Kroeber. Foremost American anthropologist offers complete ethnographic study of each group. Monumental classic. 459 illustrations, maps. 995pp. 5⅜ x 8½.
23368-5 Pa. $13.00

SHAKTI AND SHAKTA, Arthur Avalon. First book to give clear, cohesive analysis of Shakta doctrine, Shakta ritual and Kundalini Shakti (yoga). Important work by one of world's foremost students of Shaktic and Tantric thought. 732pp. 5⅜ x 8½. (Available in U.S. only)
23645-5 Pa. $7.95

AN INTRODUCTION TO THE STUDY OF THE MAYA HIEROGLYPHS, Syvanus Griswold Morley. Classic study by one of the truly great figures in hieroglyph research. Still the best introduction for the student for reading Maya hieroglyphs. New introduction by J. Eric S. Thompson. 117 illustrations. 284pp. 5⅜ x 8½.
23108-9 Pa. $4.00

A STUDY OF MAYA ART, Herbert J. Spinden. Landmark classic interprets Maya symbolism, estimates styles, covers ceramics, architecture, murals, stone carvings as artforms. Still a basic book in area. New introduction by J. Eric Thompson. Over 750 illustrations. 341pp. 8⅜ x 11¼.
21235-1 Pa. $6.95

GEOMETRY, RELATIVITY AND THE FOURTH DIMENSION, Rudolf
Rucker. Exposition of fourth dimension, means of visualization, concepts
of relativity as Flatland characters continue adventures. Popular, easily
followed yet accurate, profound. 141 illustrations. 133pp. 5⅜ x 8½.
23400-2 Pa. $2.75

THE ORIGIN OF LIFE, A. I. Oparin. Modern classic in biochemistry, the
first rigorous examination of possible evolution of life from nitrocarbon com-
pounds. Non-technical, easily followed. Total of 295pp. 5⅜ x 8½.
60213-3 Pa. $4.00

PLANETS, STARS AND GALAXIES, A. E. Fanning. Comprehensive introductory survey: the sun, solar system, stars, galaxies, universe, cosmology;
quasars, radio stars, etc. 24pp. of photographs. 189pp. 5⅜ x 8½. (Available in U.S. only) 21680-2 Pa. $3.75

THE THIRTEEN BOOKS OF EUCLID'S ELEMENTS, translated with
introduction and commentary by Sir Thomas L. Heath. Definitive edition.
Textual and linguistic notes, mathematical analysis, 2500 years of critical
commentary. Do not confuse with abridged school editions. Total of 1414pp.
5⅜ x 8½. 60088-2, 60089-0, 60090-4 Pa., Three-vol. set $18.50